The Prince and the Sell-Swords

A Warriors of Mezer Novel

By: Dustin Farris

Publisher: Dustin Farris

Edited by: Leonora Bulbeck

Cover Design: tjmbookcovers.com

I dedicate this book to all those who gave me the words of encouragement I needed to get this far

Table of Contents

Prologue: Newcomers in the Land of Warriors

G uzan sat in his chair, waiting. His fingers impatiently tapped on his desk as the time seemed to drag on. Every second felt like an eternity to him, and the tapping of his fingers became ever quicker. His fear and nervousness weren't missed by his guard. Guzan's gaze landed on him and the door he stood next to more often as the time passed.

For years Guzan had ruled the underground of EastAvri, one of the twin cities. Every illegal good smuggled through the twin cities had his touch or his influence on it. He was feared by all in EastAvri, and he himself feared no one in his city. Even the warrior families knew better than to mess with him. However, this had all changed when a lone stranger had arrived a few days back.

The stranger had been looking for passage across Avri River and had come to Guzan to help him smuggle himself into WestAvri. With the stench of alchemic seed radiating from the man, as well as the crystal-like eyes of an addict, Guzan thought the stranger an easy target. By the end of that single day, more than half of his men were either dead or permanently crippled. With each swing of his sword, the stranger had become the harbinger of death. To the stranger, it was no fight; to him, it was a dance, and with each step, another man fell, never to get up again.

After that, the stranger seemingly found a way over the bridge, and as quickly as he had appeared, he was gone. With the nightmare over, Guzan wanted nothing more than to put the events of that day behind him. Even though just thinking of the stranger made his blood boil, he knew he was no match for him. But when news came a few days later that people had arrived and were looking for the stranger, Guzan couldn't help himself.

Calling for his counterpart across the river in WestAvri, Guzan quickly made his plans. In less than half a day, Guzan was able to gather more than thirty men from the underground of both cities. Sending out whispers of the two searchers' location, he had his and his counterpart's men wait to ambush those searching for the stranger while he waited impatiently in his office.

As the night wore on, he had begun to worry that the ambush had failed and they had failed to kill the searchers, or worse, that a repeat of the previous massacre was happening.

Guzan was beginning to worry that his anger had led him down a path of no return when the sound of rushed footsteps headed in his direction. Hearing the footsteps, the guard at the door unsheathed the long knife at his side and exited the room.

Guzan waited in silence as he wondered what was going on right outside the room. Then the door opened. The guard who had just left reentered the room with his knife strapped at his side once more. A smaller man accompanied the guard. The small man was gasping for breath as if he had just run for the entire night. Guzan let out the breath he hadn't realized he had been holding when he saw who the man was.

The man was Rickens, known by all as Rickens the Rat. He neither was strong nor had a conniving brain, and when his timid personality was added, it was a miracle he had survived for so long in the murderous life of the twin cities' underground. Guzan had little respect for the man, as did anyone who met him, but he was one amazing smuggler. By greasing a few wheels here and there, and filling not just a few bridge guards' pockets, Rickens had made Guzan more money than any other person under him. While Guzan didn't respect Rickens, with his skill at smuggling, along with his acute sense of danger leading him out of trouble, he highly valued him.

"What happened, Rickens? Did the ambush work?" Guzan demanded of the gasping man, as his patience was thin from all the waiting. He couldn't wait for Rickens to catch his breath and tell him whether they had succeeded.

"Boss, not only did we succeed, we have captured one of them alive. We have him waiting for you right outside," Rickens said meekly, startled by Guzan's shout.

"Good," Guzan said with a haughty laugh. He himself hadn't taken part in the ambush. While he was filled with anger, he also feared for his life and would never take direct action against those connected to the murderous stranger.

His mood now jubilant from the news, Guzan rushed out of his office. At his heels followed his guard and the timid Rickens. With each step, his mood grew brighter. He was finally going to be able to vent the frustration he held in his chest.

When he finally made it outside, his jubilant mood instantly soured. The road was silent, and not a soul was waiting for the underboss of EastAvri.

"What is the meaning of this, Rickens?" Guzan yelled, turning toward Rickens. He turned around just in time to see his guard fall to the ground with a hideous knife protruding from his back.

Guzan was shocked into silence. Taking a few steps back, he watched as Rickens pulled his long knife out of the dead guard's back.

Cleaning off the bloody knife with a hand cloth he had pulled from his coat pocket, Rickens's face was void of his normally timid nature. In its place, his eyes shone with a cold ruthlessness.

"You rat! You dare to betray me?" Guzan shouted. Seeing Rickens's fell his guard had startled him at first, but once he had processed what had happened, he calmed down. He was stronger than the rat like Rickens, and he, too, had a long knife hidden on his person. If it hadn't been for the backstabbing, not even ten Rickens could have beaten his guard.

"Ah … Guzan. You truly are one fool of a man," Rickens said with pity.

"Shut your mouth, you rat!" Guzan yelled as he lunged at Rickens, pulling out his own knife.

The two long knives collided with each other with a subtle clink. Rickens had easily parried Guzan's thrust, and with each subsequent failed strike, Guzan began to grow nervous. He was barely able to keep up with Rickens's fast strikes, and soon his guard faltered.

An agonizing scream came from Guzan as his hand fell to the floor. Rickens had cut off Guzan's dominant hand. It lay on the ground, still gripping the knife. Not giving Guzan time to recover, Rickens drove his knife deep into Guzan's chest. Guzan's strength quickly left him as he fell to the floor. Blood pooled under him as his body grew cold. He struggled to move, but his body refused as he lost more blood.

"Don't try to get up. Your lungs are filling with blood as we speak, and soon you will die. Struggling will only make the process painful in the end," Rickens said, looking down at the dying man.

"You really think you've won?" Guzan said, coughing up blood. "You will soon regret this."

"Oh? How will I regret this?" Rickens questioningly mocked.

"I know Osborn. As soon as he hears of my death, that calculating old man will swoop in and take EastAvri for himself," Guzan spat. His voice was growing ever weaker.

Osborn was Guzan's counterpart and ruled the underground of WestAvri, across the river from EastAvri. Decades older than Guzan, Osborn had ruled WestAvri before Guzan had even been born. The old man was conniving and calculating. It had cost Guzan many concessions to get Osborn's help in this plan. When Guzan contemplated the ambush being carried out, a thought came to mind, a thought that terrified him.

"It seems that you have realized something," Rickens said as Guzan's face revealed what he was thinking.

"You're the one who helped the stranger across to WestAvri," Guzan said in hardly a whisper.

"That's right. And now those who came after will help me take care of the old man from WestAvri, as one monster will certainly herald others."

With those last words, Rickens watched the last life leave the once great underboss of EastAvri.

+

Osborn looked on in horror as a nightmare unfolded in front of him. When Guzan had come to him with his proposal, Osborn had thought of it as nothing more than a way to gain leverage from his rival and take money right out of the man's pockets. After the deal had been made, Osborn brought twenty of his best men and crossed the Avri River into EastAvri. Meeting up with ten of Guzan's own men, they lured their targets to an abandoned storage building near the docks that was a common place for illegal activities.

It all went downhill soon after the targets arrived. Two men walked into the building and were quickly surrounded by the thirty thugs. The two men wore long gray coats and dark cowls that covered their faces. Seeing the long swords strapped to their sides gave Osborn slight pause, but as they outnumbered the two fifteen to one, his worries vanished from his mind. Only the most famous and strongest warriors would be able to fight their way out against such odds. Eagar to get this over with, he gave the men the order to attack.

Seeing the swarm of men, each holding a malicious knife or club, did not faze the two cloaked men. The larger of the two men looked to the shorter one as if asking something as the thugs neared. With a slight nod, the shorter man gave his companion his answer. Stepping up, the larger man seemed as unmovable as a mountain as he unsheathed his sword, ready to face the overwhelming odds.

None of the thugs saw the man's first move as the first of them fell. As the first of the thugs neared, the man's sword cut down several in a single breath. The inability to see how their fellow thugs had died startled the charging thugs, freezing them in their tracks. In this split second of hesitation, the cowled man stepped into the group and quickly lopped off the head of another thug. Jogged out of their stupefied state, the thugs angrily charged at the man, completely forgetting the other one.

The formerly simple job for the thugs that ruled the underground of the twin cities turned into a battle for their very lives. One by one, the thugs fell to the cowled man's sword. With each clash, another thug fell to the ground, dead. Quickly moving between the mass of people, the man seemed to have eyes on the back of his head, as he narrowly dodged every strike and ambush the thugs tried. Several of the thugs resorted to pulling out crossbows in hopes of ending the man, but to their horror, the cowled man's reflexes were inhuman, and he was able to move out of the bolts' paths. In the end, all thirty of the armed thugs had been killed. Their corpses left little room on the floor to stand.

Osborn stood frozen in terror, his mind a complete blank. He was the only one left of the ambushing party. Not trusting Guzan, Osborn had brought only his strongest and most trusted men to EastAvri for this ambush, but now he regretted it. Even his most trusted guards, who were disgraced warriors, had died in the bloodbath. When the cowled man took notice of him, Osborn panicked. Turning to flee, he was met with a sword to his throat.

"Lucis, don't kill him," said the other man. During the entire massacre, he had not made a single move. Only after hearing his words did Osborn remember that there were two targets.

Hearing his companion's words, the bloodied man reluctantly withdrew his sword from Osborn's neck and firmly sheathed the blade back in its scabbard. Realizing that his life had been spared did not give Osborn any reassurance. He was fearing what the two had in store for him when the sound of clapping alerted him to a third man.

"Amazing, truly amazing. Men cut down like sheep to the slaughter. You two truly are quite fearsome," said Rickens as he came out of the shadows.

"Rickens? You … you knew this would happen?" Osborn yelled. As he was one of Guzan's most trusted and most experienced smugglers, Osborn had met the man known as Rickens the Rat on several occasions. Osborn also knew what it meant for Rickens to appear at this moment.

Hearing Osborn's accusation didn't cause Rickens to flinch in the slightest. Turning to the two cowled men, he gave them a warm but untrustworthy smile. He snapped his fingers, and the doors to the building opened, and a man quickly entered. After handing Rickens a batch of papers, the man was gone as fast as he had appeared. Osborn recognized the man as one of his own carriers.

"I have already finished my end of our deal. Here are your papers, which will allow you across the bridge into WestAvri," said Rickens, handing the papers over.

The bloodied man let his partner take the papers and read them over.

"My sources also tell me the man you are looking for has already left WestAvri and is heading westward," said Rickens.

After looking over the papers, the two men left without a single glance or word.

Once their footsteps could no longer be heard, Rickens turned back to old man Osborn. His timid nature was a thing of the past. The Rat's gaze sent shivers down Osborn's spine.

"We have lots to discuss, former underboss of WestAvri," said Rickens sinisterly.

+

"Aer, are you sure we can trust a man like that? A man with neither honor nor duty. He had no problems betraying and sending dozens to their deaths," said Lucis as he pulled off his bloodied coat and cowl, revealing a youthful face. The only blemish anyone would find was a curved scar following his right jawline.

"Weren't you the one who swung the sword? And only the foolish would trust a rat like Rickens." Aer laughed as he, too, took off his cowl. His unshaven face, along with slight wrinkles around his eyes, made the man look older than he was.

The two, while companions, looked vastly different from one another. The scar-faced Lucis looked to be a young man entering his prime. Half a head taller than Aer, he radiated the aura of a warrior. On the other hand, Aer had more normal features. Nearing the end of his prime, he had begun to show the appearance of an older man. Some gray hairs poked through around his ears.

"We had little choice in the matter. Our brother had already caused us to fall out with the local underground before we even arrived. It was in our best interest to help a third party, even though he is not trustworthy," said Aer, answering Lucis's question before Lucis could ask it.

"Even so, we might have made the situation a lot worse for the locals," Lucis said, still disgruntled about helping a traitorous man.

"You don't have to worry about that. Rickens may be a rat with not an ounce of honor in his body, but he is a survivor. That is why he has spared that old man who ruled WestAvri for so long," said Aer. "Now, let's hurry. If we haven't crossed the bridge by the end of the day, we most likely will lose Kay's trail and will have to wait till a situation like the one a few days ago happens."

Hearing Aer mention their missing brother made Lucis's face turn solemn. It had been many months since they had last seen their brother, Kay, and they had been on his trail since he had disappeared. Luckily for the two of them, their brother's erratic behavior allowed them to track him quite easily, but every time they got close, the trail ran cold until another incident happened. Being only a few days behind this was the closest the two had been to catching up to Kay.

"How long is Kay going to run? Neither of us blame him for what happened," said Lucis as he dunked his coat into the nearby Avri River to rinse off the blood.

"Who said he was running?" said Aer, stunning and dumbfounding Lucis.

"If he isn't running, then what is he doing?" asked Lucis as he threw his wet coat over his shoulder. He had thought that his brother had run away in regret.

"I thought he was running too, but with each incident Kay has caused, I have begun to think differently. Our brother isn't wallowing in regret but chasing something—or more accurately, hunting someone. And I believe it is a man we both know."

"Karsic," Lucis said, spitting out the name.

Dustin Farris

Chapter One: An Awkward Farewell

The land of the Estelles was a vast field of green stretching from one horizon to the next. Yellow wildflowers bloomed, giving the green plains streaks of gold across their winding hillsides. Untamed horses galloped across the lands, led by their majestic horned kings. Long-eared hares scurried to and from their burrows, trying to stay one step ahead of the hawks circling above.

Protruding from the rolling hills was the great southern city of the Estelles, the city of Esesa. Yurts made of animal skins made Esesa a living creature. Warriors rode their horned mounts through the city as some children cheered for the brave men. On the outskirts of the city, the vast herds of sheep, horses, and cows grazed as the herdsmen stood watch for wolves and other beasts. At the center of this great city was the grand castle of the Estelles.

Built from stone, this castle was the only constant building in this ever-changing city. Standing stories taller than the traditional yurts of the plains, the castle lorded over the city. Large horned banners adorned the castle walls, displaying the Estelles' famous horned horses. It was in this stone fortress that the Estelles, one of the founding families, lived and ruled.

Elaina Estelle watched the sunrise over the Great Plains from her window, the cold morning breeze banishing the previous night's drowsiness from her body. Her curly blond hair was a tangled mess from sleep. From her room, she could see the Talov warriors in the castle courtyard, preparing for the long ride home. When she spotted two familiar figures in the crowd beneath her, a knock came from her door.

"Your Highness, may I come in?" asked a soft voice from the door.

"Hali, there is no need for you to ask. Come in," Elaina chuckled. Hali had been her attending maiden since they were both young, and she treated the girl more as a sister than a servant.

A creak came from the door as it slowly opened. A young girl quietly entered the room. Hali was a short girl just entering her prime. While short in stature, she had a cuteness to her that caused her to be pursued by many suitors. However, when she saw the princess, her smile turned into a frown.

"Ma'am, you are of royal blood. Can you please act like a normal princess for once?" Hali asked with a pout.

Elaina couldn't help but smile at her long-cherished friend's remark. She well understood that proper ladies would never stand at their open window in their nightgown, and never would they let their attending maidens enter without normal etiquette. However, Elaina found all these proper manners and womanly etiquette to be very trivial.

"Are you going to just stand there and pout, or are you going to help me with my dress?" Elaina teased.

"Ma'am, please don't tease," Hali said, pulling out an elaborate red silk dress from Elaina's closet.

The red dress made Elaina's face scrunch up.

"Ma'am, you are seeing off Their Highnesses Crown Prince Eustace and Prince Leander today. You must look your best," Hali said.

"Fine," Elaina said in a defeated tone, knowing that she was right. Unhooking her nightgown, she let the thin garment fall to the floor.

Elated that her princess had agreed so easily, Hali began helping Elaina into the silk dress.

Normally, the princess was adamant about not wearing feminine dresses and clothing, and preferred simpler articles—clothes that didn't need a second pair of hands to put them on. Sometimes she even went around in men's trousers and shirts, even though it displeased the Archduke so.

"Not so tight," Elaina complained as Hali tightened the corset around her waist.

"Ma'am, a lady's waist must be as narrow as it can be," said Hali, wrenching the laces even more, causing Elaina to gasp.

"Perfect. Now all that is needed is the matching shoes and jewelry," Hali said, satisfied that her tomboy princess looked like a proper princess for once.

As Hali went to pick out the right shoes and jewelry, Elaina's attention went back to the scurrying people below. She found the two princes just as quickly as before. Pulling at the corset to try to breathe more easily, she saw that Prince Leander was looking toward her window. Startled, Elaina roughly pulled the curtains closed, hoping that Leander hadn't seen her.

"Is something the matter?" Hali asked as she walked back into the room from the closet, holding a pair of embroidered red shoes and a pearl necklace. When she had seen Elaina's expression, she had worriedly questioned her. It was only when her princess was upset or did something reckless that Hali dropped all forms of propriety and became Elaina's childhood friend.

Seeing that the curtains were now shut, Hali peeked through. When she saw the second prince staring at the window of Elaina's quarters, she understood. Luckily, Leander couldn't see Elaina or Hali from where he stood, and soon his attention went back to preparing for the ride home.

When the prince's attention was no longer toward them, Hali cracked the curtains a little to let some light back in and went back to helping Elaina dress.

"Ma'am, you have been friends with Prince Leander since you were little. You must tell him," Hali said, slipping one of the shoes onto Elaina's foot. "The archduke plans to engage the two of you once you come of age. If you don't tell them your true feelings, I'm afraid it will do no one—"

"I know," said Elaina, interrupting Hali. Taking the pearl necklace from Hali, she tied it around her neck herself. "I just don't know how to tell him."

With nothing else to say about her princess's troubles, Hali kept silent. Hali knew Elaina's true feelings and knew that the archduke would never allow it. Hali also knew that the archduke cared a great deal for his daughter, and it was for that reason alone that Elaina hadn't already been married away, and instead, the archduke looked for someone Elaina had feelings for. Regretfully, the archduke was wrong about his daughter's feelings for the second prince of the Talov Duchy.

"Hali, let's go. We can't keep Crown Prince Eustace and Prince Leander waiting," Elaina said as she headed for the door, with Hali rushing ahead to open it for her.

Walking through the grand hallways of the Estelle castle was breathtaking. From the walls hung magnificent tapestries replicating major victories and heroic feats. The skulls of crownes, the famous horned horses of the Estelle Duchy, and other beasts were mounted on the walls as well, some being proof of a tapestry's story.

Elegantly dressed maids and footmen went about their business, only stopping to give Elaina a respectful bow. The Estelles' personal warriors stood guard throughout the castle. Motionless, the warriors blended into the walls as though they were decorative statues. Elaina always felt pride when she strode the halls of her family's castle. Each legend that adorned the walls spoke of the greatness of the

Estelle lineage.

It took the two quite a while to reach the courtyard. By the time they had, the warriors of the Talov Duchy had nearly finished their preparations. The presence of the princess was quickly noticed. Stopping what they were doing, the Talov warriors took a step back and saluted the princess. Servants and citizens bowed; only warriors saluted.

Taking her time, Elaina took in the sight of the Talov warriors. Their light armor and colorful surcoats were quite the contrast to their own warriors, who wore heavy armor and tunics of simple designs. Her father had told her that the differences derived from how the land of the two duchies differed. Unlike the Estelles' rolling plains, the Talov Duchy was a tapestry of different geographical features and ideals. Compared to the unified Estelle warriors, the Talov warriors came from all different perspectives. A warrior family from the north of the Talov Duchy was different from the central or southern warrior families. Because of these differences, the warriors had to be more adaptable than the warriors of the Estelles, who were more horse-mounted berserkers, strong in an open battle but weak to change.

As they neared the princes, Elaina couldn't help but slow her pace even more. When she saw Prince Leander's bright smile as he gazed at her, Elaina's heart tightened.

"Your Highness. I am so glad to have you see us off," said Leander.

"Of course I came to see you off on your way home. We have known each other since we were kids," Elaina said, giving Leander a slight smile, which caused him to grin uncontrollably, much to Elaina's dismay.

"Your Highness," Crown Prince Eustace greeted her. "Thank you for your hospitality during our stay. I'll be sure to mention this to my grandfather."

Crown Prince Eustace's grandfather was the current Archduke of the Talov

15

Duchy. Elaina had heard much of the elderly Archduke, who had taken the throne once more after the untimely demise of his only son and the two princes' father. Over a decade older than when most people died, he now ruled from his bed rather than the throne.

"There is no need to. It was my pleasure," Elaina responded. She knew that what Crown Prince Eustace truly wanted to talk about was her potential engagement.

"My daughter, you don't have to be so formal with the princes." A booming voice came from behind her. "Childhood sweethearts shouldn't keep each other at arm's length."

Before she had even turned around, Elaina knew right away that the voice belonged to her father. All the warriors turned toward the voice and saluted. Hali kept her head bowed while the two princes and Elaina waited for the archduke's arrival.

Entering the courtyard alongside his two sons was the Archduke of the Estelle Duchy, Bennet Estelle. His domineering presence spoke loudly of his fame as the most feared man in the three duchies of Mezer. He stood a head taller than even the tallest of men, and his bulging muscles intimidated even the bravest of warriors. His two sons, behind him, had inherited the archduke's intimidating physique. Crown Prince Aleron Estelle stood to the right of his father, while his younger brother, Prince Felon, was to the left. Each was a behemoth, but while Aleron was as cold as ice, Felon had a raging temper.

"Father, they may have known each other since they were children, but it isn't proper for an unmarried woman to get too close to any man, no matter how close they were as children," Aleron said, seeing the frustration hidden in Elaina's eyes.

"What are you saying, brother? Their Highnesses are more like brothers to us than mere acquaintances," Felon said, hinting at the proposed marriage.

"Never mind any of that. We are here to send the princes off, for they have a long journey home," Archduke Bennet said. Then he turned to his daughter. "Elaina, you look more beautiful today than I've seen you in a while. Is there a specific reason for you to be so dressed up?" Archduke Bennet gave his daughter a nod of approval for her current appearance.

"Shouldn't I look my best when sending off Their Highnesses? Our families have been on good terms for decades," Elaina answered, trying to hint at the distance she was trying to make, but to her disappointment, her father was oblivious to the hint.

As the princes from two of the three duchies of Mezer mingled, Elaina stayed back. Leander's gaze went to her anytime it could. Elaina knew of her childhood friend's feelings for her, and it pained her that she could not reciprocate them.

"Elaina, are you all right? You look flushed," Aleron said, giving his sister a knowing glance.

"Just a light fever I woke up with. It isn't a problem," Elaina said, thankful that Aleron had noticed her discomfort.

"If you're not feeling well, you don't have to send us off. I'm already happy you came while you were ill," Leander said, worried that she was trying to simplify how sick she really was.

Hearing that Leander himself wished for Elaina to return to her room, Archduke Bennet gave his approval with a nod. Hiding a sigh of relief, Elaina gave her family and the princes a farewell before leaving with Hali.

+

"My sons and I will ride with you out of the city," said Archduke Bennet as Elaina vanished into the halls of the castle.

"Your Undaunted Majesty, I believe that the princess is more ill than she lets on," Leander said, clearly still worried about Elaina.

"If Their Highnesses don't mind me not sending them off, I'll keep my sister company," said Aleron.

When he saw that the Talov princes didn't mind, Archduke Bennet agreed. "Very well, then. Felon, the two of us will ride out with the princes," he said to his second son.

Aleron watched as his father and brother mounted their horned steeds and rode out along with the two Talov princes and their warriors.

Once there wasn't a single man left in the courtyard, Aleron went to find his sister. It was easy to find her, as she, with her handmaiden, stood watching from the top of the castle wall as her father and the Talovs made their way through the city. Not disguising his approach, Aleron was quickly noticed by Elaina and Hali.

"Were you not to send off the princes with Father?" Elaina asked.

"Prince Leander worried that you were feigning how well you were, so I offered to stay and look out for you," Aleron answered.

Elaina cringed when she heard Aleron, and Aleron saw this.

"You should have told him how you feel before they left. I know you care for him but don't love him. Now you are in quite the quandary."

Elaina didn't respond to her brother's remarks, as she knew very well the situation she was facing. Right at this very moment, the two princes were returning to Raven's Nest, the capital of the Talov Duchy, with her father's wish for marriage to bind their two great families together. When Leander had arrived with his brother as an ambassador from Archduke Ambrose, she had known of their fathers' plan for them to get closer during this time. She also knew flatly declining the engagement would lead to discord among the duchies, so she couldn't do that either. The only thing she could do was give hints at her displeasure at the engagement. Sadly, only her eldest brother noticed.

When his sister didn't respond, Aleron could only sigh and stand with them on the wall. The three watched as the troop of warriors, led by the princes, made its way out of the city to begin the long ride home.

Chapter Two: The Fall of the Talov Princes

The two princes of the Talov Duchy made good time as they made their way home. Clouds blocked the sun, keeping the day cool and their ride less strenuous. By midday of the third day, they had made it halfway to the twin cities of Avri Bridge.

As the troop made its way east, the terrain changed. Vast rolling plains turned into scattered woodlands. The woodlands in the east of the Estelle Duchy were small, and each could be traversed quickly. After half a year of only seeing the continuous plains during their stay in Esesa, the changing landscape reminded the troop of their home, and the joy of returning burned in their hearts. Out of the entire group, only a single person wasn't enjoying the ride home.

"Cheer up, Leander. You will see Princess Elaina again," Crown Prince Eustace said to his brother as they rode side by side.

"I know, but that doesn't change the fact that I miss her," Leander said with a sigh.

Ever since he had first laid eyes on Elaina many years ago, he had gained feelings for the princess. Compared to the other young ladies, who feared to get dirty and enjoyed the three arts, Elaina was more inclined to play with the boys. Leander couldn't help but crack a smile when he remembered meeting Elaina for the first time, covered in dirt after playing war with boys. At first he had mistaken her for one as well—that is, until she had unhooked her long golden hair, and he had fallen in love.

As they had grown older, his feelings had changed to ones of love. Any chance he got, he would travel to the Estelle Duchy to spend even a single moment with Elaina. He also knew she cared for him as well, so when his grandfather had proposed to engage him to the princess of the Estelle Duchy, he had readily agreed.

As Leander reminisced, a warrior rode toward them.

"Your Highness, we have been riding nonstop since we left Esesa. The horses need to rest," said the warrior. The warrior's name was Bez, and he was the crown prince's squire.

Eustace had noticed that the horses looked fatigued. "Very well, then. Have the men set up camp for the night. We will continue on at daybreak," Eustace ordered.

Saluting his prince, the squire Bez ordered the troop to halt and begin pitching camp. In no time at all, the camp was lined with makeshift tents. The servants had built a roaring fire in the center of camp and were busy preparing dinner for the princes and their warriors. All around the camp, warriors were cheerfully talking about what they would do once they made it back home to Raven's Nest.

Leander watched on awkwardly as his older brother mingled with the warriors. Eustace had always had a charisma about him, allowing him to befriend people easily. Leander envied this, as he himself was more awkward. It seemed that out of his family, only Leander had this type of personality. His grandfather was domineering, and his elder sister had inherited the Archduke's strong mentality and intellect. Only he seemed so normal and timid.

Not only were their personalities worthy of the Talov name, their skill with a sword and warfare was impressive as well. Leander's swordplay could be considered average at his best. There had been more than one occasion when Leander had thought that fate had borne him into the wrong family.

As he was lost in thought, a warrior came toward Leander, carrying a bowl. "Your meal, Your Highness," the man said, handing him a simple meal of soup and bread.

Accepting the meal, Leander looked down at the steaming bowl. He swished the soup around but was in no mood to eat. Wanting to clear his head, he decided to go out on a short walk. Hopefully, he would return only when all the merrymaking was over. Before his brother had noticed, Leander was out of the camp.

It wasn't that Leander hated his brother. On the contrary, he loved all his family, but if asked whether he was jealous of his older brother, then he would say no but inside scream yes. As he walked through the woodland in the moonlight, the music of the crickets drowned out the sounds of the camp, and Leander found his restless heart becoming peaceful.

When he reached an old spruce tree, he sat down to rest. Looking up to the moon, he marveled at its beauty, which only reminded him of his beloved Princess Elaina. In just a few days' time, he and his brother would bring the engagement agreement to their grandfather. Leander lost himself to his daydreaming. Visions of a life with Elaina. It was only with her that he didn't feel like the black sheep of the Talovs. He was so lost in thought that he didn't hear the warrior coming closer.

"Are you awake, Your Highness?" the warrior asked, but Leander didn't hear him and kept on daydreaming. It was only his instincts from years of training that warned him of the danger.

With the hairs of his neck standing straight up, Leander rolled to the side just in time as a sword swung past where he was and into the tree he had been leaning on. The traitorous warrior was shocked and tried to pull out his sword, but his strong killing blow had lodged it deep in the tree trunk. Within a breath's time, Leander had drawn his own sword and cut down the warrior just as he finally freed his weapon.

With his mind rattled, Leander pushed over the dead warrior to get a better look at him. Seeing the warrior's face caused Leander's own to turn white. He instantly recognized the warrior as one of their own troop and not from another duchy. He had even seen this very man joking with his brother not half an hour ago.

Thinking of his brother, Leander ran back to the camp as fast as he could. As he neared, he slowed his pace so as not to alert anyone to his presence. Hiding in some brambles, Leander peeked into the campsite. The scene he saw filled him with dread. Leander watched as four of the warriors went around the camp, pushing their blades into their brethren. It was then that Leander noticed that the eyes of all the warriors on the ground were wide open and glaring at the traitors.

"They've been poisoned," Leander whispered to himself. He also saw that one of the traitors was the warrior who had brought him his meal.

It then dawned on Leander why he was still fine: he hadn't eaten the food given to him. The food must have been drugged when everyone was enjoying themselves and not even paying attention to the ones preparing the meal. Leander watched as every single loyal warrior was slain, helpless to the traitors' blades.

"You vile bastards. You tarnish your ancestors' glories with your treachery," a voice familiar to Leander tried to shout.

Leander finally found his brother, who had just spoken. Crown Prince Eustace Talov had been drugged as well. A warrior stood behind him with his sword ready. The warrior in front of Eustace was his squire, Bez, looking down at his prince with ridicule. Leander knew right away who the ringleader behind this evil plot was.

"Oh, Prince, the dead don't hear or see," Bez mocked. "Unless you believe those stories the priests preach, about the Ancestral Hall."

"A traitor has no right to ridicule our faith," Eustace sharply said.

"Faith? What good will faith do for you? Or honor, for that matter. Look around," Bez said, gesturing to the camp. "Your so-called honor-bound warriors you are so proud of are dead, and you, my dear crown prince, will soon join them."

It was then that the four traitorous warriors finished killing their former friends and comrades. Their clothes and armor were drenched in blood—blood spilled dishonorably. Even drugged, Eustace was still able to clench his fist in outrage for how these warriors had died. They should have died an honorable death, with their swords in hand, not lying on the ground defenseless.

"Why didn't you just poison us and be done with it?" Eustace angrily asked through clenched teeth.

"Oh, Prince, you may find poisons distasteful and corrupting of your honor, but you really should at least know a little about them," Bez answered the prince. "No matter how subtle a poison, it always leaves clues as to its use. What has been used on you is nothing more than a muscle relaxer that healers use to keep pain away while giving treatment. Nothing will be left of it after its use."

"Why, Bez? Why betray me?" Eustace couldn't help but ask. Bez was not only his squire but a trusted aide. If their positions had been the same, maybe they could have been friends.

"Your Highness, it isn't personal. I never was on your side to begin with. Now, let us finish this," Bez said, drawing his sword.

Leander knew it was now or never if he was going to save his brother. With his sword in hand, Leander prepared to fight the five traitors, even knowing it would most likely cost him his life, but when it was time for action, he could not step out of the brush. The sight of the dead warriors, with their eyes screaming in anger and sorrow, froze Leander in place. He tried to push the thoughts out, and when he saw Bez's sword rise, ready to fall on his brother, he was finally able to take a single step.

That step must have made a sound because Eustace turned toward Leander and noticed him preparing to strike. Eustace gave his younger brother a stern glare. Leander knew that glare all too well. It was the same glare Eustace gave him every time he was about to do something foolish. Eustace saw his brother stop and couldn't help giving a slight smile of relief as Bez's sword came down.

Through tear-stained eyes, Leander watched his beloved brother fall back onto the ground. Bez's sword had cut his torso wide open. The world slowed down for Leander as he watched his brother taking his final breaths. In these last breaths, Eustace mouthed a single word several times until the light in his eyes disappeared and the crown prince of the Talov Duchy's life ended. What Eustace had tried to tell Leander was clear to him. In his final moment, his brother had mouthed the word "Go."

"What's taking Gran so long?" Leander heard Bez ask as he wiped his sword clean. "You two, go look for him," Bez said, pointing to two of the traitors.

Seeing the two heading his way, Leander burrowed deeper into the brush and hid himself just in time as the two warriors ran past without spotting him. Knowing this was his time to escape, Leander crawled far enough away that Bez and the other warriors still at the camp wouldn't see him, then made a run for it.

Leander continued running, blinded by the tears that wouldn't stop flowing from his eyes. He tripped more than once. Every one of his limbs was scraped and bruised, but he knew if they caught him, he was done for. He ran to the edge of the woodland, past the rolling plains, and through another woodland. It wasn't until daybreak that Leander ran out of strength and fell to the ground, gasping for breath.

Scrunching into a ball, he began to bawl his eyes out. His heart throbbed with pain. Memories of his past with his brother flowed endlessly. No more would he hear his brother's hearty laugh. No more would his brother be there to defend him when he got into trouble.

His whole life, Eustace had looked out for him. Even as they had gotten older and Leander had started distancing himself, he never felt his brother's love for him waver. How he wished he could have the time back. Leander wanted to rewrite his foolishness and once more, like when the two had been children, be close to Eustace, but he knew that would never happen now.

Lying in a fetal position, his eyes no longer able to spill tears, Leander felt the dawn's rays on his body. A new day had arrived, but Leander's life would never be like the past days.

+

The sun's rays broke through the woodland, making the small forest come to life with sounds, but Bez and the other four warriors heard none of it. Surrounding the body of their fellow conspirator, each had a grim look on his face. It had taken them most of the night to find the body, as it had been torn apart by scavenging beasts, but with one look, they knew what had happened.

"Useless fool," Bez cursed, kicking the man's corpse. This could only mean one thing: Prince Leander had escaped.

"What do we do now? Prince Leander survived. If he makes it back, we are done for," one of the four traitorous warriors declared.

"It doesn't matter," Bez said after a few breaths. "With Crown Prince Eustace dead, we can still go forward with our plan."

"How?" another warrior asked. "The plan was to peg Prince Leander as the culprit and claim he died trying to usurp his brother." The plan had been to have them be the only survivors of Leander's "betrayal."

With no evidence against this, as well as Prince Leander's known envy of his elder brother, their lie would be taken as truth. But with the prince's survival, their treachery could be unearthed. Betrayal in the lands of Mezer was looked down upon more than murder. Being labeled a traitor would bring down not only yourself but your whole family with you. Many families had been sentenced to death for the betrayal of a single member.

"The prince is alone and on foot," answered Bez with a vicious smile on his face. "We will ride to WestAvri and will continue with our story but report that Prince Leander killed his brother and escaped. Once word reaches our friends in Raven's Nest, they will surely know how to handle the situation. Then we will stay in WestAvri and wait for the prince to come to us. Once he is in our grasp, his fate is sealed."

Thinking that Bez's plan made sense, the warriors felt reassured and breathed sighs of relief. The only way to reach the Talov Duchy from the Estelle Duchy was either through the holy city or crossing Avri Bridge. With the holy city too far north for the prince to travel to alone and on foot, that only left the bridge.

After mounting up, the five traitors headed east toward the twin cities to carry out their dastardly plan.

Chapter Three: Rumors Fly; a Prince Is Hunted

T hat's impossible! Prince Leander would never kill Crown Prince Eustace! I refuse to believe this!" shouted Princess Aris Talov, the elder sister of the two princes of the Talov Duchy.

It had been midday when the message regarding the death of Crown Prince Eustace had arrived at Raven's Nest. A meeting had quickly been called to discuss this news. Sitting on his throne, the elderly Archduke Ambrose had been lifeless ever since he had heard the news of his grandson's death at the hands of his other grandson. Also in the throne room were the princess, accompanied by her two personal warriors, Duke Jarl Valens, several council members, and a group of the archduke's personal warriors lining the walls, standing as still as stone.

"Your Highness," Duke Valens said, "this news comes from the crown prince's personal squire, and the four surviving warriors all back up his story. Never have you let your emotions affect your decisions. That is why you were chosen to lead the council, even at your young age. You cannot let your personal feelings hinder your judgment." Some of the council members nodded their approval.

"My mind is clear," Aris said, turning to the council. "You have all watched Prince Leander grow up. You all know he would never do what that vile Bez claims."

"Ma'am, you must not condemn a man without proper judgment," one of the council members chimed in.

"Isn't that what you are all doing? Deciding that my brother is guilty before you know all the facts," Aris retorted, scoffing at the member and making the man's face grow red in anger and embarrassment.

"That is enough, Aris," the archduke said with a sigh in his voice.

"Grandfather, you practically raised the three of us since our father and mother died. You carved the ideals of honor, duty, and sacrifice into our very bones. Prince Leander would never dishonor us or himself by killing Crown Prince Eustace for his own gain," Aris said, trying to convince her grandfather that Leander was innocent.

"That is what we want too, ma'am," said Duke Valens. "That is why we wish to find Prince Leander, to prove that he hasn't murdered the crown prince."

"Is that what you are doing by sending out a warrant for his arrest to all the warriors across the duchy? You could have fooled me," Aris said with venom in her words.

Her words sent discontent muttering through the council. Her words dishonored the duke, and to those of Mezer, honor was more important than life. Not only had the princess been disrespectful to the duke, who had a high position in the Talov Duchy, she gave no face to the members of the council. They all thought the princess should control herself.

"You are out of line, Aris. Duke Valens is as concerned as we all are. You shouldn't dishonor him with your speculations," the archduke said, reprimanding his granddaughter.

Aris bit her lip and kept quiet. The former Duke Valens, Jarl Valens's father, was a sworn brother to her grandfather and a decorated hero. He had even given his own leg to save the young Ambrose Talov. It was because of this that the archduke felt indebted to the Valenses, but it also blinded him to the fact that the current duke wasn't like his honorable father.

"Does this mean I have your permission to proceed?" Duke Valens asked.

All in the throne room waited in silence for the archduke's response. His choice would decide the fate of the entire duchy. The princess hoped her grandfather could remember that Leander wouldn't harm their brother, but the archduke's answer was a splash of cold water, dashing her hopes.

"Very well. Send word to every warrior family in our duchy, that Prince Leander will be detained on sight and sent back to Raven's Nest," the archduke ordered.

"As you wish, Your Undaunted Majesty." Duke Valens saluted. "But if he resists?"

"My grandson must not be harmed under any circumstance!" the archduke bellowed. His old body was unable to take the strain, and he began to have a coughing fit. One of the warriors brought the archduke some water, and his fit stopped. "Do you understand? I must see my grandson brought back alive and in one piece."

"As you wish. We will carry out your will," Duke Valens said, giving one final salute. The warriors, council members, and even Princess Aris gave a fisted salute to the archduke.

Angered by her grandfather's decision, the princess was the first to leave, along with her two personal warriors. Storming out of the throne room, she nearly walked into a young man who was waiting just outside. When Aris saw the young man, her sour mood became even worse.

"Your Highness, what has the archduke decided to do about Prince Leander's betrayal?" the young man asked.

"I have nothing to say to you, Lord Sarus," Aris said, and she walked by without even a look back.

The young man's face twitched, almost revealing his true emotions.

Sarus Valens was Jarl Valens's son and heir, and he annoyed Aris just as much as his father did, if not more. Arrogant and unruly, he looked down on those of lower rank than himself, making the young man extremely unpopular with the other warrior families. Not only was he arrogant, but he was a regular womanizer. His father had covered up more than one incident for him. But what made Aris hate him more than anything was that her grandfather had engaged him to her against her wishes.

"Your Highness, as the head of the council, you shouldn't throw your anger at the first person you see after not getting what you want," said Duke Valens, walking out of the throne room with the rest of the council members.

Not caring for what the duke had to say, Aris continued to leave. The council elders muttered among themselves at this show of disrespect. Duke Valens kept the same expression as he watched the princess walk away.

Princess Aris made her way through the palace and into her quarters. Finally, away from the public eye, Aris flew into a rage, smashing up several items. She only stopped when a vase sliced open her hand. One of her personal warriors handed the princess a cloth to dress her wound.

"Your Highness, you shouldn't have shown your anger in the throne room just now. You know that most of the council backs Duke Valens, and with your outburst, now even more council members will flock to his side," said the warrior while bandaging the princess's hand.

"I know that, Pierce," Aris said. "But when I heard that Duke Valens wanted to place a warrant on Prince Leander, I couldn't contain myself."

Hearing his princess say this, the warrior Pierce could only sigh in response. No one in the palace knew how close the siblings were. Only a few knew that there was no way that Leander would kill his brother. Envious of his brother he was, but never would he harm him.

Just when Pierce had finished wrapping Aris's hand, the door suddenly slammed open. Striding into the princess's quarters was Sarus Valens. Seeing him, Aris instantly went cold, and her face couldn't hide her disgust for the man.

"You need to learn how to warm up to me. I am your future husband, after all," Sarus said with a devious laugh.

As he got closer, Pierce and the other warrior blocked his path. This agitated the already temperamental Sarus. In his outrage, he spat in annoyance. "What do you two pet warriors think you are doing blocking me? You two are nothing but pretty songbirds that the princess found. Don't assume you are true warriors," Sarus mocked.

The two warriors weren't fazed by Sarus's taunting and stood in between Sarus and their princess with their hands on their sword hilts, ready for Sarus to act. Their epithet "the princess's songbirds" came from their talent with musical instruments. It was meant to insult the two, as the learning of musical notes was considered feminine and a woman's study, but they took pride in the name. It was because they weren't like the other warriors that Aris had chosen them to be her warriors, and they would die before letting anything befall their princess.

"I said get out of my way!" Sarus shouted once he realized they hadn't budged. When he took another step forward, in an instant, Pierce had his sword drawn and placed at Sarus's throat. Having not expected that a warrior of lower rank would draw his weapon against him, Sarus was petrified with fear.

Aris watched the scene in amusement. Giving a light chuckle, she knew she had

33

to stop this from escalating further.

"That is enough, Pierce. While Lord Sarus did come unannounced, he is still the son of a duke," Aris said.

Almost instantly Pierce's sword left the terrified man's neck and went back to its sheath.

With the threat on his life gone, Sarus readjusted his collar and walked past the two warriors, giving them a scowl, which the two promptly ignored. Sarus tried to hold in his anger, but Aris noticed the twitch in his cheek.

"You really should train your pets better, Princess. Or I could introduce you to true warriors, better warriors—ones who wouldn't let any harm befall you," Sarus said as he gripped her hand that was bound in the bloodied cloth.

"Thanks for the offer, Lord Sarus, but I could think of no warriors better able to protect me," Aris said, pulling her hand away.

Her action infuriated Sarus, but he kept his calm. "My father has informed me of the archduke's decision about Prince Leander," he said. "He also informed me that the Third and Fourth Chivalric Orders are being sent to EastAvri to help Lord Kalfas in the capture of the prince. Rest assured, our crown prince will be avenged."

Aris's worry for Leander intensified. The Third and Fourth Chivalric Orders were warriors under Duke Valens's command. They wouldn't hesitate to kill her brother when given the chance if the duke ordered it. While Lord Hector Kalfas, the Marquess of EastAvri, the ruler of the city, was loyal to the Talovs, the number of warriors under any marquess's command was less than a single chivalric order. The marquess wasn't in any position to help if the duke's men captured Leander. She could only pray that her brother could evade their grasp.

"Is that why you are here, Lord Sarus? To tell me of my brother's impending capture?" Aris asked. Each word contained bottled-up anger.

"My father and the council elders worried that with this decision, the princess would be distraught, and they sent me to make sure you are well," Sarus said, feigning sympathy for her.

"As you can see, I am fine, so you can leave and tell the council and your father that keeping me under surveillance isn't any way for descendants of honorable warriors to act," Aris said, gesturing for Sarus to leave her quarters.

"Aris, that wasn't our—" Sarus began to explain.

"I said leave!" Aris shouted, cutting him off.

Before Sarus could say anything, Aris's two warriors threw him out of the room.

Alone with her trusted warriors once more, Aris contemplated her next move. She knew that her hands were tied with the council now being under Duke Valens's control. She also knew that when the news of Leander's supposed murder of his own brother began to spread, many warriors would believe that it was their duty to bring Leander to justice. Too many people knew of Leander's jealousy of Eustace and could see him committing the crime.

After thinking it through, she knew what she must do.

"We must have Prince Leander return here alive. Only then will his innocence be proved," Aris declared.

"What is your order, ma'am?" the warrior Pierce asked.

"Roan, you will travel to EastAvri. Find my brother, and bring him back to Raven's Nest," Aris ordered.

"As you command," the other warrior, Roan, answered, giving her a fisted salute. As he turned to leave, the door suddenly slammed open once more.

"Not good, Your Highness!" A maid ran in panting. "The archduke has collapsed!"

+

In the city of Esesa, a similar meeting was being held in the throne room of the Estelles. Sitting on his throne, Archduke Bennet looked as regal as any monarch—a vast contrast to the withered look of the Talov archduke. Unlike the meeting in Raven's Nest, only his two sons and daughter were present. Underneath the throne, Elaina Estelle stood glaring at her father.

"I will not change my mind," Archduke Bennet said. "Until we know more, I will not send men to look for Prince Leander. It could be seen as us interfering and could lead to war with the Talov Duchy if they think we had anything to do with the crown prince's assassination."

"All I understand is that the most feared general of his generation is a coward." Elaina mocked her father.

"Elaina! How could you say such a thing about our father?" the second prince, Felon, shouted.

"Am I wrong? If so, then allow me to send warriors to find out what really happened," Elaina said, trying to goad her father.

"That is enough, Elaina. If you will not be contributing to this discussion, then you should leave," her elder brother, Aleron, said, to her shock.

Realizing that her arguments were pointless, Elaina left the throne room, furious. Waiting for her at the door was her attending maiden Hali. Seeing her princess in a bad mood, Hali knew that her princess's request had been denied by the archduke. Several council members and warriors were waiting outside the throne room. They wished to ask the princess what the archduke's orders were, but Elaina left without answering, a plan silently formulating in her head.

+

The day soon turned into night, and when the moon was at the center of the sky, a figure could be seen sneaking out of the palace. Making its way to the stables, the cloaked figure went to one of the crownes. The black-coated crowne was irritated by the nighttime intruder, but when it realized who the intruder was, it calmed down.

As the figure began to strap a harness onto the horned horse, the stable door opened, and bright light illuminated the figure, revealing it to be the princess.

Blinded by the sudden light, Elaina had to let her eyes adjust before she could see who had caught her. She sighed in relief when she saw who had discovered her escape attempt.

"Hali … Kaine … what are you two doing here?" Elaina asked.

"Isn't that what we should be asking you, Your Highness?" Kaine Malis retorted, looking over Elaina. The princess was dressed in men's traveling clothes and had several bags. She was clearly attempting to leave Esesa in the dead of night before anyone could stop her.

Elaina knew that any excuse she made to the two siblings in front of her would be useless. Hali and Kaine Malis were a brother and sister who had grown up with her and were the closest people to Elaina besides her family. Kaine was also a decorated warrior, even at his age, and one of her eldest brother's personal warriors. She knew that if he was here to stop her, it would be impossible for her to leave.

"I can't just wait around and do nothing," Elaina said. "Something is wrong with this whole situation, and finding Prince Leander is the fastest way to unraveling it."

"You would go against the archduke's orders?" Kaine asked in a serious tone, while Hali stood there with a worried look on her face.

"Kaine, can you just pretend you haven't seen me?" Elaina asked with little hope.

"You can't be seriously thinking of searching for His Highness alone," Hali said, shocked by the princess's plea.

"If my father refuses to find Prince Leander, then I will," said Elaina, standing there, almost daring Hali and Kaine to stop her.

37

Seeing that Elaina was adamant about going, Kaine let out a sigh, then turned and left the stables. Not a few seconds had gone by when Kaine returned along with several others. Elaina recognized the newcomers. They were all young warriors. Seeing Elaina's confused look, the youths couldn't help laughing.

"You aren't the only one who believes we should find His Highness," Kaine said. "Everyone here is a friend of Prince Leander and Crown Prince Eustace."

"You all …" Elaina began as she watched everyone ready their steeds for the long journey. She didn't finish her words, and the young warriors didn't need to hear them.

That night, without anyone noticing, seven young men and two young women rode out of Esesa.

It was only when Kaine and the other young warriors didn't report in the next morning that they were discovered missing. By then the troop of younglings was long gone.

Chapter Four: The Prince and the Sell-Swords

The outskirts of WestAvri was a place where the beggars and homeless dwelled. Each of the twin cities had their slums, but the outskirts of the southern part of WestAvri were the worst, full of drug dealers and thieves. No one of decent upbringing would be caught dead in these decrepit streets.

Hiding in this armpit of society was Prince Leander Talov. Covered in dirt and grime, the prince looked just like any other street beggar. It had taken him several days to make it to WestAvri. During this time, he had hidden from multiple warrior parties, as he didn't know who he could trust. His fine clothes had quickly turned to rags on the way to WestAvri, and he no longer had the demeanor of a prince. He blended in quite well with the dregs of the slum.

Walking through the run-down streets, not a single person gave the prince a second glance. Some even lifted their noses at him. Leander considered himself lucky that no one recognized him as he was at that moment. As he neared Avri Bridge, the slums gave way to nicer houses. The closer to the bridge he got, the better the houses became. There were also more people roaming the streets compared to in the outskirts.

As the bridge came into sight, Leander felt as if he was almost safe. Once he was in EastAvri and under the protection of Lord Kalfas, he would not have anything to fear, and the traitors would face justice for their crimes.

Thinking of the traitors, Leander remembered that night when he had watched Bez strike down his brother. Holding in his tears, Leander kept going until he reached the bridge.

What was waiting for him was something he wasn't expecting. Lines of warriors blocked the bridge at its center. While there were always guards to inspect people passing over the bridge, it was usually only around ten from each city, and right now, there were over a hundred trained warriors standing almost motionless on the bridge, making a human wall. But what shocked Leander was a sign in front of the bridge.

Posted on the sign was a picture of himself. With his portrait were several lines of words: "Wanted for the supposed assassination of Crown Prince Eustace of the Talov Duchy: Prince Leander Talov. Archduke Ambrose calls on all warriors to apprehend the criminal on sight. Wanted alive."

Seeing his wanted poster, Leander dropped to his knees, his mouth agape. He could not believe that his own grandfather would send out a warrant for his arrest. Did his grandfather really believe that he could kill his own brother?

"Your Highness, I almost didn't recognize you," said an all-too-familiar voice to Prince Leander.

Turning around, he came face-to-face with his brother's murderer. Bez, with an evil smirk on his face, led a group of ten warriors. Leander noticed that two of the warriors were those who had conspired with Bez. The rest of the warriors had the black wing emblem on their tunics with the numeral 3 underneath, the emblem of the Third Chivalric Order.

"Bez … you slimy thing," Leander said, grinding his teeth as he spoke. "How dare you appear before me!"

"How dare I? A traitor has no right to speak to me! Arrest this man who killed our crown prince!" Bez ordered.

The warriors drew their swords and approached Leander. He knew that if these men caught him, he wouldn't survive to see tomorrow's sunrise. Bez would make sure that he "tried to escape" and was mistakenly cut down in the process. As he tried to figure out a way out of the situation, Leander was already halfway encircled.

Knowing that he had to act now, Leander ran toward the warriors. Trained to be the archduke and his family's guards before anything else, the warriors instinctively pulled back, allowing Leander to slip past. Escaping the encirclement, Leander ran as fast as he could.

"After him!" he heard Bez shout from behind.

Running through the streets and back alleys, Leander could hear the warriors right on his heels. He waded through the crowds and was able to gain some distance from the armored warriors. Sadly, his luck began to run out. After days of travel and nothing to eat, Leander had little energy to continue running.

Finding himself back in the outskirts, Leander's strength began to give. He knew his only chance was to find a place to hide, so he searched for a spot as he ran. No longer obstructed by the crowds, the pursuing warriors closed in. Leander turned into an empty alley and saw a small door hidden from sight of the main street. Just as he closed the door behind him, he heard the quick marching pace of the warriors running by.

Sighing in relief, Leander's body went slack, as he didn't even have the energy to stand. His mind and sight began to go fuzzy as he succumbed to exhaustion, but it was at that moment that he saw them. In the small room he had barged into were two others. Both had cowls that covered their heads and faces, and swords strapped to their waists.

As the two men walked toward him, Leander could no longer hold on and fainted from exhaustion.

+

"Who is this?" Lucis asked, looking down at the passed-out Leander. "He looks vaguely familiar."

Crouching down, Aer inspected the fallen young man. After finding that the young man was only unconscious, Aer lifted Leander's hand. Both Aer and Lucis noticed the calluses on the young man's palms.

"Those aren't the hands of a laborer. Those hands are made from constantly swinging a sword," Lucis remarked.

Aer nodded at Lucis's observation as he went back to looking over Leander. He pulled out a waterskin and a cloth. Dampening the cloth, he wiped off the grime from Leander's face. Getting a better look at Leander's face, Aer suddenly narrowed his eyes as he remembered where he had seen the young man.

"I know where we have seen him before, or to be more accurate, why he seems familiar," Aer said.

Peering down, Lucis still couldn't figure out where he had seen Leander before. Seeing Lucis's confusion, Aer finally told him. "He is the one from the wanted posters. The famous murderous prince," Aer said.

Realization set in as Lucis remembered all the wanted posters plastered around the city. When the duo had first crossed the bridge into WestAvri, the city had been busy but peaceful. Now, several days later, it had all changed. Warriors flowed into the twin cities constantly. The Talov warriors from EastAvri clashed with the Estelle warriors from WestAvri daily. This made finding the trail of their missing brother even more difficult, and the culprit for all of this was now passed out in front of them.

"What should we do, then? Should we hand him over to the patrolling guards or the warriors from the chivalric order?" Lucis asked.

"Something is not right with this entire situation. Even if this prince killed his brother but failed to finish off the rest of the warriors, how is he in such dire straits now? Someone ready to kill his own brother should have thought it out more thoroughly or had a backup plan," Aer said. "No. Something happened, but not in the way that people have been told."

"If you say so." Lucis sighed, then chuckled. "You and Kay were always better at reading people and situations than me, anyways."

Suddenly the two could hear many footsteps heading toward them stop just outside the door. The sound of metal armor clanking made the two realize that a group of warriors chasing the prince had tracked him here. Loud banging came from the other side of the door as those outside pounded on it.

"Open the door!" ordered someone impatiently.

Neither Lucis nor Aer felt intimidated by the man and didn't feel the need to respond. When his order wasn't followed, the man ordered his men to break down the door. Very quickly the door broke off its hinges, and five warriors ran in, each with sword in hand.

The warriors looked over the three of them who were in the room, but their attention went straight to the one unconscious. The warriors instantly recognized Prince Leander. Of the five, the one who seemed to be the leader stepped forward.

"Hand over the fugitive, and we will let you live," he ordered. Again Lucis and Aer didn't react. The leader was angered but didn't know what to do. They had been told that the prince was alone, so where had these two come from?

"Sir, these men could be conspirators. We shouldn't let them go," said one of the warriors. Aer noticed that this warrior had a malicious glint in his eyes.

43

Seeing that they had no choice, Lucis and Aer unsheathed their swords. Lucis grabbed Leander by the collar and threw the young man behind him and Aer, protecting him from the warriors. His action solidified their appearance as conspirators in the minds of the warriors, and they encircled Lucis and Aer.

Running out of patience, one of the warriors attacked, lunging with his sword at Aer. Aer was easily able to parry the strike and struck out himself, sending the warrior back. Keeping with the momentum, Aer continued to attack, with the warrior struggling to guard.

One of the other warriors tried to help, but before he could, Lucis intercepted the man. The warrior blocked, but Lucis's strike was stronger than the warrior had thought. His guard failed as Lucis's sword found its mark, cutting into the warrior's neck.

Enraged, the leading warrior charged Lucis with the other two warriors. With otherworldly reflexes, Lucis was able to dodge all their strikes and put some distance between him and the three. As the fighting between the three and Lucis intensified, Aer was able to wear down the remaining warrior and stab his sword through the man's chest.

Seeing another one of his comrades fall, the warrior leader knew that they were in trouble. The fighting had only just started, and they had lost two men, while their enemy wasn't even winded yet. The scariest part was those movements that he had just seen. No normal warrior could move like that.

As the fighting intensified, the commotion woke the unconscious Leander. He was baffled at what he awoke to. Two cloaked men were fighting warriors from the Third Chivalric Order. Leander knew that warriors chosen to be part of any chivalric order were the best warriors of the duchy. Any single member could face two warriors and come out on top. But the scene in front of him was of these strong warriors struggling to face these unknown men. Two had even been slain already.

Still dizzy, Leander tried to stand, but his legs were still asleep and refused to move. Then someone kicked him to the ground, pinning him to the floor with his foot. It was one of the Talov warriors, who had been able to make it to the prince during the fighting. As Leander's sight began to focus, he recognized the warrior standing over him. It was one of the traitorous warriors from the night his brother had been killed. The warrior's arm hung limp and bleeding, a sacrifice to escape from his opponent.

"Die!" was all the traitorous warrior said as he swung his sword at the defenseless Leander.

Closing his eyes, Leander braced himself for the blow, but it never came. Opening his eyes, he looked up at the warrior, who now had a sword sticking out of his chest. Behind the warrior stood Lucis, whose cowl had fallen back during the fight. The warrior looked down at the sword that had run him through, not believing that his life was over. Then Lucis pulled his sword out of the warrior. Blood flowed out of the hole in his chest as he fell to the floor, dying before his body hit the ground.

Lucis turned back to the warrior leader he had been fighting. Kneeling on the ground, the warrior looked at Lucis's now-revealed face as he held a bloody stump that used to be his right hand. When Lucis had noticed the warrior about to strike Leander, he, in a single breath, had cut off the leader's hand and lunged at the warrior standing above the prince, piercing him through with his sword.

But it was neither losing his hand nor knowing that he and his men were done for that had the leader so shocked. What shocked him was the scar that he saw on Lucis's face. A scar that looked older than the man who bore it. A scar that told of legendary battles and heroic feats. Not just him, but any warrior from any of the

45

three duchies would know what that scar implied. As Lucis reached the warrior leader, the leader only said one word before Lucis's sword separated his head from his torso. "Zer'sheen."

Seeing all his comrades had died, the remaining warrior didn't run or try to escape. With the wild bravery the warriors of Mezer were famous for, he continued to clash swords with Aer. While Aer was not as strong or as talented as Lucis, he was still a step ahead of the warrior, and soon the final warrior joined his comrades in the afterlife.

With all the warriors dead, Lucis and Aer sheathed their weapons. An eerie silence hung in the air. Leander was glad for being saved, but besides the dead traitor, the rest of the warriors were honorable men and dutiful warriors. They shouldn't have died in this run-down building in the slums of WestAvri. These conflicting emotions plus the last word one of the warriors had said kept Leander silent.

Looking at Lucis, Leander knew for a fact that the man was a Zer'sheen, a bearer of scars. The word Zer'sheen was old Angrelic and translated to "one who has returned." Born with scars, these people were the reincarnations of legendary warriors. With incredible strength and supreme reflexes, Zer'sheen were known to be the strongest warriors in all the three duchies.

Priests preached and taught that these scarred born were warriors who had gained approval from the Phoenix God, Calv Ridian, and rested in the legendary Ancestral Hall after their earthly demise. These great warriors of old would return bearing their scars from their past life. With most people in the three duchies worshipping Calv Ridian and believing the fables and tales, these Zer'sheen were treated as saints the day they were born.

As Leander looked over the scar on Lucis's face, one question echoed in his mind: How had a Zer'sheen been undiscovered for this long? The holy city of Ridia kept detailed records of every child born in the duchies, and when one was born, the holy city would take custody of the child, with the exception of Zer'sheen born into warrior lineages.

"Are you really a Zer'sheen?" Leander asked, breaking the silence.

"And if he is?" Aer said, taking off his cowl.

It was then that Leander got a good look at his two saviors. Both had strong builds, showing their lives as warriors, but the supposed Zer'sheen radiated strength. They each had a sword on their waist, and they wore strange foreign cloaks and cowls. As a prince of the Talov Duchy, which had strong trading links with the southern kingdoms, he saw some similarities their clothing had to that of some traders.

"If you truly are a Zer'sheen, then you are a warrior birthed from honor. I implore you, my name is Leander Talov, grandson of Archduke Ambrose and prince of the Talov Duchy. Help me make my way back to Raven's Nest," Leander pleaded, bowing to Lucis. Zer'sheen were considered the highest form a warrior could be. There was no dishonor in a prince bowing to one.

Seeing the prince bow, Aer couldn't help but give a slight chuckle. "You seem to be mistaken. While my brother is a Zer'sheen, we are not warriors. We are simple sell-swords," Aer said.

Leander was struck dumb by this revelation. He had never heard of a Zer'sheen, the greatest of warriors, becoming a sell-sword, or mercenary. Those of warrior families and lineages looked down on those who sold their sword to the highest bidder. "Warriors without honor" was a popular epithet slung around.

"It doesn't matter if you two are sell-swords. A Zer'sheen could never do anything dishonorable, so I'll ask you again. Please help me get home to Raven's

Nest. You can name any price once we get there," Leander said, once more bowing his head.

"How can we trust the words of a man who killed his own brother?" Lucis asked.

"I didn't kill my brother!" Leander shouted, but quieted himself, as he didn't want to alert the warriors still searching for him. "I was set up."

Seeing the sorrow in the prince, Aer knew he was telling the truth. Too many things didn't add up. As sell-swords, Aer and Lucis had seen many different types of people, and Aer had quickly picked up on how people thought. The prince didn't look like one of those who would slay their own blood for their own gain.

"We will agree with your request to take you to Raven's Nest," Aer said, shocking both Lucis and Leander. "But on one condition."

"As long as it is within my power," Leander said. "What is the condition?"

"I need your help finding someone, our brother, Kay. If you can help us find him, then we don't need any other payment," Aer said.

Lucis suddenly understood why Aer had agreed to the prince's request. With his power, the prince could easily find a person in the three duchies. By themselves, who knew how long it would take or whether they could even find their brother?

"Do you agree to our terms?" Aer asked once more.

Leander knew that this was his only chance to survive the way to Raven's Nest. Even though he didn't know these two or who their brother was, he quickly shouted, "Yes!"

Chapter Five: The Blood-Crazed Stranger

It had been several days since Elaina and her troop of young warriors had sneaked out of Esesa. Their steeds had made quick work of the journey, and they were only a single day's ride from WestAvri.

"Your Highness, we have been riding throughout the night. We have to let our crownes rest for a while," Kaine said as he rode next to Elaina.

"Just a while longer," Elaina said, adamant about continuing the ride.

Seeing his princess so focused, Kaine could only follow. Truly, as the king of horses, a crowne could run for several days before it got tired. Its rider, on the other hand, was a different story. Turning to the following warriors, Kaine grimaced. Most that followed Elaina on her search for Prince Leander were young warriors, closer to childhood than adulthood. While most had ridden long distances, none had ridden this long continuously. The young warriors could only hold on for dear life and not get thrown off.

When Kaine saw his sister nearly fall off her steed in front of his eyes, he had had enough. Rushing forward, he rode in front of Elaina, stopping her in her tracks. Whenever she tried to ride around, Kaine would block her.

"What do you think you are doing?" Elaina shouted, clearly upset over Kaine's actions.

"I could ask you the very same question," Kaine said with a sharp tone in his voice. "Why don't you look behind you?"

Still upset, she turned to look behind at the warriors following and was shocked. Everyone was covered in sweat and was panting heavily. Some held their reins in trembling hands, while others had a dazed look, unable to concentrate, but the worst off was Hali. She was neither an expert rider, like Elaina, nor a warrior, like everyone else. It took all her strength not to fall, but her consciousness was beginning to fade from exhaustion.

"If we go at this pace, we will be worn out before we even reach WestAvri," said Kaine.

Elaina looked away from Kaine. A slight tint of red appeared on her face. She felt guilty for pushing them so hard and embarrassed for not noticing sooner. As the daughter of Archduke Bennet, she had learned to ride before she could walk. Her riding skills were far superior to those of everyone here. She had not thought that they wouldn't be able to keep up with her.

"Very well. We will stop once we reach that grove," Elaina said, pointing at some trees not too far off.

Everyone heaved a sigh of relief hearing her agree. The trees weren't too far off, only several hundred paces away, and they would give them shade from the blistering sun. Desperate for some rest, some of the young warriors rushed ahead to the grove. Seeing some of their fellow warriors ride off, the rest followed suit, with Elaina, Kaine, and Hali at the rear.

"Elaina, do you really not have romantic feelings for Prince Leander?" Kaine asked in an informal tone now that the rest of the warriors were far away. As Hali's older brother, he had grown up with the princess and was one of her closest friends. When they were alone, the division that their positions entailed disappeared.

"I have said it before. I care for Prince Leander, but I do not love him," Elaina said with a sigh as she thought about what Leander must be going through at this moment.

"Then why take such a risk to look for him?" Kaine asked. "We did agree with you that Prince Leander should be found, but you know that we really came to keep you safe. Finding the prince comes second in our hearts."

Elaina knew what Kaine was saying. As a princess, her going out alone posed more than one danger. Her family had many enemies, and if news of this reached them, her life could be in jeopardy. So when Elaina had said that she only cared for Leander as a friend and not a lover, Kaine and the rest of the warriors had their doubts. No normal friend would risk their life and their relationship with their family for another.

"You are right, Kaine. I do think of Prince Leander as more than a friend. To me, he is more like a brother," Elaina said, looking toward the grove.

"I can understand, I too have carved brotherly bonds with my fellow warriors, but are you sure it is familial love? Are the feelings you have for Prince Leander the same as your feelings for your blood brothers?" Kaine asked.

Elaina sighed. "You are sworn to my eldest brother, so tell me, what is the first word that comes to mind when you picture him?" Elaina asked.

Kaine didn't take long to think up a word that embodied the crown prince. Anyone who had met the crown prince would use this word to describe him, and that word would be *cold*. Whether it was ordering warriors or simple conversations with his family, the prince's attitude rarely changed. This gave him the nickname "the Frozen-Hearted Prince."

"And what of my second brother?" Elaina said before Kaine could respond to her first question. "Do you think I could have a sibling relationship with Prince

Felon?"

Both Kaine and Elaina knew that a sibling relationship with the second prince was even less likely. If Crown Prince Aleron was cold, then Prince Felon burned with aggression. Wearing his emotions on his sleeve, Prince Felon seemed to try to rub people up the wrong way. There had never been a day growing up when he wasn't bruised from fighting with the other kids.

But it wasn't this personality that made the relationship between brother and sister strained. When he was five years old, Felon had watched his mother die giving birth to his sister, Princess Elaina. He had never forgiven Elaina for taking his loving mother away from him. The archduke tried to have Felon see that it wasn't Elaina's fault, but it was to no avail.

"My blood brothers treat me like no more than a stranger, or sometimes more like an acquaintance," Elaina said. "I haven't seen them smile my way, let alone act like true brothers. On the other hand, anytime we met, Prince Leander would greet me with a warm smile. He would play with me even if he was tired, or worry if I was hurt. I always feel that he has my best interests at heart when he is around." A slight smile grew as she reminisced.

"To me, that sounds like love," Kaine said, still not understanding what she was going for.

"I thought that as well when I first noticed my feelings for Prince Leander," Elaina said. "But one night, in the garden, I stumbled across two lovers embracing each other in the moonlight. It was one of the maids and a warrior I had seen in the palace. Not knowing what to do, I ran away and locked myself in my room."

"What warrior and maid? Just give me a description of the two, and I'll have them reprimanded," Kaine angrily said.

"That isn't the point," Elaina said. "Once I'd had time to absorb what I'd seen, I tried to picture Prince Leander and me in the same embrace." She gave a slight pause before continuing. "And I found that I couldn't. It was then that I knew I didn't love Prince Leander the way I know he loves me, that, to me, he would only be a brotherly figure and nothing more."

When she had finished telling Kaine how she felt about Leander, she couldn't help but show a painful expression.

After watching Elaina withdraw into herself, Kaine turned to his sister, seeing that her face hadn't changed during this revelation. It was clear that Hali had already known Elaina's true feelings.

Not knowing what to do, the three rode on in silence.

"What's going on?" Hali suddenly said, pointing toward the grove they were heading for.

Right before the grove were the young warriors who had ridden on ahead, but none of them had entered the wooded area. They all were alert and had their swords and halberds drawn. Drawing near the trio soon caught a scent of what had made the warriors alert. A potent scent of iron spread out from the grove.

"The scent of blood, and a lot of it at that," Kaine said as he, too, unsheathed his sword. He ordered his crowne forward, putting himself between the grove and Princess Elaina. For the smell of blood to be this strong, many must have died, quite recently as well.

"Myles, report what has happened," Elaina ordered one of the warriors.

"Your Highness," the warrior Myles said, giving Elaina a fisted salute. "We aren't sure. Before any of us could enter, we caught the scent of blood and prepared for a fight, but nothing has left the grove. We have heard several noises but are unable to discern what they are or what they come from."

"Then we should look into it," Elaina declared. "Myles, you will stay here and guard Hali. Kaine, you and the rest of the warriors will follow me into the grove."

"Ma'am, I urge you to wait out here as well. Unlike us, you have not trained in swordplay nor taken a man's life. I will take command of the warriors and lead them into the grove myself," Kaine said, hoping the princess was in a reasonable mood, but he was sadly disappointed. Her look told him that she was going in as well.

"If you are adamant about coming, then please let me take the lead," Kaine said, submitting to letting her go.

Nodding her head, Elaina and the rest dismounted from their steeds. She then followed Kaine and the warriors into the grove. Her attending maiden Hali and the warrior Myles watched from outside the grove as the group disappeared from sight. Hali's hands were clenched together as she prayed for her princess's safety.

The groves and woodlands of the eastern part of the Estelle Duchy were not difficult to traverse. The trees were spaced out, giving them plenty of space to pass through. As the group entered deeper into the grove, the scent of blood grew thicker. Holding her nose, Elaina did all she could to keep herself from vomiting. Compared to the youthful warriors, who had seen bloodshed before, Elaina could barely tolerate the stench.

It was then that an agonizing scream came from ahead. The scream was sharp and loud, but also quick, and no other sounded afterward. More alert than ever, Kaine led Elaina and the warriors onward.

When they made it to where the scream and blood smell originated from, the scene dumbfounded them. Even Kaine, the most experienced of the group, couldn't help but grimace at what was before them.

Bodies ripped apart littered the ground ahead of them. Mangled and bloody, each corpse held a weapon, from a sword to a spear. Some wore some form of armor, but most were adorned with simple leather gear. Each of the bodies had the same permanent expression plastered on its deceased face, the expression of pure disbelief and terror.

Standing in the center of this bloodshed was a lone man. Adorned in a long brown coat that reached his ankles and holding a broken sword in his hand, the man was covered in blood. With his back to them, they couldn't make out his appearance, and the amount of blood on the man turned even his skin and hair a deep crimson. To Elaina and the rest, the man looked as if he were death incarnate, ready to take the life of his next victim.

The arrival of Elaina and her group was not missed by the man. As he turned his blood-soaked face toward them, Elaina shivered in fright. Two bright blue eyes stared menacingly at her. Elaina couldn't help taking a step back, trying her hardest to restrain her instincts to run.

"Stay behind me," Kaine said, using his body to shield Elaina from the bloody man. "You there, identify yourself!" Kaine ordered the bloody man.

The bloody man didn't react or show that he had heard Kaine. His frustration and anxiety growing, Kaine signaled the rest of the warriors to surround the man.

Elaina didn't know why, but as she watched the warriors creeping closer to the unknown man, she felt that they were sending them to their deaths.

"Wait—" was all she could get out before the bloody man made his move.

Dropping the broken blade, the man twisted his hand around the closest warrior's arm and, with a loud pop, dislocated the poor warrior's shoulder. Screaming in pain, the warrior couldn't hold on to his sword. On its release, the bloody man nimbly caught it, swinging at the warrior, who stared in horror as he clutched his limp arm. The bloody man's strike was intercepted just in time by another warrior.

With his fatal strike parried, the bloody man quickly spun and struck the warrior who had parried his sword with a kick to the chin, knocking the warrior down and into a daze. When three of the warriors attacked the man in a team, he was able to contend with them on an equal footing. He was even pushing them back, as his strikes were faster and cleaner than the warriors'.

Seeing his fellow warriors struggle, Kaine had no choice but to join the fray. Leaving Elaina protected by the two remaining warriors, he joined the three fighting the bloody man. With Kaine's addition, the fight turned in favor of the warriors. When Kaine's sword narrowly missed the man's throat, the bloody man took the chance and dashed through the four. He was as slick as an eel as he dodged every strike. Kaine looked on in horror as the man headed straight for Elaina and the two other warriors.

"HALT!" Kaine shouted, but the man was already upon the two warriors. The man easily passed the two and was now heading toward the princess.

Shocked by the sudden situation, Elaina pulled out her sword, more out of instinct than a conscious motion. With a quick flick of his wrist, the bloody man instantly disarmed the untrained Elaina. Defenseless, Elaina could only watch as the man's sword neared. As his sword lunged at her throat, Elaina knew her life was over. She only hoped that Kaine and the rest could make it home alive from this. Closing her eyes, Elaina waited for the sting of the sword to pass her throat, but it never arrived.

Peeking out through squinting eyes, she saw the man holding his sword less than a hair's breadth from her throat. Her gaze flowed up and locked onto the bloody man's eyes. His eyes were hazy and not focusing on her. Unconsciously, Elaina placed her hand on the sword held to her throat. This motion alerted the man, whose eyes refocused and stared into Elaina's own two emerald eyes. The two stood motionless, staring into each other, neither knowing what to do.

"Release her, you fiend!" Kaine shouted as he and the warriors surrounded the two.

Elaina watched as the murderous intent faded from the man's eyes, like the morning fog dispersing over the plains. Releasing his grip on his sword, the man's knees buckled, and he fell to the ground.

Still on his guard, Kaine inspected the fallen man. "He's unconscious," he said as he checked and found the man to still be alive. Making sure they were safe from the man, Kaine bound his arms and legs with rope.

Elaina felt her legs give out as the tension left her body weak. As she gasped for breath, a cold sweat poured down the nape of her neck. That was the closest she had ever been to losing her life. She could still feel the cold steel of the sword at her throat. She raised her hand to her neck, then pulled it away when she felt a stinging sensation. Looking at her hand, Elaina felt her pulse race. Her fingertips were stained with a small amount of blood. She could only hear her heartbeat, so she didn't hear the others calling her.

"Ma'am," Kaine said, gripping Elaina by her shoulders. "Are you all right?" Seeing her in shock, Kaine worried for her mind after her near-death encounter.

"Kaine?" Elaina said, coming out of whatever trance she had been in. "I'm fine. Just a little shaken is all," she said, trying to reassure him.

"If that is all, then that is good," Kaine said, not truly believing her words, but seeing no outer forms of panic, he let it slide.

"Kaine, you need to see this," yelled one of the warriors, who was inspecting the piles of dead bodies.

Hearing the warrior, Kaine helped Elaina up, and the two headed toward the field of bodies. Elaina still couldn't believe the number of people who had been killed. As a princess and member of one of the founding warrior families, Elaina had seen death, but only as an execution or a rare duel to the death—never something this bloody and violent. Elaina once more found her gaze becoming blurry, but feeling Kaine grip her shoulder kept her from slipping back into herself.

"What is it that you have found?" Kaine asked as they reached the warrior who had called for him. The warrior was crouched by one of the bodies that was adorned in armor.

"This," the warrior said, pulling out a ripped piece of cloth. The cloth was as black as night, and a crimson sword was sewn onto the black cloth.

Both Elaina and Kaine were shocked. They knew of only one group who had a crimson sword as their symbol.

"What is a warrior of the Bloody Blade of Tarsis doing this far south?" Elaina couldn't help but say, taking the cloth into her hands.

The Tarsises were probably the most infamous family in all the lands of Mezer. The Bloody Blade was one of the more vicious orders controlled by them. The final duchy was controlled by the Tarsis family. Unlike the Talovs and Estelles, the Tarsises had no friendly relations with either of the other two duchies. The relationship was so bad that if any warrior were to pass the border of either duchy, a war would break out. It was because of the last war that the Talovs and Estelles had formed an alliance against the Tarsises. But that was a generation ago, when Elaina's grandfather had been the archduke. Since then, not a single person from the Tarsis Duchy had crossed into the Estelles' land—that is, until now.

"Nothing good comes from Tarsis," Kaine grumbled. "Check every corpse to see which are from the Tarsis Duchy, and find out who they were fighting," he ordered.

The warriors quickly went to work, searching the corpses. In the end, every corpse had the same piece of cloth depicting a crimson sword.

"If all of them are from the Tarsis Duchy, then who were they fighting?" Kaine questioned.

Suddenly a thought entered his head, and he turned to the unconscious man. The bloody man was the only person they hadn't searched.

Elaina saw Kaine's gaze, and she, too, understood what Kaine was thinking, that the bloody man was the one who had killed all the dead here. Elaina didn't know why, but whatever she had seen in those crystal blue eyes made her believe that the man could in fact cause a slaughter like the one around them.

Whatever had happened here, only one person could give them the answers, and it was the one person they all feared would soon wake.

Dustin Farris

Chapter Six: An Irritating Sell-Sword

Kay awoke to his body in pain. His head was pounding as the blood rushed to his brain. Groaning, he tried to move, only to find his arms and legs bound. Opening his eyes, Kay found that he was in a large tent. His arms and legs were tied to a wooden pole that stuck out of the ground like a spike.

Kay tried to remember how he had gotten into this situation. The last thing he remembered was fighting Karsic's men. He had trailed them for months, only to walk straight into an ambush. Luckily, he had been able to kill the lot of them, but that didn't explain why he was bound in a tent.

When he closed his eyes to try to remember, a small face appeared in his mind—a young girl in her prime, with soft features and hair of gold. She had appeared not long after he had killed the last of Karsic's warriors. Her face was the last thing Kay could remember, but it wasn't her looks that had stuck out to Kay, it was her eyes.

"Those eyes," Kay whispered under his breath as he tried to picture the young girl once more.

As he struggled with his bindings, the sound of footsteps heading toward him caused Kay to stop struggling. Through the tent flap entered the young woman with the golden hair, followed by a muscular young man and another young woman. The young man gave Kay a fierce glare, which only amused Kay.

"You're finally awake," the blond woman started, sitting down on a stool in front of Kay, with the other two standing behind her. It was clear to Kay that this young woman was the one in charge.

"Who are you?" Kay asked.

"Me?" the blond woman said, pointing at herself with one of her small fingers. "Shouldn't the crest on my chest tell you who I am?" she chuckled.

Kay then noticed the fine embroidered family crest on her tunic. A mighty horned horse adorned the woman's chest. Every warrior family had their own crest. They came in many forms, from beasts to weapons or patterns, and showed who they were and who they were allied to. Kay knew that in all the duchies, only one family had the crowne as their family crest.

"You're an Estelle," Kay said.

"That's right. And now that you know who I am, I would like to ask you the very same question. Who are you?" Elaina asked with a slight smile that she used to mask her true thoughts.

"Me? I'm no one of importance. Just a run-of-the-mill sell-sword," Kay said, giving Elaina a slight smile back to taunt her.

"An ordinary sell-sword capable of killing dozens of Tarsis warriors single-handedly? Don't treat us as fools," said Kaine, irked at how the man looked at the princess.

Kay only gave a wary smile but didn't respond to Kaine's outburst. From hunting the man, Kay knew that Karsic was connected to the Tarsises, but as someone who had only arrived in the lands of Mezer from the southern kingdoms not too long ago, Kay wasn't knowledgeable about the intricate relations. He only knew that the Tarsis Duchy was more of another world than a third duchy.

"I am what I am. It doesn't matter to me if you believe me or not," Kay said with a shrug.

"You—" Kaine started, but with a motion of her hand, Elaina stopped the angry Kaine's rebuttal.

"While we do wish to know who you are, the more pressing question is, what is your relationship to the dead Tarsis warriors?" Elaina said, her eyes narrowing, trying to notice anything out of place Kay might do as a result of the dead warriors being mentioned, but Kay showed no response to her inquiry.

"I know nothing about Tarsis warriors. The men I killed were the followers of a man called Karsic," Kay said, having no reason to hide anything. The men he had killed could have been Tarsis warriors, but that didn't really matter to him.

"Karsic?" Elaina said, turning toward Kaine. Seeing him shake his head, she knew that Kaine hadn't heard of the man either.

"Anyways, I have no quarrel with the Estelles, so why don't you untie me, and we can go our separate ways?" Kay said, indicating his bound limbs.

Kay's words brought Elaina's and Kaine's attention back to him. Seeing his slight smile angered the two of them. "Maybe before, that was so, but you still murdered over a dozen men in land protected by my family. I cannot just let you walk free," said Elaina.

"They ambushed me. I was only defending myself," Kay argued back.

"We don't know that for sure. With all other witnesses dead, it is only your word against the silence of the dead," said Kaine, clearly distrusting of Kay.

"Then what are you going to do with me, Princess? Make me your pet?" Kay teased Elaina with a taunting grin.

"You ..." Elaina said as she blushed a bright red. Never had anyone spoken to her in that way. Her hands clenched as they trembled with rage.

"How dare you speak to the princess in that way!" Hali shouted, speaking up for the first time. Next to her, Kaine placed his hand on the hilt of his sword as if waiting for Elaina's order to punish their prisoner.

"That is quite all right, Hali. As he said, he is only a sell-sword. It's a given for him to be a crude and uneducated man," Elaina said, scrutinizing Kay.

Sitting there looking up at Elaina, whose face had calmed down but still had a tint of embarrassment, Kay felt that she was very amusing to watch. He had caused many to turn red in anger or embarrassment due to his vicious tongue, but never had those people reacted the way this princess did. Seeing as she had thrown an insult back, Kay couldn't help but take his taunting up a notch.

"Crude and uneducated? There is no need for name-calling, little princess. Someone of your high stature might be mistaken for some back-alley woman with words like that," Kay said, stunning the three others in the room.

"Shut your mouth! If you say one more word, I'll cut out your vile tongue myself," Kaine said, his patience long gone.

With a smug smile on his face, Kay took in the two girls, whose faces had flushed red at his remark. He watched as Elaina went from shocked to embarrassed to trembling in fury. He was excited to see how this princess would react, but what came surprised him even more than before. Elaina's trembling stopped, and her face was no longer flushed as she looked at the bound Kay with cold eyes.

"You're enjoying taunting us, aren't you?" Elaina said with a smile that chilled Hali and Kaine. Kay didn't answer, but his face told the three that it was true. "You don't seem to be afraid of what we might do to you."

Kay couldn't help but laugh as he answered. "You wouldn't risk tarnishing your honor with my life until you knew that I was sinful, so until then, my life is quite safe."

"You're right about that," Elaina said after a moment. "We wouldn't risk tarnishing our honor with your blood, but that doesn't mean we will let you off." Elaina stood up and walked out of the tent. Hali and Kaine followed her, only stopping to turn around and give Kay a murderous glare.

Alone once more, Kay listened to the princess order some warriors outside the tent to guard him well. Now knowing who he was prisoner to, Kay couldn't help but feel relief. The Estelles were famous across the land as the most honorable people, and their warriors were the most dutiful. If he hadn't committed a crime or dishonored himself in some way, they would eventually release him. Kay hadn't lied—he truly had been defending himself, only he had gotten a little out of hand in the end.

Thinking back to the ambush and the man who he was hunting, Kay ground his teeth. He had left his brothers to search for Karsic, and just when he had been close to catching the man, he had fallen into the trap.

"For what you have done, you will pay with your life, Karsic," vowed Kay.

+

"What an uncivilized man!" Elaina angrily shouted at Hali as she vented her frustrations about the failed interrogation. Once she had made it back to her tent, she was able to remove her mask and show her true expressions. The man's words rang in her ears, only making Elaina madder as time went on.

"Your Highness, please calm down," Hali begged. She had never seen her princess get this mad before. "That uncultured man isn't worth stressing yourself over."

Hali's words calmed Elaina, and she stopped her ranting, but even so, Elaina felt vexed. She didn't know why, but the man's crystal-clear eyes made her nervous. Even with the man bound and defenseless, she felt that he was still holding his sword to her throat when she looked into his eyes.

65

When they had first entered the tent, they had been ready to press the man for all he knew. After scouring the scene, the only clues they had found were what they already knew, that all but the man were servants or warriors of the Tarsis Duchy, and that the man had somehow killed them all single-handedly. With the man as the only witness, they had been forced to wait for him to awaken so they could learn what had happened. Who could have known that almost every word out of his mouth would infuriate them?

"Do you agree with my brother, ma'am?" Hali asked. "That this has some connection with Prince Leander's disappearance?"

This theory had been brought about by Kaine. With Prince Leander disappearing near where they had found the man, along with the coincidence of Tarsis warriors, who hadn't been seen in decades, appearing this far south, not long after the prince had vanished, Kaine believed that it was all somehow connected.

"I was thinking the same as Kaine, but after talking to that man, I'm not too sure," Elaina said. While hard to read, the man clearly hadn't reacted when they had brought up the Tarsis warriors, nor was he afraid about what they would find out. All this led Elaina to believe that him having anything to do with the crown prince's murder and Leander's disappearance was a long shot, but it was their only lead.

"Your Highness, may I come in?" Elaina and Hali heard Kaine ask.

Elaina quickly called for him to enter.

"What is it, Kaine? Have you found anything to bring light to this situation?" Elaina asked, but she knew she was grasping at straws.

"I'm sorry, but I've yet to uncover anything to discover the man's identity. I believe staying here any longer would only prove to be pointless," said Kaine apologetically.

"Very well, then. Have everyone prepare to head out. I want to be on the move in a half hour," ordered Elaina, but Kaine did not move. "Is there something else you wish to say?"

"I only wish to know what we will do with the prisoner," said Kaine.

"We will take him with us," said Elaina, and the upset look on Kaine's face told her that this was a decision he was against.

"We know nothing about this man. All we do know is that he is capable of slaughtering dozens of men single-handedly. Taking such a dangerous man with us is too risky, and your safety is of the utmost importance," said Kaine.

"Then what should we do? The only other options are to release him or execute him, and we can't do either until the truth of what happened today is unveiled," argued Elaina.

Kaine could only bow his head in silence. He knew that she was right—there was no way they could let such a dangerous man loose. Who knew if a repeat of today's bloody event would occur? What Kaine wanted to do was execute the man for murder, but until they had proved it wasn't an act of self-defense, killing the man would dishonor themselves and their families.

"I'm also against bringing the man with us," Hali said, quietly speaking up for her brother's decision. "The man's eyes scare me. It was like looking into a tranquil lake but being unable to see what lies beneath."

It was then that it dawned on Elaina why the man's eyes spoke to her so. She hadn't seen a single shred of emotion coming from those crystal depths—not when he had teased her nor when Kaine had threatened him. Only an apathetic gaze came from the man.

"He's an addict … or was an addict. His gaze is the same as those addicted to alchemic seed," Elaina said.

Alchemic seed, better known as Breath, was a drug that was famous not only in the lands of Mezer. Its illegal sale was spread throughout the continent. Created by alchemists as stimulants, these seed-shaped pills would render different effects depending on the type. Some might heighten the senses, while others increased strength. Once ingested, the user would have smoke come out of their mouths, a different color for each type. This had given rise to their nickname of "Breath."

While at the beginning alchemic seed had been highly regarded, it had soon become detested once the side effects began to show. Highly addictive, it was almost impossible to stop using, even if used only once. Not only was it addictive, but over time, the drug would destroy the user's body. Those who used Breath that increased their strength would find themselves unable to even lift a fork, and those who heightened their senses would find themselves going blind, deaf, or even both.

The man's crystal blue eyes were the sign that he was a user. Over time, the user's eyes would change color and look crystal-like in appearance. The seed that this man was most likely using was known as Blue Breath, or the Heart Render. It was used by soldiers who were too timid, and it would temporarily dampen their emotions, but over time, these effects would become permanent, turning the users into emotionless husks.

"Why do you think he is a former addict and not using now?" Hali asked.

"When we searched the man, we didn't find any seed, nor did his body or clothes have the scent of Breath on them," Kaine answered his sister. "Truthfully, if Your Highness hadn't said anything, I wouldn't have thought the man was a former Breath addict."

What Kaine said made a lot of sense for both Elaina and Hali. Breath was widely known as a life ender. In a group of ten thousand addicts, there might be one who was able to quit, but it required an insane amount of willpower, which most people didn't have. Even strong warriors had fallen to their addiction.

"Ma'am, please reconsider taking this man. The first thing lost to those who use Blue Breath is their empathy and remorse," Hali said, worrying that Elaina would still let such a man travel with them even if he was bound and weaponless.

Elaina thought about what she should do. Hali was right about the dangers of a man with no remorse. On the other hand, would a man with little to no emotion left be able to taunt and tease her the way that this man had?

Steeling herself, Elaina left her tent and headed toward the tent the man was imprisoned in. Kaine and Hali followed and asked where she was going and what she was thinking of doing, but Elaina ignored them. Reaching the tent, she entered without hesitation.

Her entrance surprised Kay, as she had left not too long ago. He did not think that she would be back so soon after storming off.

"When was the last time that you used?" was the first thing that Elaina said.

Both Kaine and Hali wondered what Elaina was going for.

"It's been about three years now," Kay responded. He wasn't too shocked that the princess had discovered that he was a former addict. "Why do you ask?"

Taking a moment to ready herself, Elaina answered. "I wish to hire you."

Not only was Kay shocked, but both Kaine and Hali were stunned. They had just discovered the man was a former addict, and now their princess wished to hire him? If it got out that Elaina had hired not only a sell-sword but one that had used Breath, her reputation would be tarnished.

"Are you serious? The daughter of the Archduke of the Estelle Duchy wishes to hire a lowly sell-sword like myself?" Kay teased.

"Your Highness, it is one thing to bring him with us as our prisoner, but it is another as a hired hand. I urge you to reconsider," Kaine said, but her stern look showed that she was undaunted by the risks.

69

"As a hired sword, he could come in handy. You've seen firsthand his strength. But there is a more important reason for my decision. I still don't believe that it is a coincidence that we found him so near where Prince Leander went missing," Elaina explained to Kaine and Hali.

"And what if I refuse?" Kay said, interrupting Elaina.

"You can choose to refuse, but instead of riding with us, you will be brought as our prisoner, bound and slung over the back of one of our crownes." Elaina mischievously grinned.

Kay couldn't help but laugh knowing he was cornered. Even if he managed to escape and continue his pursuit of Karsic, the Estelles and their army of warriors would be after him. Not only that but him becoming a fugitive might bring harm to the people he cared about—his two brothers.

"Very well, but you must promise to let me go once our contract is fulfilled," said Kay, and Elaina agreed with a nod.

"Ma'am, you can't—" Kaine said, but he was silenced with a raise of Elaina's hand.

"Well, Princess, you have yourself a sell-sword. Until our contract is fulfilled, my sword is yours," vowed Kay.

With everything in order, Elaina turned to leave but stopped. "I just realized I haven't gotten your name yet," she said, turning to Kay.

"It's Kay, Your Highness. Just Kay," he said with a grin. For some reason, he was excited about working for this new employer.

Chapter Seven: Escaping the Twin Cities Only to Run into Danger

U nderneath the moonless night sky, Leander followed Lucis and Aer through the narrow back alleys of WestAvri's harbor. After being saved by the two sell-swords, they had tried to leave the city, but the entrances were sealed by a mass of armed warriors searching all who tried to pass through. Unable to leave through the gates, and with the bridge a definite no-go, Leander hadn't known what to do, but Aer had recommended an alternative route. That was what they were doing right now: heading to get the help of a smuggler to ferry them across the river.

As these were cities connecting two of the three duchies, the harbors were huge, encompassing a third of the entire city mass. Even at this time of night, sailors who traversed the river and merchants trying to make their big break went around procuring wares and making deals. On several occasions, the three had to change their route in order to avoid being recognized, as Leander's face was plastered on every wall for all to see.

Finally they made it to one of the storage areas of the harbor. The building they stood in front of was no different from the buildings all around, save for the patrolling armed thugs. Reacting to the newcomers, the thugs quickly encircled the three. Leander worried, as he had grown up on the Code of Valor, and those who lived a life of crime, to him, were savage. Capable of doing almost anything.

"You chose the wrong place to take a stroll," said one of the larger thugs as he whipped out a curved dagger from his belt.

Leander looked toward Aer and Lucis, but the two were unfazed by the threat.

After rummaging through the pocket of his coat, Aer took something out and tossed it to the thug who had just spoken. "I'm here to speak to Rickens," said Aer.

What he had tossed was a small leather purse, and when the thug opened it to look inside, his face turned pale. Closing the small purse, he quickly went into the storage building, leaving the three of them surrounded. As he had issued no orders, the thugs just stood there, not sure what to do. Soon the thug was back, and his face had gained a bit of color.

"Rickens wishes to see you," the thug said, turning to lead them in.

Thoughts entered Leander's mind as to what a storage building controlled by murderous villains would look like on the inside, but when he discovered it looked like any other storage building, he wasn't sure what to think.

"Did you think there would be drugs strewn about or some form of torture going on?" Lucis said, noticing Leander's reaction. "If they were that open about their crimes, the chivalric orders would have done away with them years ago."

Leander turned his face away in embarrassment. He truly had believed that the hideout of criminals would look eviler. He had been taught that those without honor, who lived in sin, were the vilest of people. He had never thought that they would look so normal, so inconspicuous.

"We're here," said the thug leading them, stopping at a door that led to a back room. After knocking once, then twice, the door slowly opened. An armed guard came out of the room, blocking the entrance with his large body. The large guard stared at them for a moment before moving aside to let them through.

The back room was a simple room. Besides the door they entered through, there was no other way out. In this windowless room, the only light came from candles at each corner. At the center of the room was Rickens, sitting on a simple wooden chair. Three other chairs were placed in front of him.

Seeing Lucis and Aer walk in, Rickens couldn't help but give a heartful laugh. "I know I told you that you could come to me next time you needed a favor done, but I never thought it would be so soon," Rickens joked. "Why don't you sit? I'm guessing we have much to discuss."

With Aer taking the lead, the three of them sat down. The thug who had brought them here, as well as the large guard, left the room, leaving only the four of them. Leander nervously rubbed his hands together, waiting for one of the sell-swords to speak.

"We need your help to get out of the city," said Aer. His face showed no hints of the desperate situation they were in.

"You two have gotten yourselves in one hell of a problem. Every soul in WestAvri is talking about you. I have been wondering when you would come to find me," said Rickens, his face having the same calm expression as Aer's.

"Are you going to help us or not?" Lucis angrily asked.

"I would love to help you, but with warriors from the chivalric orders scouring the city for you, it would be hard even for me to get you out without being caught," Rickens said with a sigh. "I'm sorry, but the risk is too high. I'm going to have to decline."

Upon hearing Rickens's answer, all three of them had different reactions. Leander, who was the most nervous, felt that Rickens's refusal sounded more like a death sentence. Lucis, who already found the man detestable, fought the urge to cut him in two. Only Aer looked undisturbed by Rickens's refusal to help them as he sat there with not a shred of emotion showing on his face.

"I think it would be in your best interest to reconsider," Aer said.

"And why is that?" Rickens said as a grin started to spread on his face.

"You know everything that goes on in the twin cities, and that makes it clear that you know that this man is the second prince of the Talov Duchy," Aer said, gesturing toward Leander. "If you helped us, the Talovs would reward you beyond your wildest dreams."

"That does sound grand, but there are two problems that I can see, the first being that this prince is a traitor who killed his own brother. How can I trust the word of someone who is a kin killer?" asked Rickens.

Leander wanted to argue, but Lucis stopped him.

"Let Aer handle this. It is what he is good at," Lucis whispered to the prince.

"The second problem is that there is already an exorbitant price for turning the prince in, issued by the archduke himself, the prince's own grandfather. If his own blood wants him caught, then the idea of them rewarding me in helping him escape capture sounds far-fetched," said Rickens.

The tension in the room was heavy, making it hard for Leander to breathe. The more Rickens talked, the more nervous Leander got. He wanted to say something to try to persuade Rickens, but the words eluded him. He could only hope that Lucis's trust in Aer was well deserved.

"If the prospects of wealth and fortune won't persuade you, then how about this?" Aer said as he pulled out a leather pouch and tossed it to Rickens. When Rickens opened the pouch, his eyes opened wide. Looking up, Rickens saw that the stone face Aer had been showing this entire time now had a slight grin at the corners of his mouth.

Shocking both Leander and Lucis, Rickens burst into hysterical laughter. "You really don't play fair, do you? Very well. I'll see to it that you are safely brought out of the city," Rickens said, quickly stashing the pouch in his pocket.

With the deal done, Rickens called back in the guard who had been waiting outside the door. Once he had told the guard to lead them out, Lucis, Aer, and Leander were once more walking through the narrow alleys of the harbor, only going in the opposite direction to the one they had come in. It didn't take long for them to find a safe place to hide from the searching warriors and to wait for word from Rickens.

+

Two days later Rickens didn't let them down. He personally led them to a small boat moored underneath a tall dock. The small rowboat was as unimpressive as it looked, with several holes sealed shut. It was so small that the three of them would barely be able to fit.

"I have already bribed several officials. You will have a small opening when no patrols are by the shore. Head south till you are out of WestAvri, then sink the boat to leave no evidence," Rickens instructed them.

Thanking the man, the three of them boarded the rickety boat and pushed off, flowing with the current south. Lucis took the lead with the oars and silently rowed them along. As Rickens had said, the usual lights of the patrols were away from the river, and in the darkness of night, no one noticed the small boat leaving the city.

When they were no longer within earshot, Leander asked Aer a question he had been dying to know for days. "What was in that pouch you gave Rickens that made him agree?"

Aer let out a slight chuckle before answering. "Something of little value to me but of great value for someone like Rickens."

75

"And what's that?" Leander asked.

"Rickens values his life and safety over everything—at least, that is what he wants everyone to believe. What I gave him was the key to gaining what he truly desires," answered Aer. With that said, Aer didn't answer further.

Still unconvinced, Leander wanted to continue to ask, but Lucis interrupted him. "If you have time to talk, then you take over rowing," he said, tossing an oar to Leander and Aer.

After they were a good distance from the city, they were able to stop rowing and let the river carry them. The current of the river grew stronger the farther south they went, until the old boat could not handle the fast-moving waters. Around daybreak they were forced to rowed to shore. After they were safely onshore, Lucis struck several holes in the boat and cast it out. In seconds, the small boat sank below the water's surface.

"Let us get going. We must make as much distance as we can before they discover we are no longer in WestAvri," Aer said.

The three of them continued on foot. Following the river, they trekked until the sun was high in the sky. Not used to such a fast pace, Leander was gasping for breath as he struggled to match the sell-swords' pace. While he was good with a sword, he had been mostly taught how to lead and help his brother when he became archduke, so he had never had much stamina. Even when he had been heading to WestAvri after escaping from the treasonous trap, it had taken him a while to make it there.

"I can't walk any farther. Can we please rest for a bit?" Leander said, slumping on a nearby boulder by the river. Lucis and Aer could see the sweat raining down from the prince and could only concede.

"Very well. We will rest for half an hour, but we must be up and going after that," Aer said, dropping his pack. From his pack he pulled out some dried meat and bread, and handed the food to Leander. Starving, the prince ravenously ate up the simple travel meal. Aer and Lucis also ate, but being used to long travels, they ate at a moderate pace.

After quickly finishing his meal, Leander downed his waterskin, emptying it in one go. Finding his hands dirty, he walked to the edge of the river to clean himself off and refill his flask. When he peered at his reflection, he was appalled. His former princely appearance was ruined. His face was covered in days' worth of dirt and muck. His normally smooth brown hair stuck together in clumps, and large circles had gathered around his eyes from lack of rest.

Disgusted by what he saw, Leander submerged his head into the cold water of the river. He took out an old cloth that used to be part of his tunic, and he started to scrub the filth away. Looking at his appearance once more, he could vaguely see his past self, but he still looked horrendous. Not able to do any more than that, Leander quit trying.

"Try this," Aer said from behind Leander, handing him a small bound item.

Leander almost cried when he saw what was wrapped within. In his hands was a tiny bar of soap. Compared to the scented soap he was used to, this bar was rough and had a strange waxy smell, but to Leander at this time, it was a godsend. He immediately went back to washing himself clean. Soon he was looking like his old self once again.

"Thanks for that," Leander said to Aer. He tried handing him back the bar of soap, but Aer wasn't paying attention.

Leander turned to the direction Aer was looking in. Not too far away, Lucis stood motionless. His sword was strapped to his side while his hand rested on the handle. His eyes were closed, and his stillness made Lucis look serene. Leander waited for him to move, but Lucis just stood there without moving a muscle.

"What's he doing?" Leander couldn't help but ask.

"It is a type of meditation that our brother taught us," Aer answered, but seeing Leander still had questions, he decided to elaborate. "This form of meditation is said to have been created by Kintra, the first goddess of war. Unlike normal meditation, which causes people to look inward, this meditation expands the senses outward. This strengthens the senses and heightens a person's natural instincts beyond the normal limit. Right now, Lucis is listening to every gust of wind and every motion of the blades of grass under his feet. Even the slightest change around him, he can feel."

Leander looked at Lucis, who was just standing in place, in a different light from a moment ago. Before, when he had seen the motionless Lucis, he thought what he was doing was strange, but now he found deep respect for what he was doing. Standing in one place, trying to listen to everything around him, sounded impossible to Leander.

Another thing Leander thought about was this mysterious brother they had. Ever since they had agreed to help him return to Raven's Nest, their focus had been on finding their lost brother. Besides getting a general description, Leander had known nothing about this third sell-sword, but now he had some strange knowledge about him. Somehow this third brother had been able to teach them a meditation technique developed by the goddess Kintra.

The people of the duchies of Mezer were devout worshippers of the Phoenix God, Calv Ridian. Due to their isolation from the other kingdoms and powers of the continent, there were very few other gods worshipped in Mezer. Many didn't know the other gods' names, let alone their creeds and followers. Hearing about a man who had knowledge of the teachings of another god intrigued Leander.

"Your missing brother, how did he learn this?" Leander asked Aer, only to get a slight grin back. "If you don't want to tell me, then don't," grumbled Leander, upset over Aer's smirk.

"It really isn't much of a secret," Aer said. "Our brother, Kay, used to be a warrior priest. That is why he knows this form of meditation."

Leander was once more shocked by these sell-swords. He had heard of the warrior priests. Also known as Kintra's Weapons, these priests didn't spread the words of their god, nor did they partake in religious activities. All they did, day in and day out, was master the five forms of weaponry. Even the warriors of Mezer weren't as obsessed with strength as these priests.

The warriors of Mezer followed the teachings of Calv Ridian and his Code of Valor. While strength was important, the three virtues—honor, duty, and sacrifice—were more important in the teachings. It was by following these three virtues that a warrior could transcend at their death to a Zer'sheen.

"I didn't know that there were any temples or priests of Kintra in the duchies," said Leander.

"There aren't. Or at least, I haven't seen or heard of any," responded Aer. "My brothers and I aren't from the duchies. We have only just arrived in these lands from the southern kingdoms."

"Then how is your brother a Zer'sheen? Those bearing the mark of the Phoenix God and the scars of their past life can only be born in the lands protected by the Phoenix God. It is impossible for one to be born in the southern kingdoms," Leander quickly stated.

Aer didn't give a direct answer, only saying, "Why do you think?"

Leander gave it some thought, and the only thing he could think of was that when Lucis had been born, his parents had left the duchies and gone to the southern kingdoms, but that did not make much sense to him. In the duchies, a Zer'sheen was considered higher than even the archdukes. When one was born, even their family was recognized and promoted to the warrior class. He couldn't think of why Lucis's parents would do such a thing as leave.

"His parents left when they found out he was a Zer'sheen," Leander answered, as it was the only thing he could think of. It came out more as a question, as he still couldn't believe it. When Aer nodded to confirm, Leander was still wondering why. "Why would they take him away? If they had stayed, they would have basked in praise and glory for generations. I can't see how people who were raised here could turn their backs on all their beliefs."

"You haven't interacted with the common people much, have you? If you had, then you would know that a Zer'sheen born into a common family is more of a curse than a blessing," Aer answered.

"What do you mean?" Leander asked.

"Normal people wish only to live a simple life. Many don't know how to read, let alone understand your Code of Valor. They also don't want their child to be thrown into the warrior life, one filled with death. Sadly, when a Zer'sheen is discovered, they don't have a choice in the matter. Either their lord or a priest from Ridia will take the child. So Lucis's parents made the decision to run from here as soon as they could, making their way all the way to the southern kingdoms."

"My grandfather wouldn't take a child from their family," Leander angrily said, his voice slightly high.

"Even if he wouldn't, that doesn't mean other warrior families wouldn't, and the holy city is notorious for spiriting away Zer'sheen children. Why do you think most Zer'sheen end up part of the holy city's forces? Not only that, but if Lucis's parents had been caught, they would have been executed for the crime of theft against the Phoenix God."

Leander knew that what Aer said made sense. The holy city had a shady side, and he had heard his grandfather and sister complain about the radicalness growing in its sacred halls. He also knew that of the seven Zer'sheen—eight if Lucis was included—in the three duchies, four were sworn to Ridia.

Suddenly the still Lucis's eyes shot open, and he shouted, "Get away from there!"

Upon hearing him, both Leander and Aer instinctively moved away just as a large beast pounced from the reeds by the river. The beast was a huge feline with similar features to a mountain lion, only larger. Two menacing horns grew out of the beast's temples, and a long, thin tail with a sharp tip swung behind it.

"A lixin beast," Leander said, surprised by the beast's appearance.

Hearing the prince, the lixin turned toward him. Its eyes narrowed as it neared Leander, ready to pounce once more. Leander fearfully took steps back, but his back hit a large boulder behind him. He was trapped between the lixin and the giant rock.

"This isn't good," Aer said, seeing the beast near the prince. Just as he was about to help, Lucis stopped him. "What are you doing? We have to help."

"He needs to deal with this problem on his own. The journey to Raven's Nest will be fraught with peril. This lixin beast is but the first dangerous encounter of many, and the prince has too much fear in him. If he wants to survive this journey, he must conquer that fear, or he will never reach the end," Lucis said.

Aer turned back to Leander, who was frozen in terror. He didn't argue with Lucis, because his words held truth in them. In order to avoid the warriors hunting them, they had decided to take the most dangerous path. If Leander couldn't muster the courage to face the lixin beast, then when the other dangers arrived, he would only be able to wait for his demise. It was at that moment that Leander noticed Lucis and Aer.

"Help me!" he shouted. His shout alerted the lixin, and it struck. Leander narrowly escaped by a hair's breadth, but the beast's claws tore the back of his shirt.

"You have a sword at your side. Use it," Lucis called back. "You can't just rely on us to save you every time."

Leander saw the seriousness in Lucis's eyes and knew arguing was pointless. He turned to Aer, hoping for some help, but Aer only shook his head. Neither was going to help him out of this. Leander felt that they were sending him to his death. With no other choice, Leander turned to face the lixin beast with his sword drawn.

The lixin saw the shine of the steel and became alert. It had faced warriors before and knew the dangers of a sword. As it stalked Leander, keeping its distance, the prince's shaking hands could barely hold the sword steady. The beast's sharp claws and vicious fangs had his blood running cold. When the beast swung its long tail toward him, he flinched and dropped his sword.

Seeing its chance, the lixin attacked. It barreled into him, and the prince was sent flying through the air, then hit the ground with a loud thud. Unable to breathe or move, he heard a familiar growl. Looking up, Leander saw the lixin standing over him, ready to sink its teeth into his neck. A small piece of flesh from Leander's side hung from the beast's horn from when it had charged into him.

Closing his eyes and coiling into himself, Leander knew he was done for, but instead of pain, he heard a loud yelp. When he opened his eyes, what stood above him wasn't the lixin but Lucis, looking down at him, his eyes full of disappointment. Off to the side, the lixin beast stood with one of its front legs elevated. A large gash in the beast's shoulder revealed bone.

Lucis and the lixin faced off against one another. In the end, the lixin thought it best not to face Lucis and ran off, disappearing as swiftly as it had appeared.

Sheathing his sword, Lucis helped Leander back to his feet.

"Are you all right?" Lucis asked.

Leander was about to reply, but then he remembered that Lucis had only watched as the lixin beast had attacked him, only stepping in at the last minute. Angered by this lack of help, he shrugged off Lucis's hand that gripped his wrist. "Why didn't you help?" he angrily asked. "I could have died!"

"It was for your own good," Aer said, reaching the two.

Hearing this answer from the normally reasonable one of the two shocked Leander. "My own good? How is almost dying in my best interest?" he asked.

"Why did you drop your sword?" Lucis asked back.

"What ...?" said Leander, not sure whether he had heard right.

"A sword is the soul of a warrior and his closest partner. Dropping your sword in the middle of combat is not only cowardly but shameful," Lucis coldly remarked.

"What do you sell-swords know of honor? You agreed to bring me back to Raven's Nest safely. You should have protected me," Leander argued, completely forgetting that he was talking to a Zer'sheen, an embodiment of honor and duty.

"And we can't do that if you will not even save yourself," Lucis coldly said before walking away, not even giving Leander a single glance.

Leander felt his anger swell up, but soon it turned to shame. Lucis was right. He had acted shamefully, dishonorably even. Instead of facing the lixin with his sword held high, he had given in to his fear and even dropped his sword. Picking up his discarded weapon, he held it up. The more he thought of his disgraceful act, the more anger he felt, not toward Lucis or the lixin beast but toward himself. Staring deeply into the shine of the sword, Leander vowed that he would not drop his sword again.

Chapter Eight: Karsic of the Crying Face Mask

In a well-decorated inn located in the high-class district of WestAvri, Bez paced back and forth, his footsteps voicing his worry. It had been several days since Leander had been spotted in WestAvri, but he still hadn't captured the missing prince. They had been close to catching the prince once, but out of nowhere, two sell-swords had saved the prince just as he was in their grasp.

They had searched the entire city, breaking into homes and businesses, but every lead had led to a dead end. Whoever was helping Leander escape from them knew how to hide their tracks very well. With every day that passed, Bez feared that he had failed, and he could not fail.

"Why haven't you found anything yet?" Bez shouted at the two warriors in the room with him. "If we don't find him soon, it will be our lives that are forfeit."

The two warriors paled when they heard Bez. They were part of the group that had killed the crown prince. They knew how dangerous it was for them to have Prince Leander still alive. Two of their traitorous colleagues had already perished, and they would be next if Leander survived.

"All the ways in and out of the city have been secured. The river is being patrolled constantly. It won't be long before we track them down," said the braver warrior.

Upon hearing the warrior, Bez slammed his fist into the wall. For the past few days, that was all he had heard, and every day ended the same, with no results. He was beginning to wonder whether Leander had somehow escaped from WestAvri.

"Could Prince Leander have made it out of the city somehow?" Bez seriously asked the two warriors.

"Impossible," said the other warrior. "The warriors of the Third and Fourth Chivalric Orders guard the gates. No one would be able to sneak past them."

Before Bez could say another word, a cold breeze blew into the room. The air around the inn became stale and made it hard to breathe. Bez and the two warriors grew solemn. They knew what this feeling meant. They knew what had arrived.

"They're here," Bez muttered.

From outside the door, they could hear the sound of footsteps steadily heading toward the room. Their heartbeats quickened as the footsteps grew near. Slowly the door creaked open without anyone pushing. Three figures entered the room. The one leading the three was a man wearing a metal mask, cast to look like a crying face. Of the other two, one was a muscular man dressed in black leather, with a longbow strapped to his back and a long knife hanging from his hip. The last person was a young boy who looked no older than nine. The boy looked like any other boy his age, but his young face creeped Bez out. The boy stood there showing no emotion, like a doll.

"Bez, you have greatly disappointed me," said the masked man. His voice was as cold as ice. The scent of blood permeated the air as he spoke.

"Lord Karsic, I beg you to give me just a little more time. I promise you I will have Prince Leander's body spread out for you in only a few more days," Bez vowed. He knelt before the masked man, with the two warriors following suit.

Karsic looked down at the kneeling Bez but did not speak. His mask hid whatever Karsic was thinking. On his knees, Bez was too terrified to look up.

"Is that so?" Karsic said, then turned toward the man with the bow. "Hunter, search the city. Find where Prince Leander is hiding," he ordered.

The man called the Hunter made his way to the large window. The inn they were in was in the richer part of WestAvri, and it was one of the larger buildings. The view from the window looked over most of the city. The Hunter's pupils jumped back and forth, taking in the entire city. His pupils grew and shrank, making them look like moving ink splatters. When his eyes finally stopped their strange flickering, the man said, "The prince is no longer in the city."

"What?" Bez said, startled by the man's sudden declaration. "That is impossible. The entire city is sealed. There is no way for him to leave." While he said this, Bez wasn't too convinced by his own words. He had just asked whether it was possible for Leander to have escaped. Now he was giving the same answer as the two warriors had.

"It seems you have failed me yet again," Karsic said.

"Please give me another chance," Bez pleaded, his head banging on the floor as he bowed.

"Failure must not be tolerated, and a proper punishment should be in order," Karsic said, causing Bez to almost faint from fright. "Take these two away so I can talk to Bez privately," Karsic said to the young boy.

Gesturing to the two warriors, the young boy left the room. Seeing that this was their way to safety, the warriors didn't even glance at the kneeling Bez before hastily leaving the room. Bez stared daggers at the two men as they abandoned him.

Suddenly loud screaming came from the hall the two warriors had just entered. The inn began to tremble as loud banging drowned out the screaming until Bez couldn't hear the shouting anymore. He recognized the shouting as belonging to the two warriors who had just left. Unable to control his trembling, Bez watched as the young boy entered the room, covered in blood. The boy's face showed the same empty expression as when he had first entered.

"Now that punishment has been given, tell me, why haven't you captured the runaway prince yet?" Karsic demanded.

"It isn't my fault. We had the prince in our grasp, but suddenly two sell-swords appeared and thwarted us," Bez quickly said, trying to push the blame onto the sell-swords. "But they weren't just ordinary sell-swords. The two of them were strong, able to easily kill a group of warriors and escape before anyone could stop them."

"Sell-swords …" Karsic mumbled to himself. "Do you have a description of the two sell-swords?"

"Yes. According to what we gathered, the sell-swords had arrived in WestAvri a few days prior, wearing clothing uncommon in the duchies. One was a young man with a scar across his jaw. The other seemed to be an older man in his thirties."

"A scar-faced sell-sword …" Karsic once more mumbled to himself after Bez had finished giving the description.

"My lord, do you know these sell-swords?" Bez asked. It seemed that he had discovered the identity of Leander's saviors.

The masked Karsic didn't answer him and instead turned to the Hunter. "Find the prince and take care of him and anyone who is helping him," he ordered. The Hunter neither bowed nor saluted, and only disappeared from the room, leaving Bez alone with Karsic and the murderous youth. Bez stayed as still as he could, hoping his fate would be different from that of the two warriors.

"There is no need to fear. You still have some use left," Karsic said, filling Bez with both joy and fear at the same time.

+

Standing above the largest building in WestAvri, the Hunter took in the city with his strange gaze. His eyes saw all that was happening in WestAvri. In the end, he turned toward the south.

"Have you found their trail?" Karsic asked, seemingly appearing out of thin air next to the Hunter.

The Hunter only pointed in the direction he was looking in.

"Good. I have ordered Bez to gather up a group of warriors loyal to our cause. Take them with you, and bring me back the prince's head, along with the heads of those sell-swords that are helping him," Karsic ordered.

"I'll go on my own," the Hunter said coldly. "They will only get in my way, slow me down."

"Take them. You will need some fodder if you are going to defeat the sell-swords protecting him."

The Hunter only scoffed at Karsic's remark.

"One of them is a Zer'sheen," Karsic said.

The Hunter reacted to this news but quickly composed himself. "Even if there is a Zer'sheen protecting him, he won't get away," he said. Then he jumped off the roof.

Alone on the roof, Karsic stood motionless. His mask hid what he was thinking as he looked toward the south.

"Lucis, Aer, I don't know how you got involved, but it will be the end for you," Karsic said as he continued to look southward.

+

"How about you let me wield a sword?" Kay said as he rode next to Elaina on a horse that they had been able to procure at the previous town.

"Like we would let you near a weapon," Hali said in Elaina's stead.

89

"You have nothing to worry about, little miss. Your princess has hired me, so my sword is now hers," Kay said.

Upon hearing Kay call her "little miss," Hali was about to angrily erupt, but Elaina stopped her. "Don't let him rattle you. That is what he wants," Elaina told Hali.

When Hali discovered that she had almost fallen into Kay's trap, she shot him a glare but didn't say anything. Kay was about to taunt her again, but a glare from Elaina told him that he shouldn't.

Elaina and her group continued to ride, and soon they came into sight of WestAvri. The city's walls stretched parallel with the river. As the center of trade between two duchies, countless merchants and caravans were traveling toward the city. Strangely, they noticed that none were leaving. They also noticed that the caravans that were in front of them were halted at the gate.

"What is happening?" Hali asked. Her question was in the minds of every one of the warriors and Elaina.

"Looks to me as if the city has been locked down," Kay said. "Seems they fear someone getting in—or out."

"Getting out? Could it be Prince Leander was spotted in WestAvri?" Elaina said as she looked at the city. She worried about the prince. She was also excited, as this showed that Leander had yet to be caught. "Let's go. We have to see if Prince Leander was the cause of this." With that said, Elaina rode ahead, leaving the rest trying to catch up.

As they blended into the caravans waiting to be allowed entry, they were bombarded by the constant rumors and hearsay going around, rumors that confirmed Elaina's suspicion. Leander had been spotted in WestAvri, trying to cross Avri Bridge into the Talov Duchy.

"Your Highness, what do we do?" Kaine asked as they drew closer to the gate and the checkpoint.

"Once we are in WestAvri, we will split into two groups and begin our search for Prince Leander. Remember, no one can know who we are," Elaina said. Kaine and the rest of the warriors gave a nod instead of the regular salute, afraid of their identities being discovered if they did so.

Elaina and her group waited in the line of caravans entering the city. The guards in front of the gate took their time and searched each person rigorously. Anyone who tried to fight the search was beaten and taken away by the guards for questioning. Watching all of this unfold were over a dozen warriors from the Talov Duchy.

"Ma'am, those are warriors from a Talov chivalric order," Kaine whispered to Elaina. "This is going to be difficult."

Elaina knew what Kaine meant. They, too, had chivalric orders, and the Talov warriors looked as disciplined as their own. Warriors were usually stoic and unbending. The ones who joined the chivalric orders took it up to the next level. They lived and breathed the Code of Valor, and every moment of their lives followed the three virtues. Getting past them would be a lot harder than getting past regular guards.

"Stay calm. WestAvri is still part of the Estelle Duchy. They would think twice before doing anything drastic," she said.

Elaina was right about that. Standing next to the Talov warriors were two Estelle warriors. It was obvious that they were there to supervise the warriors from their neighboring duchy. As the line proceeded, it was soon their turn. Elaina covered herself with her cloak, trying her best to hide her face.

"What is your business in coming here?" asked one of the Talov warriors. From

91

his uniform, Elaina and her group knew he was a captain in a chivalric order. As he questioned them, the rest of the warriors searched through their bags and luggage.

"Once we heard of the crown prince of the Talov Duchy's demise at his own brother's hand, we couldn't just sit back and do nothing," answered Kaine. It was the reason that they had decided on telling them, and it was the truth. Only they were there to help the prince and not bring him to justice, as it sounded.

"More glory hounds," the warrior said in contempt. Since the prince had been spotted, every honor-bound warrior within riding distance had rushed over, making their job all the harder. "Just don't get in the way of our duty," he said with a huff. He then stepped away to allow them to pass.

After they had gained permission to enter, the warriors moved out the way to let Elaina and the others past. However, as they passed the two Estelle warriors, one of Elaina's golden locks fell from her hood. Elaina tried to hide it, but it was noticed by one of the Estelle warriors.

"Halt!" the warrior yelled. "Remove your hood."

With the warrior's shout, the rest of the warriors and guards once more surrounded their group. Stuck in this situation, Elaina could only comply and removed her hood. When her golden hair was free from the hood, several gasps could be heard from those waiting to be inspected. Some were able to guess Elaina's identity from her appearance.

"Ma'am, could you please come with us?" said the warrior who had asked her to remove her hood. They had gotten word that the princess had disappeared and may be heading their way, looking for Prince Leander. Princess Elaina was famous for her long golden hair, so when he had seen the loose lock fall from her hood, he had assumed she was their missing princess.

Elaina was distraught over this. She knew that if her identity were discovered, she would be sent back to Esesa and her father. Her eyes darted back and forth, trying to find a way out of this, but the look she got from Kaine, Hali, and the rest of the warriors made her realize that it was over. As she was about to give up, a shout was heard from inside the city.

"Sister, you have finally arrived!" yelled a man running toward the gate. Several warriors stopped the man from getting closer. "Sir, could I ask what my younger sister has done to be taken away?"

"Sister? Who is your sister? And who are you?" the warrior asked, turning his head between the newcomer and Elaina. He thought that he might have been mistaken but wasn't sure. He may be a warrior, but he had never seen the princess, only heard descriptions.

"Sir, my name is Peter Remell of the warrior house Remell, and the young woman with the blond hair is my sister, Susan Remell. I sent word to my sister when Prince Leander was spotted in the city," the man known as Peter said, handing one of the Talov warriors stopping him a family crest. The warrior brought the crest to the Estelle warrior.

Taking the crest, the warrior closely examined it. He knew that the crest was real, but with so many warrior families, he hadn't heard of the Remells. He was still skeptical, but the next words the man said made him surer he was wrong in thinking the young lady was the princess.

"Sir, if you need more proof, my sister has the same crest on her as well. Susan, please take the crest out of your pocket and have this whole situation cleared up," said Peter.

Elaina didn't know what was going on. Looking at the man, she couldn't recognize him or understand why he thought she was his sister. The man then gave her a look that made her instinctively search her pocket. When she felt something

93

that hadn't been there before, she pulled it out, revealing the same crest token that the man Peter had given the warrior. Seeing the token, the warrior knew that he was mistaken.

"I'm sorry for holding you up," he apologized, giving the crest token back to Peter.

"It is no problem. You were just doing your duty," Peter said. His soft words stroked the ego of the warriors around. "Sister, if you would follow me? You must be tired from your long ride here. I have gotten us rooms at one of WestAvri's finest inns."

To keep this charade going and to avoid being found out, Elaina had no choice but to follow this stranger. Peter brought them through the main street of the city. As they got farther away from the walls, Elaina thought it was safe enough to question this man.

"Who are you? Why did you help us back there?" she asked.

Upon hearing Elaina, the rest of them took up positions around her, keeping the man a safe distance from the princess.

"Your Highness, you have nothing to fear from me," Peter said, giving Elaina a fisted salute.

"Answer the princess's question," Myles said, placing his hand on the hilt of his sword.

"Sorry for the late introduction. My name is Roan, and I'm a personal warrior of Her Highness Princess Aris Talov," Peter, now Roan, said.

"One of Princess Aris's songbirds," said Hali, but she quickly covered her mouth. She didn't mean to speak out just then, let alone call Roan by his insulting epithet, but if he took offense, he didn't show it.

"If you know who we are, then why help?" Elaina asked.

"Her Highness talks about how close you and the second prince are. I was hoping you knew where he was or at least where he could be going," Roan answered truthfully.

"If you are looking for Prince Leander, then why aren't you working with the other Talov warriors?" Elaina asked, not sure what Roan was up to.

"Ma'am, it seems that we aren't the only ones who believe that Prince Leander is innocent," said Kaine as he picked up a few things from the warrior Roan.

"That is true. Her Highness also believes that the prince is being framed for the murder of his brother. I have been sent to ensure the prince's safety. So anything you know about the prince's location will help," Roan said.

Seeing Roan's hopeful look, Elaina and the rest gave him a look of sympathy. "Sadly, we don't know where the prince is. We only learned that he was in WestAvri when we arrived," Elaina told Roan.

"Is that so?" Roan sighed dejectedly.

With everything now revealed, Roan led them to the inn that he had promised. It wasn't the fanciest inn, as he had said. It was closer to the docks than the richer districts by the bridge, but Elaina and the rest preferred this type of inn. If they had stayed in a wealthier inn, the chance of them being discovered would have increased.

As they dismounted from their mounts, a shrill scream pierced their ears.

"Oh no!" Hali shouted.

"What is it, Hali?" Elaina asked worriedly.

"He's gone! The sell-sword is gone!" Hali said. Her words had all of them realizing that Kay wasn't with them. None of them knew when he had slipped away. The last time any of them remembered seeing Kay was when they were being inspected.

They quickly searched the nearby area but only came up empty-handed. With no ideas on where Kay could have gone, they returned to the inn.

Chapter Nine: Can You Trust a Sell-Sword?

By Ridian's flame! How could I have been so foolish?" Elaina cursed, throwing her bag onto the bed in her room. "My father has always told me that sell-swords are men with no honor, that those who sell their swords to the highest bidder can't be trusted. I should never have put my trust in that blasted man."

"Your Highness, you can't blame yourself. None of us saw him sneak off either," Hali said, trying to comfort Elaina.

"But it was my idea to unbind him, which gave him the chance to escape," Elaina said as she aggressively began to undress out of her dirty clothes.

"Allow me," Hali said, and helped Elaina out of her old clothes and into some cleaner ones. "You shouldn't stress yourself over a simple sell-sword. He isn't worth it."

Elaina felt a little better once she was out of her dirty clothes. When she heard Hali's words, she didn't know what to feel. Elaina's intuition had told her that Kay wasn't an ordinary sell-sword, so she had decided to trust him and free him. Now she worried that her instincts were wrong about him.

Once she was fully dressed, Elaina put the problem of Kay to one side. Leaving her own room, she made her way to the adjoining room. There, Kaine and the young warriors, along with the warrior Roan, were waiting for her. After Elaina sat down, they began to discuss what to do to find Leander.

"Roan, you have been here longer than us. Do you have any ideas on where Prince Leander could be hiding?" Elaina asked.

"Your Highness, I only arrived a day ago. During that time, I have found no trace of the prince. I even contacted several members of WestAvri's underground, to no avail," Roan sadly told her.

"Our only option is to go with our original plan," Kaine said. "We will split up into groups. One will continue to search, while the others will listen in on the warriors of the chivalric orders to hear if they learn anything concerning Prince Leander's whereabouts."

There were a few other ideas, but Elaina agreed with Kaine and thought that this idea was the most reasonable. "Then I will lead those who will search for Prince Leander. Kaine and Roan will lead the groups to observe the chivalric warriors," Elaina said, but her decision made everyone's faces betray nervousness. "What is it?" she asked.

"Ma'am, we believe that it is in your best interest to wait here while we search," Kaine said when no one else stepped forward.

"I will not simply wait around and do nothing. It was my decision to look for Prince Leander. I won't have anyone telling me I can't," Elaina declared.

"Ma'am, I believe that my brother is right," Hali said. She knew that what she was about to say would upset Elaina, but she had to say it. "You were almost discovered at the gate. With so many warriors about, only one has to recognize you, and our search for Prince Leander is over."

Elaina held back her retort. Kaine and Hali were right. It had been a close call at the gate, and they might not be as lucky next time. "Fine, Kaine will lead the continued search for Prince Leander, while Roan and Myles will listen in on the chivalric orders," Elaina said. Then a fierce glint entered her eyes. "Also, if anyone sees that bastard Kay, send word. We cannot let such a dangerous and unfaithful man roam freely."

From the window, she watched them disperse throughout the city. As she did, she could not help but mutter, "Kay, you better not let me catch you, because if I do, then I'll make sure your life is a living hell."

+

In the alleyways of the harbor district of WestAvri, Kay felt a strange sensation run through him. *Is someone talking about me?* he wondered as he itched his nose, but the sound of groaning brought his attention back to the present.

Scattered all around Kay were the bodies of over a dozen thugs. While each was battered and bloody, they all still breathed. Turning away from the battered men, Kay's gaze fell on a familiar building. It was through this building that he had arrived here from EastAvri. As if on cue, Rickens exited the building, followed by a dozen more thugs.

"Did you really have to be so rough on my men?" Rickens said, but his tone didn't seem to be questioning Kay.

"They were the ones who tried to stop me from entering," Kay said. His words angered the thugs behind Rickens.

"Let me deal with this bastard," one of the thugs behind Rickens shouted.

"You wouldn't last a second against him," Rickens told the thug. "He's the Bloody Stranger."

When the thug heard that Kay was the Bloody Stranger, he immediately regretted his words. The Bloody Stranger was the name they gave the man who, in a single night, had killed dozens of men, only to mysteriously disappear afterward.

Many of them still remembered that night and thanked the gods that they hadn't run into him.

"I had a feeling that I would be seeing you soon," Rickens laughed.

"And why is that?" Kay asked. He didn't know why Rickens thought he would return, but it made him feel uncomfortable.

"Why …?" Rickens repeated. Seeing the questioning look Kay gave him, he asked a question. "Why is it that you came to see me?"

"I've been hired to help find the missing prince. I know that everything that happens in WestAvri eventually reaches your ear. You must know exactly where the prince is hiding," Kay said.

Kay watched as Rickens's beady eyes looked him over, trying to find out whether he was being lied to.

After seeing that Kay was telling the truth, the underground boss muttered, "Can it be such a coincidence?"

"What coincidence?" Kay asked—more demanded, by the tone.

"You really don't know, do you?" Rickens said. He still felt all of this was way too coincidental.

"Know what?" Kay asked. The uncomfortable feeling was now racing through him.

"The ones who are helping Prince Leander, the one you are trying to find, are your brothers," Rickens told him.

Kay just stood there for a moment. He knew that his brothers were looking for him, so he could not understand how they could suddenly be the ones who were helping the prince. "How did such a thing come about?"

"It seems that while escaping, the prince ran into your brothers. After rescuing the prince, they agreed to help the poor lad," Rickens explained. He then told Kay everything, how a few days later Aer and Lucis had come to him for help, and how he had helped them out of the city.

"How long ago was that?" Kay asked once Rickens was finished.

"It hasn't even been two days since they left the city," Rickens answered.

Two days may have seemed not too long ago, but Kay knew otherwise. If what Rickens had told him was true, then they had headed south on the river, toward Verilis Forest. With the speed of the current, they would have traveled quite a distance. The only positive thing was that everyone believed the prince was still in WestAvri, so the prince and Kay's brothers were safer than before.

"But I do have some not-so-good information," Rickens said. "I heard that a group of warriors rode out, heading south. It looks as if not everyone was fooled into believing the prince is still here."

The reassurance that Kay had just gained was quickly dashed by this news. Kay knew how strong his brothers were; he didn't worry about them defending themselves. It was the prince that worried Kay. While he had not been in the duchies for long, he had heard a thing or two. One of those things was that the second prince was a timid person. He feared that the prince would drag his brothers down, putting their lives in danger.

The one brother he most worried for was Lucis. As a Zer'sheen, honor and duty flowed through his veins. As he had taken the contract, it was now his duty to safeguard Prince Leander. Even if death was assured, Lucis would not abandon the prince.

With this new information, an idea came to Kay. "You're coming with me," he told Rickens.

"And where are you taking me?" Rickens asked. His tone was a little nervous. Wherever Kay wished to take him would not be anywhere good.

101

"I'm sure that my employer would like to have a word with you," answered Kay.

+

Back at the inn, Elaina's mood was just turning from bad to worse. The sun was setting, and most of their group had returned, but not even one had brought back any information concerning the whereabouts of Leander.

As she sat in her room grumbling, a half-empty wineglass in hand, her handmaiden Hali burst into the room. "We found him!" she proclaimed.

"You found Prince Leander?" Elaina asked excitedly, standing up from her seat. When she saw Hali's frown, she knew that her guess was wrong, and she slouched back into her seat.

"Sadly, not the prince," Hali said. Her frown then turned into a grin. "It's that blasted runaway sell-sword."

When she heard this, Elaina stood back up. "Where is he?" she asked. Her voice carried a hint of anger that Hali hadn't heard from her princess before. It made her stutter, so she didn't answer right away. "Hali, I asked where that bastard is."

Returning to the present, Hali blushed in embarrassment. "He is in the next room," she said.

With Hali right behind her, Elaina made her way to the neighboring room. Pushing the door open with gusto, everyone waiting in the room turned their heads toward the arriving princess. Elaina saw none of them; her attention went immediately to the center of the room, where two men were bound.

Elaina recognized one of the men as the missing sell-sword Kay. She had to rein herself in when he turned to her and gave her a silent grin. The other man she didn't recognize. He was a middle-aged man and, to Elaina, looked too sketchy to be trusted with anything.

Taking the seat that Kaine offered, she asked him, "Where did you find him?"

"We didn't find him," Kaine said. Then he went into detail. "He found us. Just strode into the inn a few moments ago."

Whatever Elaina was thinking about Kay at that moment vanished from her mind. Just a few hours ago, she had been cursing her gullibility for helping Kay escape. Now that he had returned, Elaina didn't know what to think. It was while she was pondering what to do that the other tied-up man spoke.

"You didn't tell me your employer was Princess Elaina Estelle," Rickens said to Kay. The look the man gave Kay told all that Kay had fooled the man into coming here.

"Does it really matter who employed me?" Kay said. Everyone could see that he was enjoying seeing the man's shock at this revelation.

"Have you really been employed by the princess? Then why is it that the moment they spotted you, they tied us up and brought us here?" Rickens remarked. He slouched over, regretting following Kay here.

"I would like to know that as well. Why is it that, once more, you've decided to bind me like a criminal?" Kay asked.

"Aren't you? Didn't you escape when we first entered WestAvri?" Myles angrily spat. Besides Roan and Elaina, the rest of the people in the room were glaring at Kay. To them, this dishonorable sell-sword had taken their princess's trust and used her. They all wanted nothing more than to throw the man into the darkest cell once they returned to Esesa.

"Escape? Who says I was trying to escape? And if I did, why would I return?" Kay argued back, but his voice didn't have the least bit of anger. His voice almost sounded neutral to everyone, maybe even amused by this accusation.

His words were exactly what Elaina was thinking. He had been able to escape, so why risk imprisonment in returning? He must have known that if they had found him, then all that would have awaited him was the inside of a cell.

"If you didn't run, then what were you doing?" Kaine questioned. He had never trusted Kay and didn't believe a word the sell-sword said.

When asked this, Kay only turned to Kaine before looking at Elaina. His silence cut through Kaine more than words, making him furious. Kaine felt that the sell-sword's silence was a "why do I have to explain myself to you?" type of response. Not only Kaine, but Elaina and Roan picked up on Kay's silent retort too.

"Answer Kaine's question," Elaina ordered, her tone cold, not in the mood for Kay's retorts.

"I was doing what you hired me to do. I was out searching for the missing prince," Kay said. His answer infuriated the warriors in the room. They didn't believe Kay for a second.

"If you were searching for Prince Leander, like you say, then why leave without telling anyone?" Hali asked.

"When you were all stopped at the gate, I saw an opening and secretly entered the city when the guards were distracted," Kay explained. "As for why I didn't tell you, it is simple. You all stick out way too much to get any reliable information. Just one look, and anyone can tell you are the sons and daughters of high-ranking warrior families. With how untrusting of me you all are, you would never have allowed me out of your sight. So I decided to leave without telling you."

"What are you talking about?" replied Kaine. "While we are indeed wearing warrior clothing and armor, all of it is simple. Even lower warrior households wear similar clothing. We have even hidden our crests away. There isn't a single reason for people to think that we aren't from a common warrior family."

"Then why were you almost caught at the gate?" Kay remarked, giving Kaine a pitying look, as if he were looking at a simpleton, which only infuriated Kaine more.

It took Kaine's entire willpower not to draw his sword and cut down the maddening sell-sword.

"Why don't I explain?" said Rickens. "If you continue to allow Kay to taunt you, then nothing will get accomplished."

"And who might you be?" Elaina asked. After she had calmed down, she turned her attention to the man Kay had brought with him, and she was interested in why he had done so.

"My name is Rickens, Your Highness," Rickens said, bowing to the princess. When Elaina gestured for him to continue, he explained, "As for why you all stick out, it is for one main reason. You all are too clean. Commoners and those warriors of lower rank don't have the luxuries that dukes, marquesses, and counts have. One look at your clean clothes, and you will be seen as a highborn child. If you tried to even speak to someone from the underground, that person would run before you got your first words out of your mouths."

Upon hearing Rickens's answer, Elaina looked at the clothes she had put on earlier today. While she wasn't the most girlish young woman, the one thing one could consider feminine about Elaina was her dislike for being dirty. Even during this mission to find Leander, she had brought enough clothes to change several times. When she turned toward the rest of their group, she found that they were all relatively well dressed and clean-shaven. Compared to the warriors wandering around outside, they were outlandish.

It wasn't only Elaina. Everyone looked at their fine clothes. When they realized they really did stick out, they couldn't help but be embarrassed, but how were they supposed to have known? They have been raised to be proud and honorable warriors; sticking out was fine for them. This sneaking around like a criminal was foreign and strange to them. Only Roan, who was dressed relatively simply, didn't stand out, and he was the only one who noticed something from Rickens's answer.

"You know quite a bit about the workings of WestAvri's underground," Roan said. His questioning tone made the others realize the same thing Roan had noticed.

"Your Highness, I would plead for leniency. I know all this because I am a smuggler," Rickens admitted. His timid nature revealed itself as he looked toward the floor when he told everyone he was a criminal.

The young warriors instinctively gripped their swords hilts. The innocent Hali backed away and hid behind her brother as if Rickens would pounce on her at any second. Only Elaina and Roan remained calm.

"Why did you bring this man to me? You must have valid reasoning behind this," Elaina said, looking at Kay. The contempt for the sell-sword was now gone from her eyes. Once she had found out he hadn't broken his vow, her anger had faded. Her instincts had not betrayed her, as she had thought.

"The reason is that I have information regarding the missing prince," Kay said. "And Rickens was the last person to see him."

"Where is he? Where is Prince Leander?" Elaina quickly asked. Her words shot out before Kay could explain. Before, when she had heard from everyone that there was no news of Leander, she had felt gloomy, but now Kay, who she had thought had run off, had brought her information regarding Leander. How could she not be excited over that?

"Could we maybe be untied before we tell you?" Kay said as he tried to move his hands. Elaina gave the order, and the two of them were freed from their bindings.

"Now, tell me what you know about the whereabouts of Prince Leander," Elaina impatiently ordered.

Rickens explained how, a few nights ago, he had helped Prince Leander and his two saviors escape from the city. He also told them how the prince had been rescued by the two and that it seemed that someone had discovered that the prince had escaped the city.

Once Rickens had finished telling his story, the entire room was silent.

"Your Highness, now what do we do? Now that the prince is no longer in WestAvri, he could be anywhere," Hali said. Everyone knew what she meant. They had followed the path that Leander had been taking before the incident. They had luckily been able to pick up his trail, but now that trail had run cold. Once he had left WestAvri, the prince could have gone in any of several different directions.

"That might not be so," Kay said as he pulled out a piece of paper from his coat pocket. As he unfolded the paper, it turned out to be a map of the three duchies of Mezer. "The prince will be heading south, following the river till he makes it here," Kay said. His finger following the river on the map until it reached a large forest.

"Verilis Forest? How are you sure that the prince is heading there? Wouldn't it make more sense for the prince to head north?" Kaine asked doubtfully, and for good reasons. Verilis Forest was one of the most dangerous places in the three duchies. For every ten warriors that entered, one might emerge, if they were lucky. No one in their right mind would enter such a place, and Kay had said that the prince was heading there at that moment. Not only Kaine, but the rest of the warriors thought the same too.

"No. What this sell-sword is saying makes sense," Roan said, entering the conversation as he pointed at the lands to the north of WestAvri. "As you all know, the lands north of this city are the lands of Ridia, the holy city. Ridia has total control of the lands around it. The priests who worship there would not tolerate someone accused of murdering his own brother entering their domain. The moment the prince was found out, that day would be the anniversary of his death. The lands south are a lot less populated and would allow the prince and his group to travel without the risk of discovery."

Elaina agreed that going north would be too risky, but heading south had risks that were just as dangerous. "Even if he isn't heading north, I don't believe that Prince Leander would be foolish enough to enter the woods of Verilis. Even seasoned warriors wouldn't dare to risk their lives in entering," Elaina said.

"They are definitely heading for Verilis," Kay said with full confidence.

"How can you be so sure of that?" Kaine questioned. "According to what this Rickens has told us, no one has seen the prince since he left WestAvri. How can you be so sure they headed south?" His words held anger in them, as he quite disliked Kay, especially when he saw how he interacted with the princess.

"I know because the ones who saved the prince and are traveling with him at this very moment are my brothers," Kay answered.

"Your brothers? How are your brothers the ones with Prince Leander?" Hali demanded, her voice cracking from her shock.

Elaina was also surprised at this coincidence. Who would have known that Kay, who they had hired to find Leander, was the brother of the ones who had saved Leander? Elaina couldn't help but chuckle when she thought of this new information. Her chuckle turned into laughter, and Elaina forgot her worries for the moment.

When Kaine, Hali, and the young warriors heard Elaina laugh, they were dumbfounded. Ever since she had learned of the accusations about Leander, Elaina hadn't been cheerful. She had constantly worn a solemn look on her face, but at this moment, she was cheerful for the first time in days.

"This is too much of a coincidence," Elaina said with a smile, but then her face steadied, and she recomposed herself. "Everyone, first thing tomorrow, we will head south toward Verilis Forest. Make sure the crownes are fed and everything is prepared. And as for you …" She turned toward Kay. "If you wander off again, I will make sure you will regret doing so."

Chapter Ten: Entering the Dreaded Verilis Forest

In the dead of night, two people clashed with each other. Their swords reflected the light of the campfire, giving the metal a glowing red tint. As the fighting continued, it was obvious that one was vastly stronger than the other. Every slash and jab the weaker one performed, the stronger one countered perfectly. Finally the stronger one couldn't contain himself anymore, and with a heavy swing, he knocked the sword out of the other's hands.

"If you two are finished, can you join me so we can eat?" Aer shouted at them.

Lucis sheathed his sword, while Leander picked his up to check the damage. Seeing that his sword's edge was still sharp, he sighed in relief, and he, too, sheathed his weapon. Following Lucis, Leander took his seat around the fire, where dinner was cooking. His depressed mood was noticed by Aer.

"Don't let this loss bother you. I can't even remember the last time I bested Lucis," Aer said, trying to encourage the prince.

"That is because you have never bested me," Lucis said as he bit into the deer leg in his hands.

Leander also began eating. As he ate, he thought back to the duel he had just had with Lucis. Ever since he had dishonored himself in that confrontation with the lixin beast, Leander had been training with Lucis every chance he got. At first Lucis had refused. "If you are so determined, then show me this conviction of yours," Lucis had told him. That night, Leander had practiced his swordplay until the sun began to peek out over the horizon. The next day, Lucis agreed when Leander asked once more.

Lucis didn't hold anything back as they sparred. Each day, by the end of training, Leander felt that his limbs were numb. The prince had quickly understood that the training he got in Raven's Nest was completely watered down compared to his sparring with Lucis. He understood why though: as the son of the archduke, if anything were to happen to him, the one sparring with him could lose his position as a warrior, so none came at him with everything they had.

When he thought of home, Leander turned toward the nearby Verilis Forest. The forest groaned in the breeze as if it were a beast, ready to swallow them whole. Leander knew how dangerous Verilis Forest was, but he also knew that if they couldn't cross Avri Bridge or head north into the lands of Ridia, then their only option was to travel through the perilous forest.

"Worried about tomorrow?" Aer asked, noticing Leander gazing at the forest. When they had arrived, the sun had been about to set. Fearing the nocturnal predators, they had decided to camp outside the forest for the night, then enter at sunrise. As they had set up camp, strange sounds had echoed from the forest, and even Aer had said he felt reluctant to enter.

"Yes ... no ... I don't know," Leander mumbled. While he was feeling intimidated by the forest, compared to what he had been through in the past few days, a forest seemed not as bad, but it still filled him with some fear.

"You're slowly becoming able to embrace your fear, which is a good thing," Aer said, giving Leander a nod of approval. "But don't forget your fear. It is what keeps your instincts sharp and reflexes quick. Without it, you will lose your ability to sense incoming threats one day."

Leander nodded in agreement since his mouth was full of deer meat. Every night, after Lucis had taught him how to properly wield his sword, Aer would speak to him. The topics ranged from the profoundness of fear, like today, to the reasons and desires that drove people. Leander had quickly understood that Aer was teaching him what he had learned during his years as a sell-sword. Once he understood that, Leander soaked up all that he could.

"You should be feeling fear toward these woods," Lucis said, entering the conversation. "From the howls that we heard, I could make out a few. From the grunting roar of a borune, to the high-pitched wails of giant timber foxes, to the constant howls of a huge wolf pack. If we stumble across any of those, we will be in a fight for our lives. That isn't even mentioning the dangerous terrain and strange plants that grow there. We will have to be ever vigilant once we enter."

Upon hearing Lucis talk about the beasts he knew from just their sounds, Leander was impressed. He also knew that each dangerous creature Lucis had counted was as dangerous, if not more so, than the lixin beast. Just the borune, a giant bear with fur as tough as iron, would send even the strongest warriors running for their lives.

"No need to try and scare him, Lucis. He knows how dangerous Verilis Forest is without you saying—" Aer had started reprimanding Lucis in a joking tone when, out of the darkness, an arrow flew straight at Aer, piercing his right shoulder. Grunting in pain, Aer fell to the ground.

"Aer!" Lucis shouted as he ran and knelt by the wounded sell-sword. The arrow had gone straight through his shoulder, with the arrowhead jutting out of Aer's flesh.

Leander scanned the darkness for whoever had shot at them, but with the moon clouded over, he couldn't see past the glow of the fire. As he searched, several

113

arrows flew by. Leander instinctively crouched down, only to have another volley of arrows land right where he had just been.

"Douse the fire!" Lucis yelled as he snapped off the end of the arrow that was embedded in Aer's shoulder. Not missing a second, Leander ran to the fire and quickly stomped it out. Several more arrows flew at them, but with the fire out, the arrows failed to find their marks.

Once the fire was out, whoever was shooting at them should have been unable to see them. The arrows did stop, and Leander relaxed his guard for only a moment. It was at that moment that an arrow was loosed. The only one who had noticed was Lucis, who pulled Prince Leander away at the last moment. As all three were crouching on the ground, the sound of hoofbeats was fast approaching them.

"Head to the forest. We can take cover in the woods," Lucis said to Leander. He then helped up Aer, whose arm now hung limply by his side.

Not waiting for themselves to be surrounded, the three ran to Verilis Forest. The hoofbeats grew faster as they chased after the prince and the two sell-swords. The closer they got to the forest, the closer the pursuers came to catching them. Running as fast as they could, they reached the forest's edge just as the first mounted warrior came into view. However, before they could enter, another arrow hit the wounded Aer, knocking him out of Lucis's grip and onto the ground.

Tumbling over, Aer grunted in pain. Lucis and Leander stopped to help, but Aer gave the two a look. "Go!" he shouted. When they didn't move, Aer got angry. "I told you to go!"

"I can't leave you. How could I ever show my face to Kay if I left you to die?" Lucis said. As he tried to help the wounded sell-sword up, Aer pushed his arms away.

"Whoever said I needed your help? We were hired to protect Prince Leander.

114

How can you do that while worrying about me?" Aer bellowed. Pulling himself up, Aer started limping toward the forest.

Steeling his resolve, Lucis took Leander and ran into the forest. Leander turned around, but once in the forest, he could no longer see Aer struggling behind them but could still hear him.

The brush was thick in Verilis Forest. As they clawed their way through, branches scratched at their skin, and the uneven ground slowed their pace. The dense foliage also made traveling on horseback impossible, stopping their pursuers in their tracks. This gave them some much-needed time to get away.

The deeper into Verilis Forest they went, the more treacherous the terrain became. They were lucky and able to stop themselves from stumbling into such dangers, but that luck didn't last. Not noticing an uprooted tree root as they ran over the top of a large hill, Leander tripped. Lucis tried to catch him, only to be pulled down himself.

Luckily for them, the hill wasn't too steep, so the fall didn't harm them when they landed in a grouping of bushes covered in strange yellow flowers. The second they fell into the brush, a cloud of pollen shot out from the flowers.

The thick cloud of pollen made seeing impossible and made it extremely difficult to breathe. Each breath Lucis and Leander took caused more of the pollen to stick to the inside of their throats. The pollen cloud continued to grow in size until it covered a large portion of the forest. When the animals of the forest saw the incoming pollen, they ran for cover.

Leander tried to call out to Lucis, but the pollen stifled his voice. With the pollen stinging his eyes and burning his lungs, the prince could only try to find his way out. Not knowing whether Lucis was going in the same direction as he was, Leander clumsily made his way through the pollen cloud.

+

Aer stumbled through the forest, leaving a bloody trail after him. He had lost sight of Leander and Lucis just as the two had entered the forest. He had been able to follow the sound of their footsteps until they had gotten too far ahead of him, then nothing.

Behind him, Aer could hear their pursuers as they dismounted and began to hack their way through the forest. Knowing that he couldn't escape, with his dead arm and leg dragging him down, Aer pulled his way up a nearby tree. He hid in the branches.

Nestled away, Aer could hear many footsteps below. The darkness of the forest made it so Aer couldn't see them. It also caused them to miss the trail of blood he had left behind. As he pulled the arrow out of his thigh, Aer listened in on the men below.

"They couldn't have gotten far. Spread out and search," Aer heard one of them shout.

"Sir, this is Verilis Forest, the Forest of Death. Shouldn't we wait till the rest of us arrive and search in the morning, when it is safe?" another voice chimed in. Aer could hear the fear of Verilis Forest in the man's voice.

"By that time, the prince could be far ahead of us. We almost had him at the edge of the forest. He can't be that far ahead, and you want to wait for morning?" the first voice shouted at the timid man.

"Sir, something is coming," a third voice yelled. Aer heard the unsheathing of swords but then nothing.

Trying to find out what was going on, he looked below and saw a yellow cloud rising from the ground. As he was unable to get away, the yellow cloud engulfed him. The thick pollen made him cough and feel dizzy, but soon he found his head clearing. As he looked around, a familiar voice called to him from behind.

"Aer? Is that you, my love?" a woman's voice called to him. Aer's body stiffened. He recognized the voice immediately.

Turning his head, he came face-to-face with someone he thought he would never see again. Sitting on one of the branches was a middle-aged woman looking back at him, still as beautiful as he remembered. Aer could feel the tears welling up behind his eyes. When he finally got the courage to speak, his voice cracked. His nervousness prevented him from saying anything.

"What's wrong, dear? Are you not glad to see me?" said the woman as she took a few steps toward Aer. She looked hurt from Aer's lack of response.

"Stay back!" Aer shouted, placing more distance between them. "I don't know what you are, but you aren't Fae."

"How could you say that to me? Aren't you happy to see that I'm still alive?" the woman cried.

Seeing her tears tore at Aer's heart. Fae, his wife, had been taken from him by illness five years ago. He was sure that whatever he was seeing wasn't his wife, but seeing her tearful face made him second-guess himself. He had heard that Verilis Forest wasn't only feared due to the many beasts. It was also said to be haunted. When he thought that Fae's soul could be trapped here, he quickly pushed the idea out of his mind. Fae had died in the southern kingdoms, so how would her spirit have ended up here, of all places. As his mind raced, Aer was unaware that the woman had made her way to his side.

Before he could react, Aer found himself in his dead wife's embrace. Feeling the warmth, he forgot all of his doubts and embraced her back. Her scent entered his nose. The familiar scent of lavender. Fae loved to wear that perfume wherever she went.

"I have missed you so," whispered Fae. Her hand slowly headed for the back of his head. "Never leave me alone again."

"I won't," Aer said. Then he suddenly pierced his wife's back with a dagger that he had hidden in his sleeve. He watched as his wife looked at him, not in betrayal or heartache, but in complete shock.

"Why?" she asked, barely able to hold herself up.

"I would recognize that perfume anywhere. It is a special blend I made for my wife myself. No one else knows how to make it, and I would certainly never smell it here, of all places," Aer said, pushing her away.

As she fell, Aer watched as the form of his wife changed before his eyes. His love ended up turning into a strange bug with long limbs and a sharp stinger. The hand that had been heading for his head was that very stinger. If he had been less cautious, he would have fallen prey to the insect's scheme.

Safe once more, Aer slouched on the branch. The vision of his departed wife dying once more had taken more out of him than he had thought. Even though he knew that it had been fake, it had all been too real—to even copy the perfume.

"Lucis, Leander, I hope you are all right," Aer said, looking into the vast darkness of Verilis Forest.

+

At the time Aer was facing his illusion, Leander was struggling with his own. Standing in front of Leander was his brother. Crown Prince Eustace stood there as large gashes bled profusely. Upon seeing his brother appear before him, Leander could only stand motionless, his fear and guilt pinning him in place.

"Why?" the bleeding prince asked. "Why was I the one who died and not you? You, who just stood there and watched as that traitorous squire murdered me. It should have been you who died. You! Not me!"

Leander felt that what his brother said was true. He had let Bez kill Eustace as he had cowardly hidden in the bushes. Looking at his brother, who glared at him with hateful eyes, Leander felt the pain of Eustace's death all over again. He could only watch as Eustace spoke vile words as he neared.

"I was supposed to become the Archduke of the Talov Duchy. I was supposed to lead my warriors in protecting the people of my land. But that will never happen, because of you. I, who was beloved by all, am dead, while my lowly brother survives to take my place. I will not stand for it!" the bloody Eustace shouted. Each step he took closer to Leander was one more devastating blow to Leander's heart.

"Brother ... I'm sorry," Leander said as tears flowed out uncontrollably. "I would do anything to make things right."

"Right? You want to make things right? Then give your life to me. Face it, everyone would have been a lot happier if you had died while I had lived," Eustace spat as he pulled out his sword.

With those words said, Leander could no longer think. Pain filled his heart as visions of the night his brother had died streamed through his head. Falling to his knees, Leander waited for his brother to end his life and suffering, but at that moment, something caught his eye.

Somehow his sword had freed part of itself from its sheath. Even in this dark night, the blade's glint was noticeable. Staring at his sword, he remembered the promise he had made to himself. Looking up toward his bloody brother, who was now mere steps away, Leander realized something.

As Eustace prepared to strike Leander down, the prince acted. Drawing his sword, he put all his power into this swing. There was no sound of metal clashing as Leander's sword cut through Eustace's sword. When the blade was cut through, Eustace fell to the ground in pain. He no longer had the mask of a man and soon

119

turned into a disgusting insect, whose stinger had been cut off.

Not waiting for the insect to recover, Leander cut off its head.

The insect's limbs twitched long after its death. Looking down at the dead creature, Leander felt a strange feeling well up inside him. He hadn't run, nor had he cowered. He had stood his ground and faced this dangerous insect. For the first time in his life, he wasn't the coward everyone knew him to be.

+

In another part of Verilis Forest, the sound of loud screeching could be heard. Sharp and shrill, each screech was filled with pain. It was in this part of the forest that the pollen cloud was at its densest.

In this yellow cloud stood Lucis. His sword was covered in a strange ichor that stuck to the blade like glue. Around him were the corpses of five of those strange insects. Each one was neatly cut in half. One that was still alive tried to crawl away, leaving its back half behind. Lucis quickly ended the insect with a stab through the head. The strike caused even more ichor to grip onto the sword.

"Blasted insects! How dare you show me those illusions!" Lucis swore at the insect corpses. He radiated murderous intent, which only grew when he thought about the visions he had been shown.

Around him, Lucis could hear the scurrying of more of these insects, but none of the insects dared to come out. He had made even these apex predators terrified.

Lucis wiped his blade clean with his coat sleeve and placed it back in its sheath. Not wanting to stay there any longer, he turned his back to the slaughter and simply walked away. The eyes of many insects watched him fade into the distance.

Chapter Eleven: Conflict with the Talov Warriors

E laina and her group had noticed something was wrong almost instantly. After learning of Leander's escape from WestAvri, they had left right away. Knowing that they were not the only ones after the prince made them travel at a quicker pace than before. Early one morning, they had spotted tracks that caused them to worry. The tracks had been left by dozens of horses galloping next to each other. Only warriors rode side by side at that speed.

Nearing Verilis Forest, they found that their fears were justified. At the edge of the forest camped dozens of armed warriors. Not wanting to be discovered, Elaina and her companions hid on one of the hills overlooking the camp. This allowed them to see the warriors, but the warriors could not see them.

"I don't see the prince. They must have failed to capture him and chased him into Verilis Forest," Elaina said as they spied on the camp.

"What now, Your Highness?" asked Kaine. "We failed to make it to the prince before he entered Verilis. And with all the warriors from Talov about, it will be too dangerous for you to continue after the prince." His voice sounded remorseful but steady.

"What are you trying to say, Kaine?" Elaina angrily asked.

"I'm saying that we should retreat. Now that the prince has entered Verilis

Forest, he is no longer in land controlled by the Estelles. Continuing this mission would put Your Highness in much danger. Even with us laying down our lives for you, there's a chance that you will perish, and I will not have your blood on my hands."

"I never thought you could be such a coward," Elaina spat. Her words clearly hurt the warrior, but Elaina didn't care.

"There is a difference between being brave and doing something foolish. You should remember that, ma'am," Kaine said.

If Elaina's words had hurt Kaine, then Kaine's words tore through Elaina. She knew he was right, but with Leander so close, she didn't wish to turn back now. Looking over the dozens of warriors camped out, she tried to find a way past but saw none. The second they tried, the Talov warriors would spot them.

As they looked on, someone left one of the tents. It was a man dressed entirely in dark green. He had a longbow across his back and a long knife strapped to his side. As soon as he left the tent, he began to order the warriors about.

"It looks like that man is the leader," Hali said.

"But it is strange. I have never seen a warrior dressed the way that man is, and the way he displays himself … He clearly isn't a warrior," Kaine said.

Elaina had also noticed that. She didn't understand how proud warriors could take orders from someone who wasn't one. As they watched the green-cloaked man giving orders, a short man made his way to him. Elaina and Hali found him familiar but didn't know why. When the short man turned in their direction, they saw his face and instantly recognized him.

"Isn't that Bez, Crown Prince Eustace's squire? What is he doing all the way out here?" Elaina questioned. She now knew why he was so familiar. Bez had always been just behind Crown Prince Eustace, like his shadow. They had seen him during

122

the two princes' stay with them but never spoken a single word to the man.

"Isn't he here to capture the prince?" Hali said, not understanding why everyone was shocked to see Bez here.

"How can you call yourself a Malis and not understand warrior customs?" her brother Kaine berated her. He then explained. "Squires are warriors of the lowest class. They are more like servants than warriors. Only warrior families with no ties or land would allow their children to become squires. Heck, even classless warriors look down on them."

Hali nodded, understanding now. Unlike personal warriors, who guarded their charges with their lives, squires were merely servants, who polished armor or brought meals. With so many warriors searching for the prince, there was little reason to send out a squire. Sending out a squire to catch a warrior would be something extremely foolish to do.

"Then why is he out here? It doesn't look like he is serving any of the warriors," said Myles. Looking toward the camp, they realized that Myles was right. Bez wasn't following orders but giving them, and the warriors were complying.

"This doesn't make any sense," Kaine mumbled.

"Of course it does," they suddenly heard Kay say. When they looked at him, not knowing what he meant, he elaborated. "Wasn't Bez the one who revealed that it was Leander who murdered his brother? This must be him trying to tie up loose ends."

"You're saying that Bez is the one who really murdered the prince and had Leander take the fall?" Roan said, looking at Kay in a new light. He wasn't too keen on traveling with a sell-sword, especially after he had learned of how Princess Elaina had met him, but when he heard what Kay had just said, he realized that this Kay was more intuitive than most.

123

"I'm not saying anything, but if this Bez truly is the culprit, then something must have gone wrong in his plot to kill the prince. If I were planning on killing a prince, I wouldn't let a witness survive, much less the one I claimed is responsible for the murder," Kay said.

Kay's words made sense to Elaina. She was sure that Leander wasn't responsible, but for some reason, it hadn't crossed her mind that the crown prince's own squire would be a traitor. Looking down at the evil squire giving orders to hunt down Leander, Elaina wanted nothing more than to wring his neck.

"We should leave. Our chances of being discovered only increase if we stay," Kaine warned. Even hearing that Bez was the true culprit didn't change his mind about leaving. The princess's safety was the only thing that mattered to him.

Elaina ignored Kaine and continued to monitor the activity of the warriors below. Soon half the warriors were gathered in front of the man in green. After issuing an order, the man led the warriors into the forest, leaving the other half stationed in wait. Bez also left with the warriors to search the forest.

"We have to get to Leander before them," Elaina declared. She saw the ruthlessness of the warriors. If they reached Prince Leander first, the only thing waiting for her would be the prince's corpse.

"Ma'am, I implore you to reconsider. We are not equipped for the dangers of Verilis Forest," Kaine said, but Elaina ignored him once again. She was adamant about continuing the search for Leander.

"What is that?" Elaina and the others suddenly heard Hali speak up.

Looking back, Elaina saw that Hali was pointing toward the sky. Following Hali's finger, Elaina noticed a small shadow above them. As she narrowed her eyes, the shadow came into focus as it left the cover of the sun. What flew above them was a large spotted bird with long head feathers, longer than the rest of its feathers.

Seeing the bird circling them, Elaina and the others paled.

"It's a spotted rael! We have to take cover," Myles suddenly proclaimed, but no one moved. There wasn't any cover to hide from the rael's sight.

Raels were the companions of the Talov warriors. Due to the birds' high intellect, they were difficult to tame, but once tamed, they were as loyal as the most devout warriors. There were several different kinds of these fierce and loyal birds, but the spotted rael was the most common. Its main duty was to scout ahead and alert its master to the enemy's movements. As the rael spotted them, it gave a loud screech.

The warriors who remained at the camp turned around. They saw the rael flying in circles, so they quickly mounted their horses and headed toward Elaina and the others, their weapons already drawn.

"Not good," Kay said, but he didn't sound too worried.

Out of the corner of her eye, Elaina saw that the sell-sword was smiling. His hands inched toward Myles's sword. The man wanted to fight. Elaina gave Kay a glare, stopping him from stealing the sword.

"Prepare for combat!" Kaine ordered.

The young warriors were quick to act. They readied their weapons and encircled Elaina and Hali. Their crownes snorted and stomped their hooves—their steeds were also ready to fight.

The Talov warriors drew closer. When they spotted Elaina and her warriors, they sped up their charge. As they neared, they split into two groups and quickly surrounded the young warriors. The loud beating of hooves and the sharp glint of steel made the young warriors nervous, but on their faces, they only showed courage. They had been trained since childhood to not fear death. Even if these young warriors were too green to truly be unafraid, they at least stood their ground.

Soon the circling Talov warriors came to a halt. As the two sides faced one

125

another, one of the Talov warriors rode forward. As he did, he held up his arm, and the rael above swooped down, landing comfortably on the warrior's forearm. The man was grizzly, with wild hair and a long scar across his face. He didn't look anything like an honorable warrior to Elaina and the young Estelle warriors.

"What are a bunch of smooth-skins doing so close to Verilis Forest?" said the man as he pulled out a piece of dried meat and fed it to the rael.

Being called "smooth-skins" made the young warriors tremble in anger. It was an epithet that the older warriors used for young and newly appointed warriors. It derived from the belief that all warriors should carry scars on them. So, as an insult, the elder warriors had started calling their juniors "smooth-skins," as to imply that they weren't true warriors yet.

"You bastard—" Myles started shouting, but a glare from Kaine stopped him from saying anything else. Elaina was glad for Kaine's understanding of the situation. It would do them no good to antagonize the warrior.

"I apologize for my comrade's behavior," Kaine said, taking it upon himself to represent the group. "As for why we are here, we have heard stories of Verilis Forest and wished to see if it was as perilous as people say."

"Well, aren't you a couple of brave smooth-skins," the man said, causing the rest of the Talov warriors to laugh. "Unluckily for you, our orders are to apprehend any who come near Verilis Forest. It would be in your best interests to surrender to us. Of course, you can try to resist. My men and I wouldn't mind spilling some Estelle warrior blood."

As the Talov warriors howled in laughter, Elaina held back her contempt for these men. *How dare they act like this!* she thought. The Avri River was the border between the Talov and Estelle Duchies, and they were on the west side, in the Estelle Duchy. These warriors had no right to arrest warriors of the Estelle Duchy on their own land. When one of the Talov warriors got cocky and ordered his horse to rear up, knocking one of the young warriors to the ground, Elaina couldn't take it anymore.

"How dare you act this way! And you call yourselves warriors! Who gave you the right to treat us this way?" Elaina shouted.

Her voice sounded noble and gave the young warriors strength. They almost forgot that it wasn't their archduke or their crown prince standing there, but the young princess. While the young warriors were basking in newfound courage, the Talov warriors were grinding their teeth in rage. A young woman had dared to stand up to them. This was an insult to their honor.

"Who might you be?" the bearded warrior asked. When he had heard Elaina, he had been shocked. Her tone sounded like one of a ruler. He knew instantly that this young woman was from a high-ranking warrior family, and he had to tread lightly. He couldn't allow the Estelles to find out what they were doing.

"Your Highness, don't," Kaine warned, trying to stop her from speaking. He knew what Elaina was planning, but it was of no use.

Stepping in front of all the young warriors who risked their lives to protect her, she readied herself to speak. She was so focused she hadn't noticed that both Roan and Kay were looking at her in a new way.

"My name is Elaina Estelle, daughter of His Royal Highness Archduke Bennet and princess of the Estelle Duchy. I demand you release us this instant," Elaina said. Her words shocked the surrounding warriors. They had never imagined that they would run into the Estelle princess out here, at the border of Verilis, of all places.

Elaina stood there, waiting for the warriors to sheathe their weapons and let them go. When they did not, a dangerous feeling welled up inside her. Seeing this as well was Kaine, who pulled Elaina away just as a warrior's sword swung through the air, just missing the princess.

"What do you think you are doing?" Elaina demanded, but her domineering tone was gone. Instead, she felt fear. "Do you wish for our two duchies to go to war?"

Seeing the princess frightened but putting up a courageous act made the bearded warrior laugh. "Your Highness, you are sadly mistaken. If you had been just a mere daughter of a small warrior family, then we would have detained you, but seeing as you are that monstrous archduke's child, then you can only leave your life here," the man said. The rael on his arm gave a loud screech in response.

With those words, the Talov warriors attacked. Responding in kind, the young Estelle warriors parried the murderous strikes. While the young warriors were strong and full of vigor, they were not as experienced as the Talov warriors. They were also vastly outnumbered. Soon wounds began to appear on the young warriors.

Myles, unable to parry a warrior's attack properly, was struck in the back. Screaming in agony, he collapsed. As he lay motionless on the ground, no one could tell whether he was dead or alive. As the Talov warrior went to finish the job, Kaine appeared and fended off the fatal blow that was coming for Myles's life.

As the battle dragged on, the young warriors were soon unable to contend with the Talov warriors. In the end, only Kaine, Roan, and Elaina were left in fighting condition. The rest of them were either too tired to raise their weapons or too wounded.

"This is the end for you," the bearded warrior said, charging forward. His swing knocked Kaine away, leaving Elaina unguarded.

Elaina was able to raise her sword to defend herself, but the warrior had expected this. With a swift twist of his wrist, Elaina's sword flew out of her hand. With nothing else in his way, the warrior laughed maliciously and thrust his sword toward the princess.

Knowing her end was near, Elaina closed her eyes and waited for death to take her. One second went by, then two, and soon Elaina realized that the blow would never come. Opening her eyes, the scene that she saw petrified her.

Standing in front of her was the sell-sword Kay. In his hands was a small kitchen knife. Elaina recognized the knife as one they had used for dinner, a knife so dull that it could barely cut bread, but in front of her, that was proved wrong. The small knife in the sell-sword's hand had pierced the warrior's throat. With a flick of his wrist, Kay slit the warrior's throat.

Even as he died, the warrior didn't know how he had died. He had seen Kay move in front of him to protect the princess, but the warrior had given him no mind. During the entire battle, the man had only dodged and never struck back. He saw that he carried no sword and felt confidence in slaying this man. When he had gone for the killing blow, it had happened. With a strange twisting movement, the man had moved in front of him and pierced his throat.

When the warrior fell, the rest of the Talov warriors stood in horror. This man had been the strongest of them, and he had been killed by a simple kitchen knife. They were so shocked they forgot to continue the onslaught. Only the warrior's rael attacked to avenge its master. Angered by the death of its master, it tried to sink its sharp talons into Kay, only to have the same knife used to kill its master slay it as well.

Elaina didn't know what to think when she saw Kay effortlessly kill a veteran warrior. A warrior of his stature could have defeated a dozen armed men single-handedly. She thought that she should be feeling fear, but not a shred of terror was in her body.

She also didn't understand why he had saved her. He had been hired only to help them find Leander and then go their separate ways. There was no reason for him to

129

risk his own life saving hers. If anything, her dying would only make things easier for Kay. With his strength, he could easily escape these warriors after they had finished killing the rest of them. As she looked on, she watched Kay pick up the dead warrior's sword and charge the Talov warriors.

"Defend!" one of the Talov warriors shouted just as Kay reached them. That was the warrior's last word, as Kay stuck his sword through an opening in the man's armor, into his stomach.

The rest of the warriors no longer paid attention to Elaina and the rest. They knew that if they couldn't kill Kay, they wouldn't leave here with their lives. As they surrounded Kay, one warrior sneaked up behind and attacked, his sword heading right for Kay's neck.

As if he knew, Kay turned around and, with his open hand, grabbed the warrior's wrist. With a snap, Kay broke it, and the sword the warrior held fell. Before the sword touched the ground, Kay grabbed it with his free hand. With a sword in each hand, Kay readied himself, each sword raised, waiting for the Talov warriors to attack.

One against many, Kay didn't falter. He was like a fish in water, swerving in and out, narrowly dodging strike after strike. While his enemy's swords only hit air, his spilled blood. The Talov warriors fell one by one, unable to stop Kay.

Elaina and the young warriors watched with mouths agape. They had seen the end results of Kay's strength, but seeing it firsthand was a whole different matter. Even Kaine, the most seasoned and disciplined, couldn't help but be dumbfounded by what he saw.

As Kay fought, Elaina felt something was off with the sell-sword. She had noticed that during this fight, Kay's eyes began to change. It wasn't their color or size but their depth. They began to glint in a familiar way. The same way they had when they had first discovered the sell-sword. When she saw Kay's normally mischievous face turn cold, she knew she had to do something.

Not worrying about her own well-being, Elaina ran into the fray. Behind her, the young warriors yelled for her to stop as Kaine and Roan chased after her. Ignoring the pleas behind her, Elaina soon made it to Kay, who was looking more sinister by the second. With no time to think, Elaina threw herself at Kay, grabbing him from behind.

Feeling Elaina wrap herself around him, Kay tried to throw her off. This only caused Elaina to hold on tighter. More Kay struggled, until he grabbed one of Elaina's arms and threw her over him. As she landed on the ground, Elaina tried to stand, only to have Kay's foot press down on her. Looking up, she saw that he was ready to finish her as he raised one of his swords.

"No!" Kaine shouted as he saw that Kay was about to kill Elaina. Before he could reach the princess, he and Roan were blocked by a couple of Talov warriors.

Elaina looked into Kay's eyes and saw the madness in them, but she also saw something more. She saw the struggle that was going on, the reason that was trying to break free. "You won't kill me," she said. She didn't know where this thought came from, but after saying those words, she felt more reassured.

Sure enough, she saw the madness and bloodlust being driven away from the depths of Kay's eyes. As he regained his sanity, Kay's consciousness began to fade, and he toppled over. Having seen this once before, Elaina was ready, catching the now-unconscious Kay. Elaina didn't have time to check on him as the Talov warriors found their chance to finish both Kay and her.

Elaina picked up one of the swords Kay had dropped, and readied for the fight. As she was about to engage the Talov warriors, a loud rumbling came from a distance. From the hills behind them came a large group of Estelle warriors, each wearing battle armor and riding a crowne. These warriors charged the Talov warriors.

The Talov warriors tried to flee, but it was no use, as crownes, the kings of all horses, were faster than their steeds. Smashing into the Talov warriors like a wave onto a beach, the Estelle warriors made quick work of the remaining Talov warriors.

Seeing that help had arrived, the young Estelle warriors heaved sighs of relief. They had but moments ago resigned their fates to death, only to be saved at the last moment. As they watched on excitedly, only Kaine and Elaina had different expressions on their faces. While glad to be saved, they saw something the other young warriors hadn't.

After finishing the last of the Talov warriors, the newly arrived Estelle warriors made their way toward Elaina and the rest. At their lead was a man in full armor. His helmet's visor hid his face, but the emblem on his chest told the young warriors who he was, making them all tremble in fear.

Once he reached them, the man dismounted from his crowne. A large man, he looked down at them. As he did, Kaine, Hali, and the rest of the warriors saluted the warrior. Even Roan gave the man a salute. Only Kay, who was unconscious, and Elaina didn't pay obeisance to the warrior.

He took a few steps and stood directly in front of Elaina. Taking off his helmet, he revealed a rugged yet handsome face. His blond hair was cut short in the traditional warrior style. His eyes were sharp to the point that they would miss nothing. The man gave out an aura of authority—the same aura Elaina had momentarily showed against the Talov warriors. Most women, when confronted with such a man, would blush, and their hearts would flutter, but Elaina only showed a hint of fear.

"Do you know how much trouble you have caused?" the man asked as his glare burrowed into Elaina.

Elaina tried to speak, but the words were caught in her throat. Time seemed to slow down for Elaina, but she was finally able to say a single word to the man. "Brother," she said in a voice so quiet it could barely be called a whisper.

The one who had saved them, and the one the young warriors bowed to, was her eldest brother, the crown prince of the Estelle Duchy, Aleron Estelle. The pride of the entire duchy and a warrior born of honor, a Zer'sheen. Seeing him here, Elaina knew that her quest to find Leander was over.

Chapter Twelve: The Sell-Sword and the Zer'sheen Prince

D o you have any idea how worried you made Father? When he awoke to find that you had run off, he nearly destroyed the entire castle in his rage!" Aleron shouted at his younger sister. Kaine and Hali knelt behind the princess as they, too, were subjected to this reprimanding. "And you two. Is this how you protect your princess? Sneaking her out of her home on some foolhardy quest?"

"Brother, it wasn't their idea to go. I forced them to come," Elaina said, coming to Kaine and Hali's defense, but she was wrong in her judgment. Her rebuttal only infuriated Aleron more.

"Do you really think I'm so foolish to think that you alone convinced Kaine and the rest of the young ones to go on this mission to find Prince Leander? I know that every young warrior who joined you is friends with the Talovs' second prince. These young ones are warriors; if it hadn't been their choice to go, they would never have gone," Aleron said.

What he said was true. While young, these warriors who had come with Elaina had had the Code of Valor and the three virtues drilled into them since an early age. If they hadn't believed that it was their duty to find the prince, they would never have risked tarnishing their honor by going against the archduke's command. Even if Elaina had tried to force them, they wouldn't have gone.

"I'm sorry, brother," Elaina said. Her head hung low so she didn't have to see her brother's angry glare. "I'm sorry for worrying you and Father so."

When her brother didn't respond to her apology, Elaina had no choice but to look up, only to find Aleron standing right above her. She hadn't heard him near, and now he shadowed her. Elaina watched as he raised his arm high. Thinking that he was about to slap her, Elaina readied herself. However, instead of a hard slap, she found that her brother pulled her into his embrace.

"Brother? Wha... what are you doing?" Elaina muttered. Her body went stiff not knowing what to do. She couldn't remember the last time that her eldest brother had hugged her. Once he had started his warrior training, he had grown distant and cold. Even a smile was a rarity for this cold brother of hers. For him to show this type of emotion made even Kaine and Hali stare dumbfounded.

Then, as suddenly as he had embraced her, Aleron released Elaina. Still frozen in place, Elaina looked like a stone statue. When she finally regained her senses, her brother was pouring himself a glass of wine. After quickly downing the glass, he turned his attention back to Elaina with his usual cold face. For a moment, Elaina thought that the whole embrace had been in her imagination, although her body still retaining the heat of her brother's hug said otherwise.

"Tell me, sister. What have you gone through as you've searched for Prince Leander?" Aleron asked. "I notice that you have added two more to the group you set out with."

With his cold gaze burning through her, Elaina knew that she could not hide anything, so she told him everything: how she had escaped from Esesa with the help of Kaine and the rest, their meeting with Kay on their way to WestAvri, even how they had been helped by Roan at the gate of WestAvri. Elaina noticed that when she spoke about Kay, her brother's eyes flashed with interest, but she didn't know what it meant.

When Elaina finally finished the retelling of her journey, ending with the confrontation with the Talov warriors, she was out of breath.

Aleron just stood there, looking down at his rebellious sister. Scratching his unkempt beard, he looked to be pondering something. Elaina squirmed under his gaze but knew better than to speak. Finally her brother turned to one of his personal warriors, the only other one in the tent besides Elaina, Aleron, and the two Malis siblings. Elaina recognized the warrior as Declan, a loyal but boorish warrior who couldn't understand a joke even if it was explained to him for a whole day.

"Bring me the man Kay," he ordered. Giving Aleron a fisted salute, the warrior Declan left the tent to retrieve Kay.

"Brother, you saw how he was when you arrived. He might not even be awake yet," Elaina said, trying to persuade her brother not to disturb Kay's much-needed rest.

"Now, this is interesting," Aleron said jokingly. With his face still in the same neutral expression, it sounded more like a threat. "It sounds like you are quite worried for this sell-sword's well-being."

Upon hearing her brother, Elaina blushed a bright red. "Who says I'm worried about him?" Elaina yelled, but her looks and voice made everyone in the tent believe that she was indeed worried for Kay.

Knowing that she wouldn't be listened to, Elaina shut up and looked at the floor. The questioning gazes from Kaine and Hali were making her tremble slightly. She didn't know why she defended the sell-sword. All she knew was that even with the stigma of a sell-sword, Kay had kept true to his words, even when she had lost faith in him. He at least deserved this much from her.

The four of them waited in silence, waiting for Declan to bring the crown prince Kay. Time ticked on, and Aleron's face began to twitch with impatience. The campground wasn't large. It shouldn't have taken Declan this long just to retrieve a prisoner. In fact, to keep prisoners from escaping, the tent the confined were kept in was close to the center and tightly guarded.

As his patience was running thin, the warrior Declan finally returned with Kay in chains. The warrior's appearance was quite different from when he had left. His face was bruised, and one of his eyes was swollen shut, as if he had just been beaten. The four also noticed that when he entered, he walked in with a new limp he hadn't had when he had left.

"Sorry for the delay, Your Highness," Declan apologized, throwing Kay to the ground.

Elaina noticed that Kay's face was bruised as well. It was obvious to all that some form of conflict had transpired between the sell-sword and the warrior.

"Declan, what took you so long, and why is the prisoner like this?" Aleron asked, pointing to the chains that bound Kay. When they had first arrived, they had bound Kay but only with rope, and only around the wrists and ankles. Now Kay was covered in heavy chains, unable to move even slightly.

"Forgive me, sir, but I had no other choice," Declan said. He then explained. "When I arrived to fetch the prisoner, I found him trying to escape. He had already gotten the bindings around his ankles off and was working on the ones on his wrists. I confronted him and was thoroughly beaten. Luckily, the commotion alerted the warriors guarding just outside. With their help, I was able to recapture the sell-sword and bring him to you."

Elaina felt her head pounding listening to Declan speak. She had just defended the man, and now he had injured one of her brother's personal warriors. She knew that Kay would react when he woke up and found himself tied up once more. Now her words in his favor had lost their worth, but she saw something in her brother she hadn't seen in a while. Instead of anger or fury, her brother, the crown prince of the Estelle Duchy, showed curiosity.

"A meager sell-sword was able to defeat one of my own personal warriors and did this with his hands bound together? Tell me, who taught you swordplay?" Aleron asked Kay, who was lying on the ground. Elaina noticed that her brother's sword hand clenched and released over and over, a habit Elaina recognized as her brother's eagerness to duel.

Kay didn't respond to the prince's question. He just stared back at the prince defiantly. Elaina couldn't let her brother and Kay be at odds with each other. Giving a cough that echoed through the quiet tent, she was able to get the attention of Kay, who had only then noticed Elaina being there.

When he saw that Elaina was unharmed and was even wearing more-decorative clothes than before, Kay's hard gaze relaxed. Looking back at the prince, the glint in Kay's eyes told Elaina that the man's irritating personality had returned.

"Answer the prince!" Declan yelled at the bound Kay. His patience with Kay was nonexistent. Having been beaten by Kay just moments ago, Declan really didn't like the sell-sword.

Kay looked at Aleron, then at Elaina. While the two had quite different body structures—Elaina being thin, and Aleron a hulking giant of muscle—Kay could still detect a few traces of similarity between the two. He especially noticed that the two had the same piercing eyes and sharp brows.

"You must be Elaina's elder brother. It is an honor to meet such a famous warrior," Kay said. His tone was as joking as ever. Everyone in the room heard it and knew that Kay was being sarcastic.

"Answer my question," Aleron said. His cold voice sounded irritated at Kay's behavior. "Who taught you how to wield a sword?"

Elaina and Kaine were also interested. Ever since they had first met Kay, they had known that he was monstrously strong. For him to get so strong, he must have been taught by an equally strong or even famous swordsman. They had asked him before, but each time, Kay would answer with "Just some old geezers," so they had stopped asking. Upon hearing the crown prince ask, they wished that Kay would answer seriously, but didn't hold much hope.

"Just some old geezers," Kay answered. His answer caused the warrior Declan to knock him over. Declan would have continued, but with a wave of his hand, Aleron ordered him to cease.

"If you don't want to tell me who your master is, then that is fine," Crown Prince Aleron said. "In fact, I was thinking about releasing you—that is, if you do one thing for me."

"Those are some familiar words. No wonder you two are siblings," Kay said, looking back at Elaina. The last time he had been caught and chained, he had struck a deal with Elaina for his release. Now her older brother was doing the same. "So? What is this favor that you wish of me?"

Aleron looked Kay over once more. Narrowing his eyes, he only said two simple words. "Duel me."

Upon hearing his prince request a duel, the warrior Declan stepped forward. "Sir, if I may? I would implore you not to duel this man."

"Do you believe I won't be able to defeat him?" Aleron asked. His cold voice made Declan and the rest in the tent shudder. Only Kay seemed to be unaffected, which only made Aleron want to duel him even more.

"I would never think that," Declan said. He began to sweat all over. "You are the pride of the Estelle Duchy. All warriors aspire to be like you. It is only a matter of time before you take the title of Top Sword for yourself. What I fear is that this sell-sword, a man whose sword isn't bound by duty, will not fight an honorable duel between warriors."

Elaina wanted to curse Declan out. Kay may be a sell-sword, but she had just explained that he was true to his word—an aspect that all warriors must live up to but rarely ever reached. When she realized that she was defending Kay once more, even if it was only in her mind, Elaina felt herself get a splitting headache.

"That doesn't matter," Aleron said to Declan before turning back to Kay. "From what my sister has told me, as well as being able to defeat Declan, you are a talented swordsman. Do you accept my challenge? Once the duel is over, I will let you go. I will even have my sister cancel her contract with you. By the time this day is over, you will never have to see us ever again."

Elaina looked on, wondering what Kay's answer would be. In anticipation, both Kaine and Hali were looking at their princess. Both had similar thoughts in their heads when seeing Elaina. The way she acted worried them. They agreed that the sell-sword Kay had been true to his word, but unlike Elaina, the main part they remembered about the man was he could be blood-crazed.

A blood-crazed warrior was one who became so obsessed with the bloody aspect of being a warrior that they threw away their honor and forsook their duty. Their only joy was the shedding of their foes' blood. Turning blood-crazed during this short time of peace was rare, but they had heard from older warriors that during times of strife, warriors would become so obsessed with things like revenge or other negative traits that they would easily slip into a blood-crazed state of mind. These warriors were treated with contempt, and those too far gone were given the harshest of punishments—even being hated as much as traitors. Warriors were supposed to be protectors and not people consumed by vengeance.

Kaine and Hali worried that their princess was getting too close to a sell-sword who showed signs of turning blood-crazed. So when they heard what the crown prince said, they felt relief. Once this duel was over, their princess would have no more connections to this sell-sword.

"Very well," Kay said, agreeing to duel the prince.

Aleron led them out of the tent. Seeing their prince, the warriors around the camp saluted as he passed them.

Aleron brought them to a small clearing just outside the camp. A perfect place for a duel. News of the prince's duel spread throughout the warriors, and soon every warrior that wasn't patrolling had surrounded the clearing, waiting to watch their prince put this sell-sword in his place.

In the crowd, Elaina watched on in anticipation. She knew that as a Zer'sheen, her brother was unmatched when facing all other warriors, but she had also seen the ferocity of Kay. Both were leaps above regular warriors. The duel that was about to commence was a once-in-a-lifetime experience.

Soon a warrior entered the clearing, carrying a cloth wrap. Placing it on the ground, the warrior opened the wrap. Lying there were several different kinds of weapons, from a warrior's long sword to a thief's long knife. There were even maces, as well as batons and pole weapons. After laying down the weapons, the warrior unchained Kay before returning to the rest of the spectating warriors.

"Choose your weapon," Aleron said as he unsheathed his own sword. The ring of the metal rang throughout the camp.

As he rubbed his sore wrists, Kay looked over the weapons gathered. After only pondering for a few seconds, Kay made his choice. He picked up a thin long sword, similar to a warrior's long sword, in his right hand and a long knife in his left. After swinging each a few times, Kay gave a slight smile.

"Nice distribution of weight. These will do," Kay muttered to himself. His words irked the warriors. Each of those weapons had been designed for the crown prince and his personal warriors to use. Of course they would be top quality, but Kay's words made it sound as if the sell-sword thought the weapons only slightly above average.

Kay and Aleron had their weapons at the ready. Aleron held his sword in a solid form, while Kay held each lightly, almost as if ready to drop them. The warriors around mocked Kay and his strange form. Only Elaina and Kaine looked on in worry. The duel would commence as soon as one of them took a step forward.

Kay was the first to move. Both sword and knife went for the prince's vitals. Aleron wasn't intimidated and faced the attack head-on, parrying each lunge with ease. Taking a step forward, Aleron swung his own sword at Kay's open underside. Kay was also ready and, with a twist, narrowly dodged the strike.

The warriors around cursed, saying that the sell-sword had gotten lucky. Only a few saw things differently. It wasn't that he had nearly been hit; it was that he had only moved slightly to dodge the prince's strike. Such body control was outside the capability of normal warriors.

The duel continued with Aleron's heavy and sturdy strikes against Kay's quick and nimble moves. During the duel, Elaina worried that Kay would go berserk, as before, but as time blew by, she realized that Kay showed no signs of going on a murderous rampage. By now no warriors were ridiculing Kay. They all knew that if they had been facing Aleron, they would have been defeated many moves ago.

As the two clashed again and again, Aleron's eyes sparkled even more. "You are more impressive than I thought. You may even be reaching the strength of a

Zer'sheen," Aleron complimented.

Kay's response was a strike to Aleron's open flank, but Aleron once again parried Kay's sword. The battle drew on as both sides began to show signs of exhaustion. Sweat poured down their necks as their arm muscles spasmed.

"Why are they getting tired so quickly?" Hali asked. She had seen both men fight before. Both Kay and Crown Prince Aleron had monstrous stamina. They shouldn't have been getting tired so soon.

"It's because of how skilled their opponent is," her brother answered. "Fighting someone with their level of skill requires having your concentration pushed to the limits. One minute fighting in these situations is the same as fighting normal soldiers for an hour, or even warriors for these two."

Now understanding, Hali looked in awe at the two dueling. They had been fighting for several minutes. So, according to Kaine, if they had been fighting those weaker than them, they could have been fighting for hours.

As the exhaustion began to set in, the first mistake was made. Kay rushed in too soon. Taking advantage of this, Aleron struck at Kay's hand. With no other option, Kay was forced to release the sword from his grip to escape, but he was still a little slow, and Aleron's sword left a small gash on his knuckles.

Seeing their prince take the advantage, the warriors cheered. With the duel coming close to an end, everyone believed that the prince would be the final victor, but there was no one insulting Kay anymore. They had all seen him fight evenly with their crown prince—a feat that even they could not accomplish.

"Do you concede?" asked Aleron, as he, too, believed victory to be at hand. Only Elaina looked on in trepidation.

Not giving an answer, Kay struck with his long knife. Without the sword slowing him down, Kay grew even faster, but his attack strength had grown weaker, making it harder to land a winning blow. Without the heavier blows from the sword, Aleron changed from a defensive stance to an offensive one.

One heavy blow after another came at Kay. He was able to fend them off with the long knife, but the heavy strikes were draining the rest of his strength quickly. When one of Aleron's blows knocked Kay to his knee, everyone, even Aleron, thought this duel over, but then suddenly Kay threw out his open hand. A sharp rock that Kay had hidden inside his palm flew toward the prince's head.

Being so close, Aleron was not able to defend himself in time. He was only able to move his head enough to not be hit in the eye. Stone connected with flesh, and the sharp edge of the rock gouged out a chunk of Aleron's forehead. The hit rattled Aleron, allowing Kay to seize the chance. As Aleron took a step back, Kay swept the prince's legs, knocking him to the ground.

Even knocked to the ground and disoriented, Aleron was still vigilant and kept his sword in hand, but Kay was too quick. Pinning the prince to the ground, Kay held the long knife to the crown prince's throat.

The whole clearing went silent. Everyone looked shocked about the sudden change of events. The scene of their prince standing over the sell-sword in victory hadn't happened. Instead, they saw their beloved prince hit with a rock and pinned to the ground with a knife to his throat.

"Bastard! How dare you tarnish the sacredness of a warrior's duel!" the warrior Declan shouted. Pulling out his sword, he charged toward Kay.

Seeing this, the rest of the warriors went into action. After the shock, what they felt toward Kay was hatred. He had used something that wasn't a chosen weapon in the duel. This was against the warrior code, an insult to every warrior who followed the Code of Valor. They couldn't let such a man get away with such a deed.

Exhausted from the duel, Kay could hardly stand, let alone defend himself against veteran warriors. Led by Declan, the warriors pulled Kay off their prince and held him to the ground. Elaina wanted to stop them from doing anything rash, but Kaine gripped her wrist, preventing her from stepping up.

"Let go!" Elaina demanded.

"I will not. Kay has sullied the rules of a duel and must be held accountable. If you defend him, it will only get more complicated," Kaine said.

"Sullied the rules? That would be true if the two fighting had both been warriors, but have you forgotten? Kay isn't a warrior but a sell-sword. The rules for a duel aren't the same," Elaina angrily said, trying to pull free from Kaine's steel-like grip. When she found that she couldn't pull free, she tried hitting him with her other hand, only to have that wrist caught as well.

"You may see it that way, but the warriors don't," Kaine said. His grip tightened even more. He was adamant about not letting Elaina help Kay.

"Your Highness, can't you see that my brother is only looking out for your own good?" Hali asked. "If you defend Kay now, you will be looked down upon by all the warriors here. Even your own brother might see you in a more negative light. Is all that worth stepping up for just a sell-sword?" She worried that the princess might really stand up for Kay, putting her at odds with the crown prince and his warriors.

Elaina bit her lip to keep from saying anything to hurt their long-standing friendship. While she knew that the two were doing this for her, it still didn't sit well with her. Reluctantly Elaina could only hope that her brother would be lenient.

Helped up by one of his warriors, Aleron stood motionless as he tried to regain his balance. Like Kay, the duel had taken most of his strength. Adding the blow to the head, any normal warrior wouldn't be standing. Once he was steady, a drop of blood flowed from the gash on his forehead and into his eye. Wiping it off, he stared at the wet blood on his fingers before looking over to Kay, who had been forced to kneel in front of Aleron by Declan and another warrior. Seeing Kay not looking the least bit guilty for dishonoring a sacred duel made Aleron furious.

"Chain him up, and throw him back in the tent!" Aleron ordered.

Obeying the command, the two warriors holding Kay dragged him away.

"Brother, didn't you promise to release him after the duel? Are you going to go back on your word?" Elaina shouted. Her shout only made Aleron angrier as he turned to glare at his younger sister.

"It is true that I promised to let him go," Aleron said. "And indeed, I have forgotten all the deeds he has done in the past, but this is another matter entirely. He has sinned against all warriors with his actions during the duel and will be held accountable for it."

Without giving Elaina a chance to argue back, Aleron walked back to his tent. The gathered warriors quickly went back to their duties.

As she watched her brother walk away, Elaina knew what she must do.

+

"That really was a foolish thing to do," Roan said, looking at Kay, who had been brought back. He had overheard the warrior's curses and learned what had transpired during the duel. "All you had to do was lose to the prince, and you would have been a free man. Instead, you are going to be sent to Esesa for trial and most likely imprisonment."

Kay gave an amused snort but didn't say anything in return. He knew what he had done was stupid, but during the duel, he had gotten more serious than he had thought he would. Crown Prince Aleron was indeed one of the toughest men he had ever faced. He couldn't have held back his strength. After several blows, Kay had known he would have to let Aleron lower his guard, or else the duel wouldn't have a winner. So he had let the prince knock the sword out of his hand. With the prince's attention gone from his right hand, Kay had been able to conceal a stone in his palm. By then all Kay had been thinking about was winning and not the consequences. In the end, his plan had succeeded, and he had been able to pin the prince, but he had forgotten that this was an official duel. He had only remembered that when several warriors had charged his way.

"Well, there is no turning back now, is there? At least it seems as if the princess favors you. At most you will spend several nights in jail," said Roan.

"There is no way that I'm going to Esesa," Kay said as he shifted his bound hands around. Roan looked on, curious as to what Kay was trying.

Suddenly a light click could be heard, and the chains binding Kay fell to the floor. Roan sat there, mouth agape. He didn't know how, but he saw that in the sell-sword's hand was the key to his chains.

Seeing Roan looking at him, Kay knew what the warrior wished to know. "If you are that curious about how I got the key to my restraints, it was easy. I picked them from that warrior Declan when he charged me after the duel. The muscle head probably still hasn't realized that he's been robbed."

Roan looked at the sell-sword in awe. During that small chance, Kay had been able to steal the keys from a veteran warrior without him knowing, with many more warriors looking on. "What are you going to do now?" Roan asked.

"Once night arrives, I will take my chance and escape into Verilis Forest. Once inside, I will be safe to continue my search for my brothers," Kay answered.

Roan noticed that he didn't say a single thing about finding the prince. Kay had only his brothers' safety on his mind.

"Take me with you," Roan suddenly said.

"Why should I do that?" asked Kay.

"I promised my princess that I would return to Raven's Nest with Prince

Leander, and I will not betray her trust in me," Roan said. "Besides, do you think you will be able to escape from the crown prince's personal warriors by yourself? With me helping, your chances can only increase."

Kay thought about it for a moment and soon concluded that what Roan had said was true. These warriors weren't like the ones he had faced before. He may have been able to face one or two alone, but with ten or more, he would only be facing his death.

"Very well," Kay said, untying the ropes binding Roan's hands together. "We will make our move as soon as the sun sets."

With the two of them on the same page, they began to plan their escape.

Unnoticed by them, a small shadow that had appeared sometime during their talk faded from the side of the tent.

Dustin Farris

Chapter Thirteen: The Warriors Gather in Raven's Nest

From her window, Aris watched as more and more delegates from different warrior families arrived. From the highest-ranking and ancient noble families to the small and first-generation families. It seemed that every warrior family in the duchy had sent someone to Raven's Nest during this worrisome time.

Ever since her brother's arrest warrant had gone out and her grandfather's condition had been worsening, the situation in the capital had been turning from bad to worse. Duke Valens had been up to his usual mischief and had been trying to stabilize his power. After the healer's prognosis concerning the archduke hadn't turned out to be in the archduke's favor, Jarl Valens declared that the duchy couldn't be left without a ruler. The council decided to elect a regent to govern the Talov Duchy. It was for this reason that every warrior family had sent a delegate, as every family had a vote for who would lead them as regent.

"Those muscle-headed fools!" Aris cursed as more warriors dismounted from their steeds and entered through the palace gates. "Can't they see that if a vote for regent is decided on, Valens will without a doubt be chosen?"

"Ma'am, you can't blame them. Most of them are honorable warriors. None of them have even been touched by the capital's politics, let alone have the ability to see through the duke's schemes," said her personal warrior Pierce.

Aris knew that Pierce was right, but she still felt anger at these warriors for not being able to see that they were being used. The Valenses had so much power that it even rivaled the Talovs' own might. For a while now, Aris had worried about the Valenses and had been watching their movements, afraid that they would get ambitions for the seat of archduke. Sadly, every time that she brought it up with her grandfather, he always shot her down and reprimanded her for not trusting her warriors.

"If only Uncle Devlin were still head of the Valens family instead of his son. No one would even have dared to bring up the topic of regent while the archduke still lived," Aris said, her grip on the window railing tightening.

Her uncle Devlin was the former head of the Valens family. He had also been her grandfather's most trusted warrior. During the times of strife, when each duchy had been at war with each other, the old duke had risked his life time and again to save her grandfather. He had even lost one of his feet in the process. After the war was over, her grandfather had awarded his friend with the title of Talovs Protector and, with the title, more power than even the hall masters had. Aris admitted that it had been a good idea at the time, but after the old duke had resigned, her grandfather should have taken the power he had given back.

As Aris went back to watching the continuing arrival of warriors, a sudden knock came from her door. "Your Highness, may I come in?" asked a feminine voice from outside the door.

Aris recognized the voice as one of her handmaidens. She gave a wave to Pierce, and the warrior opened the door. One of Aris's trusted handmaidens quickly entered. She was neither too ugly nor too pretty. If anyone were to say anything about this handmaiden's appearance, it would be that she was plain, someone who wouldn't be noticed in a crowd. It was for this reason that Aris had chosen her as one of her handmaidens.

"Have you done what I asked of you?" Aris asked the handmaiden, who quickly knelt in the presence of her princess.

"Your Highness, I didn't let you down," said the handmaiden, and she pulled out a sealed letter from her bosom. Upon seeing the handmaiden slightly reveal herself as she searched for the letter, the warrior Pierce turned away in embarrassment. Aris only smiled at her warrior's response. What better way for a woman to hide things from honorable warriors than in places a warrior shouldn't look?

After taking the letter, Aris inspected the wax insignia that sealed it. It was the mountain-and-gate insignia. Aris hastily ripped open the letter. She read the letter through, making sure not to miss anything. Her expression did not show what she was thinking as she read the letter. Once she was done, she sat down in front of a small table. She held the letter above one of the candles that decorated the table, and the paper instantly burst into flames. Soon there was nothing more than ash showing that the letter had existed.

"Your Highness, what did the hall master of Stone Hall have to say about this situation?" asked Pierce. He only caught a glimpse of the insignia on the letter but knew that only one family had the crest of a mountain and gate. One of the founding families and overseers of the Divide—the Altareses of Stone Hall.

"He agrees with me. A regent should not be named while the archduke is still alive and while heirs still live," Aris said, but then the light in her eyes dimmed. "He also says that with just the small amount of support our side has, we won't be able to stop the vote from happening. The Valenses have spread their influence too far. Almost every marquess has sided with Duke Valens. With the marquesses siding with the duke, all the warriors in their territories will side with him as well. With only the warriors of the Divide, we have little chance of stopping Duke Valens being named regent."

Aris had hoped that when she had secretly contacted Jukel Altares, the current hall master of Stone Hall, he would have had some insight on how to stop this. Sadly, she had been mistaken. The Divide was too far away from Raven's Nest, vastly limiting the connections Stone Hall had with the rest of the duchy. The rank of hall master may have been higher than duke, but due to the locations of the two halls, in the north and south of the duchy, the hall masters had fewer interactions with warriors besides their own.

"But we have gained support from some warriors, even several warrior families with the title of count and viscount. With Stone Hall backing us, don't we stand a chance of stopping Valens from succeeding?" Pierce asked.

"The problem is that those families aren't standing behind me. They are standing against Duke Valens. They won't let a woman rule over them," Aris said. She tried to stay calm, but her anger could be heard when she said these words.

This wasn't the first time that she wished she had been born a boy. While both men and women could hold titles and become warriors in the Talov Duchy, most men refused to let a woman control them. History had shown that every time a woman took a seat of power, she was confronted with men who refused to kneel and salute a woman. Even women of powerful families, like Temperance Morwood, had to face countless trials before being accepted.

"Lexi, when will the dignitaries from Stone Hall be arriving?" Aris asked the handmaiden who had delivered the letter.

"They will be arriving at the palace shortly, ma'am," answered Lexi.

"Then let us meet them at the gate," Aris said, standing up from her seat and heading out of her quarters, not waiting to see whether Lexi and Pierce were following her, but she could hear their footsteps following right behind her.

Aris made her way down the winding staircase that led to her quarters in the north tower. The Talovs' palace was unique in its design. Four large towers protruded out of the palace, like large fingers that reached for the sky. Connected by many covered stone bridges, these towers made the palace look like a nest made of stone. It was from the palace's appearance that this city had been named Raven's Nest. It was in these towers that the Talov family lived, and the princess lived in the northern tower.

Seeing the princess, the maids and servants running around during this hectic time stopped to bow, while patrolling warriors gave her a warrior's salute, but Aris had little time to take notice. She was making her way to the courtyard where the dignitaries were gathering at a brisk pace. Aris wished to meet those from Stone Hall personally, before Duke Valens could speak with his silver tongue.

What awaited her in the courtyard was eye-catching, to say the least. Hundreds of warriors from different families, from every corner of the duchy, had gathered. Aris recognized some of the warriors from the family crests they wore on their chests, but most of the coats of arms she did not. She couldn't be blamed for this—there were simply too many small warrior families for her to remember them all. These warriors would normally never enter the capital, much less the palace, but the vote for a regent allowed all warrior families to participate, even ones without titles or land.

Aris's arrival didn't go unnoticed. Seeing their princess right before their eyes excited the warriors. All of them saluted Aris, while over a dozen rushed to introduce themselves. Pierce had a rough time keeping them at bay.

Aris smiled at the warrior but felt upset in her heart. She knew why these warriors were trying to get acquainted with her. As her eldest brother was dead and her second brother had been accused of the murder, it was likely that Aris would become archduchess of the Talov Duchy. These warriors were hoping to get in good favor with their soon-to-be archduchess before others. She could only pray that those from Stone Hall would arrive soon, so she could excuse herself.

As if answering her call, a loud commotion was heard from the palace gates. Shock and awe echoed through the courtyard, which turned the hushed murmurs into a torrent of sound. Excited to meet the dignitaries from Stone Hall and the Divide, Aris walked to the gates to greet them, but who had arrived wasn't who she had been expecting.

Nine men on eerily pale horses dismounted. Each man was covered head to toe, wrapped up in black cloth so that not even a single part of their skin could be seen. Even their eyes were hidden, covered by the wrappings around their heads and strange glass hidden beneath the bandages. Aris knew who these people were, as did everyone in the courtyard.

"Why are the warriors from Hollowell here? I thought they never leave their own territory," Aris heard a warrior next to her whisper to a fellow warrior.

"Don't ask me. This is my first time seeing someone from Hollowell," answered the other warrior.

Aris was similarly stumped by the arrival of people from Hollowell. Hollowell was located in the southernmost part of the Talov Duchy, even farther than Red Hall. It was formerly a grand mine that stretched deep into the bowels of the land, and the people of Hollowell were former slaves who had worked the mine. They spent most of their lives in these tunnels. Some never even looked up to the sky during their lives. When the mine had dried up, the owners had simply left. Without their masters, and knowing nothing besides the darkness, most had stayed, renaming the mine Hollowell.

As the years had dragged on, the people of Hollowell grew more and more comfortable living in the darkness of the underground and interacted less and less with the above world. This, in turn, had started to change them, giving them unique traits. In order to live in the dark and impoverished mine, the people's eyes had changed, allowing them to see in this perpetual darkness. Their bodies had grown used to the moss and fungus, and allowed them to survive and eat most plants, even ones poisonous and fatal to others. However, not all changes benefited the Hollowell denizens.

After spending countless generations underground, the sun had become their enemy. Even on cloudy days, the rays of the sun ravaged their now-pale skin, forcing them to cover their entire bodies before venturing into the daylight. Their eyes, which were so perfect in the dark, were blind in the light. In order to see, they used strange tinted glass, placed over their eyes to dim the bright light of the sun.

With these afflictions, only once in a century would a resident of the old mine venture out into the above world. They had become so scarce that they were all but forgotten. If it hadn't been for one who had befriended the Phoenix God, becoming one of his most trusted warriors, they would probably still be unknown.

The mummified men strode through the gazing warriors until they reached Princess Aris. Caught off guard by their arrival, Aris reacted late, giving them a quick but courteous greeting. The Hollowell warriors didn't seem to notice and returned the princess's greeting with a warrior's salute.

"It is a pleasure to see you again, Your Highness," said the leading man. His voice sounded like silk to Aris's ears and made her feel uncomfortable. The duchies of Mezer were lands of warriors, and men with such feminine voices were regarded with contempt.

"Apologies, but I can't seem to remember ever meeting you, sir ..." Aris said, but she couldn't finish, as the man hadn't given his name.

"It's Oh'ash, Your Highness, and with how we cover ourselves above ground, it is easy to understand why you couldn't recognize me," the man said, but with his face hidden, Aris couldn't tell what he was feeling. However, she did know the name and couldn't help but take a step back.

It wasn't only Aris who stepped back after hearing his name. Every warrior in the courtyard retreated from the mummified man. Oh'ash was famous throughout the three duchies. Known as the Pit Viper of Hollowell, the man was considered one of the three strongest warriors in all the duchies, rivaling even the Sword Child, Isolde Isgate, and the current Top Sword, Brana Ulfenn, both of whom were true-blooded Zer'sheen. A man who can rival a Zer'sheen was rarer than Zer'sheen themselves.

But that wasn't the only reason that the warriors backed away. They retreated because the warrior Oh'ash was renowned for being obsessed with the warrior arts. As a young warrior, Oh'ash had traveled across the duchies, challenging every warrior he could find. Even when he was refused, he would wait for a time to ambush them, forcing them into a duel. More than one warrior had lost their life, and many others had vowed to stop Oh'ash's rampage. One by one, warriors had turned from being challenged to being the challengers, but every time, Oh'ash had stood the victor.

During this troubling situation, an unknown warrior had stood against him. Being from a warrior family with the rank of baron, none believed he could win. The fight didn't last ten moves before Oh'ash was shockingly defeated. With that loss, the domination of Oh'ash ended, and the warrior who had defeated him was raised to the top of all warriors. This warrior was now the current Top Sword, Brana

Ulfenn.

Aris was about to speak, but a sudden voice interrupted her. "The famous Pit Viper of Hollowell. It is our honor for you to visit us in these troubled times."

Aris recognized the haughty and arrogant voice and did not need to turn around to know who had just arrived. Striding forward with over a dozen of his personal warriors was one of the men she thought of as vile, her fiancé, Sarus Valens. Seeing the man's wide grin, Aris had a hard time holding in a scowl that threatened to come out.

When he reached Aris and Oh'ash, he neither bowed nor saluted the two. He acted as if he were above them, as if he were of princely blood while Aris wasn't. Many warriors felt vexed seeing this disrespectful display but didn't say anything. Sarus was the one who was to wed Princess Aris, and in doing so, he would become the next archduke.

"The great warrior Oh'ash. I have dreamed of meeting you face-to-face for a long time. I grew up hearing stories of your many battles," Sarus said. His flattery made many around believe that the disrespect he had shown just moments ago had only been a mistake, a misstep brought on by meeting someone he admired.

Oh'ash only looked at Sarus for a moment before his attention went back to Aris. "I apologize for not sending notice of our joining this gathering. It was a personal decision on my part," he said.

Being completely ignored angered Sarus to no end. A vein in his forehead protruded and beat heavily. It took all Sarus's willpower to keep his wide grin from breaking away into a scowl. He had to rein in his displeasure at Oh'ash and the Hollowell warriors, as he had been sent here for a reason.

Aris watched the turmoil in Sarus with amusement. Sarus's arrogance knew no bounds, and watching him go through this made the princess's mood grow slightly better.

"Oh'ash, if you would please follow me. My father has requested your presence," Sarus said.

The warrior Oh'ash turned his gaze back to Sarus, but the man's gaze was different from last time. Suddenly the man's body exuded waves of pressure. Under such a presence, Sarus tumbled backward, landing on his back. Even Aris felt it become hard to breathe, even though the pressure wasn't directed at her. Just being in the vicinity caused people to shudder in fear of this mummified warrior.

"Duke Valens requests my presence? What gives him the right to ask that of me? Last time I checked, he still hasn't been named regent," Oh'ash said. His reprimanding words showed he cared little for giving Duke Valens face. No longer caring for the cowering young man, he turned his attention away from him.

With the help of his personal warriors, Sarus was able to get back to his feet. His face was a mix of different shades of red, from the bright red of embarrassment to the deep red of rage. If Sarus had been vexed before, he was downright mad with anger now. He wasn't about to let this ridicule go.

"My father doesn't have the right to ask for you? Who do you think you are? My father is one of the three dukes. Even the hall masters of the Stone and Red Halls must give my father face. You are just a warrior of an old mine, a man who cowers before the sun. My father has no right? As his heir, I have more than enough authority to drag you to my father if need be!" Sarus shouted in a hysterical rage.

Sarus's words came out without filter. The warriors gathered looked at the young Valens with a mixture a pity and contempt. Even a levelheaded warrior wouldn't be able to stand this amount of insult, let alone the infamous Pit Viper. His words were simply asking Oh'ash to cut him down.

Aris looked at Sarus with a bewildered look, her eyes almost popping out of her head. She knew that Sarus was arrogant and unruly, but she didn't think he was so suicidal as to pick a fight with one of the three strongest warriors in the duchy—the most temperamental warrior at that. She could hardly look when Oh'ash turned his attention back to Sarus for the third time.

Seeing Oh'ash looking at him once more, Sarus stepped back in fear. His personal warriors, sturdier hearted than their lord, stepped forward to defend him. None of the warriors believed they could defeat Oh'ash. They only wished to buy time until help arrived.

Oh'ash, undisturbed by the warriors, strode forward. Each step sent shivers down everyone's spines. Aris wanted to stop the bloodbath that was about to happen, but didn't know how. If Oh'ash had been someone who could be reasoned with, he wouldn't be as feared as he was.

Finally one of Sarus's warriors couldn't stand the pressure. With a shout, he struck out at Oh'ash. The warrior was young and in the prime of his life, but his recklessness made everyone mourn the young warrior as he fell. No one had seen when, but Oh'ash had drawn his sword. The cold steel of the sword looked devious to all the onlookers as it dripped with the blood of the fallen warrior.

Aris's worst fears came true with the death of the warrior. Spilling blood in the palace was an offense. Even a simple fight could have a warrior banned from entering for life. Aris looked around to see all the warriors gathered trembling with a mixture of fear and rage. If it had been anyone besides the dreaded Oh'ash, the gathered warriors would have attacked by now.

"How ... how dare you kill one of my warriors!" Sarus stuttered. He tried to sound authoritative but couldn't help taking even more steps back.

Murdering the warrior hadn't stopped or slowed down the Pit Viper's pace. He calmly inched closer to Sarus. The warriors protecting Sarus had little choice. While they knew they had no chance, they had vowed to serve the young Valens. All at once, the warriors charged, but Oh'ash was undaunted. With several swings, he forced the more than a dozen warriors back. Before they could regroup, he had his sword to Sarus Valens's neck.

"You … you can't do this to me." Sarus tried to speak up, but his voice came out so cracked the words were gibberish.

"Can't I?" Oh'ash said, his sword cutting a small gash in Sarus's neck. The young Valens nearly passed out from the fear.

"That is enough!" a voice bellowed.

All the warriors turned to see who would dare get in the way of the Pit Viper.

Walking out of the palace was a group of men. Ranging from middle-aged to elderly, these men had an aura of authority about them. These men were the members of the council that oversaw the duchy, and leading them was Duke Valens himself.

Upon seeing the men, Aris felt fury rise in her chest. With them arriving together, it was clear that they had just come from a meeting—one without her. It seemed that she wasn't welcome in the council anymore.

Duke Valens didn't look disturbed by seeing his heir at the point of Oh'ash's sword. As he made it to Oh'ash and his son, he took a quick glance at Aris. Aris glared back, but the duke's eyes stayed as calm and unfathomable as always. The duke's attention then went back to his son, who was looking at his father with pleading eyes, hoping that his father could save him from Oh'ash's wrath.

"Dishonorable!" Duke Valens yelled, giving a heavy-handed slap to his son. The force of the slap was so strong that Sarus slammed to the ground. The watching warriors all wished to laugh. A warrior being slapped would bring him much shame, but they all held it in. Laughing would offend the duke.

Sarus didn't know what his father was thinking, shaming him like this in front of so many warriors. He was about to speak, but Duke Valens wouldn't allow that.

"Do you think this is unfair? Then think before you act. Your actions showed no respect for Oh'ash, who is the current leader of Hollowell. Now leave my sight, and think about how foolish your actions have been!" Duke Valens bellowed, and waved his hand.

Instantly several warriors appeared and ushered the shocked Sarus away before he could say anything else.

Sarus wasn't the only one shocked. Everyone was baffled by what they had just learned. The bloody and sword-hungry Pit Viper was now the leader of Hollowell. While the information on Hollowell was limited, the head of such a great force was commonly known. The current leader should have been Oh'ash's uncle. Even Aris, the princess, hadn't known of this sudden change in power.

"Seems that Duke Valens has eyes and ears everywhere, to even hear things from the depths of Hollowell. One of the reasons I have come to Raven's Nest is to announce myself as the new leader of Hollowell to the archduke," Oh'ash said as he sheathed his sword. When he did, everyone breathed a sigh of relief that no more blood would be spilled.

"I only hear whispers from such a remote place as Hollowell, but the ascension of a new leader would have eventually reached Raven's Nest sooner or later," said Duke Valens. "But I regret to inform you that the archduke's condition is deteriorating. I'm not sure if he will be able to recover, much less receive you."

"Then I see no reason for me being here," Oh'ash suddenly said, and turned around to leave. He only stopped to give Aris a slight bow before he left along with the rest of the warriors of Hollowell.

Aris watched them leave as swiftly as they had arrived. When they were out of the gate, she turned to face Duke Valens. The man had his usual calm face, but Aris had been fighting secret battles with this man for years and could see slight differences in his mood. The slight narrowing of his eyes and the scrunching of his brows that only lasted a second, Aris saw it all. To the princess, the duke was clearly vexed from Oh'ash's dismissive attitude toward him.

Aris mocked the duke in her mind. Duke Valens may have seemed to be kind and understanding, but he was the same type of man as his son. He simply had more control of his emotions than his son did. They both had grand ambitions hidden in their hearts, and the same arrogant demeanor that didn't allow others to look down on them.

"I'm sorry you had to see my son's unruly behavior," Duke Valens apologized to Aris. "It seems blood rushed to his head when he was mocked by Oh'ash in front of the woman he loves."

When the warriors gathered heard the duke, many who had previously had negative thoughts about Sarus changed their minds about the young Valens. Warriors could tolerate much, but being shamed in front of his woman would make any of them fly into a rage. With new information in their minds, Sarus became a hot-blooded warrior standing up against the disrespectful Oh'ash, not a little tyrant flaunting his power.

Aris once more scoffed at these warriors and their simple minds. In only a few words, Duke Valens had been able to change their minds about his son. Watching this, Aris felt that Duke Valens was more dangerous than she had first believed.

Upon seeing Duke Valens grin, Aris had to keep herself from arguing with the man. She felt her control slipping, so she turned and left without responding to Duke Valens's apology. The warriors loyal to Duke Valens quickly began talking, discontented with how the princess acted toward the duke. Aris heard all this and knew her quick decision to leave was a mistake, but she knew that making a scene would be worse. So, without looking back, she returned to the palace.

"Your Highness, where are you going?" the warrior Pierce asked, realizing that she wasn't heading to her quarters in the northern tower.

Aris didn't answer, but as they headed deeper into the palace and heard the commotion ahead, Pierce didn't need to ask her again. As they reached the door the commotion was coming from, it suddenly slammed open, and a maid was tossed out of the room. Not expecting this, the maid landed right on the princess, knocking the two of them to the ground. Dizzy from being tossed from the room, the maid looked down to see who she had landed on, only to freeze in terror.

"Your Highness! I beg you to forgive my transgression," the maid said, quickly getting up and kneeling on the ground. She was so terrified that she couldn't contain her tears, and they flowed out of her.

"It is quite all right," Aris said as Lexi helped her up. "Besides, I know that this wasn't your fault." As she said this, she looked into the room, where the commotion continued. Inside the room, Sarus Valens was trashing all that he could get his hands on. His personal warriors looked on, unable to stop him.

"That bastard! How dare he ridicule me in that way! He is nothing more than a man who should live his entire life rotting away underground. Does he think he is something now that he has become the leader of Hollowell? Compared to the power my father and family have, that measly title is nothing. I'll make him watch as I strip him of his rank and title once I am archduke!" Sarus howled as he threw a vase against the wall, smashing it to pieces.

Hearing Sarus declare that he would be archduke caused Aris to tremble in fury. Not hesitating, she stormed into the room, her face showing how livid she was. "How dare you declare yourself the heir to the Talov Duchy! Since when has your

165

family name been Talov?" Aris shouted. Her sudden appearance shocked everyone in the room.

Turning to the princess and seeing her look at him like that caused Sarus to smirk. "Am I wrong? With the crown prince murdered and the second prince being the murderer, I, as your future husband, will be Archduke of the Talov Duchy," Sarus said with pride, which only made Aris even more angry.

"Do you honestly believe that just by marrying me, you will become archduke? Even if you marry me, the only thing you will be is husband to the archduchess," Aris said. She watched as the words sank in for Sarus.

"My father and the rest of the council will never allow a woman to rule the duchy. Once my father becomes regent, he will make me archduke the day the two of us are wed," Sarus argued back.

Aris gave a scornful laugh at Sarus's statement.

Driven to near insanity by Aris's taunts, Sarus couldn't rein in his anger anymore. He drew his sword and was ready to strike down the princess, much to the horror of his personal warriors. Before he could, Aris's own warrior Pierce stepped between the two.

"Get out of my way!" Sarus screamed as he slashed at Pierce. He was so mad that all reason had left the young Valens.

Pierce effortlessly blocked Sarus's strike and countered with a knee to the stomach. The contents of Sarus's stomach left him as he collapsed to the floor. Before he could get up, Pierce landed another heavy kick, which sent Sarus flying across the room. Luckily, one of his personal warriors was able to catch him before he landed on the broken glass scattered all over the floor.

"Let me go!" Sarus yelled at the warrior who had rescued him when the warrior kept his grip on his shoulders. "I must kill this wench!"

"Calling your fiancée and the princess of the Talov Duchy a wench. Do you not care that you are committing treason? I guess it shouldn't come as a shock from a family that would plot their own prince's murder," Aris said, in her taunting manner once more.

"What if we did? The Talov Duchy will fall into our hands eventually!" Sarus shouted, but he immediately knew that he shouldn't have said that.

Even Aris was shocked at what Sarus had just spat out. She was sure that the Valenses were using the death and framing of her brothers to rise in power, but she never would have thought that they had planned the whole thing. She was only trying to goad Sarus into admitting that they were using the prince's death for their own gain. The rest of what she was going to say didn't matter. The truth was out. Sure, the thought had flashed in her mind, but never had she believed a family with the rank of duke would plot rebellion.

Even some of Sarus's own warriors couldn't believe it, but after the initial shock, the warriors surrounded the distraught Valens and soon had him pinned down. Aris grew excited: she now had a way to fight back against Duke Valens.

"I wish you hadn't heard that," a voice suddenly said from behind the princess.

Quickly turning, Aris came face-to-face with Duke Valens. He had the same calm look he always had, even after learning that his plot had been revealed. Behind the duke were three other members of the council and a half dozen warriors from the Third and Fourth Chivalric Orders. Aris knew that these men were fellow conspirators and traitors.

"My foolish son. Can never keep his mouth shut. It was for this reason that we refrained from telling him our plan till after it was executed," Duke Valens said, striding into the room.

Pierce immediately went to protect Aris.

As the two sides faced one another, screams of pain came from where Sarus and his warriors were. Suddenly half of the warriors attacked their fellow comrades. Caught unprepared, the half that knew not of this treachery were quickly slain. Free from his captors, Sarus propped himself up, but upon seeing his father's cold gaze directed at him, he looked at the floor. He might have been arrogant and unruly, but in front of his heartless father, he could only cower.

Surrounded on both sides, Aris, Pierce, and Lexi were in dire straits. The only way out was through the door they had entered, but Duke Valens, along with six warriors from the chivalric orders, was blocking the way. If they tried to force their way, the warriors behind them would immediately attack.

"Duke. I always knew you were dishonest, but I never pinned you for a traitor," Aris spat. It wasn't hard to understand why she was so angered. The ones who had caused her family such suffering stood in front of her.

Duke Valens didn't respond to Aris and only gestured to the warriors behind him. "Take them, but the princess must be captured unharmed," he ordered.

At once the warriors rushed into the room, swords drawn. Pierce, who was waiting, met their challenge head-on. Aris unsheathed a hidden blade from her wrist. The slender and short blade was made specifically for women from warrior families to use, able to be kept on them even while they were adorned in intricate womanly attire.

With both Pierce and Aris fighting, the warriors struggled to capture them. The orders to take the princess unharmed meant they couldn't use their full strength on her. Aris took advantage of this: anytime they had the warrior Pierce in their grasp, she threw herself in front of them. While the two held their ground, they couldn't escape. It only got more disastrous for Aris and Pierce when Sarus's warriors joined the fray. One of the warriors' strikes found its mark as a sword went hilt-deep into

Pierce's stomach.

"Pierce!" Aris shouted. Before the warrior who had stabbed Pierce could retract his sword, Aris imbedded her blade into his temple. Grabbing her personal warrior, Aris was so distraught that she didn't notice the remaining warriors had sneaked up behind her. One of the warriors grabbed the princess from behind, pulling her away from Pierce.

Struggle as she might, the warrior's grip didn't waver. She could only watch as two more warriors stood over Pierce and, with two more thrusts, ended her trusted warrior's life. Aris felt sorrow eat at her, but even more than the pain, she felt a burning sensation grow from within. Looking up at Duke Valens, who looked as calm as ever, she wanted to take her blade and gouge out the man's eyes.

"Take the princess and lock her in the eastern tower. Have four of you keep watch. I do not want anything to befall the princess before her wedding day," Valens ordered, completely ignoring the glare that Aris was giving him.

As she was dragged away, Aris looked one last time into the room where this had all happened. She saw Pierce lying in a pool of blood, along with the warrior she had killed. She also saw Duke Valens looking over his son as he spoke with his fellow conspirators. What she didn't see, and what everyone failed to notice, was that the room was missing the presence of a certain handmaiden. Turning her head down, she looked at the floor to hide the calculating glint in her eyes.

Dustin Farris

Chapter Fourteen: Falling into the Enemy's Grasp

Hidden among the old tree's branches in Verilis Forest, Aer awoke. Forgetting where he was, he had to catch himself from falling out of the tree. As he got his bearings, Aer noticed the corpse of the strange insect that he had killed the night before. Even dead, the creature's eyes shone with intelligence.

"The creatures and life-forms of Verilis Forest are truly terrifying. Even the insects here are so fearsome," Aer mumbled to himself. As he was about to descend from the tree, Aer heard several footsteps heading his way.

Out of the brush came a half dozen warriors. Peeking down from above, Aer saw that they were warriors from the Talov Duchy—most likely the same who had chased him into Verilis Forest in the first place. The warriors below took their time as they neared, poking and prying into every bush they came across. Aer saw all of this from the tree canopy and knew that they were looking for Prince Leander and the ones who were helping him.

Aer felt his heart ease when he saw the warriors searching. This told Aer that they still hadn't found the prince, as there would be no meaning to continuing the search just for some sell-sword. This also meant that Lucis, who was with the prince, was safe as well. From his vantage point, Aer waited until he could no longer see or hear the warriors before he made his way down the tree.

Landing on the ground, Aer had to catch himself from falling over. The landing irritated his wounds. Pain once again shot through him, causing his whole body to ache. Feeling that his shoulder wound was bleeding again, Aer pulled his tunic away to look. His shirt was glued to the wound by the dried blood. Gritting his teeth, he freed his flesh from the fabric. When he looked at his wound, Aer grimaced. The wound was already festering and showed signs of infection. He knew that if he didn't get treatment soon, he may lose his life, or at least, his arm would have to be amputated.

As he struggled with the pain, Aer slowly made his way away from the searching warriors and deeper into Verilis Forest. The forest was quite different during the day compared to the previous night. It almost seemed tranquil. If it hadn't been for the occasional animal corpse, Aer would have thought this place was a peaceful one.

Aer continued his slow pace, ducking into brush whenever he heard a sound, until he came across a small stream. Kneeling by the flowing water, Aer began to cleanse his wounds. It was painful, but he had to remove the rotten flesh from the healthy flesh.

Then, from somewhere among the brush, he heard a branch snap underfoot. Turning, Aer came face-to-face with a man. The man in question had his bow drawn with an arrow nocked, ready to release if Aer tried anything.

The man wore a large green coat that covered most of his body. His hood was raised, concealing his face. The man looked nothing like a warrior, from his simple leathers to having no warrior crest adorning his chest. There was one thing that Aer knew as his gaze fell onto the readied arrow: this man was the one who had shot him.

Weak and wounded, Aer had no chance against this man. He was unable to fight back, so his hands were bound and his sword discarded. After his hands were secured, the green-cloaked man dragged him through the forest. While the man did drag him, he wasn't heavy-handed. Whenever the pain from Aer's wounds irritated him, the man would stop to let Aer catch his breath. The closer they got to their destination, the quieter the forest became. It was like the vicious beasts of this forest dared not come close to this place. With their moderate pace, the two of them finally made it to wherever the green-cloaked man was taking him.

Aer was brought into a clearing in the forest. The clearing wasn't any different from any other part of the forest, but it was engulfed in a feeling of danger. This feeling came from the two people standing in the clearing. One was a young boy with a face more like a mask than real flesh, like a life-size doll. The second was a man in a long black coat. His face couldn't be seen, as it was covered by a steel mask depicting a crying face. Aer's veins bulged, and anger flared up inside him when he saw the man in the mask.

"It has been a while, Aer," the masked man said. His face couldn't be seen, but the tone of his voice made it sound as if he was mocking Aer.

"Karsic," Aer said through grinding teeth. He would never forget this man in his entire life—the man his brother Kay was so desperately trying to hunt and kill.

"Are you still mad over that little incident?" Karsic said with an unenthused sigh. "You three brothers are so simpleminded."

"How dare you insult my brothers!" Aer roared. As he secretly struggled with his bindings, he was able to get one of his thumbs free. No longer wishing to look at Karsic, Aer turned his attention to the boy. The boy looked vaguely familiar, but Aer couldn't remember why.

Seeing this, Karsic brought the boy closer to him and patted the boy on the head. "Do you remember this boy?" Karsic asked.

"Why should I?" retorted Aer, but deep down, he was dreading what Karsic was about to say.

"This boy is the son of that warrior Henri," Karsic said, releasing the boy from his grasp.

Upon learning this, Aer's eyes bulged as he looked to the boy. Henri had been a warrior that they had met when the three brothers had first arrived in the duchies of Mezer. They had owed the man much but had been unable to repay him before his untimely death. Now the man's son stood in front of him, but Aer saw the strangeness of the boy and grew worried for the young child.

"What did you do to him?" Aer asked as he got half of his left hand free.

"Let me show you," Karsic said, and he waved his hand.

Suddenly the young boy's body trembled fiercely. His neutral face twisted into one of pain and agony. Aer watched as the pain in the boy's face turned to rage. His tiny body started bulging and soon began to grow at an alarming rate. The thin clothes he wore ripped from his body as he transformed. The boy's pale skin turned a dark gray, and his eyes a crazed crimson. Aer went from looking down at the boy to looking up at a monster. Now standing in front of him was a hulking beast with muscles of iron that only faintly resembled a person. The once boy and now beast gave out a roar that caused Aer's ears to ring and the remaining animals to scatter.

"Marvelous, isn't he?" Karsic said, looking at the muscle-bound beast. "What was once a weak boy is now a creature of immense power."

"You're mad! How can you do such a thing to a child?" Aer shouted at Karsic, but his gaze never left the beast.

"You only say that because you do not understand. This boy has undergone my lord's baptism and received his reward for doing so. Now he will live the remainder of his days as my lord's weapon, an ogre," Karsic proudly said. His voice echoed his worship of this great lord of his.

Aer knew what an ogre was. They were the by-product of the time the Sage Kings had used their vast power to dominate the world. Unfeeling beasts that held no remorse, these creatures were thought to have been long extinct, the way to produce them having been lost through the passage of time. Who would have thought that an ogre would appear now and that they were created by using humans? Aer felt the rage inside him intensify as he thought of the young boy, who could only be called a monster now.

"I will make you pay for what you have done!" Aer yelled. With a final tug, he broke free from his restraints. Lunging at the masked Karsic, Aer pulled a concealed knife from his sleeve. With a forceful yell, Aer attempted to pierce Karsic through, only to feel himself thrown through the air.

When Aer had rushed Karsic, the ogre had grabbed Aer by the leg and thrown him almost out of the clearing. Landing on the ground, Aer felt his wounds reopen and his ribs crack. He was overshadowed as the ogre stood above him with raised fists. Before Aer could get himself up, the ogre was upon him. The beast slammed its humongous fists down on Aer again and again. Blood sprayed all over, and after a few more strikes, Karsic called the ogre to cease. The blood-covered Aer couldn't move a muscle and fought to stay awake as the ogre dragged him back to Karsic.

"You disappoint me, Aer. If it had been Lucis or Kay, they would have put up more of a fight or maybe have been able to kill the ogre. Sadly, your strength is far below your younger brothers'," Karsic said with a sigh, as if he had been hoping for more of a show.

"If it had been my brothers facing this beast, even one-handed, they would have emerged victorious," Aer said, spitting out a mouthful of blood.

"Maybe, but that doesn't change the fact that you are in my hands now, and soon

175

your brothers will meet the same fate. I will especially enjoy finishing off Kay. To think he dared to try and hunt me down," said Karsic. As he spoke, he pulled out a strange steel rod from nowhere. The rod's tip was sharpened to a point, and specks of dried flesh stuck to it. "Let's talk about something else. You are going to tell me where Prince Leander is. You can try to resist, but that will only make this more enjoyable for me."

With that, he thrust the rod into Aer's shoulder, the same one the hunter had pierced with an arrow the night before. As the rod entered Aer's shoulder, agonizing pain shot through him. He spasmed as pain continuously entered him through the rod. The quiet forest was soon echoing with Aer's painful screams. The agony only stopped when Karsic removed the rod from Aer's shoulder.

"Now, tell me what I want to know, and you will be given a swift death," Karsic said. When Aer refused to speak, he thrust the rod into Aer's side, sending that unbearable pain through his body once more. When Aer was about to faint, Karsic removed the rod. He waited until Aer could speak.

"I will never betray my brothers," Aer said. His words came out as only a whisper, as he had little strength to even breathe, much less speak.

Karsic said nothing as the rod entered Aer's chest this time. The pain seemed to double, and Aer felt his mind begin to fade. His wretched screams ripped apart his vocal cords. As the pain took over, Aer saw the faces of Lucis and Kay before only agony remained. He tried to mumble their names, but another shot of pain made him scream yet again.

+

In another part of Verilis Forest, the atmosphere was completely different. The sounds of many creatures could be heard. The weaker beasts hid, while the greater beasts rested from the night's hunt. Walking through all this was Lucis. With one

176

hand readied on the grip of his sword, Lucis's keen senses were fully at work as they scanned the area for any approaching danger.

As he continued, something caught his eye. A lone twig on a bush, neatly broken in half. Kneeling on the ground, he brushed aside some fallen leaves and twigs. In the muddy ground was a footprint.

"It seems that the prince has been through this way," Lucis mumbled to himself before continuing to follow the prince's trail.

As he journeyed farther into the forest, Lucis felt a sudden shiver come over him. He didn't know why, but a feeling of dread welled up inside, as if something had happened, but he didn't know what. Looking back, he wondered whether he should head back, but remembering his vow to the prince, he decided against it.

No longer looking back, Lucis continued his search for the missing Leander.

Verilis Forest was famous for its deadly creatures and dangerous terrain. It was also due to this that no one ever ventured so deep into the forest. In the past hundred years, they were likely the first to venture so deep. The forest's core was so dense in foliage that Lucis struggled to make his way through. The bright side was that the trail Prince Leander had left behind grew ever more transparent, as there were more twigs snapped and brush pushed away from his trekking.

As he continued to follow the prince's trail, he suddenly heard something moving in front of him. The sound was coming closer, and Lucis readied his sword, waiting for whatever beast to pounce. When the creature did reveal itself, he let out an annoyed huff.

"Lucis. By Ridian's flame, I have found you," Leander said as he burst out of the brush.

"Your Highness, you can't be kicking up so much noise in this forest. You will attract all forms of dangerous beasts," Lucis reprimanded the prince as he sheathed his sword.

Leander looked downtrodden after hearing Lucis, but he was still glad to see a familiar face. After escaping from that strange insect that had disguised itself as his brother, Leander had searched for Lucis and Aer. During this time, he had had to hide himself from all sorts of creatures. He had seen bears that were larger than crownes, and strange vipers with two heads. He now knew why this forest was so infamous. It was home to beasts only heard of in folklore.

"Quit your daydreaming," Lucis said. "We have to make it to the other side of the forest as soon as we can."

Leander was stunned and looked back at where Lucis had come from. "But what about Aer? He is injured, possibly in danger. We can't just leave him here," Leander said, not realizing his voice was growing louder.

"We have no choice. This forest is too large. It is a miracle in itself that I found you. If we go back to search for Aer, we will only be heading straight into the warriors who attacked us last night, and even if you ignore that, the chances of finding Aer are slim. We have a higher chance of meeting up once we are free from this maze of trees, so we must continue our journey."

Leander saw the resolve in the Zer'sheen's eyes but also saw how his hand slightly trembled when he talked about leaving his injured brother behind.

"It isn't that I have no good news," Lucis said when he saw the prince still wasn't convinced. Pulling down his collar, he revealed two strange tattoos that looked like ink drops. "These marks were created by an earth sage my brothers and I met back in the southern kingdoms. Both Lucis and Kay have the same marks. These marks connect the three of us to one another. As long as they are alive, the mark will not fade."

Leander looked at the marks closely, as if to try to see the magic that the sage had imbued into Lucis's flesh, but he couldn't tell the difference between this tattoo and other, normal tattoos.

Seeing the prince becoming frustrated, Lucis pulled up his collar, hiding the marks once more. "You are just going to have to believe me on this," he said.

With nothing else keeping them there, the two of them headed deeper into Verilis Forest. While Lucis had said all that, Leander did see the Zer'sheen secretly look back a single time. To Leander, it looked as if Lucis was sending a silent prayer to his brother before they continued their journey.

Chapter Fifteen: A New Trio Is Born

Are you ready? I don't have to tell you that we only have one shot at this," Roan said, looking at the sell-sword Kay as the man fitted on the armor of an Estelle warrior.

After Kay had shown that he could free them from their bindings, the two had quickly decided to escape. Their plan was simple, and the first part had gone off without a problem. Free from their restraints, the two of them had been able to overpower the warriors who had come to bring them their meal. The second part of the plan was next. After donning the warriors' clothing, they would blend in with the rest of the warriors, find some weapons and equipment, and make it to the forest's edge before the Estelle warriors even realized that they had escaped.

"I don't know how you warriors fight wearing this," Kay complained as he worked on fitting himself into the chain mail.

"Most warriors aren't monsters like you and Crown Prince Aleron. They need this armor to protect themselves. Now hurry up before the guards out front notice that something is wrong," Roan said.

Kay worked on the armor but, in the end, gave up on getting it right. With the helmets on, the two looked like every other Estelle warrior. Giving a nod, Roan walked out of the tent first, followed shortly by Kay.

As they left the tent, the guarding warriors gave them not a second glance and went back to guarding the prisoners, not realizing that they had failed in their duty. After escaping the tent, Roan and Kay made their way toward where the supplies were located. Warriors went about doing their jobs in the camp, making the two of them duck around the tent in hopes they wouldn't be noticed.

After sneaking through the camp, they made it to the tent where the supplies were gathered. It was unguarded, and they quickly stepped into the supply tent before anyone could notice.

"We have to be quick," said Roan. "The sooner we are out of this camp, the farther we will be when they find out that we are gone."

Kay only shrugged, as this wasn't the first time Roan had said this. When they had been going over the plan, Roan had said these same words several times.

They quickly filled two packs full of items such as food and blankets and bandages. They filled the two packs with anything they thought they would need. When they had everything, they threw the packs over their shoulders.

"Now comes the difficult part," Roan said.

He pulled out a flint and a smooth stone, then struck the two together. Sparks soon appeared, and very quickly the supply tent was ablaze. Needing to get to safety, Kay and Roan ran out of the tent, taking shelter inside a nearby tent. The supplies in the tent were the perfect tinder for the flames, and the tent was engulfed in fire, which began to spread to tents nearby. The warriors around the camp soon took notice of the inferno.

"Fire! Fire!" shouted several warriors. Soon the entire camp knew about the supply tent catching fire.

"What is going on? How did the supply tent catch fire?" asked Declan, but no one knew the answer. When the tent right next to the blaze caught fire as well,

Declan's face turned grim. "We cannot let this fire spread."

With that said, Declan began to give orders for some warriors to gather water and for others to begin taking down the tents in close proximity to the flames. He even sent some warriors to protect the prince and princess during this chaos.

The warriors sent to the siblings didn't get far, as both Princess Elaina and Crown Prince Aleron were hurrying toward the fire. Seeing the blaze growing ever more intense, Aleron frowned. Elaina's gaze stretched throughout the camp, as if searching for something.

"How did this happen?" Aleron asked Declan.

"We aren't sure right now," Declan answered his prince. "I have already dispatched warriors to gather water and make a clearing between the fire and the rest of the camp. Once we have the fire under control, we can discover how it started."

Aleron, satisfied with Declan's decision and quick responses, gave a nod of approval. He then turned to his sister and then to her attending maiden. "Take the princess to one of the farther tents, and keep her safe," Aleron ordered Hali.

Bowing to the prince, Hali dragged the princess away. Elaina was still scouring the campsite with her gaze as she left.

With every warrior distracted by the fire, Roan and Kay made their move. Blending in with those sent for water, the two made their way out of the camp. Each warrior was hauling items to fill with water. This made the bags the two were carrying hardly noticeable.

Reaching a small creek that ran right by the campsite, the warriors went to work filling their gathering of containers with water. Not to be noticed, both Roan and Kay took out several pots to fill with water and handed them to warriors who could only find things like cups and other things too small. Giving their thanks, the warriors ran back to the camp, unaware that the two hadn't followed behind them.

"That was a lot easier than I thought. Let's hurry to the forest," Kay said, but at that moment, something came rushing from behind.

Turning around, Kay unsheathed his sword and parried just in time as a strike from behind came close to opening his back from top to bottom. Not being one to let a grievance go, an infuriated Kay struck back heavily, sending the attacker back several paces. The sword in the attacker's hand trembled from the impact, but the assailant held it firmly.

"Well, I didn't expect to see you here, Kaine," Kay said, taunting his attacker with a grin. "How did you realize?"

Upon seeing Kay act so nonchalant, Kaine gave a loud snort. "After traveling with you for so long, how could I not understand you, if only a little? You would never allow yourself to be dragged back to Esesa. As soon as I heard of the fire, I went to your tent and found the warriors you had knocked unconscious and tied up. By now the entire camp knows it was you who started the fire, and soon you will once more be in our custody."

"You really think you can handle the two of us on your own?" Roan asked, trying to get the warrior to realize he was outmatched.

"I only have to hold on till reinforcements from the camp arrive," Kaine said. He wasn't going to back down.

"Then you will have to forgive me," Roan said as he, too, drew his sword, ready to face Kaine two on one.

"Aren't you the personal warrior of the princess of the Talov Duchy? Facing a lone warrior while you have help. How can you still have your honor after such a deed?" Kaine said. While he was mocking Roan, it was obvious to Roan that Kaine was only stalling for time. Getting enraged would cause Roan to not think clearly, and someone not thinking straight would easily lose track of what was important.

"To me, my duty to my princess takes priority. She has given me the order to find Prince Leander and return him safely. I will not disappoint her," Roan declared, taking a step forward.

"Then prepare to—" Kaine started, but he couldn't finish his sentence, as he was given a heavy smack to the back of the head. The blow to the head knocked the warrior out cold. Only the slight movement of his chest showed that he was still alive.

Unlike Roan, who was still looking at the downed Kaine, the sell-sword Kay was looking at the one who had knocked him out. Standing in front of them was Princess Elaina. In her hands was her sword, which she had used to hit Kaine over the head. The princess was wearing her traveling clothes and had a bag over her shoulder. Seeing the princess's stunned expression for what she had done, Kay couldn't help but chuckle.

"What do you think you are doing, Princess?" Kay asked, slightly amused by the princess's antics.

Kay's words brought Elaina back to reality. Looking at the sell-sword and his mischievous grin, Elaina wanted to shout at him but held herself back. She knew now wasn't the time. Instead, she sheathed her sword and took steps forward until she was mere inches from Kay. Looking up at him, Elaina said, "Take me with you."

"Absolutely not," Roan instantly answered. "Your Highness, I beg your pardon, but if you leave with us, they will think that we have kidnapped you to use as a hostage. This could potentially cause relations between our duchies to crumble."

"You have nothing to worry about. I have left behind a letter with Hali that will explain everything to my brother," Elaina said proudly.

Roan was tongue-tied. It seemed that the princess was determined to go with

185

them—so determined that she completely ignored Roan's advice. Even if she had left a note, she was still leaving with a sell-sword and the personal warrior of Aris Talov. The relationship between their two duchies might not crumble, but it would certainly strain.

On the other hand, Kay had a grin plastered on his face. He was feeling the exact opposite of what Roan was feeling. It was obvious that he didn't mind having the princess join them and probably thought it would make the journey more interesting. "Just give up already, Roan. Even if you wanted to refuse her, we couldn't be as aggressive with a princess as we were with Kaine over there," Kay said, pointing at the unconscious Kaine.

With no other choice, Roan relented with a long sigh. "Very well, but, Your Highness, I must warn you that we are no longer going to be in land governed by your father. Once we are in the Talov Duchy, your status as a princess won't account for anything," Roan warned, hoping his last threat would dissuade Elaina, but he was sadly disappointed.

"You don't have to worry about me. I can take care of myself," Elaina said, pushing out her chest to show her bravery, which only made Kay cough up a laugh. Elaina glared at the sell-sword, and Kay's single chuckle turned into full-on laughter.

"Let us be off, then. We have wasted enough time already," Roan said, and before the two could say anything, he ran into Verilis Forest.

Kay gave Elaina one last grin before he, too, disappeared into the forest. Left on her own, Elaina gave one last look at the camp, the fire now subdued. Steeling herself, Elaina ran to catch up to Kay and Roan.

+

Back in Crown Prince Aleron's tent, the atmosphere was suffocating. Crown Prince

Aleron stood there, his face a furious shade of red. A crumpled letter was clutched in his hand. Kneeling in front of Aleron were three people. From left to right, it was Declan, Kaine, and the attending maiden Hali. None of them had the courage to speak. They knew the first one to do so would take the full brunt of their prince's fury.

When the fire had been quenched, everyone had heaved a sigh of relief, but before they could rejoice, the news of the prisoners was learned. Instantly the warriors searched the camp, but upon discovering that they weren't there, they went to the forest's edge in hopes of cutting off their escape. The only thing they discovered there was a disoriented Kaine, who told them that they had already escaped into Verilis Forest.

Crown Prince Aleron wasn't too happy when he found out that his prisoners had escaped, but when his sister's attending maiden handed him the note Elaina had left for him, telling of her decision to leave with them willingly, he went berserk. By the time he had calmed down, nothing was left undamaged in his tent. He immediately ordered for the edge of the forest to be searched again, hoping that they hadn't gone far, but with the lead the three had, they were unsuccessful.

With failure hanging overhead, the three kneeling could only wait for their prince's punishment.

"Declan, you are one of my most trusted warriors. How do you think I should punish you three for your failures?" Aleron finally said, staring daggers at the kneeling warrior.

"Your Highness, you left me in charge of the camp as well as the prisoners. I take full responsibility for this incident," Declan said with his head bowed. He was determined to take all the responsibility for this blunder.

Hali trembled hearing Declan's words. Declan's full name was Declan Malis, and he was blood related to the siblings Kaine and Hali. While related, Declan was a distant relative. He had only gained the last name Malis after proving to the siblings' father that he was worthy of it. It wasn't only because of this distant relationship that Hali felt so distraught. Declan had practically helped raise the two Malis siblings. He had even been the first one to teach Kaine how to wield a sword. With such a relationship, Hali couldn't help but speak up for her distant uncle.

"Your Highness, the responsibility isn't all Declan's. Her Highness told me of her plan, and I chose to go along with it instead of telling you. It is my fault that the princess was able to escape with the prisoners," Hali said.

"Don't listen to her. I was overseeing the camp. Whatever happened was due to my oversight," Declan quickly said, trying to shift the blame back to himself. When Hali tried to speak again, Declan shot her a glare that stilled her tongue.

"So, the two of you wish to take the fall for this disaster," Aleron said, then turning to Kaine, who was the only one not to have spoken up yet. "What about you, Kaine? You were also in charge of protecting the princess. What do you have to say about this?"

Declan and Hali turned toward Kaine. The two knew that whatever Kaine said would most likely decide who would take the fall. As everyone waited for Kaine's answer, the warrior lifted his head and spoke. "Your Highness. Please let me wash away this dishonor. Allow me to lead a group into Verilis Forest to bring back Her Highness and the two escaped prisoners."

Both Hali and Declan gasped slightly at Kaine's answer. Hali was more shocked, as she knew how much Kaine hadn't wanted to enter the forest before Crown Prince Aleron arrived. Now he was asking to lead a group into one of the most dangerous places in the three duchies. If it hadn't been to bring back the princess, he wouldn't have chosen this route.

"You wish to erase your failure and the dishonor you have brought upon yourself by doing this noble deed," Aleron said. "But my answer is no. I will not send anyone into Verilis Forest in search of my sister and the two prisoners."

"Sir, I beg you to please reconsider," Kaine said before Declan could stop him from speaking.

"I will not change my decision. My sister has chosen her path. I will not risk men who have put their trust in me because of one of my unruly sister's whims," Aleron said. His tone told that he would not be changing his mind anytime soon. "Now, leave me and await your punishments. Declan, you stay. I have some more words I would like to say to you privately."

Hali almost had to drag her brother out of the tent, as he was still adamant about going into the forest to bring back Princess Elaina. It was only his training and duty as a warrior that kept him from saying what he shouldn't and allowed Hali to pull him out of the tent.

Alone with his prince, Declan looked at the furious Aleron.

"Prepare the men to ride," Crown Prince Aleron ordered. "I want them ready to head out as soon as possible."

"May I ask where we are heading?" Declan asked, but seeing the prince looking north, he had a rough idea.

"We are riding to the twin cities. If my foolish sister survives the perils of Verilis Forest, she will exit in the territory of the Talovs. We must cross Avri Bridge and make it to the other side of the forest before she leaves," Aleron answered.

Declan had always known that the prince wouldn't abandon his sister. No matter how much the world saw the prince as cold and distant, Declan knew how much the prince cared for his family. Even the second prince, who he butted heads with constantly, the crown prince had a soft spot for.

"As you command. I will prepare your steed for the journey," Declan said, but before he could leave, Aleron spoke.

"That won't be necessary. You will lead the warriors to WestAvri in my place. I will follow my sister into Verilis Forest," Aleron said, stunning Declan.

"Sir, I urge you to reconsider," Declan said. It was his turn to try to persuade the prince, but he would have equally disastrous results. "If you do, then allow me and several other warriors to go with you."

"No. I need you here. My warriors know that you speak for me. I will also not risk any of my warriors' lives. If they do lose their lives, it should be defending their home, not fighting against some beast in a forest."

"I still refuse to send you on your own into such a dangerous place," Declan said. He was not backing down, even if it meant being on the wrong side of his prince. It was his duty to protect the prince, and that sometimes meant even from himself. "At least take one warrior to accompany you."

"Very well," Aleron said, relenting to Declan's demand. "Kaine said he wishes to redeem himself. I will take him."

"As you wish," Declan said. While he should have been worried for his distant nephew, he also knew that Kaine was a step above most warriors, even when compared to the prince's own personal warriors. If there was anyone besides himself who could protect Crown Prince Aleron, it was Kaine.

Chapter Sixteen: Illusions Strike Again

The trio of Kay, Roan, and Elaina made their way deeper into the treacherous Verilis Forest. They had already learned the hard way to tread lightly when trekking through this forest after nearly walking into the jaws of a hungry borune. The large bear only let them be because it had already snagged a meal. It had only glared in their direction before going back to feasting on the poor deer's carcass. After that they slowed their pace and kept their eyes and ears alert for even the tiniest hints of danger.

Having lived her entire life on the golden plains of her duchy, Elaina was having difficulty traversing the twisting landscape. More than once did she trip on a tree's roots. Her skin was covered in little scrapes and bruises, and the back of her head stung from where a branch she had pushed aside had swung back, striking her.

Kay hadn't been able to contain his laughter when he had seen the princess tumble over, holding the back of her head.

"You damn sell-sword! Have you no honor in the slightest? Shouldn't you help a maiden when you see her fall over?" Elaina had snapped at the snickering Kay, unaware that calling herself a maiden made Kay almost fall over in laughter.

"Did you forget that I am a sell-sword? My sword is given to the highest bidder," Kay answered back.

"Can you two please stop arguing, and could we get a move on?" Roan said, putting himself between the two.

Kay gave a light laugh before continuing, with Elaina grinding her teeth in anger before she, too, followed.

The Talov warrior couldn't help but rub his forehead in frustration. Ever since they had entered Verilis Forest, the two of them had been arguing. This time it was Kay who had started it, but before, Elaina had said something that had made Kay argue back. Roan was beginning to regret his decision on teaming up with either of them.

Princess Elaina cursed under her breath but didn't say another word. Not wanting to see the sell-sword's face, Elaina had gone on ahead, with Kay and Roan following close behind.

The group ventured deeper into the forest. The trees grew closer together, and the branches blocked out most of the sun, cloaking them in shadows. Elaina and Roan stayed on full alert, while Kay whistled along merrily, as if he were walking down a simple village street.

"You know, you could at least try to look serious, and can you stop purposely upsetting the princess? This isn't the place for being at each other's throat," Roan whispered to Kay, so Elaina couldn't hear him.

"But it is so much fun watching all of her different reactions," Kay said with amusement in his cold blue eyes.

Hearing Kay joke around at the princess's expense, Roan couldn't connect this sell-sword to the blood-crazed killer he had seen just a few days before. When he had first joined the princess and her group in WestAvri, he hadn't known what to think about the Estelle princess hiring a sell-sword. The man was whimsical and could barely be trusted to follow orders. To Roan, the man had looked as if he would get in the way rather than help. It was only when they had been surrounded by the Talov warriors that he had seen the man's true strength.

Even for Roan, a seasoned warrior, just thinking about the scene sent shivers down his spine—how Kay had easily slaughtered over a dozen warriors in no time at all, his cold eyes full of murderous intent. Roan could honestly say that seeing Kay like that had made him feel more afraid than at any other time in his life.

As he was thinking, Roan heard a commotion from just ahead. Both Kay and Elaina were at it again. When he wasn't paying attention, the two began their stream of constant arguing. Roan had had enough of trying to play peacemaker and decided to let the two argue until they tired themselves out. At least then there would finally be some peace and quiet.

"How can you say such things?" Elaina yelled at Kay for a comment he had just made. "Without honor, a warrior is nothing. No matter how strong he becomes or what he accomplishes, a lack of honor will always leave a shadow in his heart."

"Princess, if I lived the way that you say I should live, I would be dead ten times over by now," Kay replied, brushing off Elaina's words. "Also, I'm not a warrior, so your Code of Valor doesn't apply to me."

"Even those who aren't warriors should live their lives honorably," Elaina retorted.

"Not this argument again," Roan sighed. His headache, which had been going away, came right back. Warriors and their honor was the topic the two argued about the most. Already this day, they had had two arguments due to this topic.

"Princess, you are too naive," Kay said. "The world is a lot more complicated. Your rules and ideas on how people should live don't apply to everything. Then again, what can you expect from a pampered princess?"

Elaina stuttered in anger, her fury rising in her chest. She hated when people called her spoiled or pampered. Her father had been strict when raising her and her two brothers. Never mind spoiled, she had had to beg her father for a new dress on her birthday. So when Kay called her pampered, she felt offended. She wanted to yell and scream at the sell-sword, but she knew that would only give him the reaction he wanted. She decided on a different course of action.

"You're right. I am pampered if you compare me to a scoundrel like yourself. I swear, if those brothers of yours are as blackhearted as you, I should fear for Prince Leander's safety," Elaina said. As the words left her mouth, she regretted them. She didn't know these men but had decided on insulting them only by how their brother acted. It wasn't how someone raised with a warrior's honor should act. With the words already said, she could only stand her ground and not show on her face her regret.

The grin that was plastered on Kay's face instantly faded. The mischievous twinkle in his eyes vanished, and only the cold blue remained. Elaina took a step back, as her instincts told her that he was in a dangerous mood now. She had clearly upset the man by talking about his brothers like that.

"You can say all you want about me, but my brothers are not me. They uphold your so-called virtues more than most of the warriors I have met," Kay spat. After saying those words, he seemed to calm down, but he kept his gaze away from Elaina.

Elaina didn't know what to say. This was an entirely different person from the Kay she knew. Before, Kay had been either an unserious jokester or a blood-crazed killer. Elaina felt guilt for what she had said and finally took it upon herself to apologize.

"Sorry," she said with her head hanging down.

"Well, I can understand you calling my brother Aer blackhearted. He does have a perceptive mind that tends to look at things in a darker light," Kay joked, as if his seriousness had never existed. "But for someone to call my brother Lucis blackhearted … I never thought I'd see the day when someone could think of a Zer'sheen as blackhearted."

Elaina's jaw dropped when she heard Kay. "Your brother is a Zer'sheen?" she almost screamed. Even Roan was looking at Kay with a face that showed that he thought he had heard wrong.

"Did I forget to mention that?" Kay said. "Why else do you think my brothers and I traveled such a great distance from the southern kingdoms to make it here?"

Both Elaina and Roan felt like shouting their loudest at Kay. Forgetting to tell them such a vital detail about one of those who were helping Prince Leander? It was obvious that he had deliberately hidden this from them. Elaina especially felt vexed by this. If her father found out that she had called a Zer'sheen blackhearted, he would lock her in her quarters until she was married. But how was she to have known that one of Kay's brothers was a Zer'sheen? Kay had said that the three of them were from the southern kingdoms, and Zer'sheen were only born in the land of Mezer, where the power of the Phoenix God dwelled.

As the three continued on, Roan suddenly stopped. Sniffing the air, he couldn't help but frown. "Do you smell that?" he asked.

Kay, too, smelled what Roan had smelled, and his face returned to being stern. "The smell of blood," Kay answered.

Elaina tried to smell what Roan and Kay smelled but was unable to. The scents of the forest kept her from smelling anything. She thought the two might be exaggerating. In a forest this dangerous, the chance of running into an animal corpse was high. They had run into a borune not long after entering. She thought that even if they did smell blood, the most likely thing would be that the blood came from a beast. It was only a few moments later that she was proved wrong.

The three of them found themselves in a small clearing. The peaceful-looking stretch of forest was coated in splatters of blood. Bits of cloth and other items told that this was not blood from an animal. Several small critters licked at some of the blood that had pooled. The scene was haunting and sent shivers down the princess's spine. She felt that this scene was all too similar to the one in which they had first met Kay, only the culprit was gone, and there were no bodies that they could see. Even if there were corpses, the creatures of the forest had most likely taken them as an easy meal.

Roan quickly began to inspect the clearing, looking for hints of what had happened. Right when Elaina was about to enter, she noticed that Kay paused before entering the clearing. She saw that within the man's eyes, there were hints of the blood craze that she had seen before. Worried about him going violent again, she grabbed the sell-sword's shoulder.

"Are you all right?" Elaina asked in a concerned voice. "You can keep your distance while Roan and I look around."

"Just let me get used to the blood. I'll be fine," Kay answered, and smiled back to Elaina.

Elaina stayed by his side, feeling that she shouldn't leave him at this moment.

Just as the last tints of madness left Kay's eyes, Roan shouted at them from the other side of the clearing. "You two need to see this." His tone was quite high-pitched and sounded nervous.

When the two reached Roan, they knew why he had sounded so nervous. There, in the mud, was a footprint larger than any that Elaina had ever seen. It looked human, but the toes were spread out more like a monkey's, and no monkey could leave a footprint this huge. Judging by the footprint, the creature was likely larger than even the borune they had seen.

As Roan and Elaina were still mesmerized by the monstrous footprint, something caught Kay's attention. In a patch of brush next to the footprint, there was something brownish gray in color. He picked up the item, and it turned out to be a small pouch, one worn around the waist. It was a common item, but when he laid eyes upon the pouch, Kay's face turned a deathly white.

"What have you found?" Elaina asked when she noticed Kay holding something. When she saw what he was holding, she was puzzled. "A waist pouch?"

"This pouch belongs to my brother Aer," Kay answered. His voice came out broken, and his body was visibly trembling.

Elaina gasped and looked over the pouch again, but the brownish-gray item had no identifying features. It looked to be an ordinary waist pouch, worn by most commoners. "Are you sure that the pouch belongs to your brother? Could you be mistaken?" Elaina asked.

"I'm sure of it. The appearance might be simple, but the material used can only be found in certain places in the southern kingdoms. I am sure that this pouch belongs to Aer," Kay answered.

Elaina watched as Kay gripped the tiny pouch in his hands. She wanted to reassure him that his brother was fine, but seeing all the blood around, she didn't dare. With so much blood lost, there was little chance for anyone to survive. She could only stand in place as the man she had just been arguing with was on the brink of a breakdown.

As she looked over Kay with pity, the sell-sword suddenly rushed forward. Elaina saw the desperation in his eyes. When he was about to charge out of the clearing, Roan suddenly stood in front of him.

"Get out of my way!" Kay shouted. He was clearly agitated and unable to think straight.

"You need to calm down," Roan said, but he didn't move out of Kay's way.

"I'm as calm as I need to be. Now, are you going to get out of my way, or do I have to make you?" Kay said, tightening his grip on his sword. Elaina was worried that in his state of mind, he may actually attack Roan.

"If you were as calm as you say you are, then you would have noticed that the three of us are surrounded," Roan said, pointing to the surrounding brush.

With that said, Elaina and Kay looked around. Sure enough, within the dense brush and bushes, they could see several pairs of glowing yellow eyes. They also noticed that the sounds of the forest had stopped, but it wasn't silent. They could hear a strange clicking and snipping sound coming from all around them.

"What are these things?" Elaina asked as she drew her sword. She had also been absorbed in Kay's drama and hadn't noticed the creatures' arrival.

"I don't know. I can't get a clear view," Roan cursed. While he had noticed the creatures' arrival, they had already surrounded them. He then turned and saw that Kay was still standing in a daze. "Kay, wake up! If we don't get out of this, how are you going to save your brother?"

Roan's shout brought Kay back. After putting the small pouch in his pocket, the sell-sword finally drew his sword as well. Around them, the clicking sounds grew ever louder, and more eyes appeared. Soon there were over a dozen yellow eyes staring menacingly at the three of them.

The three stood ready for a fight, but the creatures didn't emerge from their hiding places. The clicking grew louder and louder, until their ears were ringing. The sound made them dizzy and nauseous. With the increased sound, the brush started to erratically shake back and forth. From the brush came a strange yellow fog of pollen that instantly covered the entire clearing.

"Cover your mouth. It is most likely toxic," Roan warned.

Sadly, his warning came too late. The cloud of yellow pollen had already been inhaled by all three of them. The pollen quickly filled their lungs, making them cough uncontrollably. Soon the pollen cloud got so thick they could hardly see each other.

Elaina looked around fearfully. Neither she nor the other two knew what was going on. All they knew was that they had fallen into these creatures' trap. From out of the corner of her eye, Elaina saw something appear from the yellow fog. As it approached, the silhouette took on the shape of a person. Looking at the shadowed form, Elaina felt something crawl inside her head. Sharp pain shot through her skull. She endured the pain, and as quickly as it had started, the pain vanished as if it had never been.

Not knowing what had just happened, she turned to see that both Kay and Roan were acting strangely. They were looking at the shadowy silhouette with longing and fear. While Roan recoiled away from the figure, Kay took a step forward.

"I … I'm sorry. I couldn't stop. Please forgive me," Kay begged the figure. Elaina didn't know what was going on nor why Kay was acting so familiarly with the thing. The silhouette may have looked human, but the way it moved said otherwise.

Roan wasn't doing much better. He was crouched down with his arms over his ears, trying to block out something that only he could hear. Elaina could hear him mumbling something, but it was too faint to tell what the warrior was saying.

Too many things were happening, making Elaina unsure of what to do. The strange shadow stopped getting any closer but stood there, beckoning them to approach. Kay kept on mumbling apologies as he slowly inched closer to the silhouette. When he was less than a foot away, the shadow began to change.

To Elaina's horror, the shadow suddenly grew a long serpentlike appendage.

Along with it, the shadow also grew an extra pair of limbs. Seeing Kay in danger, Elaina sprang into action. With a swing of her sword, she severed the long, twisting appendage.

As the limb fell to the ground, a pain-filled shrill rattled Elaina's brain. Before she could reorganize herself, the shadow launched itself at her. Knocked onto her back, her sword flung to her side, Elaina found herself pinned to the ground with a grotesque-looking insect biting at her. She tried to push the insect away, but the creature's sharp limbs dug into her, tearing at her flesh and making her struggle more difficult.

As the insects protruding fangs nearly took a chunk out of her face, Elaina spotted her dropped sword not too far off. Reaching for her sword, she fended off the insect with only a single hand. The insect saw the opportunity and bit into Elaina's defending hand. Fighting through the pain, Elaina was able to grab her sword. Before the creature could remove its fangs from Elaina's hand, she had already separated the insect's head from the rest of its body.

The body of the insect spasmed and fell off her. The head seemed to not know that it was dead, and the fangs bit deeper into Elaina's hand. Bracing herself, Elaina ripped the head off her hand. While she got the head off, a couple of the insect's fangs were still lodged in her skin.

Free from the current danger, Elaina propped herself up, but when she looked around, her face turned pale. Both Kay and Roan were still in their strange trance, with Roan now acting more like Kay. What made her terrified was that the shadows had increased. Now several of those shadowed silhouettes surrounded them, beckoning to them. Seeing that they were in extreme danger, Elaina ran toward Kay, who was nearest to the shadows. When she reached the mesmerized sell-sword, she raised her hand.

"Snap out of it!" Elaina yelled, and slapped Kay right across the face. The slap seemed to do the trick. The glazed look in his eyes faded, and he looked at the princess, not knowing what had just happened.

Before Kay could ask, Elaina ran to Roan, who was getting a little too close to one of the shadows. Elaina pulled Roan away just as the shadow's serpent appendage struck right where Roan had been standing. The pull was too forceful, and both Elaina and Roan fell to the ground. Luckily, the fall jogged Roan out of his trance.

"What is going on?" Roan asked, moaning in pain from the fall. Looking around, he saw all the strange shadows surrounding them. "What are those things?"

"Now is not the time. We have to escape," Elaina said, pulling Roan to his feet. Before they could stand, one of the shadows struck out.

Not too far away, Kay, who had regained his mind, saw the shadow attack. Before the shadow could reach Elaina and Roan, Kay cut it in two. A loud shrill rang out from one half of the shadow. The shadow disappeared, and the corpse of a large insect remained.

"What in the world?" Kay said, shocked by the shadow's true appearance.

"There's no time. We have to leave now!" Elaina shouted. Both Kay and Roan agreed, and the three headed toward the opening in the encirclement created by the death of the insect that Kay had killed.

Seeing another of their own cut down, the shadows vanished, revealing the insects' true form. The insects ranged in size, from the size of a dog to ones nearing a horse's height. With their stingers whipping behind them, the insects charged, their pincers and fangs aimed right at the backs of the fleeing Kay, Elaina, and Roan. The three just made it out of the clearing, dodging the vicious attacks of these horrifying insects.

They continued to run away as the insects gave chase. The insects, terrifying as they were, were slow. The distance between them only grew. The insects were ambush predators and normally lay in wait, chasing their prey as a last resort. In the end, the insects were too slow to catch the humans. Outraged, the insects gave one final screech of anger before returning to their lair.

Safe from the insects, the three fell to the ground, exhausted both physically and mentally.

"What just happened? One moment, I'm ready to fight whatever is about to come, and the next ..." Roan started, but stopped. Whatever he had seen in his mesmerized state, he did not want to talk about it.

"It was the pollen," Kay answered. "It seems that the plant that produces the pollen has a symbiotic relationship with those bugs. The insects use the pollen to confuse their prey, while the plant soaks up the nutrients left over from the insects' meal." He shivered when he thought about how close he had come to being the insects' next meal. He then turned to Elaina. "I need to thank you, Princess. If it hadn't been for you, I wouldn't have broken out of my spellbound state."

Elaina blushed at hearing the uncharacteristic words coming from Kay. She didn't expect to be thanked for her help, especially by Kay. They didn't have the best relationship, and even though they had gotten to know one another, Elaina still felt that Kay kept her and everyone else at a certain distance. While she still felt that he kept them away, she felt the distance had shortened a bit.

"I agree. We owe you our lives, Your Highness." Roan gave the princess a bow of gratitude. "If you hadn't broken free from your trance, we would have died without knowing how. By the way, how did you break free?"

Elaina thought back. When the pollen had surrounded them, both Kay and Roan had fallen victim to the hypnotic effects. Elaina could only remember the pain that she had felt for the brief moment. Seeing both Kay and Roan still recuperating from their hypnotic state, Elaina knew that she hadn't been affected in the slightest. That thought scared her more than the close call they had just had.

"I don't remember much. All I do recall is seeing some vague images, then waking to see you two in your trancelike states," Elaina lied. She didn't know why she lied, but she did.

"Seems that you inhaled less of the mesmerizing pollen than the two of us. That meant you were not hypnotized correctly and were able to break free," Roan said, beginning to understand why Elaina had woken up first. If she had only gotten a small dose, then the visions could have been weaker and maybe even too brittle for the insects to fool her.

Elaina just nodded and sighed in relief that her lie hadn't been exposed. As she relaxed, she noticed Kay's gaze on her. His questioning look told her that, unlike Roan, Kay did not believe her words. She tried to keep her emotions in check, but when he started toward her, she felt her heart leap. She prayed that Kay would not call her out on her lie, but what came next was unexpected.

When Kay reached her, he quickly grabbed her wrist. He revealed the nasty wound that still bled. Even worse was the fact that there was still a small fang sticking out of it. Elaina had tried to pull out the fangs while she had run, but one of them had been too small and too deep to get a good grip while they had been running for their lives.

"Wha... what do you think you are doing?" Elaina said, trying to pull her hand away, but Kay's grip was too strong.

"Quit squirming and let me get this insect's fang out. If you leave it in too long, it will only get worse," Kay answered.

Ceasing to struggle, Elaina allowed Kay to pull the fang out of her hand. Elaina watched Kay work, seeing another side of the sell-sword. He was being gentle as he worked on getting the fang out. After removing it, Kay didn't let go and began wrapping the wound. Seeing him concentrating so hard, Elaina felt her face flushing. When Kay had finally finished, her face was turning a noticeable shade.

"Thank you," Elaina said, rubbing her now-bandaged hand.

Seeing the two of them acting this way made Roan uncomfortable. "Now that we are safe, does anyone know exactly where we have run off to?" he asked.

Remembering that she and Kay weren't alone, Elaina felt even more embarrassed. As she looked at Kay, who had returned to his nonchalant attitude, Elaina felt like beating the man half to death. Holding in her desire, she decided to try to find out where they had run off to.

Almost instantly the three realized that this part of the forest was vastly different from the places they had been in so far. While the deeper parts of Verilis Forest were denser and more perilous, both the edge of the forest and the center had the same foreboding feeling. However, this place gave them a tranquil and peaceful feeling.

Soft sunlight cut through the dense canopy as singing birds perched up above. Small critters, such as forest rabbits and other adorable animals not seen in the other parts of the forest, scurried around. Several different kinds of wildflowers bloomed around them, and butterflies danced with the sway of the petals.

"Is this another illusion?" Roan asked, not believing that this scene was from the dreaded Verilis Forest.

"It shouldn't be, as we are all seeing this," Elaina answered, but she, too, was a little skeptical of it being real.

"Do you two hear that?" Kay suddenly asked.

Both Elaina and Roan closed their eyes and tried to hear what Kay had heard.

Underneath the birdsong and the light patter of butterfly wings, they could hear the sound of splashing.

"Is that the sound of water?" Elaina said. With the sound discerned, she tried to find out where it was coming from. "It seems to be coming from directly ahead of us."

Pushing through the brush, the three headed toward the sound. The closer they got, the more the sound of water could be heard. When they pushed through the last of the brush, what they found left them speechless.

Chapter Seventeen: Grave of the First Zer'sheen

The three stood before a grand lake. The lake stretched away, and the trees on the other side looked like shadows. The water was so clear that they could see the bottom, which wasn't very deep. The lake stayed the same shallow depth throughout and would barely reach a man's calf. In these clear waters, tiny fish launched themselves out of the water as if welcoming the three. The scene looked like something out of a fairy tale, but what really stood out was the center of the lake.

Protruding from the middle of the water was a huge weeping willow. The tree stood proud as the ruler of this strange lake, rooted deep into a small island. The willow's branches hung over the lake, casting their shadows over the water. Stabbed into the tree's twisted trunk were dozens of swords, all different shapes and sizes. The scabbards lined the large roots as if waiting for their partners to leave the tree.

When Elaina saw the tree and all the swords stabbed into its trunk, a certain story flashed through her mind. It was a story that her father used to tell her before she went to sleep, a sad story that always made Elaina tear up after hearing it. Even so, it was one of her favorites, and she would ask her father to tell it again and again. Now seeing the legendary tree in person, Elaina found it difficult to breathe.

Roan was also feeling the same pressure as the princess. As a musician and one of Princess Aris's songbirds, Roan knew many stories. The moment he had seen the tree with all those swords embedded in its trunk, Roan knew where they were. He tried to stay calm, but inside, his emotions were fluctuating rapidly.

The only one who didn't react this way was Kay. Unlike Roan and Elaina, the sell-sword had lived most of his life in the southern kingdoms and heard the stories and fables common there. Due to this, he only thought the tree strange. However, he did notice how his two companions acted upon seeing it.

"What is it? Do you recognize where we are?" Kay asked.

"We have to leave now. This isn't a place we should intrude upon," Roan said. His voice was hardly a whisper, as if he was terrified as to what may hear.

Seeing that Roan wouldn't answer him, Kay turned to ask Elaina.

She looked at Kay, then toward the weeping willow on the lake. "This is the Grave of the First Zer'sheen," she told him.

Kay finally understood why the two were acting this way. Even Kay, who hadn't been in the lands of Mezer long, had heard the stories of the First Grave. It was said that after unifying the lands of Mezer, the first king, Calv Ridian, had mourned the losses that the unification had caused. Many of his friends and trusted warriors had been lost. Even his most valiant warrior had lost his life in the final battle.

Wishing to honor his fallen warriors in some way, Calv Ridian brought their weapons with him as he traveled his newly founded kingdom. He continued this way until he made it to a lake hidden in the dense Verilis Forest. When he gazed at the weeping willow that reigned over the lake, Calv Ridian knew what he must do. One by one, he plunged the weapon of each of his fallen comrades into the trunk of the tree, turning the entire lake into a grave for the fallen warriors.

When he was done, the king prayed for the souls of his fallen. As he did, the godhood that had lain dormant inside awoke. That day, the man Calv Ridian was no longer, and the god Calv Ridian rose, but that wasn't all. With the king's ascension, he used his power to call his departed warriors back. Thus, the first Zer'sheen were born. After that day, Zer'sheen, with the scars of their past lives, would be born in the lands of Mezer, and the legendary grave was carved into their history.

"We can talk once we are away from this place, else we will never leave," Roan said, urging Kay and Elaina to leave this famous grave.

"Going so soon?" a voice suddenly said from somewhere behind them. The three turned to face who had sneaked up on them, but they saw nothing. The peacefulness of the place only made them even more nervous as they tried to locate the person who had spoken.

"It's no use. No matter how much you search, you will never find me." The voice spoke again, elongating each *s*, giving those words a hissing sound to them. Along with the voice, several trees shook abruptly. Elaina thought she spotted something, but it was too dark and fast to catch a real glimpse.

"We apologize for trespassing," Roan said, trying to smooth over the situation. "We had no idea that we were entering the tomb of the first Zer'sheen. My name is Roan, and I am a sworn warrior to Her Highness Princess Aris Talov. With me is Her Highness Princess Elaina Estelle and a warrior from the southern kingdoms."

"I am the caretaker and guardian of this place. I am also the reaper for all who defile this place with their presence," the voice hissed. "While you may not have meant to come here, it matters not. Your bodies will become nutrients for the willow."

"The guardian of the First Grave is real," Roan couldn't help but proclaim out loud.

"What guardian?" Elaina asked Roan. "I have never heard stories about a person guarding the First Grave." She had grown up listening and learning about the legendary characters of their land. This so-called guardian had never been in any of the histories nor the stories.

"You wouldn't. The guardian was purposely kept out of all stories and records, as it was considered heresy by the holy city," Roan answered. "I only learned of this due to stumbling across an old children's song from the time of the second king's reign—before Ridia grew in power."

"Blind men who think they know the will of their god," the voice said, insulting the priests and the holy city. "Now, relinquish your lives, and I will make your deaths painless."

With the declaration of the guardian, the entire forest began to shake. The earth trembled, as if a giant were rampaging near.

With fear gripping her heart, Elaina stepped forward. She couldn't let herself die here. "Honorable guardian of the First Grave, my name is Elaina Estelle, descendant of Travis Estelle. In remembrance of my ancestor whose weapon decorates the sacred willow, please have leniency," she said, giving a bow, not even sure whether the person talking was in that direction.

The quaking stopped as the guardian took a moment to think it over. "It matters not if you are a descendant of those honored here. In accordance with my master's order, all who trespass must die," the voice declared.

A tree near them suddenly came crashing down. The three jumped away just in time as the tree fell right where they had been standing. If they hadn't moved, the three of them would have been crushed.

"Wait a moment!" Roan yelled out. "If the stories are true, then I ask you, let us take the test."

Once more the forest went silent as the guardian began to think Roan's words over.

"What is this test that you are talking about?" Elaina asked. She wasn't sure, but she didn't like the sound of it.

"According to the song, those who trespass on this sacred ground will be given a test. If they pass, not only are they free to go, they also leave with the blessing of the first Zer'sheen. At least, that is how the lyrics of the song go," Roan answered.

"Does the song at least tell us what type of test it is?" Kay asked, finally chiming in. During this whole confrontation with the guardian, he had never said a word.

"Sadly, the parts that would have explained it were too damaged for me to recover," Roan depressingly said. "The only thing that I could discover was that the test has something to do with the lake itself."

"The lake?" Elaina said, puzzled by what that meant. The lake was beautiful to behold, and the clarity showed that there were no hidden dangers in its shallow depths. There were even fish and other creatures swimming about, so the water wasn't poisonous or tainted.

Before she could see anything suspicious about the lake, the guardian's voice rang out again. "Very well. I will allow you to take the test."

After the guardian spoke, a large shadow began to move. Light from the sun somehow reflected off the moving shadow. As it came closer, the three realized that the shadow was actually black scales. When the guardian finally revealed itself, none of them spoke. Even Kay had his mouth open in awe.

The guardian was a giant serpent. Its body was so long that they couldn't see the end of the beast. The serpent was covered in black scales that glistened in the sunlight. A pair of piercing red eyes looked down upon them. Opening its jaws, the serpent revealed a pair of fangs larger than a pair of broadswords.

Elaina let out a gasp. "It can't be. The guardian is a serpent of the Moaa race!" She finally understood why all information relating to the guardian of the First

Grave had been lost, or hidden by the holy city.

The Moaa race was a race of giant serpents with intelligence rivaling—in some cases, surpassing—humanity's. These giant snakes were feared throughout the world for their cunning minds, which loved to plot, and their massive strength, capable of crushing a fully armored man to death. But the main reason they were so feared was that they were one of the surviving Ninn species.

The Ninn were considered the archenemies of mankind. Coming in all shapes and sizes, the Ninn were more of a grouping of species and races than one, like humanity. When one was discovered, crusades would amass to vanquish the evil. If news that the Phoenix God and founder of their warrior way was in league with the Ninn were to get out, the results would be disastrous.

"What does the test require of us?" Elaina asked. She tried to hide her fear, but those large crimson eyes saw all.

"It is quite simple. All you must do is reach the weeping willow at the center of the lake. If a single one of you makes it, you will all be free to leave," the giant serpent answered, its forked tongue twisting with each word. "Now, step into the lake."

With the giant serpent watching their every move, the three of them had no other choice but to do as it said. The moment their feet stepped into the clear water, it turned murky. The formerly clear water, which had been alive with lively fish, turned into a black swamp.

Elaina turned to the serpent, wishing to ask it what was happening, but the serpent had already disappeared from sight.

"What do we do now?" Kay asked.

"We have to proceed toward the willow. The moment we stepped foot into the lake, we had only this choice. That is the reason the guardian has left us alone. It knows we can't leave otherwise," Roan answered.

Startled by this, Elaina tried to take a step back and realized she couldn't. It was as if her feet turned to stone when she thought to retreat. Oddly enough, when she lifted her foot to take a step forward, her foot lifted naturally. With no other way to leave, Elaina took the first step toward the willow.

When she took that step, she noticed something. The amount that she had sunk was a little bit greater than when she had first stepped into the lake. Normally, this wouldn't shock her, but before the water had turned murky, it had been the same depth all the way to the small island where the willow grew. It wasn't only her that sank. Both Kay and Roan had slightly sunk into the water as well.

"What is going on?" Elaina asked Roan, but the warrior was also confused by what was happening.

"This lake reflects the hearts of those who enter." The guardian's voice rang out, revealing the true meaning behind the test. "Those who enter its waters will sink according to how weighted their heart is. Only one whose heart is free of burdens can reach the grave, and those with heavy hearts will be consumed by the lake."

Elaina wasn't sure what the guardian meant. Did having a heavy heart mean someone with a guilty conscience or someone who had sinned? If that were true, then Elaina would have no problem passing the test, but that sounded almost too easy. She also didn't know what the guardian meant by *burdens*. The words were too vague to get any true meaning from them until they traversed more of the lake.

Once more the three of them continued toward the willow, and like before, Elaina found herself sinking into the murky waters. After making it not even a tenth of the way there, she realized they were in trouble. Next to her, Roan was in a similar situation. He had even sunk all the way to his knees. Looking at the willow, which was still so far off, Elaina knew they would not make it.

Step by step, they approached the tree, and with every step, they came closer to their doom. When the water had reached her waists, Elaina panicked. She could feel the lake trying to pull her under, and for some reason, she felt the temptation to let it. Closing her eyes, she felt herself beginning to sink rapidly into the water. Just before her head had completely submerged, a hand grabbed her shoulder and yanked her up.

Forcing her eyes open, Elaina found that her savior was the sell-sword Kay.

"Are you so weak willed that you would let something like this best you? If so, then I am extremely disappointed," Kay said. His eyes showed a strange fluctuation in them that Elaina could not grasp.

Looking at Kay, she noticed something that made her mouth fall open. The sell-sword was standing in water that only reached his ankles. It seemed impossible, as Kay was right next to her, and Elaina was near neck-deep in the murky water.

"How—?" Elaina began to ask, but she was cut off.

"It is really simple once you realize it," Kay said, giving her his usual grin, which told her he wouldn't answer. He then turned to the central tree and began to head toward the willow alone. Elaina thought she would see him sink a little, but every step, his feet sank to the same depth. It was as if the lake was back to its former shallowness.

If Kay had looked back, he would have seen Elaina's and Roan's stunned expressions. After what looked like a simple stroll, Kay reached the island where the weeping willow stood. The tree seemed to welcome Kay, as the light around it began to grow, until it was too bright for Elaina and Roan to continue looking. When the brightness faded, they turned back, but all they could see was a strange fog that blocked their view.

"I never thought that someone could actually make it to the island." The guardian's voice suddenly rang out. The large serpent had reappeared behind them at some point. Elaina and Roan could hear the surprise in the its voice.

"What is happening to Kay over there?" Elaina asked as she and Roan magically began to rise from the lake, until they were only ankle-deep, as Kay had been.

Whether the serpent had heard Elaina or not, the Moaa didn't answer as it stared into the fog that Kay had disappeared into.

Turning back to the fog, Elaina could only wait for whatever was happening to end.

+

On the island, Kay watched as the light made a barrier between himself and the others, leaving only him and the island. Divided from Roan and the princess, Kay tried to leave the island, only to find himself walking back onto it. He tried once more and knew that he couldn't leave the same way he had come.

Making his way to the sword-pierced willow, Kay slid one of his fingers over one of the swords jutting out of its trunk. Pulling his hand away, he watched as a small trickle of blood flowed out of a small cut at the tip of his finger. Even after all these years, the swords the first Zer'sheen had used were still as sharp as the day they had been stabbed into the tree. It seemed that the Phoenix God had imbued the tree with some sort of magic, keeping his fallen warriors' weapons from degrading.

"After all these years, someone has finally reached the willow." A voice suddenly came from the willow.

From the way that it spoke, Kay thought it was the guardian, but the voice was feminine, while the guardian's voice was undoubtedly male. Looking up, he spotted who had just spoken. Winding its way through the tree's limbs was another member of the Moaa race. With scales as white as the branches, it almost blended in perfectly with the willow. It was only due to it coming toward him that Kay had noticed it, or else he wouldn't have seen it, even if he was mere inches from the giant serpent.

This serpent wasn't as daunting as the black one. Instead, it held a mesmerizing feeling. Its golden eyes seemed to hold wisdom above that of even wizened sages, and its scales glowed in a mystical way.

"During these long years of waiting, I have wondered who would be the first to reach this willow. First, I thought that it would be either Ridian's descendants or maybe a Zer'sheen. Then I broadened my guesses as the years grew long, to include the founding families. Sadly, those who did find their way here never passed," the serpent said as it made its way off the tree and began to circle around Kay, inspecting him. "That is, until you. What makes you so special that you could pass a test that even those with a god's blood failed?"

Kay didn't find this as intimidating as he should have. Staring back at the serpent with his crystal blue eyes, he answered. "The test isn't all that hard once you realize the truth of it." His words almost mimicked the words he had said to Princess Elaina only a few moments ago.

"Yes, the test is quite simple once you know, but even knowing how to pull it off is no small feat," the white serpent said with a hissing laugh. "A heavy heart means just that, but it doesn't mean one racked with sin or many responsibilities, does it?"

Kay knew the serpent wasn't really asking. It was only wishing for Kay to say the right answer. "The answer is connections, or to be more precise, bonds."

"That is correct. While bonds make us strong, they also make us weak. One without bonds will not have a heart and will be devoured by my brother. While those with too many will sink into the lake," the serpent said. Its body spiraled around Kay, ecstatic that someone had finally passed.

Kay thought back to the test and understood. There had been two tests, not one.

The first had been to get the black Moaa to agree to let them take the test. If the serpent had seen that they held nothing in their hearts, it would have deemed them unworthy, and they would have been mercilessly slaughtered.

"In fact, I'm surprised that someone like you would be the first to pass. I have lived a long time and know what those eyes mean. Those addicted to anything have heavy hearts, warped by their addiction, but you ... you have a heart lighter than anyone else," the white serpent said as it looked Kay straight in the eye. As it peered into Kay, it found something that shocked it beyond belief. "Impossible! How can someone with that stigma have a light heart? It is simply unfathomable!"

Rage instantly erupted in Kay's heart. Without missing a beat, he unsheathed his sword. The stigma that he carried with him was a great taboo, a secret that only a few knew about. He didn't care that the giant serpent could swallow him whole. Anyone who brought up his stigma must be dealt with.

"You won't be able to hurt me with that sad excuse for a weapon," the white serpent taunted Kay. With a swing of its tail, the Moaa broke Kay's sword right in half. "Why don't you try one of the weapons from the willow? You may have better luck."

After his initial outburst, Kay was able to calm down. Looking over the many weapons that decorated the giant tree, Kay felt he was being drawn to them. Forgetting his desire to slay the snake, Kay walked around the tree.

The weapons were the most amazing he had ever seen. The metal had a blinding sheen, showing the blades' sharpness. Some had precious and mystical gems embedded in their hilts. Others had magnificent carved hilts and guards. The weapons were more like works of art than actual weapons, and the pressure they gave off indicated more than weapons that had seen endless bloodshed. Any person would desire any of these weapons, but Kay felt that they didn't match him. These weapons were for some great lord or honorable warrior, not a sell-sword like him.

As he ducked under a low-hanging branch, he almost ran straight into a sword stabbed into the limb. The sword immediately caught his attention. Unlike the rest of the weapons, this sword's blade was dull, almost gray, as it held no shine. There was no guard, and the hilt spiraled out of the metal to wrap itself at the pommel. With its whitish appearance, the sword looked more like a misshaped branch than a weapon.

Another thing that made this weapon different was the fact that Kay felt nothing coming from it. All the other swords felt as if they were calling to him, tempting him to pull them out of the tree. Only this weapon was silent. To Kay, its silence was shouting that he was good enough to wield this weapon.

Kay felt that this sword matched him more than the swords fit for a king. Determination building, he gripped the sword's hilt and pulled. The sword was stubborn and refused to leave the willow. Time and time again, Kay tried to pull the sword out of the tree, to no avail, but his determination never wavered. With all his strength, he gave the sword one last pull, and with strain, the sword came loose from the tree.

Immediately after he had obtained the sword, the tempting of the other weapons stopped. There was no need for them to continue—Kay had already chosen. With his new sword in hand, Kay noticed the sword felt right in his grip. Its struggling was all but a thing of the past as he swung the blade, getting a feel for it.

"Congratulations on your new partner, but it seems you still need something," the white serpent said, appearing right next to Kay. Not a second later, the sound of twigs snapping came from above. Sensing danger, Kay stepped back just as one of the branches fell and landed where he had just been standing.

Lying on the ground was a sheath. The wood was white and spiraled, just like the grip of his sword. Kay knew that this was the resting place for this sword. After picking up the sheath, Kay slid the sword in, and with a click, it fit perfectly.

"Now that everything is finished, it is time for you to go," the serpent said. The fog that surrounded the island began to encroach upon Kay.

Before Kay could do anything, the fog was upon him. The tree, which was right next to him, disappeared, and when he reached through the fog, he found that the willow had truly disappeared. The fog grew denser, until he couldn't even have seen his hand if he had placed his palm right on the tip of his nose. Soon the dense fog began to disperse, and Kay found that he was somewhere else entirely.

All around him were trees and vegetation. The lake and weeping willow were nowhere in sight. He couldn't even hear the sound of water that had allowed them to find their way there in the first place. He didn't know how, but the white serpent had transported him away from the First Grave and back into Verilis Forest.

"Kay!" a voice suddenly shouted from behind him. From out of the brush came Princess Elaina and, right behind her, the warrior Roan. Kay noticed the relief in her eyes. "Thank goodness you are all right."

Kay felt his heartbeat quicken upon hearing that the princess had been worried for him. It also made him confused. Ever since he had dulled his emotions with Blue Breath, he had only ever had warm feelings toward his brothers. Shaking the strange sensation off, he gave her one of his usual smirks.

"You don't have to cry about it. I'm fine," he said, teasing Elaina. "Anyways, how did you find yourself here?"

"Who's crying? As if I would be upset over what happens to some lowly sell-sword," Elaina said angrily. She then looked at him questioningly. "As for how we arrived here, we haven't got a clue. The light that cloaked the island suddenly grew brighter, and before we could regain our sight, we found ourselves back in Verilis

Forest. What happened on that island?"

Kay then told them what had transpired on the island, leaving nothing out. He felt no reason to hide any of the facts. The only thing he kept to himself was the knowledge of his stigma. After a few minutes, Kay finished speaking, ending with him hearing Elaina shout out to him.

"Can I see the sword?" Roan asked. He could hardly contain himself. He wanted to see a weapon that one of the first Zer'sheen had used.

Throwing the sword to Roan, Kay allowed him to see his new weapon. Elaina also wished to see the sword, but Roan had beaten her to asking. Excitement showed on Roan's face, but when he tried to pull the sword out of its sheath, it didn't budge.

"I should have warned you about that. The sword is a little arrogant. Just try a little harder," Kay said with a laugh.

Roan tried to do as Kay instructed, but no matter how hard he pulled, he couldn't free the sword from its sheath.

"Let me try," Elaina said, taking the sword out of Roan's hands.

"Your Highness, not to sound arrogant, but if I couldn't free the thing, I don't think that you—" Roan had begun to say that, with her frame, it would be impossible, but then, in front of his eyes, the sword slid easily out of its sheath.

Kay had to stop himself from laughing as Roan's face showed a strange expression upon seeing Elaina succeed just as he had been saying she wouldn't be able to. Kay himself hadn't known that others would be unable to unsheathe his sword until Roan had tried. But as Elaina demonstrated, it seemed that some people could.

With the sword drawn, Elaina stared at the dull-looking weapon. The blade had not a hint of shine to show that it was sharp, and the metal was a grayish color. It was the most unappealing sword that she had ever seen. The strange thing was that the sword fit perfectly in her hand and felt quite light for being made of steel. The more she held it, the more the sword looked like a true treasure in her eyes.

"It is a good sword," Elaina finally said, sheathing the blade and passing it back to Kay, who nodded in agreement.

Watching this interaction between the princess and Kay, the warrior Roan didn't see what the two of them saw in the dull sword. He had seen simple guards carrying weapons that looked to be in better condition than this one. If it hadn't been a weapon supposedly used by one of the first Zer'sheen, then Roan would have thought that the sword was a commoner's weapon used for self-defense.

With the three of them having successfully escaped the Grave of the First Zer'sheen, they began the venture out of Verilis Forest. Heading east, they hoped to make it through the forest without any other life-threatening situations.

+

On the island where the gray willow grew, the white Moaa stared at a part of the tree. A small indentation was all that hinted at the sword that had once been there. As if obsessed, the serpent sat motionless, transfixed by the place Kay had pulled the sword from. The white serpent was so transfixed that she hadn't noticed the black Moaa reaching the island, his long body slithering through the lake.

"The three of them are making their way east. By their speed, they should make it out of the forest in three days," the black Moaa said. Not long after the white Moaa had sent Kay, Elaina, and Roan away, she had asked the black Moaa to follow them until they were out of their territory.

"That is good" was all the white Moaa said.

The black Moaa noticed his companion was distracted. Following her gaze, he saw the empty spot where a sword had been stabbed into the willow. Unlike the white Moaa, who lived on the island with the willow, the black Moaa very rarely interacted with the grave. He may have known the names and identities of the swords and their previous owners, but he didn't know where the swords were placed in the tree, so he didn't know which sword had chosen Kay.

"Which sword finally made its way free from this place?" the black Moaa asked. He was honestly curious about this. As the first sword to leave the tomb, it was bound to create a scene in the future. Whether it was Bant's unassuming heavy sword, able to cleave steel plate in two, or Frell's soft sword, which could bend and find the chinks in an enemy's defense, they all would be worshipped as priceless heirlooms by the warriors of Mezer.

Finally taking her gaze away from the empty branch, the white Moaa looked at her comrade. The black Moaa felt something strange was going on. As the caretaker of the willow, the white Moaa had a duty to keep the tree healthy and help the swords find those worthy of wielding them. Accomplishing her task for the first time should have been a great achievement, but all the black Moaa saw in her gaze was uncertainty.

"Which sword left the willow?" the black Moaa asked once more. Then a certain realization struck him. "It can't be that he took *that* sword. That is impossible. No man can be the owner of that sword."

"Impossible as it sounds, it has come to be," the white Moaa said, answering the black Moaa's doubts with the truth.

The black Moaa didn't believe it. Winding his way around the willow, he hoped to find the certain sword. He came across Bant's heavy sword and Frell's soft sword and dozens of other weapons, all of which were not the one he was searching for.

After three times around the willow, the black Moaa gave up his search. The sword was no longer in the grave but out in the world.

"We should bring it back. Let him take several weapons instead. There is no telling what a sword like that can do if it falls into the wrong hands," the black Moaa warned, eager to find Kay and return the sword to the willow.

"There is no need for that. What is done is done. We are to allow the swords to find rightful owners, as per Calv Ridian's orders," the white Moaa said. She wasn't as worried that the sword was out in the world.

"Our duty is to find partners for the weapons the Phoenix God has left in the willow," the black Moaa said. "But that sword is different. It wasn't forged or tempered through flame and iron. It grew out from the willow tree itself. A sword born naturally will have powers that we can't even imagine. Do you honestly think it is wise to allow them to leave with a sword like that?" If the white Moaa didn't agree, then the black Moaa would not be able to leave the grave, and the sword would eventually be impossible to reacquire.

"Let's just see what happens. I don't believe that those three reached this place by accident. I believe that fate may have something in store for them," the white Moaa said. Her calm words meant one thing to the black Moaa: they would allow them to leave with the sword.

"I hope that you are right," the black Moaa said. Slithering away, he disappeared into the forest.

Watching her companion vanish, the white Moaa let out a long-held sigh. "As do I," she whispered before returning to the willow tree's canopy, also disappearing from sight.

Chapter Eighteen: Plans in Motion in Raven's Nest

T he Grand Hall of the Talovs was a spectacular sight to behold. Able to hold hundreds of people, and with the statues of every archduke that had come before lining the walls, the room could be quite intimidating. This day, the normally empty hall was packed with people. Representatives from every one of the warrior families sworn to the Talovs had gathered today to discuss the issue of the ailing archduke and the worry of having the seat empty, even for a short while.

Sitting at the center of the room was the one who had called for this gathering, Duke Valens. Next to him was his son and heir, who sat by his father proudly. Beside the Valenses sat the two other dukes, Duchess Morwood and Duke Aleo. Both were as intimidating as Duke Valens, their warriors standing behind them. Then came the two hall masters, who each ruled over the north and south of the duchy. Jukel Altares, hall master of Stone Hall, sat with his own son, who had inherited his father's physique along with his name. Only Illas Orkiss, hall master of Red Hall, sat alone. The feared hall master of Red Hall was known for his strange behavior, but no one expected him to arrive with only a single warrior as an escort. That warrior had even been sent away once the hall master had arrived.

The three dukes and two hall masters made up the main strength of the Talov Duchy. After those five came the marquesses, counts, viscounts, and barons. Warriors without titles were standing behind their respective lords. All waited patiently for Duke Valens to begin the gathering.

At the farthest part of the Grand Hall were the warriors of Hollowell, and at their front was Oh'ash. Their bound bodies were quite noticeable, but only the bravest of the warriors looked in their direction. Due to them not being under the control of the archduke, their seats were farthest away. Many feared that the warriors of Hollowell would take offense, but when Oh'ash had led his people into the hall, they had taken their place quietly.

"I thank you for coming in this desperate hour," Duke Valens began. His voice caused all muttering to cease. "As many of you are aware, I have called for this gathering to discuss the recent tragic incidents that have plagued our duchy. Our beloved crown prince was cruelly murdered by his own brother. Learning of this, Archduke Ambrose has fallen ill. In order to quell the chaos, I recommend we elect a regent until everything calms down."

"And I suppose that you believe that you should be regent," shouted one of the marquesses who wasn't on good terms with Duke Valens.

"Who else besides His Grace can lead as regent? Not only is he one of the leading figures of the duchy, but his family's power is second only to the Talovs themselves," one of Duke Valens's supporters argued back.

The entire hall quickly began to argue over who should reign as regent. Each warrior that wished it was given time to speak. Either giving their reason to be named regent to those saying one of the dukes should rcign. No one spoke up for the hall masters, as they never left their domains unless called upon, like today. No one even needed to ask about the members of Hollowell, who watched the commotion with little interest, their emotions hidden under all the wrappings. In the end, two groups were formed, one supporting Duke Valens as regent and one taking a stand against him, and the arguments intensified.

"His Grace is the only proper choice to be named regent," yelled another one of Duke Valens's supporters.

"How can you say that? Someone who relied on his father's achievements to get where he is will never make a good regent," retorted someone on the opposite side.

"How dare you say that about His Grace! To uphold His Grace's honor, I challenge you to a duel," the supporter yelled back as he drew his sword, pointing it at the one arguing with him.

Soon more warriors began to issue challenges to one another. With tensions rising, some of the onlookers began to worry that there would soon be a bloodbath. When a couple of warriors stood to charge their foes, Lord Jukel Altares slammed his fist on the table in front of him. The strike cracked the table, and the loud boom got everyone's attention.

"If all of you are finished making fools of yourselves, I need to remind you of something," Altares said in a harsh tone. "A regent can only be named when there is no one of Talov blood who can take the throne. As I recall, Princess Aris is still alive and well, and she is sharp enough to lead us."

Everyone began to look at one another. They all knew that Princess Aris Talov was bright and had done a great job on the council. However, even with all her achievements, no one really thought of her as someone who could lead them, and for one important reason.

"A woman cannot rule the duchy," someone finally shouted out. After the first, many others voiced their opinions, most of which were agreeing with the first shout.

"That is right. A woman is not strong enough to lead warriors into battle," one warrior shouted. He was large and covered in scars from his years of serving his lord.

"Never in the history of our duchy have we been ruled by a woman," another warrior, with the title of count, argued.

"I will not kneel for a woman even if she has the blood of the Talov line," a more aggressive voice chimed in. Many were shocked by the declaration and took a few steps back in order to avoid being roped in with this warrior.

Just as they had feared, when Temperance Morwood heard the warrior yell that he would not kneel, she was outraged, but unlike the hotheaded men, she became cold. "So, if all of you think a woman cannot lead, then what about me? Since my husband's untimely demise, I have been ruling over Morwood Forest for the past decade. Could it be you honorable men can't see past your own egos to see that?" the duchess said. Each of her words came out calm but vicious, causing the warrior who had said he would refuse to kneel to step back and hide behind the others.

"Duchess, none of us are saying that you haven't done an exemplary job as Duchess of Morwood Forest. We all know that your lands have flourished under your guidance," Duke Valens said, trying to calm down the duchess.

Temperance Morwood was quite famous in the three duchies. After her husband's passing, and her only son being a toddler, she had taken up the title as duchess, even without being a member of the Morwood bloodline. Many had been against this, and the former duke's brothers had tried to take control of Morwood Forest, but the duchess was more intelligent than her departed husband. She easily outwitted the usurpers and went to Raven's Nest to personally ask for the archduke's blessing. Impressed by this brave showing, Archduke Ambrose gave her the right to rule until her son came of age. Since then the Morwoods had prospered beyond what anyone could have imagined.

"What are you trying to say, Duke?" Duchess Morwood said sarcastically. She and the duke had never had a very friendly relationship in the first place. She wasn't going to allow him to gain power now.

"Duchess, we are only worried about the stability and prosperity of the duchy," Duke Aleo said.

"And when did you become Duke Valens's lackey, Sergei?" Duchess Morwood mocked the duke, calling him by his first name as a form of insult. "I guess I shouldn't expect better from some young blood like you."

"I am no one's lackey!" Duke Aleo shouted furiously. The vein on his forehead thumped angrily, which was obvious due to the duke's bald head. "I may not be a descendant of a founding family, like the Morwoods, but I have my own honor for my family. I will not let you smear it by speaking false accusations."

Sergio Aleo was the descendant of Marth Aleo, a man who had earned his warrior status during the Splintering War, which had given rise to the three duchies. His family was the youngest of the high-ranking warrior families. The term *young blood* was an insult given to warrior families who came about after the Splintering War. There was always tension between the two sides, and the Aleo family was considered the leader of the said young bloods.

With the duke and duchess seeming ready to rip each other's head off, one of the marquesses who was in support of Duke Valens suddenly asked the question some were beginning to form in their heads. "Where is Princess Aris, anyways? We are discussing the very future of the Talov Duchy. It isn't proper for someone of the Talov lineage to not be present at this gathering."

More voices began agreeing with the marquess, and soon people were outright insulting the princess for not appearing. Those who were against Duke Valens felt that this was all too coincidental for them all to speak up at once.

Before they could say anything, Duke Valens answered. "Regretfully, the stress has been too much for our poor princess, and yesterday she suddenly collapsed. I wanted to keep this confidential, but with so many wanting to know her whereabouts, I can only relent." He gave a heartfelt sigh as if he were truly worried for the princess.

"If she cannot even stand all that is happening now, then she won't be able to handle the responsibilities of being the Archduchess of the Talov Duchy," one warrior shouted out.

Soon those who were not sure who to side with began to side with Duke Valens. Even if he was out for himself, he had proved his skills in politics and warrior law. The princess was similar but had only joined the council last year, and even though she did a good job, many were still unconvinced. Before long, three-quarters of the gathered warriors were in support of the duke.

With everything going his way, Duke Valens asked for a vote. With no way of stopping it, those who didn't wish to see Duke Valens reign as regent could only hold their tongues and watch as the votes were cast in the duke's favor.

Applause echoed through the hall when the final vote was read: the duke had a majority of the votes. As the duke's side cheered, the other side sat in silence. Some didn't even try to hide their displeasure at seeing the duke named regent. The duchess had one of the worst scowls plastered on her face as she watched the warriors cheer.

"These fools don't know that they are cheering a usurper," Jukel Altares II, son of the Stone Hall master, muttered under his breath, so that only his warriors could hear him.

"Son, you can't slander someone like that without proof," Lord Altares warned his hotheaded son.

"Father, you can't honestly believe his story of the princess falling ill due to stress. That woman wouldn't stop working even if she had an arrow through her chest," the young Jukel said.

"Sir, calling the princess 'that woman' is improper," one of the Stone Hall warriors remarked.

"I didn't ask you, Knox. Why don't you continue doing what you do best, licking my father's boots?" young Jukel scoffed. He clearly didn't care for the warrior called Knox.

"Now isn't the time for infighting," Lord Altares declared. "We must figure out what has happened to Princess Aris and find a way to contact her. Knox, once this gathering is over, I want you to search for anyone connected to Princess Aris."

"Yes, my lord," answered the warrior Knox, giving his lord a fisted salute.

Jukel only gave a snort of displeasure at his father for sticking up for Knox. Knox had always been his father's favorite warrior, and his father trusted him more than any other warrior. Even his own son didn't have as much sway over the hall master as Knox did.

Having no reason to stay there any longer, Lord Altares and his warriors stood to leave. This didn't go unnoticed, and those on the duke's side grimaced, as the Stone Hall master was one of the main opponents of Duke Valens.

"Congratulations, Your Grace, for being chosen as regent, but I must advise you get the holy city's blessing as soon as you can," Lord Altares said.

"Not to worry, Lord Altares. I have already dispatched word to the holy city for a priest to come and bless my inauguration as regent," Duke Valens answered with a laugh. He, more than anyone, knew the importance of Ridia's backing. Without it, the title of regent was only an empty title.

"Then it seems my concerns are unnecessary. My warriors and I will take our leave, then," Lord Altares said.

"Lord Altares, please stay. I have prepared a feast for this occasion," Duke Valens said. His words drew in the warriors. Many began to look at the Stone Hall master with contempt.

"Thank you, but I don't see this as an occasion to celebrate," Lord Altares responded. "And by the looks of it, I am not the only one who thinks that way."

Looking around, everyone realized that there were a few people missing from the Grand Hall. When no one had been aware, Oh'ash had disappeared with his warriors. Not only were the warriors from Hollowell missing, the hall master of Red Hall had left, as well as Duchess Morwood.

Duke Valens's smile fell when he saw the empty seats. He had been so caught up in his triumph that he hadn't noticed them leave. While the hall master, who had come alone, would have been able to leave undetected quite easily, the Hollowell warriors and Morwoods had come in a large group. Someone should have told him when they had left. He gave his followers a slight look that made them look away in embarrassment for not noticing the two groups' departure.

"Then don't let me keep you any longer," Duke Valens said. He had lost some of the delight he had just acquired from becoming regent and wasn't too keen on keeping those who were against him here, anyway.

Once the Stone Hall warriors and those who took the chance to leave with them were gone, the mood changed to a celebratory one. None of them thought it was wrong to toast the duke's luck. They turned a blind eye to what was really happening for the chance to gain more wealth and power. Duke Valens watched them all with a smirk that had returned to his face. It was his time, and he wouldn't let anyone get in his way.

+

Locked away in the eastern tower of the palace, Aris looked out through the small window. From there she could see dignitaries from across the duchy arrive for the gathering. She didn't have much hope that Duke Valens wouldn't be named regent. The scheming man had laid out everything too perfectly. The moment someone brought up her right to the throne, they would make some excuse for her not being at the gathering, painting her as the one at fault. Without her, Duke Valens would easily gather the neutral warriors to his side.

Just as she had thought, the first ones out being the Hollowell warriors and Red Hall master told her Duke Valens had succeeded. As she watched them, she thought she saw Oh'ash glance in her direction. Startled, she stepped away from the window. When she turned back, Oh'ash was walking out of the courtyard, making Aris believe that she must have been mistaken. Where she was, it would have been impossible for Oh'ash to have noticed her.

After the Hollowell warriors and hall master came Lord Altares with the Stone Hall warriors. Several other warriors also departed alongside the Stone Hall master. Aris made sure to remember these warriors. Seeing those who had stood up against Duke Valens gave Aris some hope to turn this around. All she needed to do was figure out a way to get in contact with them.

As she watched all this through her small window, she heard footsteps heading toward her room. The door, which was locked from the outside, clicked and, without even a knock, was slammed open.

A warrior walked in carrying a tray of food. Aris knew this warrior and gave him a look of disdain. The warrior was one of Duke Valens's, and she could remember in vivid detail when this man had used the sword that was at his waist to kill Pierce.

"Food from the festivities below," the warrior said, dropping the tray on the small table. Half of the bowl of soup splashed out and dampened the rest of the

233

meal, but the warrior didn't care in the least. His job was to bring the princess her meals, and nothing more.

With his job completed, the warrior turned and left the room, treating Princess Aris not unlike a normal prisoner. He was so determined to have his job finished quickly he hadn't noticed the shadow that had entered along with him, staying behind when he left.

"It is good to see that you are all right, Lexi," Aris said.

From the corner of the room, the princess's handmaiden Lexi revealed herself. Walking to the princess, she knelt at Aris's feet. "Your Highness, please punish me for leaving you behind and escaping on my own that day," Lexi said, bowing. Her head stayed bowed as she awaited her princess's punishment.

"Raise your head, as there is no need for punishment. If you had stayed and fought, then you would have ended up dead as well," Princess Aris said. Pain filled her when thinking about the deceased Pierce.

Roan and Pierce had been personally picked by her to become her personal warriors. When she had come of age, her grandfather had tried to present her with honorable warriors to be her personal warriors. Sadly, not a single one had Aris taken a fancy to, and they were sent away only a few days later.

When the archduke was at his wits' end, he ordered her to find her warriors herself. Aris was delighted by the idea and went through each warrior barracks and each chivalric order personally. She traveled throughout the duchy in search. In the end, she found her two warriors.

The funny thing was that while the two of them were strong and had strong wills, neither of those attributes was the reason that Aris had chosen them. When she had arrived at a small town, one close to Morwood Forest, she had accidentally stumbled on the two of them practicing, but it wasn't their swordplay; it was their instruments.

Aris was intrigued by the notion of warriors practicing one of the three arts and secretly listened in. By the end of the song, Aris knew that these two would be perfect warriors to stay at her side.

The two proved to be just the right fit and became the princess's right and left hands. It was partly thanks to them that Aris had been able to get so far, but now she was locked away; Pierce was dead; and she didn't know whether Roan had accomplished his task of finding her brother. He may have ended up with an arrow in his back from one of the warriors in league with the treacherous Duke Valens.

"Ma'am, are you all right?" Lexi asked. When she had gotten permission to lift her head, she had discovered that her princess had tears forming in her eyes. Bewildered, she could only think to ask whether she was all right.

"I'm fine. Apologies for making you worry," Aris said, wiping a tear from the corner of her eye.

"Not at all. My duty is to serve you to the best of my abilities no matter what. If you ask me to, I will do whatever you wish of me," Lexi responded. Her words echoed the conviction Aris heard in her tone.

"There is something I need you to do for me," Aris said. Making her way to the small desk, she jotted down a letter and, with some wax from a nearby candle, sealed it before handing it over to Lexi. "I need you to deliver this letter for me."

"Yes, ma'am," Lexi said, giving Aris a bow. "And who do you wish for me to give this letter to?"

"Bring the letter to Lord Altares of Stone Hall. He has always been someone who can see the bigger picture. He will be needed if we wish to stop Duke Valens from taking over the duchy," Aris said, her fist trembling in rage at the thought of Duke Valens.

With the letter in hand, Lexi gave Aris one last bow before hiding in the corner of the room. Knowing what to do, Aris called for the warrior guarding the door—the one there to prevent her from escaping. The lock clicked and the door slammed open.

"What is it?" the warrior demanded, looking at the princess.

"You can take that away. I'm not in the mood to eat," Aris said, pointing at the meal the previous warrior had brought.

Grunting in frustration, the warrior entered and took the tray of food. When he did, Lexi took the opportunity to sneak out. The warrior didn't know that he had been fooled as he carried the tray away, slamming the door shut behind him.

With her plan beginning to be put into motion, Aris once more looked out the small window. In her mind, she began to weave a plan to foil the duke's evil scheme.

Chapter Nineteen: Those Who Wait and Those Who Search

The town of Hensgrove was like any small town in the Talov Duchy. The men went to work the fields, while the women stayed in town, doing the chores and chasing after the children who went around playing warriors. The only thing that this town had that made it different was its proximity to the treacherous Verilis Forest. In this quiet town, without a single warrior family, no one would ever think that the most wanted person in the three duchies was drawing water from the town well like any other commoner.

Prince Leander Talov carried the pail of water back to the home of one of the villagers, who had graciously allowed them to stay with him. The villagers stared at the prince with looks of interest and curiosity. Some of the young women who were whispering to one another blushed as Leander looked their way, their whispering and giggling growing. The young men who saw the women act this way gave the prince a look, trying to intimidate him and show their own masculinity. Sadly, the prince was not intimidated in the slightest, and the young men looked more like children trying to threaten an adult.

As he neared the house they were staying at, Leander noticed a small crowd that had formed around the house. Parents lifted their children to allow them to see over the crowd. Pushing his way through, Leander found what had caused the gathering.

Sitting on a stump in front of the small house was the sell-sword Lucis. He sat there as he sharpened his sword, unaware of the crowd that had gathered. Every time he pushed the stone over the steel of his sword, it made a smooth sound. Leander saw this and knew why the crowd had gathered. Simply by moving the whetstone, Lucis was able to captivate the villagers into watching such a mundane task.

"You're late," Lucis said to Leander, not looking up from his sharpening, making all the villagers wonder how he knew that Leander had returned. Broken from their trance, the villagers dispersed.

"Then you go get the water. It was your idea to stay here. I wanted to leave days ago," Leander said, placing the pail by the door for the day's use.

After they had escaped from Verilis Forest and the pursuing warriors, they had found themselves at this town. The villagers were at first shocked to see the two of them leaving the forest, as they had been told since childhood that the forest was a dangerous place, but Leander was quick-witted and told them that they were warriors who had gotten lost. The villagers, who hadn't seen a warrior in some time, took them in as guests, an offer that the two accepted with gratitude.

Leander thought that once they had regained their strength, they would continue for Raven's Nest, but the next day, Lucis announced that they were staying. When asked for how long, Lucis had replied, "Until Aer finds his way here." Leander wanted to continue, as he worried for his sister and grandfather, but Lucis was adamant about waiting for his brother to arrive.

"I told you that both Aer and I agreed to escort you back to Raven's Nest. If you wish to continue alone, then go ahead," Lucis replied as he sheathed his sword, which shone from the care he showed it.

Leander had been through this before and knew he would not convince the man, so he kept his mouth shut.

Lucis saw the frustration in the prince and sighed. "Let's go get a drink. The tavern will soon be quite packed, as the men will be finishing their work soon," he said, patting the prince on the shoulder.

With that, the two of them headed to the tavern. Due to the village's small size, it didn't have amenities like an inn or even a store. Most of the villagers bartered or traded with one another rather than used money. The tavern was the only place that sold anything and operated like establishments in the larger towns and cities. It was not as grand as the winehouses that warriors drank in, but it was impressive for a village of this size. It was also the gathering place of the men who would drink and merrymake after a long day's work—until the day turned to night and their wives dragged them home.

Entering the tavern, they were greeted by a bunch of half-drunk men filling their stomachs with ale and cheap wine.

"Lucis, Rick, over here. I have already ordered a pitcher for each of you." One of the men called the two of them over.

When they had decided to stay in the village, they had also decided that using the prince's name was too dangerous. So they thought up the name Rick as Leander's false identity.

The man who had called them over was a large man with muscles gained from years as a farmer. The village was poor and didn't have luxuries such as oxen and horses. The only livestock that they had were pigs and some chickens. Due to this, the men had large upper bodies from the manual labor that they endured.

"Thank you very much, Ernest," Leander said, sitting down at Ernest's table. Ernest was the one who had opened his home to them. He was a kind man but a rather wild drunk. They had learned that one night, when Ernest had tried to pick a fight with Lucis, only to find himself flat on his face with a mouth full of dirt. With all that, he was still a good man, husband, and father.

The table they sat at was one in the corner, away from the rest. Both Lucis and Leander liked the distance, as they never knew when someone might realize who they were. On the other hand, Ernest sat there at the request of the tavern owner, to avoid Ernest starting any more brawls in the tavern.

"It's no problem," Ernest said, slurring his words. The number of empty tankards on the table showed that he was quite drunk, and if that didn't give it away, the smell of alcohol that poured from him certainly did.

As they began to drink, more and more men entered the tavern, and soon a dozen conversations echoed around them, from how one farmer's field was doing poorly to the rumors that someone's wife had been seen with another man—simple topics for men with common lives. The random conversations mixed with the alcohol lightened Leander's mood—that is, until they overheard a certain conversation between two farmers.

"It's true, I tell you. I learned about it when I went to Bellfast to sell some of my crop. Seems Duke Valens has been named regent," the farmer said. His words were picked up by Leander and Lucis, who listened in, ignoring the rantings of their drunk tablemate.

"Why would that be? I know that the archduke is ill, but wouldn't one of his descendants be named regent instead of a duke?" his drinking partner asked.

"What descendants? One prince is on the run for the murder of the other. The only other person left is the princess, and I hear that she had a breakdown. It seems that she didn't even show up for the gathering," the farmer said to his friend as he took another chug of his ale.

Hearing all this, Leander felt his hands tremble, causing him to spill his ale all over the table. Ernest called him out for wasting the precious ale and continued drinking before passing out, unaware of the dark mood Leander was now in.

"Drink. You won't get anything accomplished by getting emotional now," Lucis said, pushing his own tankard over.

"This is why I said that we needed to leave days ago. If I had been there, then I could have proved my innocence, and my sister would be fine. Now that snake Duke Valens is going to be named regent," Leander spat, knocking over the tankard that had been given to him.

"Or you would be locked up, awaiting your execution," Lucis retorted. "The only one who can help you is your grandfather. Without him, do you expect the warriors who are demanding your blood to simply let you speak? Even if you get some people to stand beside you, it will only cause more people to lose their lives with you."

Leander knew what Lucis was saying was right. During this downtime in Hensgrove, Leander had thought about this whole situation. He didn't believe that a single treacherous squire was the one pulling the strings. To get his grandfather to issue a warrant against his own grandson meant that someone with a great amount of power must be the mastermind—someone who was at least a marquess, or even a duke.

When he thought the word *duke*, he immediately thought of the person whose name he had just overheard, Duke Valens. As someone with power close to the archduke, he was the prime choice for regent. Not only that, but his son was engaged to Leander's sister, Princess Aris, and with the way things were going, that would make Sarus the next archduke. The one who would gain the most from all of this would be the duke.

241

With this realized, Leander didn't know what to think. This whole time, he had thought that the evil from the Tarsis Duchy had somehow crossed the border into their own duchy. Now it seemed to be much worse than that. A duke turning traitor would be devastating to the entirety of the Talov Duchy. He may have disliked Duke Valens, but he would never think that someone born into such an honorable warrior family, like the Valenses, could do such a thing.

As he was lost in his thoughts, Lucis suddenly tugged on his sleeve. "Get ready to leave town," Lucis whispered in his ear.

"Leave town now?" Leander said, puzzled. Lucis was the one who wanted to stay and wait for Aer, but now he wanted to leave just before dark?

Not answering, Lucis pointed toward the bar. Turning, Leander saw three men cloaked in hoods talking to the tavern owner. What Leander instantly noticed, and what Lucis was warning him about, was the swords that were strapped to their waists.

"Warriors," Leander said under his breath. "How did they find us?"

After their reunion in Verilis Forest, Lucis and Leander had been cautious to not leave anything behind. They had already been tracked all the way to the forest without realizing, so they had made sure their tracks were dealt with, but it looked as if that just hadn't been enough.

Sure enough, they heard one of the warriors ask, "We are looking for a group of three men who should have left Verilis Forest a couple of days ago. It would be appreciated if you could tell us anything." Leander heard coins hitting the bar—a bribe, most likely.

The tavern owner pocketed the coins before speaking. "I don't know about a group of three, but two warriors arrived not that long ago. They are staying at Ernest's place, just down at the end of the main road," the tavern owner said, not even hesitating to sell out the two of them for a quick coin.

The three warriors didn't thank the man and turned to the exit. As they did, both Lucis and Leander turned away, as they were now in view of the three men. Luckily, the drunk Ernest was perfect cover, making them look like regular villagers. The warriors walked by without noticing that their targets were sitting in the corner of the tavern.

Once the three cloaked warriors were out of sight, Lucis and Leander stood and left the drunken Ernest to his delirious mumblings. Taking the roundabout way to Ernest's house, they found that the warriors were already there, asking Ernest's wife about them. They were too far away for Lucis and Leander to hear anything, but only a few seconds later, the three warriors turned to leave. Ernest's wife looked upset and slammed the door in their wake.

Sneaking around to the back of the home, Lucis and Leander jumped in through a window, scaring the poor older woman half to death. "Yikes! You boys scared the living daylights out of me!" the old woman, Nancy, proclaimed. She grabbed at her chest to stop her heart from beating out of control.

"Sorry. We had no other way of entering without being seen," Lucis said, apologizing to the woman who had let them stay with her.

"Who were those warriors just now?" she asked. "They said they were looking for three people, but the two of you match their descriptions perfectly. Why are warriors hunting for you?"

She looked first to Lucis, but the man kept his mouth tight, and when she turned her attention to Leander, he wanted to tell her. This kind woman had opened her home to them, and now they had brought their trouble with them. It would be dishonorable for him to lie, and it seemed that Lucis agreed. That was why the Zer'sheen remained tight-lipped. Speaking would hinder his duty to protect

Leander, while lying would dishonor him.

"Sorry, Nancy. We have been dishonest with you," Leander said. "My name isn't really Rick. My true name is Leander Talov, prince of the Talov Duchy."

When old Nancy heard this, she took a few steps back. "Prince Leander? The very prince who killed his brother to try and gain the throne? The most wanted person in the three duchies? *That* Prince Leander?" Nancy said, covering her mouth in disbelief.

"I didn't kill my brother, but yes, I am he," Leander said, feeling sad that even in small villages like this, news of his alleged crimes had arrived.

"Wait here," Nancy said. She then rushed into the back rooms. Leander was wondering whether she was looking for a way to escape in order to find those warriors who she had just sent away, but not a second later, the old woman returned with their belongings in her arms.

"You two have to leave before the warriors realize you are still here. I told them that you left this morning without telling anyone," Nancy said, pushing their gear into their arms.

"Why are you doing this?" Leander couldn't help but ask.

"For the past few days that you have been staying with us, I have learned much about you. Not only do you help around the house, but you are always polite. You might have been a little antsy, but now I know that you are the infamous Prince Leander, I can understand," said Nancy. "Someone like you wouldn't be able to kill his own brother."

Leander didn't know when they had started, but tears were falling from his eyes. Since he had been forced to watch Bez kill his brother, no one had doubted the squire's words. Everyone believed that Leander had killed Eustace. Only this old woman, who had only met him a few days ago, believed that he was innocent.

"Thank you," Leander muttered. "Thank you so much."

"Now is not the time. I told them that you had headed north, so head east. There is an abandoned farm only a few miles out. The barn is surrounded by woods and undergrowth, making it completely invisible from the road. You can hide from the searching warriors there," Nancy said.

After saying their goodbyes, Lucis and Leander made their way back out the window they had crawled in through. The setting sun cast large shadows over the village, making their escape a relative breeze. Outside the small village of Hensgrove, they carefully made their way through the farmland, keeping just off the road to avoid being seen. When they found their way to the abandoned barn the moon was high in the sky.

The barn was overgrown and had half collapsed. While the barn would give them an appropriate amount of shelter from the cold wind, if they compared it to the warm but tiny home of Ernest and Nancy, it was quite the downgrade.

The inside was almost as bad as the outside. The part of the roof that had collapsed had littered the ground with rubble. Cobwebs coated the barn like a white blanket over a bed. They could hear the scurrying of rats or other small rodents trying to hide from the trespassers. If there was one thing good about this barn, it was that it was warm and dry compared to the wilderness outside its rotting walls.

"I'll clear out a space for us to sleep," Lucis said, putting down his pack. Dust shot up when the pack hit the ground. "Grab some dried meat out of your pack to eat tonight. We will have to make do with just our coats. It will be too dangerous to light a fire, as it might draw the attention of the searching warriors."

As Lucis started picking up some of the rotting boards that covered the ground, Leander reached into his pack and grabbed a piece of dried pork and shoved it into his mouth. The meat was stale and salty, not like the warm meals that Nancy had cooked for them.

After finishing up the dried pork, Leander helped Lucis finish clearing a place to sleep. They moved the fallen boards around, making a barricade, allowing only one way to enter the barn. If anyone did discover the barn, they wouldn't be able to sneak up on them.

Lucis offered to take the first watch, leaving Leander to try to get some rest, but sleep eluded the prince. Every time he closed his eyes, he would think about what he had heard in the tavern. Returning to the capital was already a dangerous task, but with Duke Valens now regent, it had become a suicide mission, especially if the duke was the mastermind behind his brother's murder.

Unable to sleep, Leander made his way over to Lucis, who was leaning against the entrance of the barn. The sell-sword didn't show that he noticed Leander approach, but Leander knew that Lucis had most likely known he had been awake the entire time.

Lucis looked up at the night sky with longing. Leander knew that if it hadn't been for the warriors searching for them, then Lucis would have stayed in Hensgrove until Aer appeared, or until the mark on his chest vanished. Due to the mark on Lucis's chest, they knew that Aer was still alive. The problem was the mark only told them that Aer was alive. He could be injured and unable to move, or he could have been captured by the Talov warriors hunting them. They just had no way of knowing what fate had befallen Aer.

"Go back to sleep. You will need all your energy when tomorrow comes," Lucis said, looking over to Leander. The scar that framed one side of his face was quite eye-catching, but in the moonlight, Leander felt that the scar looked less menacing in some way.

"I know I need to. Problem is, too much has happened today, and I haven't had the time to process it all yet," Leander answered, sitting down next to the leaning Lucis.

"Is this about what you overheard in the tavern?" Lucis asked.

"I know my sister well. She has a stronger will than either Eustace or myself. Even Grandfather has said that it is a pity she wasn't born a boy, as she has the strength and mind to rule the duchy. I just can't believe that a woman who makes the members of the council tremble in fear would have had a mental breakdown. It just doesn't make sense," Leander began ranting.

During his travels with this Zer'sheen who was also a sell-sword, something had happened that Leander hadn't realized right away. He had begun to desire Lucis's approval and wanted to know what a man who had gained the recognition of the Phoenix God thought.

"You think that someone is plotting against the princess," Lucis said, understanding what Leander was going on about. "Do you think it is this Duke Valens, who has been named regent?"

"I think so. Duke Valens has always been one who desired more power. If it hadn't been for his father, who is a sworn brother to my grandfather, he wouldn't have been able to move so freely and gain support so easily. Still, the idea of someone from a high-ranking family, like Duke Valens, turning traitor makes me sick."

"Desire is in all of us," Lucis answered. "Most can't control themselves and are driven by their desire, and the desire for wealth and power is one of the strongest desires a man can have. From what you are telling me, you shouldn't be shocked by this duke's betrayal."

"But that isn't the warrior way," Leander argued back. "Warriors aren't supposed to desire things like rank and power. We are given those responsibilities when we prove ourselves worthy of them. Aren't you a Zer'sheen? You, more than anyone, should understand the ways of a warrior."

"Before they are warriors, they are people, and people are susceptible to the pull of temptations. Don't forget, being a warrior doesn't make you higher than others. It just makes you a warrior," Lucis answered back.

The Zer'sheen's words struck a blow to the prince. He had always believed that those who followed the Code of Valor were above normal citizens. Every warrior grew up with this twisted feeling of superiority. They may have been the protectors of the lands of Mezer, but deep down, they all thought the commoners should be worshipping them as heroes.

"Besides, me being a Zer'sheen doesn't make me impervious to the many temptations around. I, too, have fallen to my desires before," Lucis said. He went quiet after saying that, as if remembering his past mistakes.

Leander felt a little disillusioned by Lucis's revelation about Zer'sheen being just men. Zer'sheen were revered by all who lived in the three duchies. Even hearing this from Lucis, a true-blooded Zer'sheen, he held some doubt. Zer'sheen were the Phoenix God's chosen warriors. If he agreed with Lucis's remark, then he would be doubting the very god that watched over the land of Mezer.

"I just can't agree with you on that," Leander said, standing up firmly, looking Lucis directly in the eye. "We were given the Code of Valor and the three virtues so we can walk the correct path and join our god after our deaths. You may be tempted like the rest of us, but you are still a Zer'sheen."

Lucis was quite shocked at the prince's sudden declaration. He looked at the normally quiet and timid prince with wide eyes. He honestly hadn't expected Leander to argue this with him.

"Why do you say that? Does me being a Zer'sheen make me better than other warriors, or people for that matter?" Lucis asked. His gaze narrowed in on the prince, seeming to drill into Leander.

"No, it doesn't," Leander said. Then a revelation hit him. "I now understand what you mean." It was as if a veil had been lifted off him. It made him feel bare and vulnerable, but also lighter.

A slight smile appeared on Lucis's face. "A warrior's belief is hard to change, as they are too stone headed to see any other way. This can be a good thing as well as a bad thing. Just don't think being a warrior means your something more than what you are—a man. The warrior code is there to better oneself, to keep one from going down the wrong path."

Leander stood there, contemplating everything that he had seen and been through in the days after his brother's murder. While being chased, he had never hated the warriors chasing him, as they were just doing their duty. What he really hated was those like Bez, who plotted and murdered under the cover of shadows. This mentality came from all his years listening to the priests and learning of the three virtues.

However, he had also seen things, and done things, that most warriors would shun. He had been helped by criminals while in WestAvri. The Code of Valor said to take nothing from a man who stained his hands with crime and greed. This would also apply to Lucis, who sold his might for money. The code didn't take into account the characteristics of the criminal or the sell-sword, as it painted them all as evil.

Lucis hadn't said that the code was wrong. He had even said that it would lead them to the right path. He wasn't attacking the code but the warriors who turned their backs to its teachings. Just as there could be good found in the criminal world, evil could lurk in the warrior ranks.

Suddenly a flock of birds scattered from a bush not too far away. The flock flew overhead and past the barn. Looking at Lucis, Leander knew that he was thinking the same thing—someone or something was heading their way.

Ducking back into the barn, Lucis and Leander peered out through the cracks of the rotting walls. From the brush came two figures, illuminated in the moonlight. From the newcomers' cloaks, they could tell it was two of the three warriors who had been asking about them in Hensgrove.

"How did they find us?" Leander whispered to Lucis, but the Zer'sheen was in no mood to respond. His hand was on his sword hilt, and his eyes shone with determination, ready for whatever was to come.

The two warriors caught sight of the old barn and decided to check it out. As they neared, Lucis spoke. "Hide behind the fallen door. When they enter, I'll distract them. Take that chance to escape."

"What are you talking about? There are only two of them. If we work together, we can finish them before they call for reinforcements," Leander said. He didn't like the idea of escaping on his own again, not after leaving Aer behind.

"These two are different from ordinary warriors," Lucis answered in a hushed tone. "Even comparing them to all the others, they are a cut above the rest. Just seeing them is making my blood boil with desire to face them, especially the one on the left. He might even be a match for me."

Leander looked back toward the warriors but couldn't see what Lucis was going on about. Sure, they looked mysterious, with their cloaks that covered their faces, but that was it. Also, Lucis hadn't reacted this way when they had first seen the warriors in the tavern. Had something changed in that short amount of time?

As Leander watched them near, the part of the wall he was leaning on cracked. One of the approaching warriors turned and looked right in Leander's direction. Even hidden behind the wall, Leander felt that the warrior was able to see him. A cold chill came over the prince, and he ducked away from the crack he had been peering out of. Gasping for breath, Leander knew that he wouldn't be a match for that warrior.

"Fine, but only if you agree to come after me once I am far enough away," Leander said, looking Lucis square in the face.

Lucis thought for a moment before nodding. His duty to help Prince Leander trumped the desire to duel these two warriors. With Lucis agreeing to Leander's demands, the prince took his position behind the rotten door in the corner of the barn.

The warriors outside quickened their pace toward the barn. Each of their steps could be heard in the silence of the night. As they neared, some clouds covered the moon, making the situation even more treacherous.

Hiding behind the door, Leander could only wait for the warriors to enter. His heart tried to jump out of his chest with each footstep made by the warriors. As Leander waited, Lucis took his position at the back of the barn with his sword drawn, ready for the face-off that was about to commence.

Then Leander saw them, still covered in their cloaks. From their positions, the warriors couldn't see Leander hiding, but they could clearly make out Lucis's silhouette in the back. As the small amount of light bounced off Lucis's sword, the warriors became alert and drew their own weapons.

The one that struck fear into Leander drew out a strange sword. It had neither a guard nor a shine like a normal sword. It looked rather dull and seemed to be unable to cut through anything, but in the warrior's hands, the sword looked to be a reaper of souls, just waiting to claim Lucis's life.

In this decrepit barn, the two warriors and Lucis began their duel. The warrior with the strange sword lunged so fast that Leander almost missed the attack.

Luckily, Lucis was able to see the coming blow and parried the lunge.

With his first attack thwarted, the warrior pushed on. His and Lucis's swords clashed and danced around one another. Leander was in awe watching the two. The warrior truly was as skilled with a sword as Lucis, and maybe even a tad quicker with his strikes. Leander strained to see what was going on between the two in the darkness of the barn, but he could make out their figures as well as the sound of their clashing swords.

While Leander was amazed by the duel going on in front of him, he was quite distressed as well. Looking toward the entrance, he saw that the other warrior was still standing there, watching his partner duel Lucis. Leander cursed under his breath, as he wouldn't be able to escape at this rate, and if he were found, then the situation would only grow in favor of the warriors.

Luckily for the prince, Lucis was able to knock away the warrior he was facing with a heavy blow. While the blow didn't harm the warrior in any real sense, it did cause the other warrior to join the fray.

As the three of them fought, Leander waited until Lucis had baited them far enough into the barn to make his escape. Leaving the safety of the door, Leander crept soundlessly out of the barn, giving Lucis one last look before exiting.

Once outside, Leander began to run with all his strength. He felt guilty over leaving Lucis like that but knew that with his skill, he would only be in Lucis's way.

Making his way east, Leander stayed to the side of the road, in the brush, to keep from being spotted by any other warriors. This made his travel time slower, but seeing several warriors patrolling the road made Leander realize that this had been the correct decision.

Every time Leander heard a noise, he looked back, hoping to see Lucis chasing after him, but every time, he was disappointed. He knew that Lucis had a hard fight on his hands, but to ensure the prince's safety over his own, he had sent Leander away from the struggle.

Since he had watched his brother being killed before his eyes, he had begun to hate this cowardly and weak side of himself. During his time with Lucis and Aer, he had only shown this side to the sell-swords, and when the time had come for him to be of help, Lucis had sent him away. He may have discovered a stronger side to himself inside Verilis Forest, but that didn't make up for how weak he still was.

As he pushed some branches aside, Leander suddenly halted in his tracks. He had noticed something out of the corner of his eye. Not sure he had seen right, Leander fought inside over what to do. In the end, he decided to find out whether what he had seen was real.

Making his way deeper into the wooded area around the main road, Leander found what he had seen, and it turned out he was right. Sitting on a large boulder, wearing a long-hooded cloak, was the third of the three warriors who they had seen in Hensgrove. The warrior sat on the boulder as if waiting for someone. Leander guessed that this warrior must have been separated from the other two.

Only having one shot at surprising the warrior, Leander slowly drew his sword. Leander silently neared the defenseless warrior, but before he could make it all the way, some small animal scurried out from behind him, causing the warrior to turn and see the prince.

Without any other choice, Leander charged him. The warrior jumped to his feet and was able to draw his sword just as Leander struck. As he had been unprepared for the sudden battle, the impact sent the warrior spiraling to the ground, his sword knocked out of his hands. When the warrior tried to reach for his dropped weapon, Leander was already upon him. Slamming his foot onto the warrior, he pinned him to the ground. Just as Leander was about to finish him, the warrior turned around, revealing a face that he would never have believed in a million years would be here at this moment. Rubbing his eyes to check whether he was seeing things, Leander found that what he was seeing was true.

"Elaina? How can it be you?" Leander asked, shocked and unable to get his mind over who he had pinned to the ground with his foot.

The warrior who he had tried to kill with all his strength turned out to be the very princess he wished to marry and spend the rest of his life with. He was so stunned by this, he froze and forgot to move his foot off the princess. Only when he saw her struggling to get up did he realize his mistake and release her.

Leander stammered out an apology. "S-sorry. I just can't believe that it is really you."

The princess didn't answer the prince. Picking herself up, Elaina turned to look straight at Leander. Leander knew that he was in trouble. Elaina was famous for her temper when she got angry, and seeing as he had knocked her down and almost killed her, Leander closed his eyes and waited for the lashing to begin.

He waited, but nothing came. Instead, he felt two arms wrap themselves around his waist. His eyes shot open and looked on in amazement as Elaina buried her face into his chest. Wanting to feel more of her warm embrace, Leander returned Princess Elaina's hug. He felt Elaina's warmth enter him through their embrace, and Leander felt a feeling of peace that he hadn't felt in a long time.

"Elaina, what are you doing here?" Leander asked a second time when he was able to think clearly again. Elaina looked up, and Leander could see that the princess was holding in tears.

"Why else would I be here? I came to find you," she answered. Then she tightened her grip on him. "I'm sorry about what happened to Crown Prince Eustace. I know that you would never harm your brother in any way."

Leander almost broke down upon hearing Elaina's kind words. Knowing that it wasn't the time to be emotional, he let go of his grip on the princess. As she felt Leander release her, Elaina did the same.

Looking her up and down, Leander was quite shocked by what he saw. The Princess Elaina in his memories might have been less feminine than other noble ladies, but she had always worn dresses and other womanly clothes. The princess standing in front of him now was decked out in warrior garb, from the sword on her waist to the leather boots on her feet. She was also covered in grime and dirt. Leander couldn't even imagine what she must have been through to get so filthy.

"By the way, where in Mezer did you get that Talov warrior coat? Because of that, I almost did something I would never be able to take back," Leander said, pointing to the coat covering Elaina. He couldn't help but shiver when thinking that he had almost murdered the woman who held his heart.

"When Kay, Roan, and I made it out of Verilis Forest, we ran into some warriors hunting you. We decided that it would be easier going around in the guise of Talov warriors, so we stole their coats," Elaina answered.

As he listened, Leander was shocked. First of all, the princess had made it through Verilis Forest, as he and Lucis had. Then there was the fact that the princess was not traveling with warriors of her own duchy. He might not know who this Kay was, but the name Roan rang a bell. That was the name of one of his elder sister's personal warriors. He thought about it for a moment but just couldn't think of a reason for Roan, who was supposed to be guarding his sister, and Elaina to be traveling together.

"Wait a moment. Did you say that not only you but your two companions had donned Talov warrior coats as well?" Leander asked with sudden realization flashing through his mind. When he saw Elaina nod, he cursed out loud.

"What is it?" Elaina asked, wondering why Leander suddenly looked so strange.

"Follow me. I'll explain as we run. Hopefully, we are not too late," Leander said as he turned and ran back the way he had come.

Not knowing why, but trusting Leander, Princess Elaina chased after him.

As they raced back to the barn, Leander explained what had transpired there. Elaina's face paled as she, too, realized that the warriors that Lucis was fighting were most likely her two comrades. With no time to waste, they made it back to the collapsing barn.

From the barn, they could hear metal clashing. They rushed in and saw Lucis struggling to fight against the two warriors. While Elaina didn't look too shocked at this, Leander was surprised beyond belief. While he did feel that the warrior wielding the guard-less sword was strong, Lucis was still a Zer'sheen. Zer'sheen were blessed with strength and talent beyond normal men. He shouldn't be struggling so much that several pieces of his clothing were torn, revealing bleeding flesh.

Finally Lucis's sword couldn't take any more, and on a heavy swing from the cloaked warrior, it snapped in two. Not expecting his sword to break on him, Lucis left himself open. The warrior took advantage of this and, with a kick to the chest, knocked Lucis to the ground. As a similar scene to the one Leander and Elaina had just been in was about to unfold, the two knew they had to stop this.

"Lucis!"

"Kay!"

"Stop!"

Chapter Twenty: Reunion Interrupted by a Less-than-Friendly Reunion

T he warrior standing over Lucis froze after hearing the princess's shout. Standing there as if stunned, he removed his hood, revealing someone Leander didn't recognize. He thought that he might remember who this warrior was after seeing him, but now he knew he had never seen the warrior before in his entire life.

"Lucis," muttered Kay, shocked as he looked down at his opponent, realizing that it was his own brother. He then gave the defeated Lucis a grin and offered him his hand.

"I should have known it was you. I knew that I recognized that style of swordplay," Lucis said, accepting Kay's hand.

Seeing that the two knew each other, Roan sheathed his sword, and Leander gave a sigh of relief. They had made it just in time. Any later, and Lucis would have been finished for sure. He was so relieved that he hadn't realized that Lucis, a Zer'sheen, had just been bested, even if it had been two against one.

While Leander breathed out his sigh of relief, Elaina made her way to Kay, Roan, and Lucis. During their time in WestAvri, she had learned that Kay's brothers were the ones helping Prince Leander, so, without being told, she knew that this must be one of the brothers. Her presence wasn't missed by the Zer'sheen, who looked at her with wariness.

"There is no need to be on guard," Kay said with a laugh. "Elaina, this is my brother Lucis. Lucis, this is Elaina Estelle, princess of the Estelle Duchy."

Hearing that Elaina was a princess, Lucis quickly changed his mood and gave her a salute. "My apologies. If I had known, I would not have acted this way toward you," Lucis said with an apologetic look.

Watching this from the side, Leander was feeling conflicted. When his identity as a prince had been discovered by Lucis and Aer, they hadn't acted as Lucis was acting right now. He felt slightly vexed, but seeing as it was Elaina that Lucis was acting this way toward, Leander was able to calm down, and the next words out of the sell-sword Elaina called Kay cleared up any lingering feelings he might have had.

"Princess, my brother here worships the deeds of your father. You might even say he has an unhealthy obsession with Archduke Bennet," Kay said, mocking his brother's actions.

Lucis gave Kay a glare, but the glare didn't conceal the happiness of finally finding his long-lost brother. Sadly, not everyone was there to celebrate. "If only Aer were here. He has been worried sick about you since you left," Lucis said. When he was preparing for Kay to ask where Aer was, he saw that Kay's face grew pale. For a person whose emotions were all but destroyed, it was strange. Feeling that something was off, Lucis asked, "What is it?"

"Lucis, I need you to stay calm as I tell you this," Kay began as he searched for something in his coat pocket. "When we were traveling through Verilis Forest, we came across a clearing. It was covered in blood. When we searched through the clearing, I came across this." Kay pulled out a small and dirty pouch and handed it to Lucis.

Watching this, Leander didn't know what to think. To him, the pouch was something you could find on any person. When he turned to ask Elaina, he saw that her face was gloomy, as was the warrior Roan's. Clearly, they knew what the pouch represented, so Leander chose to keep quiet and listen.

With the pouch in his hand, Lucis's face turned the same shade as Kay's. Looking at Kay, he asked, "This is Aer's pouch, isn't it?"

When his question got an affirmative nod from Kay, Lucis's hand that held the pouch trembled. "Did you see anything else in the clearing? Like whom might have taken him," Lucis asked.

He didn't ask whether they had found Aer's body, as the mark that bound them together was still inked onto both Lucis's and Kay's chests. Sadly, the mark only told them that Aer was alive and not what condition their brother was in at that very moment.

"No. The only thing we discovered in the clearing was strange tracks from a creature I have never seen before," Kay answered. His voice grew quieter when he said the next part. "Lucis, the amount of blood in the clearing wasn't small. If all of it belonged to Aer, I'm afraid he might be …" Kay didn't wish to continue.

Elaina felt sorry for the brothers. While she didn't know this Aer and had only just met Lucis, she had been traveling with Kay for a while now. During this time, he had shown only two emotions: his annoying mocking and his blood craze. She had only seen this sadness when they had first discovered the pouch, and during that time, Kay had been at a loss. Now that things had settled, only the raw emotion remained, and for someone with little emotion left, the pain was far greater than for others.

Elaina wasn't the only one feeling bad for them. Leander looked at Lucis, who was also showing his pain. The prince had been with Aer and Lucis for days and had grown close to the two sell-swords. He himself felt sorrow from hearing that Aer might have been tortured half to death.

Lucis stood there in silence and misery, but over time, he was able to rein in his emotions. "It's all right. As long as Aer is alive, we will find him again," Lucis vowed, grasping at the part of his chest where the mark was.

The resolve and control Lucis showed impressed all of them. Elaina turned to Kay and gave the man a mocking smirk. Kay rubbed his head, as he knew what Elaina was thinking: he had acted foolishly in the forest when he had discovered the pouch, while his brother was able to stay calm and reasonable.

With everything settled, the newly formed group of five decided to finish the night in the forgotten barn. Lucis and Kay sat by one another, talking, while Roan sharpened his sword, as it had been damaged during the duel with Lucis. Elaina took a seat next to Prince Leander, who fidgeted slightly when she sat down. She saw this but didn't say anything. Her whole reason for leaving Esesa had been to find Leander, and she had succeeded. The problem now was what to do. With everything that had been going on, Elaina hadn't had time to think that far ahead yet. She had learned of Leander's plan but wasn't sure whether she should join him, as it might cause their two duchies to begin fighting once more.

"Are you sure that you planned this out? If Duke Valens really is the mastermind behind all of this, as you say ... Now that he has been named regent, Raven's Nest is under his complete control. You will most likely be walking straight into a trap," Elaina said. She wanted him to change his mind and follow her back to Esesa and the Estelle Duchy. Once there they would be safer and would have her father, the archduke, watching over them.

"I have to go," Leander answered. "Both my grandfather and sister are there, and

I don't believe that they will stay fine for long once Duke Valens is on the throne. In order to save them, I must expose the duke for everything he has done."

Elaina saw the determination in Leander—determination that she hadn't seen when he had been visiting Esesa with Crown Prince Eustace only a few days prior. It looked as if going through all that Leander had in these few days had changed him. Elaina felt slightly gloomy seeing this transformation in her childhood friend.

As if feeling Elaina's mood change for the worse, Leander quickly changed the subject. The two talked about what they had been through and what they had seen. When Leander told Elaina about his fight with the lixin beast, Elaina gave Lucis a glare for putting Leander in danger.

"It's all right," Leander said, reassuring her that he was reconciled with what had happened. "If it hadn't been for what happened, I wouldn't have been able to confront myself."

Their discussions continued and soon turned to the topic of their unlikely companions. Elaina had learned in WestAvri of how Leander had met Lucis and Aer, but Leander had no idea of how Elaina had somehow joined up with his sister's personal warrior, as well as a sell-sword who turned out to be Lucis and Aer's missing brother.

However, Leander soon regretted this as Elaina continued to speak. The princess didn't realize it, but every other sentence, she talked about Kay. Most of it was complaining and insulting the sell-sword, but hearing Elaina talk about a man so much was a first for Leander.

Not wanting to hear any more, Leander stood. "We should get some rest," he said. Not waiting for the princess's response, he lay down a few feet away, his back to her.

"All right," Elaina said, confused about Leander's sudden mood swing, but she

261

couldn't disagree about needing rest, so she, too, lay down to get some shut-eye. "What about a lookout?"

"The three of us can keep watch. You and the prince need to replenish your strength," Lucis said, indicating that both Kay and Roan would keep lookout with him, allowing them to rest the entire night.

With everything set, Elaina was the first to fall asleep. Hearing her light breathing, Leander turned to his other side so he could see her. Seeing her sleeping face made Leander feel peaceful. He forgot all about the jealousy he felt for the sell-sword as he, too, fell asleep.

+

Elaina felt someone nudge at her shoulder. Not wanting to be disturbed, she brushed the hand away and went back to sleep, but when the nudging continued, she looked up, annoyed, only to see Kay's face intimately close to her own. Being so close to Kay startled her awake.

"What are you doing?" she tried to shout, but Kay held his hand over her mouth, preventing her from speaking.

"Quiet," Kay whispered, putting his finger to his lips, signaling her to not speak. "We are surrounded."

Elaina bolted up from the ground. Next to her, she saw Lucis waking Leander, who also jumped awake after hearing that they were surrounded. "How did they surround us? Weren't you keeping watch?" Elaina asked, pushing Kay's hand away from her mouth.

"I don't know how, but it seems that they already knew that we were hiding here. By the time we noticed them, they already had the barn surrounded," Kay answered.

Elaina peeked through a hole in the old barn's wall. It was still dark, with only the slightest light coming from the horizon telling of the incoming morning. Even in this darkness, Elaina could see the silhouettes of a dozen warriors from her vantage point. Most likely, there were more flanking them from behind. Elaina guessed that there must be at least a few dozen warriors out there.

As she watched the figures begin to move, from the several she could see, three of them stepped slightly ahead of the rest. The one in the center, who looked to be in charge, shouted to them. "Prince Leander, why don't you come on out of there? It isn't appropriate for a prince such as yourself to stay in such a decrepit place."

Elaina felt that the man sounded familiar. Turning to Leander, she saw him trembling in rage. His nails dug into his palms, and veins appeared at his temples. Leander had recognized the man from his voice.

"Leander, who is that person?" Elaina asked.

"Bez. That vile little worm," Leander cursed, spitting out the name of his brother's former squire as if it were toxic.

Elaina looked back through the hole and stared daggers at Bez's silhouette. Leander had told her that Bez was not only the one to stage the murders of him and his brother but was also the one who personally struck down Crown Prince Eustace. She couldn't see the vile man's face, but from his tone, Elaina could feel the man smirking toward them.

"Are you just going to hide in there? Hide away just like you did when your brother was murdered? It seems that hiding is the only thing a worthless prince like you is good at," Bez's voice called out once more.

"I have to face him," Leander suddenly said. Elaina and the rest looked at him, wondering what the prince was thinking.

"If you leave the barn, you will be vulnerable to their archers. You can't let the man goad you like this," Roan said, trying to persuade the prince, but the prince shook his head. He was determined to face his brother's killer.

Walking up to some rotten floorboards, Leander pulled one away. Holding it like a makeshift shield, he turned to Lucis and Kay, and asked, "I can't order you to follow me out, but I will ask. Will you join me?"

Seeing the prince's resolution, Lucis, too, pulled out a board to use himself.

Kay, on the other hand, gave a slight laugh. "You never came across as a madman," Kay said. "But I like it."

"If the three of you are going out, then I can't be hiding in here," Roan said, agreeing to venture out into battle with the prince and sell-swords.

As the four of them readied themselves, Elaina felt something well up inside her. She had felt this strange emotion before—the feeling of her blood rushing through her veins as her senses went on overdrive. When she had first met Kay, she had experienced this same feeling, and now she knew what it was.

As she took her place next to Leander, the prince looked at her with cold eyes. "You will not be going out with us," he declared.

Elaina felt shocked, then hurt, by what Leander had said. What had been the reason for her to go on this mission if not to help Leander in times of need? Ever since she had left Esesa, she had been ready to fight. Looking away from the prince and to the entrance, Elaina said, "I don't need your permission."

Leander didn't want to insult Elaina. He only wanted to keep her safe. He wanted to say more, but Leander felt a hand grasp his shoulder. Turning, he found the sell-sword Kay gripping him.

"You may think it is safer in the barn, but being with the four of us will be safer than alone in a barn that might be broken into," Kay said.

Leander thought it over for a second and believed that Kay may be right. During the confrontation with the warriors, if any could get to Elaina when she was alone, she would be in more danger than she would be in outside with them. Not only that, but both Lucis and Kay were strong. With them by the princess's side, Leander wouldn't have to worry about Elaina as much.

Taking the lead, Leander left the safety of the barn, followed by Lucis and Kay. Roan stood by Elaina, who was several paces behind the sell-swords and the prince. Once out of the old barn, they were able to see the warriors that surrounded them. Besides the warriors who had been visible through the holes in the barn walls, they caught another dozen or so making their way to the barn from the opposite side.

Standing in front of them was the traitorous Bez. On one side of the former squire was a man wearing a green coat. He had a longbow in his grip. On his other side was a young boy. The boy had a blank look on his face, almost as if the boy were a life-size doll rather than a human. Elaina felt herself grow cold when she peered into the young boy's dead eyes.

As he watched Leander and the rest exit the barn, Bez felt quite pleased with himself. He may have failed to catch them in Verilis Forest, but now that they were trapped, there was no way for the prince to escape. After he saw Leander and the sell-sword Lucis, he turned his attention to the rest of the group. Thanks to the Hunter, he knew that there were three other people in the barn with the prince and Lucis. He didn't recognize Kay, who had walked out with the prince, but he did recognize the other two. Roan was Princess Aris's personal warrior and was quite well known in Raven's Nest. He knew that Roan had been sent to find the prince, but he was still surprised that the warrior had accomplished his task. If he was shocked by seeing Roan, he was struck silly when he saw Princess Elaina Estelle walk out with Roan.

"Princess Elaina," Bez said with a salute and bow.

His voice sounded respectful, but the words directed toward her made Elaina want to vomit.

"Don't you speak my name with your vile tongue," Elaina snapped at the treacherous Bez, whose smug smile cracked at her words.

The princess's words had struck a blow to the man's ego. Holding himself together, Bez recovered his grin. "Your Highness, I don't know what this traitor has told you, but you can't believe a word from his mouth. A person who can kill his own brother cannot be trusted. I ask you to step aside so we can fulfill our duty," Bez said.

Elaina scoffed at the man. She had never seen someone so shameless. Looking at Bez in contempt, she answered, "I have heard what you have to say, and I have heard what Leander has to say, and between the two of you, I choose to believe Leander."

Bez was now trembling in rage. He no longer had a smile on his face and instead had a scowl. "Fine, then. If you wish to perish along with the prince, then so be it. My master may even reward me when I bring him not only the head of Prince Leander but the head of the daughter of Archduke Bennet," he said.

"Do you honestly expect Duke Valens to be happy with Princess Elaina's death? Killing her would only cause the duke nothing but headaches, as he is still trying to take over the duchy," Roan spoke up.

Bez turned to Roan with disgust. "A warrior like you dares to speak up to me? You may be Princess Aris's personal warrior, but to everyone else, you and that bastard Pierce are nothing more than disgraces," he said, spitting when he had finished.

"You …" Roan said, unable to speak from how furious he had become at the traitor's words.

"As for your worries, I don't care if the duke finds the princess's death troublesome," Bez answered, looking down at them with murder in his eyes.

The warriors around unsheathed their swords and awaited Bez's orders.

Leander and Roan were too enraged to hear the underlining meaning in Bez's words, but Elaina did. She heard in his tone how much Bez feared and respected the one he called his master, but when he spoke of Duke Valens, all she heard was contempt. Someone so devout should have been unable to even think a devious thing about their lord, much less speak about them in such a tone. The only answer that Elaina could think of was that Bez wasn't under the duke's control. That must mean there was someone else in the shadows, making all this happen.

Elaina wasn't the only one who had realized this. When she looked at Kay, she saw that the man had a pondering look in his eyes, and she knew that he must have noticed Bez's slipup as well. Lucis also noticed a second later.

"Bez, Karsic has ordered us to find the prince and kill him, not for you to goad and mock them," the man with the bow said. He was speaking up for the first time. The words came out calm and monotonous. It was as if he were not speaking of murdering the heir to one of the three duchies of Mezer.

When Lucis and Kay heard the name Karsic, their moods changed. They had already been on high alert, being surrounded by warriors, but they now produced a murderous intent so powerful that Elaina had to take a step back, and even then, she could feel a cold sweat that flowed down the nape of her neck.

"You are one of Karsic's men," Kay said in a venomous tone.

As Kay glared at Bez, he caused the latter to take a few steps back in fear. When Bez remembered that they had overwhelming numbers compared to just the five of them, he turned crimson in shame. Composing himself, Bez barked out, "Lord Karsic warned me about some sell-swords who might be traveling with the prince, and who know of his existence. You must be one of them. No matter. You will just end up like that brother of yours—at the mercy of my master."

Those words rattled both Kay and Lucis. "What did you just say?" Lucis finally said through clenched teeth.

Bez looked at Lucis and felt the feeling of being superior to this man run through him. "You heard me. When we were tracking you through Verilis Forest, we came across your brother. I believe his name was Aer. The blasted man refused to tell us your location no matter how much he was tortured. As a man who sells his services for coin, he was foolish," Bez answered.

Kay had had enough of listening to Bez and took several steps, but as he was about to charge the man, an arrow flew straight toward him. Reacting with inhuman reflexes, Kay was able to move his head out of the way, and the arrow flew past his ear. Kay glared at the cloaked man who had shot at him.

"Where is my brother?" Kay demanded. Elaina noticed that the madness of the blood craze was once more appearing in Kay.

Bez felt more ecstasy from seeing them all squirm than he had ever felt before, and he decided to tell them, hoping to see them writhing in agony more. "After refusing to tell us anything, it was decided that he will be tortured to within an inch of his life. Only when he cannot stand living will he be put out of his misery," Bez said as he laughed like a maniac. Even some of the warriors he had brought were looking at him in disbelief and disgust, but Bez was so self-absorbed that he failed to notice.

"I will make sure that today will be the day you take your last breath," Prince Leander declared.

His voice was strong and rattled the warriors surrounding them. Being Talov warriors, many had seen the prince, but none had seen him this courageous before.

"I would like to see you try," Bez mocked. Then, with a wave of his hand, he ordered the warriors to attack.

Several of the warriors, who were proficient with a bow, rained arrows on the three, while the rest made their way toward the barn. Using the broken planks, they were able to deflect the arrows. Kay, who hadn't grabbed a board, moved out of the way, barely avoiding being stuck by the oncoming arrows.

"Back to the barn!" Lucis ordered.

No one argued. They were sitting ducks if they stayed out in the open. They may have avoided the first volley of arrows, but the chances of them being unharmed by the next were slim.

Back inside the barn, Elaina found herself the one farthest from the entrance. Leander was standing beside her, while Kay, Lucis, and Roan stood at the front. They didn't have to wait long before the first of the enemy warriors charged through the entrance, but before they could do anything, Lucis and Kay were upon them.

The two sell-swords struck one warrior down after another. The warriors left were quick to react, and the fighting commenced. Roan joined the fray to try to even the odds, but even with his help, the three of them were fighting three on one, and there were more warriors awaiting them outside the barn.

Two warriors who weren't confronting the three noticed Leander and Elaina at the back. Seeing this as their chance, they rushed the prince and princess. Roan saw this and tried to reach them but was blocked by more warriors.

As the warriors drew near, Elaina prepared herself, but before she could, Leander stood in her way. "You stay back. I should be able to face two warriors on my own," he said to her.

Elaina wanted to argue, but Leander had already moved to face the two warriors. Seeing their prey come to them, the warriors lunged at the prince. Swords clashed, and Leander was able to hold off the warriors' attack, but the warriors weren't intimidated by this. They saw how the prince's hands quivered after their strikes.

As the warriors continued their assault, Leander found himself in a precarious situation. He was able to hold them at bay for a few rounds but found himself taking several scratches and cuts in order to keep fighting.

Finally Leander made a mistake and overswung his sword, leaving his back to a warrior's mercy. Leander knew he was done for and braced himself for the impact of steel cutting into his flesh, but the strike never came. Instead, he heard a loud groan from behind him. Turning, he found the warrior dead, with Elaina standing over the man's motionless body.

Elaina looked at Leander for only a second before turning her attention to the remaining warrior, who was keeping his distance. She had seen Leander struggling during the fight, and waited for the right time to move. When Leander had been vulnerable, the warrior had taken the opportunity, but it had left him defenseless. With no one paying her mind, Elaina had been able to sneak up and run the warrior through.

Her sword slid free when the man's body fell to the ground.

"Elaina? What …?" Leander stuttered, not knowing what to say. He had never expected the princess to kill someone. It was for that reason that he had told her to stay behind him. Now he felt like a fool for doing so.

"Hurry and get up!" Elaina barked at the prince. "This is far from over."

Leander obeyed and jumped to his feet. Against the two of them, the warrior left was in trouble. As they were about to strike, an arrow suddenly burst through the wall, heading straight for the prince. Luckily for the prince, the arrow's trajectory shifted off course, and it only grazed him, but it still left a deep cut in his forearm.

Trying to find who had shot the arrow, Elaina saw another fly through one of the holes in the barn wall. "By Ridian's flame! The bastard is shooting through the wall," Elaina cursed, pulling Leander to the side, making the arrow miss its mark yet again.

As the fighting grew ever more intense, bodies began to line the barn floor. Already nine warriors had met their end in this old barn, away from any glory or honor. Several of the deceased had faces showing reluctance as their lives ended, unable to fulfill their hopes and dreams. Elaina would normally feel pity for these lost warriors, but she was too busy fighting for her life.

+

"What is going on in there? Why is it taking so long to kill the five of them?" Bez shouted as he ordered more warriors to rush into the barn.

The leader of this squad of warriors answered. "Sir, the barn may be old, but the walls still hold strong. Any hole big enough to fit through has been blocked, making the only way in the front entrance. Our warriors can only go in two at a time, making our numbers all but useless. Also, the ones protecting the prince seem to be able to rival even the best of our duchy's warriors." He was secretly cursing Bez under his breath for such poor leadership.

"Then why don't you just set the barn on fire? Make it so that they have no choice but to exit," Bez half asked and half ordered.

The warrior had to keep himself from rolling his eyes at such a foolish idea. Seeing as Bez didn't know why it was so foolish, he elaborated. "That won't work. The wood making up the barn is too damp from the night and won't ignite."

As Bez continued his cursing, the Hunter nocked another arrow and loosed it at the barn. The snap of the string made Bez jump, and when he realized that it was only the Hunter and his bow, he was furious.

"Would you quit doing that? All you are doing is wasting arrows shooting at the barn like a madman!" Bez shouted at the Hunter. The Hunter didn't argue back and only strapped his bow over his shoulder and stopped shooting. If Bez had known that the Hunter was able to shoot through the holes in the wall, he might not have ordered him to stop, but the morning was still dark, and the barn wall looked quite solid covered in shadows.

As Bez's anger was about to burst once more, a warrior came rushing from the barn. Seeing the warrior, Bez shouted, "What is it? Why are you running here instead of continuing the attack?"

The warrior wasn't expecting to be shouted at but was able to compose himself. "Sir, we have already lost a dozen men. If we continue like this, I'm afraid most of our warriors will perish."

"Useless! All of you are useless!" Bez yelled in anger. In his rage, he pulled out a strange bell from his pocket. The bell was pitch-black and one solid piece, making it so that it wouldn't produce a sound no matter how hard it was rung. Seeing the bell, the Hunter's eyes widened, and the emotionless young boy's body trembled.

"If warriors can't do the job, then perhaps this can," Bez said with an evil grin as he stared at the bell.

"We still have warriors inside the barn," the Hunter warned.

"Necessary sacrifices," Bez answered. Putting the bell to the young boy's face, he rang it soundlessly.

The two warriors who were also there didn't understand what the bell was, but seeing how the Hunter acted and how Bez had called their comrades "necessary sacrifices," they knew it wasn't anything good. They wanted to stop whatever was about to happen, but they had their orders from the duke and weren't about to turn traitor.

As Bez rang the bell, the young boy's body trembled uncontrollably. His muscles spasmed and grew at an incredible rate. His raggedy clothes tore away from his body as it grew to over the size of an adult male's. The two warriors looked on in horror as the young boy turned into a dreadful ogre.

Only Bez looked at the monstrosity with pride. Pointing at the barn, he ordered, "Go. Kill and destroy everything in that barn."

With its order received, the ogre let out a roar and charged the barn. It was then that the two warriors understood what Bez had meant. That monster would rip through friend and foe alike once it reached its target.

+

In the barn, the fighting continued. The bodies littering the floor caused both groups hardship. More than once did someone trip over a severed limb or slip on some bodily fluids. It really was turning into a scene out of a nightmare.

Elaina felt the sweat drip from her forehead as she pulled her sword out of her defeated foe. The fighting hadn't been going on long, but their enemies were trained warriors. Elaina had been trained by her father, but like all women, she hadn't been expected to become a warrior. The only reason she was able to continue to fight was due to Leander and the rest of her comrades supporting her.

Suddenly, outside the barn, a loud roar of a beast was heard. It was so loud that it drowned out the noise of the fighting. After the roar, the earth started to tremble, and a sound similar to stampeding horses could be heard heading toward them.

Before they could figure out what was happening, the wall of the barn was smashed open. Entering through the now-gaping hole was a monster Elaina had never seen before. The hulking monstrosity towered over everyone in the barn. Its large arms, which reached the ground, looked as if they could tear a person in half with ease.

"What kind of monster is this?" Elaina heard one of the warriors they were fighting shout.

The ogre looked around, then gave another earth-shattering roar as it entered the battle. With a swing of its giant limbs, the beast sent a warrior flying. His body was impaled on a piece of protruding wood. Enraged, another warrior attacked the creature, swinging his sword at the huge beast's side. His strike was true, but before the warrior could celebrate, the beast had him in its grip and, with a pull, ripped the poor warrior in half.

Elaina felt fear the likes of which she had never felt before. She had seen the warrior's strike hit the monster but had also seen that a full-force strike from a warrior had only left a small cut, one that was hardly noticeable on the giant beast's flesh. Taking a step back, Elaina stepped on a board, causing a loud cracking sound and alerting the beast to her presence.

With another roar, the monster charged the princess. Unable to get away, Elaina raised her sword, her hands trembling. Just as the beast was about to reach her, it gave a howl of pain and turned around. Elaina saw that the beast now had a large gash running down its back. The beast bared its teeth at the one who had harmed it, the sell-sword Kay.

"Get out of here now!" Kay yelled to Elaina as the beast charged him, killing several other warriors as it made its way to Kay. Ready for the beast, Kay narrowly dodged by rolling to the side. He gained some distance and started to lure the beast away from the exit, creating an escape route for everyone else.

The remaining warriors were now terrified beyond belief. They began to climb over one another to make their way out.

Elaina felt Leander tug on her wrist as he pulled her toward the hole the beast had made. "We have to go now," the prince said.

"We can't just leave Kay to face that horrific thing alone," Elaina said, trying to stop herself from being dragged any further.

"We aren't strong enough to survive facing that thing. We will only get in the way," Leander said. He knew full well what would happen to them if they tried to face the creature. "Besides, it doesn't look like he will be alone."

It was then that Lucis made his move and struck the beast, slicing a good chunk of flesh out of the beast's leg. While not as deep as the wound Kay had somehow managed to inflict on the beast, it still made the beast howl in pain.

Knowing that Kay had Lucis, a Zer'sheen, by his side, Elaina let herself be dragged out of the barn, with Roan beside them. The warriors they had just been facing ignored them as they fled for their lives. Elaina could hear the fighting and collisions coming from behind them.

The moment they stepped foot out of the barn, Elaina heard Leander wail in pain. Turning, she found that the prince had an arrow straight through his left shoulder. If it had hit just inches lower, it would have gone straight through his heart. Sadly, they didn't have time to think about how lucky they had just been.

"Good to see you again, Your Highness," Bez said as he walked toward them. With him was what remained of the warriors, all of whom had pale faces from seeing their comrades being torn apart by the monster Bez had summoned. "I wonder how long your sell-sword friends can last against one of my master's beasts."

"It was you who brought that monstrosity here," Elaina proclaimed in horror and anger. She hadn't thought that her opinion of this vile man could get any lower, but now she had been proved wrong.

"My master thought we might have difficulties when facing the prince, with all the help he has acquired. So before my master left, he lent me this ogre, along with the way to control it," Bez said as he laughed, savoring his victory.

Elaina knew that they were in trouble. Not only were they exhausted from the fighting, but both Kay and Lucis were keeping the ogre at bay. With their two strongest comrades unable to help, even if Bez only had half his warriors left, he would still be able to kill them with ease.

"I won't hold this up any longer," Bez said, then gave the order. "End them."

Elaina braced herself for the fight, with Leander and Roan on either side of her, but then suddenly something flashed across their vision. A wail of pain came from one of the warriors as he found himself impaled on a spear. The warrior died not knowing who had killed him.

"Who's out there?" Bez yelled, looking around into the surrounding shadows for who had killed one of his men.

Out of the shadows came a man. The man was larger than life as he towered over even the largest among them. Elaina noted that even her father and brothers were shorter than this man, but this man wasn't all muscle, like her family. He was lean and had long limbs. A broadsword was thrown across the man's back, and a short sword was sheathed at his waist.

As the man drew closer, his appearance came into view. He had a chiseled face and several light scars near his eyebrows. He had slight stubble from not shaving for a few days and a pair of gray-green eyes. He was adorned in warrior's armor colored crimson with an emblem in the shape of a chain around a sword.

"A warrior from Red Hall," Elaina said, recognizing the emblem.

"Not just any warrior from Red Hall." Roan spoke as he recognized the man himself. "Only one warrior from Red Hall brings with him a broadsword, spear, and short sword. The Top Sword, Brana Ulfenn, the Executioner of Red Hall."

Upon hearing Roan, everyone looked at the Red Hall warrior in a newfound light. The warriors whose comrade had just been killed by Brana took steps back in terror. They feared becoming the Top Sword's next target. Bez looked at the warrior and had a scowl on his face.

"Brana Ulfenn, not only as a warrior but as a warrior of the Talov Duchy, you should know that Prince Leander Talov is wanted for the murder of the crown prince. What do you think you are doing interfering with us?" Bez shouted at Brana. The warriors looked at him as if he were a fool, and took several more steps back, but this time, away from Bez instead of Brana.

Brana didn't answer Bez and instead drew the broadsword from his back. The warriors looked at the sword, and Elaina could hear them whispering, "The Tombstone."

Tombstone was the name of Brana Ulfenn's famous broadsword. The blade was said to be so heavy that only Brana could wield it. Those who found themselves facing Brana and his sword were crushed by the great sword's mountainous weight.

Bez was now pale with fright. He was sure an honorable warrior like Brana wouldn't interfere with them, as it would smudge his honor, but he found that he was mistaken. "Kill the prince, quickly!" Bez ordered.

The warriors heard the order and had no choice but to obey. Their lord had told them to follow Bez's orders to the letter.

The leading warrior shouted to the remaining warriors, "You all take the prince's head. I'll keep Brana busy." With that, he ran at the Top Sword, the strongest warrior in the three duchies, ready to die. He held no hope of victory. He only hoped to fulfill his lord's will.

Brana took up the challenge, and the two clashed. As the two began to fight, the rest of the warriors began their assault on Leander, Elaina, and Roan. Being injured, Leander could only stand back as he was protected by Roan and Elaina.

With the pressure of Brana interfering with their judgment, the Talov warriors were sluggish in their movements. Taking advantage of this, Roan was able to slay two of them. Seeing their friends continue to die cleared the warriors' minds, and the fighting grew ever more intense.

"Dammit!" Bez cursed, seeing the favor of the battle slowly turning to the prince's side. He then turned to the Hunter. "Hurry up and kill them!"

The Hunter didn't answer, but he still obeyed. He pulled out another arrow from his quiver and shot at the injured prince. Elaina saw all of this and knocked Leander out of the way of the deadly arrow. Both tumbled to the ground.

When she looked up, Elaina found a group of warriors standing over them, about to strike. She raised her sword, but the downpour of heavy hits made her arm go numb. One quick strike knocked Elaina's sword out of her grasp. As the warriors were about to finish the prince and princess, a loud roar came from the barn behind them.

Suddenly the rotting wall of the barn exploded, and a dozen wooden fragments shot toward them. While Elaina and Leander were relatively unharmed by the shards, the warriors weren't so lucky. One in particular got a shard of wood in the neck, causing him to fall on top of Leander, bleeding to death.

Without the wall, the barn couldn't hold up its roof, and it began to collapse. Elaina was looking on in worry for Kay and Lucis when the two of them launched themselves through the opening. Before she could breathe a sigh of relief, the monstrous ogre bashed its way out after them.

The ogre was covered in wounds. One of its bulging arms was limp at its side, only being held on by some fleshy tendon. The injuries made the creature even more intimidating, as its eyes were glazed over in madness. A river of blackish blood was flowing through its sharp teeth.

When Kay saw Elaina sitting there, looking at the ogre with wide eyes, he pulled her and the prince to their feet. "Get away from here now!" he ordered.

Elaina came out of her stupor and, with the prince limping against her, made her way outside the battle.

On the other side, Brana had finally killed the head warrior and came to help Roan, who was busy with the last two warriors. With a swing from his broadsword, Brana cut down the remaining warriors. The two quickly went to support Lucis and Kay's fight against the ogre.

Seeing that there was no way for them to accomplish their goal, Bez began to retreat. Both Leander and Elaina, the closest ones to Bez, saw this. Pushing himself away from Elaina, the prince charged Bez.

"Who said you could go?" Leander said, appearing next to Bez. Holding his sword at the ready, he wasn't going to allow the one who had killed his brother to escape.

"Do you really think you can stop me with your pathetic skill?" Bez laughed. "I should be thanking you for placing yourself in my grasp."

Bez drew his sword and attacked the prince, but Leander was able to parry the move with ease. Seeing his first attack fail didn't daunt Bez as he targeted Leander's wounded side. After several collisions, Bez realized that he had underestimated the prince. Somehow Leander's swordplay had improved in the days he had been on the run. Even injured, Bez could not harm the prince.

"Die!" Bez shouted. Seeing that he couldn't beat the prince, Bez pulled out a black bell from his pocket.

Elaina, who was watching Leander and Bez duel, saw this and felt a chill well up inside her. Her sight never left the black bell once her gaze caught the strange item. Elaina felt a menacing presence coming from the bell. To her, the bell looked more menacing than the monster Lucis and Kay faced.

"Watch out!" Elaina screamed.

"DIE, PRINCE LEANDER!" Bez shouted, ripping his vocal cords in the

279

process. Bez shook the bell with all his might, and even though it didn't make a sound, Leander felt that something had happened.

In response to the bell, the ogre let out a savage roar. It abandoned the fight and charged Leander. It didn't care that it left itself vulnerable and was now bleeding even more from the wounds the four had inflicted on it. All that mattered to the beast was fulfilling its order.

The ogre was upon the prince before he could think. All he could do was roll out of the way as the beast thrust out its remaining arm, trying to catch him. As Leander dodged, the ogre instead grabbed Bez, who was still gloating from watching the ogre about to finally kill the prince.

"Let me go!" Bez demanded as he tried to shake the bell, but he couldn't due to the great pressure the ogre was squeezing him with. As more pressure was put on him, Bez screamed. His bones made a clear-sounding snap, and he coughed up blood. Looking at the prince, Bez's eyes showed fear as he said in a hoarse voice, "Save me."

But Leander didn't save him. All he did was sit there, watching as the ogre squeezed the life out of the traitorous squire. Finally Bez couldn't hold on, and with one final snap, his body went limp. Thinking that its order had been accomplished, the ogre released Bez and fell to the ground with a thunderous thud. The giant beast let out one last groan before it, too, died, succumbing to its many wounds.

Watching the ogre die, Elaina didn't know why, but she felt that it was relieved to be dead. The feeling only lasted a second, and she couldn't understand why she felt that, but she also thought she saw the beast smile when it died.

As everyone felt the tension leave them from the difficult battle, no one realized the danger still lurking. Before anyone could notice him, the Hunter, who had disappeared sometime during the fight, appeared beside Leander with his short sword drawn. With no one able to stop him, the Hunter struck downward. Leander was able to pick up his sword just in time and blocked the blow.

With his sneak attack failing, the Hunter began to retreat before the rest could reach him. Elaina, who was the closest, wouldn't allow him the opportunity to escape. Picking up her sword, she placed herself between him and his escape route. Roan yelled for her to not confront the man, but she wouldn't listen. She knew that this man was the most dangerous of the group—even more so than the monstrous ogre.

The Hunter didn't have much time before the rest reached him. With no other choice, he stabbed at the princess. His sword aimed to quickly deal with her. Elaina was too tired from the previous battle to defend herself from the attack. The Hunter's sword easily knocked Elaina's own out of the way. Before she could regain herself, Elaina felt pain in her stomach. Looking down, she found the Hunter's sword had pierced her gut.

"Elaina!" she heard someone shout.

As she fell, Elaina saw Kay reach the Hunter and begin fighting the man before she fell into unconsciousness.

Dustin Farris

Chapter Twenty-One: Red Hall and the Sage

After falling unconscious, Elaina woke up on several occasions, but a high fever kept her in a delirious state, preventing her from understanding what was going on. All she knew was that she was moving. On one occasion, she peeked out to see Prince Leander standing over her, a damp cloth in his hand. She also thought she saw Kay behind the prince, but she wasn't sure.

Days blurred into each other for Elaina, but most of the time, she slept. As she slept, she was racked with nightmares. She saw Prince Leander die when he reached Raven's Nest. She saw her father and brothers perish on a battlefield somewhere far from home. She saw a dark figure, and with a wave of its hand, it spread shadows throughout the duchies of Mezer. She couldn't get a good look at the figure, but when it turned around and she saw the thing's eyes, she felt that this thing was more of a monster than the ogre.

It was during one of her dreams of the shadowy figure that Elaina awoke in a cold sweat. Elaina found herself lying in a warm bed with quilts as fine as the ones from her own room back in Esesa. Sunlight crept in through cracks in the curtains, which kept the room dark and cool. Not knowing where she was or where the others were, Elaina tried to sit up. As she did, pain shot through her abdomen.

Pushing the quilt off, she found that her stomach was neatly dressed and bandaged. There was little blood on the wrappings, likely from the wrappings being changed regularly. Elaina felt slightly embarrassed thinking that someone had undressed her while she was unconscious.

As her fingers stroked the bandages around her stomach, the door suddenly swung open. "Thank the zer'! You are awake." A familiar voice came from the doorway.

Looking up, she found that it was Leander who had entered. He was carrying a damp cloth and a small bucket of water. The prince had dark circles around his eyes, most likely from being unable to sleep due to worrying about her well-being.

When Elaina tried to sit up once more, Leander sprinted to her and softly pushed her back down. "There is no need for you to get up. Just lie there and rest. We are safe here," the prince said, trying to reassure her.

"Where are we?" Elaina asked, not seeing anything that would tell her where she was.

"We are in Red Hall. After the battle, Brana Ulfenn brought us here," Leander answered. He then glanced at her bandaged stomach with a frown. "You were lucky. Any deeper, and you wouldn't be with us."

It was then that Elaina remembered the battle with the warriors, the appearance of the monster Bez had called an ogre, and the scene where she had stopped the strange man with Bez from escaping, only to end up bleeding to death on the ground. She couldn't help but bless her luck that she had somehow been able to pull through.

As they talked to one another, the door opened once more. This time it was the famous Brana Ulfenn who entered.

Seeing him, Elaina spoke up. "Brana Ulfenn, I must thank you for saving my life, as well as my companions."

"I was just doing what my lord ordered of me, Your Highness. There is no reason for you to thank me," Brana responded. The giant among men was cold, and his voice held little emotion. During all the times Elaina had seen the Top Sword, she had never seen him show any emotion other than indifference.

"Even so, I wish to thank you," Elaina said.

"If you insist, Your Highness," Brana said with a grunt. He then looked to her wound, as Leander had before him. "How's your wound? Will it keep you from moving about?"

Elaina sat up and twisted her waist a little. The pain was there, but it wasn't as agonizing as she thought it should have been. "I should be all right, as long as it isn't too strenuous," the princess answered.

"Good. Then Your Highnesses can follow me. My lord is awaiting your presence," Brana said as he walked back to the door.

"Princess Elaina is not ready to be up and about. She needs to stay here and rest," Leander shouted, not wishing for Elaina to push herself too much.

Elaina was quite impressed with Leander standing up to Brana, of all people. Before all this, she had never seen the prince ever push his thoughts or opinions on others, but now he seemed to have gained the courage to do so. Even so, she did not wish to stay in bed, playing the weak princess, while the rest fought for their lives.

"Leander, it is all right. I should be fine, so long as I don't push myself," Elaina said, putting her hand on his shoulder.

When he tried to argue with her, Elaina's face grew cold, and Leander kept his thoughts to himself.

Seeing him downcast, she said, "If you are so worried about me, then why don't you help me walk?"

Having been unable to convince her to stay in bed, Leander reluctantly lent his hand to help her out of the bed. After putting on her coat, and with Leander's help, Elaina made her way out of the room.

Following behind Brana, Elaina and Leander made their way through Red Hall. Having heard stories but never having seen the famous hall, the two of them soaked in everything they could see. Red Hall was made of large and sturdy stone from the south, excavated from deep within the Savage Lands. Elaina could hardly see a scratch on these walls, much less any part that was crumbling away, like in most centuries-old buildings. Even her family's palace, back in Esesa, wasn't as domineering as this place.

Another thing Elaina noticed was that there weren't any windows that she could see. The only window that she had seen was the one in the room that she had been resting in. Instead, the halls were illuminated by candles hanging from the walls.

As they walked, they passed a corridor that had no light coming from it. It was as if the darkness in the corridor would swallow any light that entered it. Elaina hadn't noticed that she had stopped walking and was staring deeply into the dark corridor.

"That path leads to the cells, Your Highness," Brana said, appearing next to her. "It is best we be on our way."

Taking the hint, Elaina focused her attention away from the corridor and continued following Brana.

Elaina knew that besides being the home of the Orkiss family and the warriors of Red Hall, this place had another important duty. This was a prison for warriors. If a warrior was deemed to have broken the three virtues, either by dishonoring themselves or by forsaking their duties, they would be sent here.

Elaina had heard stories of Red Hall ever since she was a child. They ranged in meaning, but one truth rang true in all of them: warriors sent to Red Hall were warriors who shouldn't see the light of day ever again.

As she tried to clear herself of such thoughts, they finally reached their destination. Brana had stopped in front of a large door. The great door looked as if it would take four men to successfully open the humongous thing, but Brana was more than just an ordinary warrior. With a great push, Brana pushed the massive door wide open.

Sunlight poured in through the open door, blinding both Elaina and Leander, who covered their eyes from the sudden brightness. As their eyes adjusted to the light, they were able to see through the door. Marveling at what they saw, they took their first steps through the door.

They found themselves in a garden. Many different flowers and trees were spread all around them. Birds sang from the tree branches, and some furry critters dashed about in the brush. If it hadn't been for the stone walls that towered over and surrounded this beautiful garden, they would have forgotten that they were in the most infamous prison in the three duchies.

"What is this place?" Elaina asked.

"This is the hall master's personal garden, Your Highness, built directly in the center of Red Hall. Only those he has given permission may enter here," Brana answered.

As she took in the garden, she spotted a familiar sell-sword lying underneath one of the trees. "Kay!" Elaina shouted, waking the sell-sword from his slumber in the shade.

When Kay spotted her, Elaina thought she saw relief in his eyes, but then she saw the usual grin on his face and thought she must have imagined it. Sitting up, Kay made his way to the three of them.

"About time you woke up. I was beginning to think you enjoyed sleeping in strange places," Kay joked.

Elaina felt herself blush. "It seems you are still as immature as before," she retorted.

Leander watched their interaction with much envy. All his life, he had wished to speak to his beloved princess so freely, but he could not. Either his own timid nature prevented him, or his duties as a prince of a neighboring duchy did. All in all, he began to feel jealous of this wayward sell-sword.

After the reunion with Kay, the four of them made their way deeper into the garden. They found themselves in a clearing with several stone benches. Sitting on the benches were the missing members of their party, Lucis and Roan. Also in the clearing was a thin man with pale skin. His long brown hair was tied behind his back. The man was sitting opposite Lucis and Roan. He was busy painting on an easel. He was so engrossed in his work, he didn't register the newcomers entering the clearing.

"Lord Orkiss, I have brought Their Highnesses Prince Leander and Princess Elaina," Brana said to the thin man, giving the man a salute.

"Thank you, Brana. You may leave us now," the man said, not looking up from his work in progress.

Brana gave one more salute and left Elaina and the rest with Lord Orkiss, not even looking back. If he had, he would have seen the confused looks on Leander's and Roan's faces.

Finally the man seemed to be satisfied with his work and put the paintbrush down. Lord Orkiss suddenly spoke, not really speaking to one person in particular. "Did you know that the three arts were originally practiced by warriors and not women? Calv Ridian spread them to temper the minds of his warriors, to teach them patience and perspective. It was only after the splitting of the Mezer kingdom that warriors abandoned this practice, and the arts became the domain of women."

Roan spoke up. "Who are you, sir? I am the personal warrior of Her Highness Princess Aris Talov and have met the hall master of Red Hall on several occasions, and you are not him." His words made those around look at the man with caution.

It wasn't only Roan who had noticed this. As a prince of the duchy, Prince Leander had met every man who held power, and Lord Orkiss was a large and silent man. This thin man was nothing like that in the least. He wouldn't even be able to swing a sword with those skinny arms, much less be the warden of dishonorable warriors.

"Ah yes, you must mean Piers," the man said. "The man you have met is nothing but my double. A face for the crowds, if that explains it better. But I assure you that I am the real Illas Orkiss. Who else can order Brana Ulfenn besides the lord he serves?"

"Then why does the world think that this Piers is you?" Lucis asked.

"As warden of Red Hall," Lord Orkiss answered, "I am bound to gain many enemies—from warriors released after serving their sentence, to their family and loved ones. In order to survive, a hall master many years ago had the idea of having doubles be the face of the hall master, while the real hall master hides away in Red Hall. Only the archduke is to know the truth about the hall master's identity."

If anyone wasn't shocked by this revelation, it was probably the sell-sword brothers. They hadn't been in the three duchies long enough to know the stories, but Elaina and the rest did. The Red Hall Master was famous for one main reason, besides being the warden of Red Hall, and that was being unable to be killed. Whether it was the current hall master or previous ones, there had never been a time when the hall master of Red Hall had died.

Many thought that they were protected by the Phoenix God himself, but that could not be farther from the truth. It turned out that it was only the doubles that died, and the hall masters only had to go out and find a new one. To describe them as the "face of Red Hall" was correct.

"If you are really the hall master, then why would you help us? Isn't it your duty to carry out the orders of the archduke and capture the prince?" Elaina asked. She wasn't quite sure of everything that had been happening. Brana's sudden appearance exactly when they needed him felt questionable.

"A warrior must pursue truth no matter what they may find," Orkiss said, quoting a part of the Code of Valor. "Not everyone has been fooled by Duke Valens's plot. They have only kept quiet, awaiting the right time to strike."

Leander suddenly shot up from his seat. "Duke Valens is truly the one behind all this? He is the one who ordered my and my brother's deaths?" Leander asked. He needed confirmation, to put a face to his true enemy.

"I believe that we should await our final guest before taking this any further," Orkiss said, refusing to answer the prince.

With that said, they had no choice but to wait. No matter what they said, Lord Orkiss refused to answer any of their questions. Everyone but Kay grew frustrated with the hall master, until finally Brana returned. Following the Top Sword was the man they had been waiting for.

The newcomer was an old man with a gray-peppered beard that reached his chest. His face was covered in wrinkles, and he wore gold spectacles to help him see. The old man wore strange robes with a star pendant pinned across his chest. He looked so fragile, as if he could fall to a slight breeze, but he walked straight, without so much as a limp.

Upon seeing the old man, gasps sounded out from all that were there. Suddenly standing from their seats, everyone began to bow. Lucis and Kay were slightly slower, as they didn't recognize the old man, but seeing the respect that both the prince and princess showed him, they decided to follow suit.

"Master, I have done what you have instructed and brought the prince and his companions here," Orkiss said to the old man. The hall master, too, stood and bowed to him.

The old man nodded to the hall master. He had a warm smile when he started to speak. "Prince Leander, Princess Elaina, it is good to see the two of you again." The old man spoke with a mellow tone.

"It is our honor to be in your presence, Sage Arvandus," Roan said respectfully.

Sage Arvandus looked at the bowing warriors and royals. "Please lift your heads. How will we be able to talk to one another if I can't even see your faces properly?" Arvandus said with a light chuckle.

Elaina and the rest raised their heads. Of all the people in Mezer, she would never have expected the famous Sage of the Star Tower to be the one that Lord Orkiss had been waiting for. As the only sage in the entire land of Mezer, Arvandus was one of the most respected people in all the duchies. Even the archdukes weren't as famous as this old man.

The Sage of the Star Tower had existed during the times before the founding of the kingdom of Mezer. When Calv Ridian had first declared his initial plans to unite the scattered tribes, it had been the sage who had first declared his right. Without the sage's help, Calv Ridian may never have been able to unite the tribes, and the kingdom of Mezer would never have been born.

After the founding of Mezer, the sage still held quite a strong presence in the kingdom. Highborn warriors would ask Arvandus to read the stars and name their children and heirs. Both Elaina and Leander had been named by this old sage.

After the initial shock of Arvandus's arrival had subsided, everyone retook their

291

seats. Arvandus sat on the bench next to Lord Orkiss, while Brana stood behind the two of them with his arms behind his back.

"I am glad to see you alive and well, Prince Leander," Arvandus finally said.

Leander's body jolted from being the first one to be called by the wise sage. "It is only due to luck and the help of my comrades that I made it this far," Leander quickly stated. He was so nervous his words barely came out, due to his stuttering.

"Is that so?" Arvandus said, looking over the rest of them. His eyes seemed to see what no one else could. When his gaze landed on Princess Elaina, he gave her a smile. "Princess Elaina, you are quite a way from home. Does the archduke know of this?"

Being called out by Arvandus made Elaina blush in embarrassment. She waited for the sage to say more, but his attention had already left her and made its way to the remaining three. His gaze passed by Roan quickly and landed on Lucis.

"I was beginning to wonder when I would be meeting you, Zer'sheen," Arvandus said to Lucis, instantly recognizing Lucis as a Zer'sheen.

"You know me?" Lucis asked defensively.

"I saw your birth in the stars, as I have every Zer'sheen before you. Usually the birth of a Zer'sheen is a celebration, but it seems that your parents didn't see it that way, as they left for the southern kingdoms immediately after your birth," Arvandus said as he stroked his speckled beard.

He then finally made his way to Kay. As he looked the other sell-sword over, Elaina thought she saw the sage's eyes widen for a second, but before she could be sure, the sage was back to normal. Kay, too, had noticed the sage's expression, as he was now giving Arvandus a cold look.

"Interesting," Arvandus said as he turned back to Leander. "It seems that your luck is quite good, to be able to find a group of comrades like this." The sage's praises weren't usually given out so easily, so the prince and princess were tongue-tied. Even Lord Orkiss looked at his master in surprise.

"Your words strike true," Leander said, giving another bow. He then looked up with determination in his eyes. "Sage Arvandus, you will know exactly what is going on in Raven's Nest. What has happened to my family, and why is Duke Valens being named regent of the duchy?"

Arvandus gave a sigh. "I may be able to see much, but I am not omniscient. I foresaw upcoming adversity but failed to see the treachery that was abound. Duke Valens has plotted with dark forces to take the throne for himself. Those who are against him are already feeling the pressure, and if they don't concede to his reign, they will face his wrath."

Leander found the truth still inconceivable. He may have guessed and said that the duke was behind all of this, but hearing it from the sage himself was a complete eye-opener. In his heart, he had still held a tiny trace of hope that there weren't traitors among his grandfather's subjects, but that last hope was dashed.

"What about the archduke and Princess Aris? Are they alive?" Roan asked, worried for his princess's well-being.

"The archduke is in bad shape," Arvandus said. "His health is deteriorating fast, and the duke is keeping any real help from reaching him. As for the princess, word is that she, too, has fallen ill, but she is being held prisoner until they can force her to wed the duke's son. After that, I'm afraid they will have little need for someone who has Talov blood running through their veins."

While the news about Aris and the archduke wasn't anything good, they now knew that at least they were alive for now. Leander had to grip his seat to keep himself from falling off. Elaina placed her hand on his shoulder to try to comfort him.

As everyone was taking in the news, a voice suddenly cut through the silence.

"What about this dark force you speak of?" Kay asked. His voice was calm and didn't show any concern for Leander's dismay. Elaina gave the sell-sword a glare, but to Elaina's surprise, he didn't simply scoff or mockingly grin at her. Instead, he stared down Arvandus, waiting for the sage's answer, but it was Lord Orkiss who answered.

"We don't know much, but what we do know is that a man wearing a mask depicting a crying face has been in contact with the duke. He seems to be the one the duke is conspiring with. Other than that, the man is like smoke. None of our people have been able to track him."

That gave both Kay and Lucis a jolt. They both stood at the same time. Elaina saw the hate that flowed out of both sell-swords after hearing about the masked man. No one needed to tell those gathered that both Lucis and Kay knew the mysterious masked man, the same man behind the plots against the Talov family.

"Kay, who is this masked man?" Elaina asked.

Her voice seemed to reach Kay, as he began to calm down before sitting down once more. Lucis, too, retook his seat after seeing Kay sit.

"The man with the crying mask, his name is Karsic. A vile and vicious man whose existence stains this world," Kay spat.

Elaina knew this name. When she had first met Kay, he had been hunting that very man. Elaina could still smell the iron stench of all the blood, as well as see the scene of Kay covered head to toe in his enemies' blood. The ones who had ambushed Kay turned out to be warriors of the Bloody Blade of Tarsis. Elaina had been too caught up with finding Leander to think anything of it, but now it seemed that there truly was a connection between that and the plot against the Talovs.

Lucis spoke up. "When we first arrived in the land of Mezer, we had little knowledge of the duchies. Luckily, we befriended a warrior from a small warrior family in the Talov Duchy. He was called Henri, and the man taught us much of what we needed to know about the traditions and common sense in the duchies." His voice held much respect for the warrior Henri, but soon it turned cold.

"But not long after we left the warrior's home, he and his entire family were slain in a single night. No one knew who had committed the crime. When we heard of this, we rushed back, only to find ruins where a kind family had once lived. A single survivor was pulled out of the wreckage, one of the servants. He said he had overheard Henri arguing with someone. When the arguing grew intense, he heard Henri shout the name Karsic before the wall suddenly fell on top of him. That misfortune turned out to be in the man's favor, as the wall hid him. Otherwise, he might have joined those killed that night," Lucis said, finishing his story.

"I understand why you would harbor resentment for this Karsic," Elaina said, but then she turned her attention to Kay. "But why was Kay the one chasing him while you and your brother Aer searched for Kay?" She may have been looking at Kay, but her question was targeting Lucis.

She had a valid point. If what Lucis had told them was the truth, then there was no reason for Kay to hunt down Karsic on his own. If the three of them had searched instead of Lucis and Aer having to look for Kay, they would have been a lot more productive. The sell-sword brothers weren't fools, so why had this situation come about?

"That is because Kay has met Karsic before," Lucis answered. Of all the answers that could have come, no one had been expecting this.

"If this man really can control the Bloody Blade of Tarsis, then he must be someone with great power in the Tarsis Duchy. How can a single sell-sword meet a man like that?" Leander asked.

Everyone looked to Kay for the answer. Kay was undisturbed by everyone's attention on him, so he answered casually. "I met him when I was still taking alchemic seed. He seemed interested as to why I could take so much and not die. His questioning disturbed me, so I never returned after that. Not long after, we met with Henri, and all this happened."

"You told me it has been three years since you last indulged in seed," Elaina accused Kay.

Kay looked at the princess and said, "I lied."

Elaina felt hurt and betrayed. Kay had been annoying, and terrifying at times, but never had she believed she couldn't trust him. It was curious that she could trust someone so quickly, but before she had known it, Kay had gained her trust. Sadly, that trust had begun to crack with this discovery.

"So, this Karsic was interested in you. Why would he be interested in a drug-addicted sell-sword?" Leander more demanded than asked. He had never really liked this brother of Aer and Lucis. Learning that not only was he an addict but he had lied to Elaina, Leander felt this Kay was more dangerous than he had first believed.

Kay looked at Prince Leander with a cold gaze that sent shivers through the prince. Everyone waited for Kay to answer, but he only turned his gaze away. Leander felt enraged from this show of disrespect and stood, his hand nearing the hilt of his sword.

Elaina saw the confrontation that was about to happen and moved in between the two of them. Others might not have noticed, but Kay's cold look slightly changed when Leander stood to confront him. Elaina saw the murderous glint in his eye and knew that Leander would die if they really did fight.

Luckily for Elaina, Lucis also saw the changes in his brother and stood between him and the prince as well. "Kay, that is enough. If you won't tell them, then I will," Lucis said.

Kay reluctantly turned away, but the murderous glint in his eyes had yet to vanish.

With the newest crisis averted, everyone returned to their seats. Elaina was able to pull Leander to his seat but was unable to calm the angered prince. Only Lucis stayed standing where he was.

"What Kay should have said is that we don't know why Karsic took an interest in him. All we know is that Henri refused to tell him where we went, and in his fury, Karsic slaughtered Henri and his family," Lucis said. He then turned to Leander. "You worry that Kay is somehow connected to the ones who plotted against you, correct? Let me take that worry from you. Kay's emotions have been so diluted by drugs that even the greatest temptations wouldn't interest him."

Lucis's words didn't persuade Leander, but the prince gave the Zer'sheen some face and kept his mouth shut. He did, however, send one final glare at Kay, who had decided to no longer pay attention to the conversation and instead looked at a pair of birds nestled in the branches of a nearby tree.

Elaina also looked at Kay. She knew from their first meeting that he had taken alchemic seed and that this particular one was an emotion dampener. But traveling with the cocky and mischievous Kay had made her completely forget that he shouldn't be able to show these emotions. Seeing Kay being distant and cold now, she could see some part of that emotionless side to him.

With no other great news to go over, Orkiss ordered Brana to bring them back to their rooms. As they left the garden, Elaina took one last look at the hall master and Arvandus before the door closed behind them.

+

"What is it that you are planning, master?" Illas Orkiss asked Arvandus. "I don't understand why you asked me to send Brana to personally bring the prince and his group back here. Wouldn't a single squad of warriors have worked just as well?"

Illas couldn't understand what his master was thinking. This wasn't new to the hall master. When he had first been taken in by the sage to be his disciple, he had gotten firsthand experience of how knowledgeable the old sage truly was. Over time, he had been able to get closer to his master, but Arvandus always seemed one step ahead. However, this situation with the prince really confused Illas.

"Times are changing. Before, there was no reason to doubt your warriors, but now ..." Arvandus said with a sigh. He then looked at the painting that the hall master was working on. "You've finally finished."

"Not that it does me any good. I have no idea what it is supposed to mean," Illas said with a sigh.

"Let me see," Arvandus said.

After handing his painting over to Arvandus, Illas watched his master look the painting over. The painting was completely chaotic. Colors mingled with one another, crossing over each other seemingly without reason or planning. If you looked closely, you could make out certain figures hidden in the chaos. Then, as soon as you thought you saw something, you would find that it had somehow disappeared.

"Looks like I still need more training before I can unravel the truth and knowledge from the stars like you do, master," Illas said dejectedly.

"Nonsense. This is quite impressive," Arvandus said. "Many stargazers twice your age would be hard-pressed to do something this splendid. All you need to do is learn how to interpret the chaos to find what is hiding beneath. Look at it yourself, and I'll show you."

Studying his chaotic painting, Illas wasn't sure what he was searching for. Arvandus suddenly lifted his thin finger and tapped the painting. At first nothing, but then Illas saw a streak of blue move. Then the green and red spiraled about the canvas. Finally, the painting came to life.

In the flowing colors, Illas saw three ravens, one old and two young. As they flew, darkness surrounded them, trying to devour the free-flying ravens. From the darkness, swords manifested, along with the roar of a beast. The two young ravens turned to face the darkness with their talons outstretched. The swords swung, trying to strike down the ravens, but before they could, Illas had to look away. The vision was too powerful and caused his head to feel as if it were breaking in two.

"What did I just witness?" Illas asked.

"Something that is to come," Arvandus said, looking at the painting with a solemn frown on his old face.

Chapter Twenty-Two: Evil Plots

Locked away in the highest room in the eastern tower, Aris sat by the small window, reading a certain letter. As she read the letter, Aris felt some tension leave her—there had finally been some good news brought to her. "Leander, Thank the zer' that you are alive," Aris said. The letter in her hands was to inform her that Prince Leander had escaped pursuit and his current location was unknown to Duke Valens.

After finding out that her brother was all right, she continued reading the second half of the letter. At the bottom, there were several family seals, along with a signature underneath each one. Aris's finger traced over each one, remembering names to go along with the family crests. As she did this, she suddenly heard footsteps heading her way, along with the sound of keys entering the door lock.

Stashing the letter in her bodice, she hid it just in time before Sarus barged into the room without so much as a knock. Looking at the young man's arrogant face made Aris want to stab out her own eyes rather than look at this vile man.

"I guess your father skipped over teaching you etiquette and instead taught you the way of a rat," Aris said. Each one of her words shot venom at the duke's heir.

Hearing his fiancée speak to him this way made Sarus's face contort into a scowl. "My father has been named regent. He is now the most powerful man in the Talov

Duchy. You will not disrespect my father in front of me," he coldly said, taking a seat by the table where Aris sat. His glare only made Aris glare back.

"Your father isn't regent yet," Aris responded.

"True, but the priest will be here to confer the title on him in a week's time. He will also be marrying you and me on that same glorious day," Sarus declared as he reached over to place his hand on her thigh.

Aris was repulsed by the very idea of marrying this conniving and scheming man. "I would rather marry a hog," she spat, swatting Sarus's hand away.

Sarus didn't take kindly to Aris's words. Grabbing the princess by her chin, he yanked her so that her face was mere inches from his. "As if you have any choice in the matter," he hissed.

Aris wanted nothing more than to beat this arrogant man to death, but she knew that it wasn't the right time to be letting her emotions run wild, so she held her urge in.

Finally Sarus released her from his grip. Rubbing her chin, which was now bruised from Sarus's rough handling, Aris gave the young Valens one last glare before looking away from him. She didn't wish to look at him any longer.

"You'd better learn to try and get on my good side. Once we are married, you, and this duchy, will be mine," Sarus said with an evil laugh.

Aris ignored his remark, but her hands tightened into fists underneath her long sleeves. Sarus was about to speak once more, but a knock on the door stopped him. The door opened, and one of the warriors guarding the princess entered. With him was another warrior, who was too busy panting to salute Sarus.

"What is it? I thought I told you I didn't wish to be disturbed," Sarus said, angered that this warrior had ignored his direct orders.

"Your father requests your presence immediately," the breathless warrior answered.

While Sarus wanted to harass Aris longer, he feared his father's wrath and decided it would be best not to let his father wait. Giving a loud huff of displeasure, he stood and made his way to the door. Behind him, he heard Princess Aris suddenly give a light chuckle.

"So scared that your father will be angry with you that you come running the moment he calls. You truly are a one-of-a-kind man," Aris mocked him as he left.

Sarus froze in place and turned around, outraged by Aris. The princess knew just the right words to anger him. The warrior who had been sent for Sarus saw this and frowned. "Sir, the regent has been waiting for a while as we searched for you," the warrior said, hoping Sarus would quickly follow.

With his fear of his father overwhelming the anger he felt for Aris, Sarus left the room, slamming the door as he left.

When Aris heard the lock snapping back into place, she felt relief from being away from the young Valens. Picking herself up, Aris, through gritted teeth, swore, "I will not let your treachery succeed."

Looking out of her window once more, she took in the sight of the city below. On one of the rooftops, Aris noticed a flash of light. The light flashed once, then twice, before several seconds of nothing, and then flashed once again. A smile grew on Aris's face.

+

"You wish to speak to me?" Sarus asked Duke Valens as he entered the room.

Jarl Valens sat at the desk of the archduke, looking over several documents. The room they were in was the archduke's personal study. After getting the approval of most of the warrior families, Duke Valens had immediately made himself quite at home in the palace. There was even his family's emblem, hanging on the wall of the study, instead of the black feather emblem of the Talov family.

"You went to trouble the princess again," Duke Valens said, not looking up from his work. The duke's words weren't asking Sarus but stating a fact. "Didn't I warn you not to cause trouble till after I'm conferred the title of regent?"

Sarus looked at his father with a hint of disdain. He didn't know why his father was still so wary after everything had already fallen into their hands. "The princess is locked away. Even if I did decide to do something dishonorable to her, no one would know," Sarus said, as if it were a matter of fact.

Duke Valens looked up from his paperwork and stared coldly at his son. Sarus couldn't help but tremble slightly under his father's gaze. "I will say this only once more. Keep away from the princess. You can have your fun after you two are wed," Duke Valens said before looking back to the piles of paper.

Sarus looked at his father in confusion. "Is that all you wanted to talk about, Father?" he asked. While his trips to harass Aris upset his father, they didn't warrant an immediate summons.

Duke Valens didn't answer his son. All he did was gesture for Sarus to take a seat. Only able to comply, Sarus sat down and waited. The duke neatly organized his papers before finally being satisfied. Sitting up, he looked at his son.

"Lord Karsic wishes to meet," the duke said to his son.

Sarus would have fallen over if he hadn't already been sitting. If Sarus feared his cold father, he was absolutely terrified of the masked Karsic. Sarus could still remember the day that his father had brought him to meet Karsic for the first time. He had walked in arrogantly, only to tumble away, shivering in fear. To Sarus, Karsic was less of a man and more of a monster wearing the skin of a man.

Sarus followed his father out of the study. The two Valenses made their way through the Talov castle until they reached the far end. Here there were no servants running about, nor were there any guards patrolling. This part of the castle was old. Hardly anyone ventured into these hallways. Only the occasional servant came to clean, but that wasn't scheduled to happen until days later.

Duke Valens finally stopped before a certain door. Sarus felt an eerie chill coming from beyond the door. The duke gave the door a light knock and waited. Soon the door slowly crept open. Peeking out of the door was a young boy without a hint of emotion on his face. Seeing the duke and his son, the boy pulled the door open.

Duke Valens walked in with gusto, leaving his son behind. After taking a deep breath to raise his courage, Sarus followed his father. Once the two entered, the young boy closed the door behind them.

The room was one of the old guest rooms before the castle had been expanded. As a never-used room, the drapes were shut, preventing light from entering, making the room dark and difficult to make things out in. Sarus strained to find the one they were about to meet. Then the drapes were pulled open, causing him to close his eyes in pain.

When Sarus opened his eyes again, Karsic stood before him and his father. Even in the sunlight coming in through the window, Karsic looked as if he were cloaked in shadows. The crying mask that covered Karsic's face looked straight toward them. Sarus wanted nothing more than to cower behind his father, but fear pinned his feet to the floor.

The duke gave a polite bow, one that was given to equals. "It has been a while Lord Karsic. We are honored by your presence," the duke said. If anyone else had seen this, they would have been surprised. Duke Valens was a prideful man, and it took a lot for him to bow to Karsic and treat any man as an equal. Only Sarus knew how much his father resented treating this masked man as one of equal footing.

"You have done well in gaining control of Raven's Nest," Karsic said, but he didn't sound pleased. In fact, he sounded furious.

"Most of the marquesses and lower-ranked warrior families have decided to stand behind me, whether through fear or personal gain," Duke Valens said. "Duchess Morwood reluctantly consented, and Duke Aleo has no real power in the capital to worry about. Only a handful resist, but they will soon kneel or find themselves and their families without a future."

"Is that so?" Karsic said, looking out of the window. When he turned back to them, Sarus almost jumped out of his skin. "Then what about the hall masters and Hollowell? It seems that they don't agree with you being regent."

Sarus saw his father's fist tighten. Ever since the hall masters of both the Stone and Red Halls had left after the gathering, he had tried to call for them but had been outright refused. Oh'ash had even taken his warriors back without even a hint or warning. When his father had found out about this, he had almost lost his constant composure.

"You have nothing to worry about. The hall masters may be powerful, but they have no say in Raven's Nest. Hollowell, even less so. It is rare for those underdwellers to even leave the mine, much less venture out to contest my claim," Duke Valens stated. He then thought of something. "Why are you asking me this?"

"Prince Leander has escaped our grasp and made it onto Talov soil," said Karsic. "He was also somehow able to kill the ogre I sent with my hunter, who also seems to have perished. He will soon be heading here to prove his innocence."

Both Valenses were shocked to hear this. The last report they had been given regarding the prince was that he had narrowly escaped the warriors they had sent out, by escaping into Verilis Forest. Knowing how dangerous the forest was and how weak the prince was at swordplay, they believed that he would never leave that forest alive. He had already been lucky when he had escaped from WestAvri, and before that the assassination. After this last stroke of luck, Duke Valens even thought that the prince might be blessed by the Phoenix God himself.

Sarus, on the other hand, was smoldering inside with rage. If Prince Leander reached Raven's Nest and got the help of the warrior families, then his life would be over. Sarus could see the future of him sitting on the throne evaporate in front of his very eyes. In his anger, he forgot that he was in the presence of the man who terrified him. He was about to speak up, but his father noticed and quickly shot him a glance to keep quiet.

"I have already begun switching out the guards and warriors around the gates to the city with ones loyal to me. The moment Leander enters through one of the gates, we will know. His homecoming will only bring about his demise," Duke Valens said, assuring Karsic that he had everything in order.

"It won't be that simple," Karsic told the duke. "I have uncovered the identities of the ones helping the prince. They are a trio of brothers by the names of Kay, Lucis, and Aer. I have already taken care of Aer, but the other two are a far more dangerous threat."

"Then I will send my strongest warriors to stand watch over the gates," Duke Valens answered. Karsic wasn't someone to exaggerate someone's strength. If he thought that these two sell-swords were that much trouble, only the duke's most valiant warriors would be able to match them.

"Then you will be sending them to their deaths," Karsic said, shocking the duke and Sarus. The duke's strongest warriors weren't to be taken lightly. In the past, they had even competed for the title of Top Sword. Normal warriors wouldn't stand a chance, and even veteran warriors would fall to their swords.

"Are they really that dangerous?" asked Duke Valens.

Karsic didn't answer at first as he gazed at the duke, his cold eyes hidden in the darkness of the crying mask's eyeholes. Finally he said, "More dangerous than you can imagine. The sell-sword Lucis is a Zer'sheen."

Sarus trembled in fear after learning that Leander had a Zer'sheen helping him. He felt his legs go weak and could feel the cold steel of the executioner's sword at his neck. Not knowing what to think, Sarus looked to his father for support.

The duke took the news in, different plots and ideas tumbling through his mind. To the side, Sarus saw this and grinned. When his father had this look, it meant someone was in for a lot of pain and disaster. Just like that, Sarus could see himself sitting on the throne once more. The young Valens had to hold in his laughter as he thought of his bright future. He had no fear of Prince Leander now, even knowing that he had a Zer'sheen on his side.

As Sarus was fantasizing about becoming the next archduke, Duke Valens thought up a plan. When Sarus heard his father's plan, he felt a little pity for Leander. The prince had no idea what was waiting for him.

"Very well. I will get you what you need, but if you fail to finish off the prince, I don't see a reason to keep our alliance going," Karsic said, agreeing to the duke's plan but at the same time threatening him.

With no reason left to stay, Karsic walked out of the room, the strange boy right at his heels. Sarus listened as Karsic's footsteps grew fainter, until they finally became silent. He could feel the room warm as the distance from the terrifying Karsic grew.

Standing next to his son, Duke Valens had a cold glint in his eyes as he watched Karsic leave. He then turned to his son. "Fetch Mikael and Drenn. I need to speak to them immediately," the duke ordered.

Sarus quickly left to find the two.

Just as the duke was growing impatient, Sarus returned with two muscular men wearing warriors' armor.

Mikael and Drenn were the duke's two most capable warriors, and the duke trusted them more than his own son. As the commander and second-in-command of the third chivalric order, they had fought for decades, and their names were famous as two of the strongest warriors in the city of Raven's Nest.

"Your Grace," Mikael said, giving the duke a warrior's salute.

"Prince Leander is on his way to Raven's Nest as we speak," the duke said, letting the shock sink in for his two warriors. "How is the transfer of the guard coming along?"

This time it was the warrior Drenn who answered. "Most of the guards at the main gates have already been changed to those under our command. We are getting some resistance from some of the warriors, but it won't be long before they submit."

"Good. With that out of the way, I need you two to do something for me," the duke said. He then began to explain his plan.

Dustin Farris

Chapter Twenty-Three: Gifts Given

In Red Hall, besides the hall master's personal garden, there were few places of comfort. The stone building had been designed to be a prison, after all. No warm sunshine nor calming breeze was able to pass through the hall's stone walls. However, the land outside Red Hall was quite different.

The hall had been built within several large hills. Away from the roads and villages, the land was untouched by man. Small woodlands were scattered about, and a small stream flowed near the hall. Red Hall's dreariness completely contrasted the natural serenity of the land.

Sitting by the stream, watching the water continuously flow, was Prince Leander. His mood mimicked Red Hall's dreariness. The prince watched as the small fish in the stream swam to the surface to feed on the bugs flying over the flowing water.

Ever since he had learned what had been happening to his family back in Raven's Nest, he had felt overwhelming sadness. Unable to cope with it within the walls of Red Hall, he had asked to be allowed to walk around outside. Lord Orkiss had given the prince permission, so long as he kept the hall in sight. Leander should have been grateful, but while he had sat there, he had noticed the Red Hall warriors keeping their eyes on him. It seemed that Lord Orkiss still didn't trust him not to do something reckless and had placed warriors to watch him.

"Damn it!" Leander cursed at the top of his lungs. He felt so powerless. He needed to vent his frustration, even if it meant yelling to the wind. His shout came suddenly and scared away a flock of small birds nestling in the trees nearby. Taking a couple of swings at the stream, he cursed loudly, "Damn it! Damn it! Damn it!"

After a little while, Leander began to breathe more heavily. Slouching back down, he watched as the water in the stream went back to its usual, tranquil flow. Leander wished that his own life could do the same.

"Leander," sounded a worried voice from behind.

Turning around, Leander found Elaina looking at him with worry in her eyes. She was no longer wearing warrior attire. She wore a sleeveless dress that reached her ankles. With her hair done up in a simple fashion, she had returned to looking like the princess she was once more.

Elaina sat down next to the prince and rested her head on his shoulder. "It is all right to feel sad. With everything going on, no one would blame you," she said in almost a whisper.

"I'm not sad. I'm angry," Leander said with a solid tone that Elaina hadn't been expecting. "I'm mad at the duke who plotted with others to kill my brother and overthrow the duchy. I'm angry at the ones who conspired with the Valenses for their own gain. I'm angry at the warriors who follow him, not realizing they are following a traitor. I'm even angry at my grandfather, who was too blinded by his trust in his warriors to see the treachery that was brewing." His voice had grown louder, but suddenly he became quiet. "But most of all, I'm angry at myself. Unable to help when my brother was killed right in front of me. Unable to stop the Valenses from taking over Raven's Nest. Unable to be there when my family needed me the most. No, the one I have the most hatred for isn't the Valenses but myself," Leander said in all but a whisper.

Seeing Leander like this, Elaina wanted to comfort him as she had before, but she found that she couldn't. For some reason, the words that had come naturally before failed to leave her lips. It might have been that she couldn't grasp his feelings of loneliness or his anger, as she herself had never gone through such turmoil. Unable to say a word, Elaina just sat there with Prince Leander in silence.

The two watched the stream flow ever onward. As time went by, Leander was able to grasp his emotions and stabilize his mind. When he turned and saw Elaina looking back at him, Leander felt himself blush.

"Sorry for that," Leander said, apologizing for his wild outburst. Remembering that Elaina had seen him acting like that made him blush even more. "I don't know what came over me just now to act like that."

"Don't be sorry," Elaina said, gripping Leander's hand. "You've had to hold in your emotions this whole time. It is all right to let them out, or else they may come back to harm you." She spoke in a calming tone.

Leander felt himself break free from all the emotions that swam inside his heart. The calm and beautiful scenery, which hadn't helped him before, began to work wonders. The anger and sadness that plagued him was like a distant memory as he basked in the warm sun and Elaina's kindness. He then turned and looked deeply into Elaina's eyes. The words that he had been too timid to speak for years came out so easily.

"Elaina, I love you. Ever since I first laid eyes on you, I have had feelings for you. I know that our families were planning our engagement before all of this transpired, but I now realize that I never asked you," he said. Then he said the famous four words. "Will you marry me?"

Elaina wasn't expecting a confession to come right at this moment, and she wasn't able to answer. She opened and closed her mouth several times, not knowing what to say. Finally she looked into the prince's hopeful eyes and spoke.

"I'm sorry, Leander, but my answer is no. I care about you, and growing up, we became as close as siblings, but that is all. I do not love you in the same way that you love me," Elaina answered.

Elaina watched the hope die in Prince Leander's eyes, and the sight was painful to her. She didn't want to hurt him so, but she couldn't fabricate her feelings. She had said that he was like a brother to her, and that was true. He was even more of a brother than Aleron or Felon most of the time. When she had learned of their pending engagement, she had tried to grow feelings of romance for Leander, but in the end, she had failed to do so.

"I should have known," Leander said with a painful little chuckle. "From the way you interact with Kay, I should have guessed that you wouldn't feel the same way for me."

Elaina didn't know what to do or say, so she quickly stood up. "What do you mean by that? Are you suggesting that I have feelings for that man?" she said. Her words came out jumbled from how fast she was speaking.

"You don't?" Leander asked. "But the way you speak to each other—"

"I speak that way because he drives me mad," Elaina said, cutting off Leander. "If you had spent as much time as I have with Kay, then you would understand. He also lied to me. He told me that he was no longer taking alchemic seed, only now I know that wasn't true. How can I have feelings for such a man?"

"Doesn't sound like you don't feel anything for Kay," Leander mumbled. The more that Elaina tried to deny it, the more Leander felt that it was the truth.

"I ..." Elaina said, beginning to argue again, but a sudden pain shot through her from her stomach. Crouching down, Elaina held her abdomen in pain. The wound caused by the man with the bow was still fresh, and any sudden moves caused her pain.

Seeing Elaina bent over in pain, Leander helped her to the ground. He immediately regretted speaking to her like that. He might have been brokenhearted after his failed proposal, but he shouldn't have confronted her like that—at least not while she was still injured.

Leander was so worried for Elaina that he didn't notice that someone now stood next to them. When he did, he looked up to see Sage Arvandus looking down at them with a smile. The old sage reached into his pocket and took out a small vial.

"Have her drink this. It will numb the pain," Arvandus said, handing the vial over to Leander.

Leander quickly broke the seal. A bitter smell came from the liquid, which gave off a strange sizzling sound as it splashed about. After handing it over to Elaina, he watched as the princess finished the bitter medicine in a single gulp. Almost instantly Elaina's face relaxed, showing that the medicine was doing its job.

"Thank you," Elaina said as the final twinges of pain left her. Handing the now-empty vial over to Arvandus, who pushed it back into his pocket, she was grateful to this old sage for helping her once more.

"No need to thank me for something so minor," Arvandus said with a laugh. His hearty laugh dissipated the tense atmosphere that had come after Leander's failed proposal, almost like magic.

"That isn't so," Elaina disagreed. "One must show thanks for even the minor things."

"I always forget, you highborn warriors really are a stiff bunch," Arvandus said with another laugh. "Actually, I came out here to find you, Princess."

"Me? What is it that you wish of me?" Elaina asked, not sure what she could do for the sage. As she waited for his reply, Arvandus pulled out another vial and tossed it to her.

Elaina caught the vial and looked it over. Unlike the previous vial, the liquid in this one was dark in color, almost black. Elaina also noticed that the liquid was bubbling, as if it were over a fire.

"This is …?" Elaina asked, not knowing what type of elixir was in this vial. Just by the looks of it, it seemed a lot more precious than the first one she had been given.

"That isn't any elixir or man-made medicine," Arvandus told her. "That is the heart blood of a hundred-year-old winter deer. Rare doesn't even begin to describe the value of the contents of that vial. Drink it, and even fatal wounds will heal, given enough time. In your case, the blood would mend your wound overnight."

Elaina looked back at the vial, but this time her eyes looked at it as if it were a treasure. "Does this mean that if I drink this, then my wound will have healed by tomorrow?" Elaina asked.

After waking up from being injured, she had realized that she might have been saved, but the wound in her stomach was keeping her nearly stationary, or else it tended to open back up. With her being so wounded, there was no way that she would be able to leave Red Hall anytime soon. Elaina knew that Leander was planning on heading to Raven's Nest any day now. Elaina didn't want to be left behind, but in her condition, it looked as if she had no other option. Now the sage was giving her one.

"But I must warn you. While the heart blood of a winter deer is a miracle cure, your body will try to reject it. You will be in constant pain until your wounds are healed. Some have died before they could get better, due to the pain," Arvandus warned.

Elaina didn't mind the drawbacks and was about to swallow the bubbling blood when a hand swiftly took the vial away from her. Angered by this, she glared daggers at the one now holding the vial.

"What do you think you are doing, Leander?" Elaina asked. In the prince's hand was the vial she had gotten from the sage.

"I should be the one asking you that, Elaina. You heard Arvandus. People have died from taking this. There is no way that I will let you consume such a dangerous substance," Leander said with absolute conviction.

"That isn't your decision," Elaina barked back, forgetting that the reason she wanted to consume the blood was to help the one she was now yelling at. "Now, give me back the vial."

Leander didn't budge and simply stood there as Elaina glared at him with her hand stretched out. There was no way that Leander was going to let Elaina risk herself for him. Even if she had refused his proposal, he couldn't stop loving her all of a sudden.

Finally Elaina couldn't take it anymore. With a huff, she stormed off, leaving Leander and Arvandus watching her walk back to Red Hall.

With a sigh, Leander turned to Arvandus. "I am sorry for that, but I won't let Elaina do such a dangerous thing to herself if I can stop it," he said, giving the vial back to Arvandus. Afterward Leander, too, followed Elaina back to Red Hall.

+

Standing alone next to the small stream, Arvandus watched as Leander quickly faded out of sight. During this entire time, he had never lost the grin that was constantly on his face.

"Are you going to stay hidden? Why don't you come out so we can talk?" Arvandus said, looking toward the small row of trees not too far off.

Suddenly someone jumped down from the branches. After landing quite nimbly, the newcomer made his way over to Arvandus. If Elaina or Leander had still been there, they would have recognized the man as the sell-sword Kay. But Elaina would have noticed that there was no smug grin on his face, as she was used to seeing. Instead, Kay had a cold aura radiating from him. From how wary he was of Arvandus, it seemed that Kay hadn't thought that he would be noticed by the old sage.

Arvandus wasn't intimidated by Kay's coldness in the slightest and gave the sell-sword a smile. "You really need to learn to get along with others better. If your brothers or Elaina aren't around, you can barely tolerate people," Arvandus said. He emphasized Elaina's name as he spoke.

Kay's eyes narrowed as if he was getting ready for a fight. "How did you know I was listening in?"

"You are just the way I pictured you to be," Arvandus said, avoiding Kay's question completely. "One who hides their viciousness deep inside. But from what I can tell, the drugs are no longer keeping that murderous rage in check." He looked over Kay thoughtfully.

"What do you know about me?" Kay barked back. He was beginning to feel disturbed by what Arvandus was saying.

"Not much," Arvandus said. "But I do know that most people with the Dragon's Stigma either go mad or are murdered before they become an adult. I've never heard of one living as long as you have."

Before Arvandus could say another word, he found Kay's sword at his neck. He had just blurted out one of Kay's most closely guarded secrets. Kay had the urge to kill this famous sage right at this moment. He could feel the stigma throbbing under his skin, urging him to finish the job. His crystal blue eyes showed the eerie red tint of his berserk state. Only Kay and his brothers knew that it wasn't the blood craze or madness but the dreaded Dragon's Stigma that caused him to become this way, so bloodthirsty.

Sage Arvandus wasn't fazed by Kay beginning to lose control. He seemed more interested in the sword at his neck. Just as Kay's sword pushed into his neck, Arvandus shouted, "That is enough!"

The shout came with a force that drove the murderous urge away. Kay had to take several steps back and was panting fiercely. He looked at Arvandus, shocked about what had just happened.

"How did you ...?" Kay began to speak, but a coughing fit stopped him from speaking more.

"If you want to know how I knew of your condition or how I was able to quell the bloodthirst, then sit down, and let's talk," Arvandus said, taking a seat on a rock next to the stream.

With no other choice, and being interested in what Arvandus knew, Kay also took a seat.

When he saw Kay waiting there impatiently, Arvandus gave a laugh. "Seems you want to know after all."

"Of course I do," Kay said angrily. Being a bearer of the Dragon's Stigma was his closest kept secret. He didn't want this knowledge to fall into other hands if he could help it.

The Dragon's Stigma was known throughout the entire world. After their fall, the dragon race cursed humanity. From then on, those with the stigma were born. Carrying the aggressive nature of dragons inside them, they slowly lost control of their emotions and went into rampages. After humanity had learned the truth of the Dragon's Stigma, they began to kill any who held the stigma, even if they were children or newborns, saying that it was a mercy for them to die this way rather than become like wild beasts.

All his life, Kay had to keep his emotions in line. Once his parents learned of his condition, they had sent him to one of the goddess Kintra's monasteries in hopes that he could learn to control the murderous tendencies. The teachings of the warrior priests helped, and Kay finally felt free of his curse. Sadly, he was wrong, and after a tragic incident, he was forced to leave the priesthood.

Not long after that, Kay discovered alchemic seed—in particular, Blue Breath. With the help of the drug, Kay began to control his emotions, but the Dragon's Stigma would not let up. He grew resistant to the drug, and his emotions were dulled. This kept him from losing control in most cases, but whenever blood was shed, he would still go into a frenzy. Only in the presence of his two brothers was he able to keep himself from going into a frenzy, and to this day, Kay couldn't explain why this was.

"If you want to know how I knew of your condition prior to meeting you, then the answer is the same as how I knew where to send Brana to find you. I read it in the stars," Arvandus explained.

"You're a stargazer?" Kay asked, but he didn't need Arvandus to reply to know that this sage was one.

Those that could read the past, present, and future in the constellations in the night sky were known as stargazers. Almost every prophecy was written down by those with this rare talent. Hearing that the sage Arvandus was one of these select individuals, Kay understood how he could know so much about him without having ever actually met. It also made him wary of what else the sage had read in the stars.

"You don't have to worry about me telling anyone of your condition. In fact, I have something for you," Arvandus said, pulling out a bracelet from his pocket. Kay wondered what else the sage had stored in his seemingly bottomless pockets.

The bracelet was dark and looked almost rusted. Taking the bracelet, Kay saw that it was covered in Angrelic symbols. Kay recognized the ancient gods' language, as he had seen it in scrolls when he was still at the monastery of Kintra.

"What is this?" Kay asked.

"That is an enormously powerful amulet, carved with protective wards during the time of the Sage Kings. Put this on, and you will no longer be consumed by the Dragon's Stigma when you fight," Arvandus answered.

Kay looked over the bracelet once more. Then, without hesitation, he put it around his wrist. As he did, the carvings lit up and emitted a bluish glow. The bracelet began to shrink until it fused with Kay's wrist. As it did so, Kay could hear a furious roar inside him as the stigma tried to fight off the power of the enchanted bracelet. When everything was done, the glow faded away, along with the dragon roar.

Kay could feel the strength of the stigma fading. It was as if a weight had been lifted off his chest. The anger and bloodlust he normally had to keep in check all but disappeared.

Before Kay could say anything, Arvandus spoke once more. "I must warn you though. The magic inside that bracelet may be strong, but it is limited. The bracelet can only be taken off two times. After the third, it will become an ordinary trinket, so you must be careful not to remove it," he warned.

After speaking those words, Arvandus walked away, leaving Kay looking at his newfound gift in deep thought.

Chapter Twenty-Four: The Hunter's Identity

E laina found sleep hard to come by. She tossed and turned for hours. Only when the moon was high in the sky did she fall into a deep slumber. When she awoke the next morning, she quickly got dressed and went to find Leander and the rest.

However, when she entered the mess hall, she saw not even one of them. Some of the Red Hall warriors sat at the long tables, eating. Elaina noticed that they were looking in her direction, but when she turned to check, they were back eating.

Searching through Red Hall, Elaina couldn't find even a glimpse of her four comrades. Unable to take it any longer, she went to find Lord Orkiss. She found the hall master in his office.

"What do you mean they left?" Elaina shouted.

"I mean exactly that. Early this morning, Leander and the others left, alongside Brana and some of my warriors, to Raven's Nest," Orkiss answered.

Elaina had to steady herself after hearing this news. She couldn't understand how they could do this to her. Sure, she and Leander had fought the day before, but she never would have thought that he would do something like this. She tried to reason in her mind that Orkiss must be mistaken, that they wouldn't leave her after being through so much together, but the look on Orkiss's face told her the truth.

They had left her behind.

"How could they do this to me?" Elaina said, slouching down into one of the chairs in the office. "After all the struggles, all the dangers we faced together. How could they leave me without so much as a word?"

Seeing Elaina so depressed, Orkiss sighed. "They only did this because they care about you. In your condition, you wouldn't be able to ride a horse, much less face what awaits them in Raven's Nest," he said.

Elaina still didn't want to believe it. As she wallowed in self-pity, for some reason Kay's face appeared in her mind. "What about Kay? Did he have anything to say about leaving me here?" Elaina asked. She didn't notice it herself, but her voice had a tinge of hope in it—hope that the sell-sword Kay had stood up for her but been outvoted, or something like that.

Sadly, her hopes were dashed almost as soon as they had come. "He didn't say anything when Prince Leander brought up the subject of leaving without you. Both Lucis and Roan agreed with the prince, and that was that. The four of them were out of sight before the sun left the horizon," Orkiss told her.

Elaina felt anger boiling inside her chest—anger for both Leander and Kay. Leander for having the gall to bring up leaving her, and Kay for not saying anything and going along with it. In her heart, she knew that if they were in front of her right now, she would not let them know peace.

"Where's Arvandus? I need to speak to him," Elaina said. It was fine that they had left her. All she had to do was take the blood Arvandus had offered her yesterday and make it to Raven's Nest before they did. With her riding skills, she didn't believe it to be that much of a challenge. Most children in the Estelle Duchy learned to ride as soon as they could walk.

Orkiss didn't seem shocked at hearing that Elaina wanted to see Arvandus. With a light chuckle, he said, "My master thought you might. He has instructed me to take you to him the moment you ask."

Leaving the office, Orkiss led Elaina deeper into Red Hall until they reached a familiar hallway. Elaina knew this hallway, as Brana had told them about it before. This was the path to the cells where the criminal warriors were incarcerated. Elaina couldn't understand what Arvandus was doing there or why she was being brought there.

As they entered the dark hallway, Elaina found herself descending deeper and deeper. The number of steps must have taken them underground as they continued onward. This part of Red Hall was vastly different from the rest. Not only was there even less light, but there was a solemnness that hung in the air. At the bottom of the stairway was a pair of strong doors. Several warriors stood guard, only moving to open the doors once Orkiss had ordered them to.

Finally they made it to the famous holding cells. Dozens of metal doors stretched out along each wall. Unable to hold in her curiosity, Elaina peeked through the small window in a door. She was shocked by what she saw.

The cell wasn't as horrible as she had thought it would be. In fact, it looked slightly cozy, even if it was behind a steel door and underground. She saw a nice bed with soft sheets, a small table and chair for eating. There was even a rug on the stone floor. On one side, the warrior who was locked in was busy swinging his sword as he practiced his swordplay.

"Shocked by what you see?" Orkiss suddenly said, startling Elaina and causing her to jump back from the door.

Looking to Orkiss, she asked, "Isn't this supposed to be a prison? How can you let an inmate keep their sword with them? Aren't you afraid something might happen?"

As a princess, Elaina's father had shown her the prison cells of their own palace. There the inmates had no such luxuries as warm sheets or tables and chairs. They were lucky to get a rough and patched-up blanket, and never would they be allowed weapons.

"Red Hall may be called the warriors' prison, but that isn't all it is," Orkiss began to explain. "This level is for warriors whose crimes of dishonor are minor. They are allowed to keep their weapon and are given fair meals. The lower levels have more intense restrictions, but no matter what, they are always allowed their sword."

"Why is it like this?" Elaina asked.

"It is because, besides a few exceptions, this prison is also a place to rehabilitate warriors who have strayed from the honorable path. The sword is a warrior's soul. Taking it away won't help them find their way back to the three virtues," Orkiss said.

He then pointed at a strange mark above the metal door. Elaina noticed that every door had this mark. "This is a mark carved by the Phoenix God himself. Once a warrior finds his honor once more, the door will open, and they will be allowed to leave," said Orkiss.

This only made Elaina even more confused. "But no warrior ever leaves once they are imprisoned," she said. This was known by all in the three duchies to be true. Not a single warrior sent to Red Hall had ever returned. If what Orkiss had said was true, then the warriors who proved themselves would find themselves free and would find their way back to their homes. "Does that mean that not a single warrior has been able to salvage themselves after sullying their honor?"

Orkiss laughed. "On the contrary, at least a dozen find their doors open every year. In fact, on our way down here, you saw some who have regained their honor," he said.

Elaina knew what Orkiss was implying. The warriors guarding the cells were warriors once living in these cells. She then understood how Red Hall could have so many warriors under its banner. These warriors were all once inmates here, and after proving themselves, they had begun to serve Lord Orkiss and Red Hall.

"Now is not the time for us to speak of this. My master is still waiting for us on a lower level," Orkiss said, hinting that it was time to continue.

The next level was almost an exact replica of the previous floor. The only difference that Elaina could tell was that the metal doors that led to each cell no longer had small windows. Instead, they had a small latched opening at the bottom of each door, most likely to insert food and withdraw waste.

It was in front of one of these doors that Elaina spotted Arvandus. The sage didn't notice their arrival at first and was looking toward the door as if pondering something. As they reached the sage, Lord Orkiss gave a respectful bow to him. Arvandus didn't respond and only stood there staring at the door, rubbing his chin in deep concentration.

Just when Elaina had gotten up the nerve to ask him why she was there, Arvandus spoke. "Orkiss, you may leave us" was all he said.

Giving Arvandus another bow, Orkiss left the two of them alone. Elaina stood there watching as Orkiss disappeared. Turning back to Arvandus, she found the sage looking back at the cell once more. She waited longer, but Arvandus still didn't speak, so Elaina decided to.

"Sage Arvandus, I have a request," Elaina said. "I would like to use the winter deer blood that you offered me yesterday. I can't just wait here while Kay, Leander, and the rest risk their lives while I stay safe."

"Do you know who is being held here?" Arvandus asked, completely ignoring Elaina's words. The sage saw Elaina's face twitch a little from being ignored, and he laughed. "Why don't I just show you?"

Arvandus knocked on the door. The heavy metal door opened slowly by itself, as if by magic. Giving Elaina a glance, Arvandus walked in. With no other option, Elaina followed suit.

The cell was similar to the one she had seen before, minus the table and chair. The bedding and rug were still there. Sitting on the bed was someone Elaina was familiar with, someone she hadn't expected to see. It was the man with the bow from their encounter with Bez and the ogre.

Without any good feeling toward this man who had tried to kill Leander, Elaina's already bad mood turned worse. "Why did you want to meet here?" Elaina asked Arvandus.

Arvandus looked at her and asked, "Do you know who this is? Or more accurately, the blood lineage that runs in his veins?"

Elaina noticed that what Arvandus had said caused a reaction from the man, but the man remained tight-lipped and refused to say a word.

Finally, curious as to why they were here, she asked, "What is his last name?"

Arvandus looked the man in the eye and said, "This man is the last surviving member of the Glaeseker line."

"Glaeseker?" Elaina said, astonished. "Didn't that family die out during the Splintering War?"

The Glaeseker family was probably the most well-known warrior line in the entire history of the kingdom of Mezer. Not only had they been the first to follow their first king and future god, Calv Ridian, but they were also famous for having the most Zer'sheen to ever come out of a single warrior lineage. No fewer than twelve Zer'sheen were recorded to have come from the Glaeseker line. It was even believed that the Glaesekers had had some mystical powers that had helped guide them to achieve these great deeds.

Sadly, this great family had been the first target of the Tarsises during the Splintering War. Before anyone could react, the Tarsis forces had surrounded Hel'ves, the ancestral home of the Glaesekers. The Tarsis warriors slaughtered every man, woman, and child that carried this heroic bloodline. Not long after the war, people tried to find even a single member of the Glaeseker line, but to no avail.

"How did you …?" The man on the bed finally spoke. He was shocked that his history had been uncovered.

"Every Sage of the Star Tower has tried to read in the stars if the Glaeseker line still lasts, and every time, we find the Glaeseker star dim but still flickering. That, to us, is more than enough proof that the Glaeseker line persists to this day, even if it only has one descendant left," Arvandus answered.

"But how do you know that this man is the last Glaeseker?" Elaina asked, still not convinced that this man was a descendant of the famous Glaeseker family. It was every warrior's hope that the Glaesekers still lived, but Elaina didn't wish it to be this man who fulfilled that hope—a man who had hunted them down for the treacherous Tarsises.

"It is in the eyes," Arvandus said. "You must have heard that the Glaesekers have some magic in their blood. This power derives from the eyes. With the help of their magical eyes, they can see what others cannot."

Elaina looked into the man's eyes, and the man looked back. As she peered into his black pupils, they suddenly began to move—not like normal people's eyes, which widened and shrank, but more like the waves of a tide, flowing back and forth until his irises were no longer circular but changing into all shapes and sizes.

Elaina was so startled by the man's changing eyes that she unintentionally took a step back. It was only when the man turned away that she was able to relax.

Arvandus saw all this, but his face didn't show what he was thinking. Before Elaina knew what was happening, the sage had already pushed her out of the cell and slammed the door shut.

"You should be careful when looking into the eyes of someone with a magical gaze," Arvandus warned. He then turned and looked at the cell once more and sighed. "I hope he can redeem himself soon."

Elaina felt anger welling up inside her. "What was all that about? Why did you tell me all this? And why did you make me meet that man?" she asked as she ground her teeth, trying not to say something she might regret later.

"I wanted to show you this for you to understand. The one you are going up against isn't just some traitorous duke. It is a darkness that Duke Valens has allied with. This darkness isn't something he can handle, and it will consume the Talov Duchy if not stopped."

Arvandus's words sent shivers down Elaina's spine.

"What is it that you want?" Elaina asked. She hadn't been brought up in the Estelle palace for nothing. She knew when someone was trying to persuade her into doing something.

Arvandus gave her a smile and said, "Elaina, what I want from you isn't something most people can do. But for Elaina Estelle, the task might be possible." As he spoke, he pulled out a familiar-looking vial and placed it in Elaina's hands.

After getting the vial of blood so easily, Elaina investigated Arvandus's gaze. When she saw the determination in the sage's eyes, she knew that she would agree, even without knowing yet what Arvandus wished of her.

+

A few days' ride from Red Hall, a group of riders was heading toward Raven's Nest at a daunting pace. Those on the road had to jump out of the way to keep from being stomped to death by the many horses. Some wanted to curse them, but upon seeing the crest of Red Hall adorning the riders' clothes, even the bravest men kept their mouths shut.

Unbeknown to those watching, the one leading the Red Hall warriors wasn't one of their own but the infamous Prince Leander Talov. The prince was covered from head to toe in the warrior attire of Red Hall, and his face was covered by a hood, making it impossible for those warriors still hunting him to notice him among the Red Hall warriors.

Along with Leander and the rest of the group was also the famous Top Sword, Brana Ulfenn, as well as over a dozen of Red Hall's strongest and most honorable warriors. When Leander had declared that he was leaving, Lord Orkiss had offered to send Brana along with them. With Brana's presence, no one dared to questioned them as they traveled to Raven's Nest.

"Your Highness, at our pace, we will reach Raven's Nest by nightfall," Brana said to Leander, preparing the prince for what was to come.

Prince Leander nodded to the warrior before he returned his gaze back to the road. Leander knew exactly where they were. Growing up, he and Eustace used to sneak out of the city and ride their horses along this very street. Whenever they returned, their grandfather would give them a tongue-lashing, but Leander and Eustace would just do it again. Remembering this happy memory caused Leander to sigh. Those playful and innocent memories seemed so far away now, and Leander knew that they would never return.

They continued to ride onward. When the sun was beginning to set, Raven's Nest came into view. Sitting on top of a large hill was the largest city in all the duchies, the capital of the Talov Duchy, the city of Raven's Nest. The capital of the Estelle Duchy, Esesa, and the holy city of Ridia were right behind in size, but with one look, anyone could tell that the two cities were completely overshadowed by the immensity of Raven's Nest.

Large spires and towers stretched up from the ground, as if trying to grasp the clouds in the sky. Mimicking these tall structures, the houses and buildings each stood over four stories tall. The largest of these was the Talov family palace, to the east of the city, and the temple to the Phoenix God, to the north. From this distance, the city looked more like a small mountain range.

Seeing Raven's Nest, the place he had been dreaming of returning to since this whole disaster had begun, Leander started to tear up. After heartache, dangerous encounters, and struggles, he had finally made it.

"I've finally returned," Leander whispered to himself. With that said, he and the rest of his group rode toward Raven's Nest.

Chapter Twenty-Five: Those Who Fight against Treachery

D ark clouds loomed over Raven's Nest, cloaking the city in a thick veil of darkness. The once peaceful night was long gone as squads of warriors loyal to Duke Valens patrolled the narrow streets, staring down any who got in their way. Even with all this, the normal citizens were too busy whispering and chatting about the upcoming wedding of Princess Aris Talov and Lord Sarus Valens, as well as Duke Valens's crowning as regent.

Sneaking through these streets, Roan kept his back to the walls as several warriors passed him by. It was only once he could no longer hear their footsteps that he continued, only to have to hide again a few moments later as another patrol walked by. This had been going on all night, and the constant threat of being caught had caused Roan to sweat profoundly. Hiding behind a couple of garbage bins, Roan couldn't help but curse under his breath.

After reaching Raven's Nest, they had made it through the gate quite easily. The guards didn't dare to get in the way of the Top Sword and had let them through. Once inside the capital, they had soon discovered that Duke Valens was to be named regent the next day, and afterward he would personally preside over his son and Aris's wedding ceremony.

As the princess's personal warrior, Roan couldn't let that happen and volunteered to try to gather as much information as he could. As the warriors of Red Hall and the rest were too conspicuous, Roan was the only rational choice. That was how Roan found himself dodging patrol after patrol, trying to learn as much as he could.

Sneaking through the alleyways and streets, Roan finally made it to his destination. In front of him was a large building. This building was one of the city's guard quarters. It was also a place where Roan could quickly learn of what was going on in the city.

In front of the entryway stood two guards, warriors with the Valens crest on their tunics. Upon seeing this, Roan didn't panic. Instead, he made his way away from the building until he was standing in front of a wall in a nearby alleyway. He placed his hand on the wall, and his fingers slid over the stone until they brushed past a crack.

Drawing his knife, Roan proceeded to carve around the stone brick until he finally got it loose. With one last nudge, the stone popped free, leaving a small opening, just large enough for a hand to fit. Inside was a strange wooden lever. After looking around and seeing no one, Roan twisted the lever until it made a click. As it did, a part of the ground by the wall lifted, revealing a secret trapdoor. Before anyone noticed, Roan returned the stone and slipped into the trapdoor, with the trapdoor closing behind him.

Beyond the trapdoor was dark, and the air was stale. Keeping his footsteps soft, Roan made his way through the secret passage, the only light coming from cracks in the floor above him. Roan could hear the floorboards above him creak as the soldiers and warriors of the guard quarters walked about. Their voices came to Roan almost unhindered.

The deeper he went, the fewer voices and footsteps could be heard. Finally Roan made it to the end of the crawl space. Above him, the voices of only two men were discernible. Placing his ear to the boards above him, Roan listened in on their conversation.

"Nothing from any of the patrols?" one of the men asked. Roan recognized the voice's owner as Drenn, one of Duke Valens's most trusted warriors and confidants. He knew he had struck gold when he heard this man speak.

"Not yet, but my men are sweeping the city as we speak. If Leander truly has already made it here, then we will find him shortly," the man answered. From his tone, he must be high up in the chivalric order under the duke. Hearing that their entry into Raven's Nest might have already been discovered worried Roan, but hearing that they were only speculating gave Roan some comfort that their plan had still not been found out.

"Continue to scour the city," Drenn ordered. Roan could hear the tapping of the warrior's fingers, as if Drenn was thinking of something. "I hear that Brana led a group of Red Hall warriors here. Check to see if the prince could have sneaked in alongside them."

"Sir? You want me to raid the manor of Lord Orkiss?" the man asked with a trembling voice. If anyone else had been asked to do this, they, too, would have been fearful. Who in their right mind would purposely antagonize the Top Sword and the warden of Red Hall?

Drenn seemed to ponder the idea before speaking. "No need for that. Just keep them under constant surveillance. I don't want a single Red Hall warrior unaccounted for," he said, deciding against a direct conflict with one of the most powerful forces in the Talov Duchy.

Sighing in relief, the man soon excused himself to continue his duties. Listening to the man leave, Roan wasn't worried about the prince being found. As soon as they had entered Raven's Nest, the prince, along with Kay, Lucis, and Brana, had found a safe house away from the Red Hall manor. The only ones that they would find there were normal warriors, along with the fake hall master.

Underneath the floor, Roan realized that Drenn was alone. As one of Duke Valens's arms, if Drenn were to die, then the duke would lose a powerful ally. Deciding that the chance was too great to pass up, Roan was preparing to ambush Drenn when suddenly Roan found a knife to his throat.

"I wouldn't do that if I were you," said the one holding the knife. "Why don't you release your grip on your sword before you do something foolish?"

Roan was stunned speechless. He hadn't even noticed someone sneaking up behind him. Unable to retaliate, Roan released his grip on his sword. He could feel the murderous intent coming from the one behind him. If he didn't let go of his hilt, he knew the person wouldn't hesitate to slit his throat.

As he let go, the person behind him retracted their knife from his throat. With the danger averted, Roan turned to face his ambusher. When he saw who it was, he was stunned once more, and so was the one who had ambushed him.

"It's you," Roan and the ambusher both said, speaking at the same time.

+

Located several blocks away from the Red Hall manor was a building like all others around—a normal housing structure where several families lived. The families living there had no idea that their prince was hiding out on the top floor of this four-story building.

Sneaking a peek through the curtains every few minutes, Leander was getting nervous. It had already been a few hours since Roan had left to find out what was going on in the city. It was already past the time he was supposed to have returned by, and now Leander had started to fear that he had already been caught or killed.

"You need to relax. Working yourself up like this won't do you any good. You must have a clear head if you want to stop Duke Valens from taking over the duchy," Lucis suddenly said, appearing next to Leander and pulling the curtain shut.

"We shouldn't have let Roan go out alone," Leander said. He knew that Lucis was right and that he had to calm down, but Roan was his sister's personal warrior, and Leander had known him since he was young. Thinking that Roan might be dead made him feel more anxious than ever.

"You know that it would only have been riskier if anyone had gone with him. Alone, he has more of a chance to sneak by all the patrols," said Piers, the fake hall master.

Leander knew that to be true, but reason rarely trumped emotion, especially when it came to those close to you. Leander had already lost so much and wasn't about to lose another person close to him.

As he sat down, Brana entered the room.

"Roan has returned," Brana said. As he spoke, the man himself walked in after Brana.

"I have safely returned, Your Highness," Roan said, saluting Leander.

"Thank the zer' you are all right," Leander said as he rushed to the warrior and clasped the man by the shoulders. After the relief he then became serious and asked, "Did you find out anything about my sister and grandfather?"

"I shouldn't be the one to answer you," Roan said. He then turned to a person standing next to him. It was only when Roan gestured to them that Leander realized that someone was there. Next to Roan was a woman. Even standing there she had no presence, as if she was simply air. Leander had to think for a moment before he remembered who this woman was.

"You're my sister's handmaiden Lexi, aren't you?" Leander said, shocked to see her here.

The woman gave the prince a bow. "I am glad to see that Your Highness is safe. I am indeed Her Highness's handmaiden," Lexi answered.

Leander then thought of what Roan had just said. "Do you have any news on how Aris is faring?" he asked.

"Sir, Her Highness is still well and is fighting with everything she can, but she is still a prisoner of the Valenses. Several warrior families are still resisting and trying to figure out how to rescue her. I had been sent out to gather intel when I ran into Roan here," Lexi answered, giving Roan a smile. She was glad to see that her old friend and comrade was still alive and well.

Leander felt more relief learning about his sister's well-being, as well as learning that there were still those not fooled or corrupted by Duke Valens. "What about my grandfather? Have you heard anything about the archduke?" Leander asked.

Lexi frowned and shook her head. "I'm afraid not. Duke Valens has the archduke under constant guard. No one can get into his quarters. All that we know is that the duke seems to be keeping the archduke alive for now."

"No news can be considered good news," said Roan, seeing that Leander's mood had changed after hearing of the archduke's unknown situation.

Leander heaved a sigh. "I guess you are right," he said. He then turned back to Lexi. "You said there are others working to rescue Princess Aris and stop Duke Valens. Can you take me to them?"

"Of course, sir," Lexi answered.

+

Lexi led them through the city. The woman seemed to know when and where the patrols would appear as they quickly made their way, passing one after another. As they continued, Leander noticed that they were getting closer and closer to the palace. The homes and buildings here all belonged to highborn families or those with great power or wealth. The Red Hall manor was located here, but with it being too conspicuous, they had decided to find a safe house away from here, and after hearing Roan's report, they had found that this was the correct decision.

Lexi led them to one of the large manors. Upon seeing the manor, Leander was shocked and looked to Lexi for confirmation. When she nodded, Leander felt more determined than ever to rescue Aris, as this manor wasn't any ordinary warrior family's manor. This was the manor of Lord Jukel Altares.

Lexi did not lead them in through the front entrance. Instead, she brought them to the back, where there were fewer eyes that could notice them. Once there, Lexi gave several knocks at the back gate in a particular rhythm. As she finished, the gate suddenly opened for them, and Lexi led them through.

Three warriors stood guard at the gate. They gave Lexi not a second look, as if seeing her was normal, but they gave Leander and the rest inquisitive looks. Due to the hoods and cowls Leander and the rest wore, they couldn't recognize them.

They made their way through the hallways until they reached a certain door. Leander could hear a heated discussion on the other side. Lexi gave the secret knock one more time, causing some of the voices to hush.

"Lexi, why don't you hurry up and enter?" a loud voice called out from the other side of the door.

Opening the door, Lexi led them in. The room was filled with warriors, all of whom were surrounding a large table. On the table, there was a map of the city, with several points and a certain route marked out.

As Leander and the rest were taking the warriors in, the warriors noticed that Lexi hadn't returned alone. Some of the warriors were quick to draw their swords, as they feared what these newcomers entailed. In response to them, Kay and Lucis were about to draw their swords as well, but Leander waved them off, making them release their grips on their weapons.

"Lexi, who are these people you brought here?" said a man with a full beard. The man towered over most of the warriors there—not as tall as Brana or Archduke Bennet, but still a giant if compared to most men. It was obvious by the way he spoke that this man was the leader. Leander grew excited.

"Lord Altares," Leander said, pulling his hood off to reveal who he was. "I'm glad to see you here."

"Your Highness," Lord Altares suddenly proclaimed. Bowing his head, the hall master gave the prince a warrior's salute.

The rest of the warriors, who were shocked at seeing the prince, realized their mistake and bowed their heads. Leander looked at these warriors and felt pride. "You all need not bow to me, as you have all shown that you hold true honor in your hearts," Leander said. He didn't know where these words came from but knew them to be true.

"Your Highness, how is it that you are here?" Lord Altares asked. "Duke Valens's men control the gates, and the city guard are under his control as well. How did you get past all the searching patrols?"

"I have Brana to thank for that," Leander said, turning to Brana, who had also taken off his hood. Many of the gathered warriors looked toward Brana in worship.

After the initial reaction, and after everyone had settled down, Leander explained as fast as he could what had transpired. He told them how his brother had actually been murdered and how the Valenses were plotting with those of the Tarsis Duchy to overthrow his grandfather. By the end, every warrior in the room was seething with fury.

"How dare they!" one of the warriors shouted. "Not only have they plotted against their lord, but they aligned themselves with the Tarsises. They have completely besmirched their honor."

More words were shouted, cursing the duke for his treacherous deeds. Some of the warriors felt betrayed after learning of all the things a duke of their duchy had done. It didn't help that Duke Valens was the son of the famous former Duke Valens, who to this day was the archduke's sworn brother. His betrayal could be considered a betrayal of his sworn uncle.

When the shouts and curses were beginning to get out of hand, Lord Altares couldn't take it anymore, but before he could speak, Prince Leander beat him to it.

"Silence!" Leander shouted. His sudden yell caused all the warriors to end their discussions and not let out a peep. "We are not here to discuss all of Duke Valens's crimes. We have gathered to rescue Princess Aris and to stop Jarl Valens from becoming regent."

Seeing Prince Leander like this, Lord Altares was first shocked, then pleased. "Right, now is not the time for this. We must prepare for tomorrow," he said.

The warriors gathered themselves, then went back to the map on the table.

As Leander took his spot around the table, Lord Altares whispered to him, "You've grown, Your Highness."

Upon hearing the compliment, Leander felt a slight feeling in his chest but pushed it aside, as now was not the time. "What have you found out?" he asked.

Lord Altares's son and heir pointed at the palace on the map. "Tomorrow morning, Princess Aris will be escorted along this path," the young Jukel Altares said as his finger went over the lined route. "If we want to rescue the princess, then hitting them on route would be the best opportunity. Of course they know this and will have Princess Aris heavily guarded. We need to make them drop their guard, and the best time is when they think they have successfully reached the temple."

Some of the warriors nodded and spoke in agreement with the Stone Hall heir. Even Leander thought what Jukel had said made sense.

Then a voice suddenly spoke out. "I respectfully disagree with the young master," said a warrior standing next to Lord Altares.

Jukel didn't take being criticized well and frowned. "Knox Ambermond," Jukel said through grinding teeth. "What is it that you disagree with?"

"Duke Valens isn't a fool. He will know that this would be the best time and place for us to strike, and he will have plans laid out to counter us if we move. The only way we can escape the duke's plotting is to do something even he would not expect," the warrior Knox answered in a respectful tone.

"Where should we strike, then?" Jukel asked, clearly upset over Knox disagreeing with him. It didn't help that he saw his father nodding in agreement with Knox, making his dislike of Knox grow even more.

The warrior Knox either didn't notice Jukel's anger toward him or decided to just ignore it, but he pointed at the bridge on the route. "We should strike here, just when they are starting to cross. This will make it so that the warriors in front will have difficulty reinforcing the rear. This gives us enough time to rescue the princess and make our escape," he answered.

After hearing Knox, all the warriors turned to Lord Altares for guidance.

"I agree with Knox's proposal," the hall master said, and all the other warriors began to agree as well.

"Now we need to discuss our next move. Taking down Duke Valens before he is named regent," said Leander.

Everyone's attention went toward the Phoenix Temple, where the ceremony for the wedding and Duke Valens's naming would be happening. They all knew that rescuing the princess was only a part of the mission. If they failed to stop the duke from being named regent, the man would hold all the power of the duchy. His word would become law, and those who fought against him would be rounded up and killed without fair trial or judgment.

After talking it over, everyone agreed. They decided to split into two groups, one going to rescue the princess while the other would confront Duke Valens and stop the naming ceremony. The group that would rescue the princess would be led by Roan and the hall master's son, Jukel, while the ones who were going after the duke would be led by Prince Leander and Lord Altares.

The only one unconvinced was the young Jukel Altares. After having his idea thrown out by his own father, he kept silent, and when it was decided he would rescue the princess instead of confronting Duke Valens, he scowled but kept quiet.

Leander looked at the map of the city lying in front of him. He couldn't help it as his body trembled in anticipation. In only a few hours, they would begin, and the battle over control of the entire duchy would commence.

Chapter Twenty-Six: You Can Never Underestimate a Plotter

Aris awoke with a heavy heart. She had been told that today was to be her wedding day. The day that most girls dreamed of, Aris looked at it with contempt. After throwing off her blanket, she picked up her hand mirror and looked through her small window.

She used the mirror to reflect the morning light once, twice, then once again. Afterward she waited, not breaking her gaze. Finally, from one of the building's rooftops, Aris spotted two small flashes of light. Her frown turned into a slight grin.

As she stood by her window, a sudden knock came from the door. She heard keys and the click of the lock. The door swung open, and three maids walked into the room before the door closed again, the lock clicking back into place.

"Your Highness, we are here to help you prepare for your wedding," said the head maid, giving Aris a bow, with the other two bowing soon after. Aris noticed that these maids only gave a slight bow, not a bow that a servant should give to royalty, but the princess knew why. These maids were servants Duke Valens had brought from his own home, and they were loyal to the duke.

Aris didn't say anything, and just let them work, undressing her and getting her dress ready. She knew that fighting at this moment wouldn't do any good, and knowing Duke Valens, it wouldn't be beneath him to have a warrior force her to wear the dress. Princess Aris wouldn't allow such humiliation to befall her.

The maids did quick work and had her in her wedding dress in no time. As they slid on her gloves, Aris caught a glimpse of herself in the mirror on the wall. She was wearing the same dress that her mother wore on her own wedding day. The silver silk dress flowed down her body like an elegant rainfall. The embroidery on the long sleeves and edges of the dress, along with her makeup, gave her an heavenly look. Seeing herself in the mirror, Aris had to admit that the maids had done a good job at making her look the part of a happy and beautiful bride.

After finishing with their work, the maids swiftly left, and a group of armed warriors arrived to escort her out of her room. They led her down to the courtyard, where a carriage awaited them. Along with the carriage, there were dozens of mounted warriors adorned with armor, their swords hanging on their hips, ready and waiting to be used. If anyone saw this, they would think that they were escorting a dangerous prisoner to jail, not a bride to her wedding ceremony.

Issuing orders to the waiting warriors was Duke Valens's personal warrior Mikael. When he saw his warriors bringing along the princess, Mikael walked over to meet them. "Your Highness, I will be the one escorting you to the temple," he said, not even attempting to bow to Aris.

"Sending one of his most trusted warriors to oversee my arrival at the temple. Duke Valens must really think much of this princess," Aris said. Her snide remark had little effect on Mikael as the warrior ushered her into the carriage.

Taking her seat, Aris found herself sitting next to two warriors. The warriors were there to keep her from making a scene as they proceeded through the city. From her seat, Aris could hear Mikael give the order to move out. She felt the carriage jolt as it began to head toward the Phoenix Temple. The dozens of hooves sounded like thunder as they reverberated off the stone roads.

It wasn't only the horses that she could hear. As today was the wedding of the only princess of the Talov family, many had come out to take part in the festivities. Some of the crowd were cheering and shouting to see the princess, but when she went to pull the curtain back, one of the warriors stopped her. She gave the warrior a hard glare, but the warrior was unfazed. Disgruntled, Aris sat back down and closed her eyes, listening ever so closely to all that was going on.

The carriage made its way through the busy streets of Raven's Nest, never stopping. The warriors pushed the crowd out of the way as they made their way to the temple. In her head, Aris was silently counting, her fingers tapping with the count. The warriors guarding her were unaware that Aris was doing this. They only saw the finger tapping as her being nervous for her upcoming wedding.

Finally, as she reached the end of her counting, Aris stopped her repetitive tapping. As if in response, the carriage suddenly ground to a halt. The two warriors looked to each other, confused. This sudden stop was not part of the plan. Before they could find out what was going on, loud shouts could be heard from outside the carriage. Citizens were screaming, and the sound of clashing steel altered the warriors' instincts.

"Go and find out what is going on. I'll stay here and watch the princess," said one of the warriors. As he did, he eyed Princess Aris with a questioning gaze, thinking that she must have some knowledge of what was going on. Aris saw this and kept her face neutral.

The other warrior nodded and rushed out of the carriage. As the door swung open, Aris caught sight of several warriors fighting with unknown assailants. Before Aris could see more, the remaining warrior slammed the carriage door shut.

"Tell me what is going on. I know that you know who these attackers are," the warrior yelled at Aris, convinced that she was responsible for the ambush. The warriors fighting for their lives were comrades of his. He felt anguish having to babysit the princess instead of fighting alongside them.

"How should I know?" Aris said calmly. "In case you've forgotten, I have been locked away for days. How can I plot anything locked inside a tower? Has your brain become nothing more than a decorative piece?"

Enraged by the princess's insulting words, the warrior smashed his fist into the carriage, barely missing Aris's face in the process. It was at that moment that Aris acted. Pulling out a pin in her hair, she stabbed the warrior's eye.

The warrior flailed away, howling in pain. Not letting this chance slip, Aris pulled a knife from the warrior's belt and slit the man's throat before he could react. All the warrior could do was look at the princess with his remaining good eye in horror as his blood flowed from his neck. His last sight was the princess he looked down on looking down on him in return.

With her guard taken care of, Aris pulled the warrior's sword free from its sheath. The sword was heavier than what she was used to, but she was a Talov princess and knew how to use it. With sword in hand, Aris pushed out of the carriage and into the conflict outside.

The warriors who were part of the guard were fighting off the assailants and weren't expecting the princess to suddenly jump out of the carriage, but the assailants were. As soon as she landed, the group of attackers surrounded the princess. One in particular caught Aris's attention. Aris gave him a smile.

"Roan, I'm glad to see you," the princess said, looking gratefully at her personal warrior who had come to her rescue. She may have known about the ambush but didn't know the exact details. She had no idea that Roan would be the one to lead the assault.

"It is good to see you as well, Your Highness," Roan answered back. As they spoke, some of the warriors who were guarding the princess noticed that Aris was escaping, and tried to stop them, but before they got close, Jukel and some Stone Hall warriors intervened.

"Now is not the time to talk," Jukel shouted at Roan. "Hurry up and get the princess out of here." After yelling, Jukel ran back into the fray.

Not wasting a moment more, Roan, along with several other warriors, began fighting their way out. Not wanting to slow them down, Aris also fought. Soon the group made it out of the fight and started heading toward the mazelike alleyways of Raven's Nest.

"Don't let them get away!" Mikael yelled from among the battling warriors.

Seeing Princess Aris escape, Jukel suddenly shouted, "Disperse!"

The warriors who were fighting suddenly ran in all different directions. Their mission was only to rescue the princess, not to fight their enemies to the bitter end. With them outnumbered it was only their sudden ambush that had given them the necessary time to get the princess away.

As the warriors retreated and spread throughout the city, they also lured the pursuing warriors away from Aris, allowing her to safely escape. Soon Aris and the rest could no longer hear warriors behind them. They had successfully escaped. Turning a corner, they decided to take a quick breath before continuing. All but Roan made a perimeter around Aris.

As he panted, Roan looked at Aris and bowed. "Your Highness—" Roan started, but as he spoke, Aris suddenly hugged him, causing him to freeze. In the end, Roan hugged Aris back and said, "I'm sorry I wasn't here."

Aris looks up to him and shook her head. "There is no reason to apologize. It was on my order that you left," Aris answered. Then her face turned solemn. "And

349

if you had stayed, you would have ended up like Pierce."

Hearing his comrade's name made Roan tremble. When he had met up with Lexi, he had learned of Pierce's demise. He hadn't had time to process it, but seeing the princess he had sworn to protect in front of him, he realized that he would never see his friend or hear his wonderful music ever again.

Aris then remembered why she had sent Roan off in the first place. "If you are here, then Leander must be here as well. Why isn't he with you, then?" Aris asked.

"You have nothing to fear. His Highness is safe. He is leading a group of warriors alongside Lord Altares and the Top Sword to stop Duke Valens from being named regent," Roan reassured the princess. "You should be proud. His Highness has grown up quite a bit since you last saw him."

As they spoke, one of the warriors suddenly ran back. Behind him was another group of warriors. Leading these new warriors was young Jukel Altares. He walked toward them in an arrogant and prideful fashion. When he reached them, he gave Princess Aris a slight bow, with the warriors behind giving a full bow.

"Your Highness, it is great to see you once more. I have heard much of Your Highness's fine accomplishments over the years," praised Jukel, trying to get on the princess's good side before anyone else could.

Aris saw through this and had to keep a frown from showing on her face. "We should speak once we have made our escape," she said, and as she did, the pursuing warriors could be heard coming closer.

Not wanting to be spotted, Roan and Jukel led Aris and their warriors through the alleyways of Raven's Nest. The group circled the Stone Hall manor a few times in order to make sure there was no one tailing them. Once they were sure no one was, they began to make their way toward the manor.

When the manor came into sight, some of the warriors were already celebrating their successful rescue of Princess Aris. Aris was also feeling that they had succeeded, but suddenly Roan forced them to halt.

"What are you doing?" Jukel demanded of Roan.

"Something isn't right," Roan said as he pointed toward the large twin doors in front of the manor. The two doors were slightly cracked, which they shouldn't have been. The silence coming from the manor was eerie and made the warriors, while not sure why, alert. As if feeling everyone's stares, one of the doors swayed, broke off its hinges, and slammed to the ground with a loud bang.

Through the opening the fallen door had left, they could see one of the warriors in charge of guarding the manor dead on the ground, lying in a pool of his own blood. Every warrior instantly drew their weapon, ready for whatever was to come out of the manor.

"You made me wait quite a while. I was beginning to wonder if you had failed to rescue the poor Princess Aris." A voice came from the manor. A young man suddenly walked out of the manor, presumably the one who had just spoken.

Seeing the young man, Aris and the rest recognized him instantly.

"How are you here?" Jukel shouted.

The young man was the son of Duke Valens, the vile Sarus Valens. The young Sarus looked toward Aris and the warriors with contempt and mockery. When his sight fell onto Aris, he laughed.

"You thought that you could escape from us so easily," Sarus laughed. "My father truly is the only one who can be called a genius. Every move you have made, he has anticipated, and you all fell right into his ploys."

Everyone's hearts dropped. They knew that with Sarus here, that only meant that they had underestimated Duke Valens. He had somehow learned of their plans and taken measures to counter them. Aris felt fear tug at her heart. If they had known of the plan to rescue her, then they must know of the plan to stop the naming ceremony.

"Vile snake! I will kill you!" a warrior from the Divide suddenly yelled, charging Sarus. Looking closely, Aris noticed that the enraged warrior had similar features to the one lying dead. The two must have been from the same warrior family, maybe even siblings.

The man held his sword high, ready to kill the arrogant Sarus, but the warrior never had his revenge, as his body became a pincushion. Over a dozen arrows were shot from the windows of the manor, killing the warrior before he could fall to the ground. The dead warrior fell not three paces from Sarus, who laughed and stomped on his head.

"That is what you get for going against me," Sarus laughed.

His laughter and actions caused the warriors around Aris to tremble in rage. They had just seen one of their comrades and brothers killed dishonorably, then watched Sarus disgrace the warrior by stomping on his corpse.

"If you are such a great and powerful man, then why don't you prove it?" Roan shouted, pointing his sword at Sarus. "Duel me. Prove to us all that you are a warrior and not some conniving little brat."

Roan's taunts truly enraged Sarus. He wanted to prove Roan wrong, but Sarus was a coward. He also knew that Roan was a skilled swordsman, one of the best in the Talov Duchy. If he did agree to the duel, that would be quite literally handing his life to his enemies.

"There is no need for me to humor someone who is about to die," Sarus spat. Taking a step slightly to the side, he revealed a young boy. The boy looked toward Aris and the rest with a dead stare.

The strange boy's sudden appearance confused Aris and the warriors. They didn't know what Sarus was planning by having a boy who looked not even past the age of nine appear now. As Aris was wondering, her personal warrior Roan stepped in front of her, as if to shield her from a monster and not a child.

Aris saw that Roan's face was as pale as a sheet when looking at the young boy. "Roan, who is that boy?" asked Aris. Seeing how Roan reacted, she could honestly guess that Roan knew the boy somehow and feared him.

"Your Highness, no matter what, you must not leave my side," Roan said with his sword at the ready.

Hearing the seriousness in his tone, Aris stepped closer but did not hide behind him. She stood side by side with her personal warrior.

Sarus didn't like the fact that his betrothed was pointing a sword at him. Taking out a black bell, he shouted, "Kill them!" and rang the bell.

The bell didn't let out a sound, but as soon as Sarus swung it, the young boy transformed into a giant, hulking monstrosity. The giant ogre gave a violent roar before charging Aris and the rest of the warriors, each of the beast's steps crushing the stones beneath it.

Having not expected the young boy to suddenly turn into a monster, Aris and the warriors were momentarily stunned, allowing the beast to reach them before they were ready. Aris felt herself being pulled away just as the creature's large arm swung right where she had been standing, killing two warriors instantly.

Seeing two warriors die in a single strike from the ogre, Sarus began heckling like a madman. "Die! All of you, die!" he shouted.

The ogre responded to Sarus's crazed behavior and let out another roar before attacking the warriors. However, this time the warriors were ready and were able to defend themselves. Even so, the ogre was able to break one warrior's arm.

"Divide and surround!" Jukel ordered.

In unison, the warriors separated from one another, preventing the ogre from attacking all of them. Using this approach, they quickly encircled the beast.

Being a simpleminded beast, the ogre attacked only the warriors in its sight, leaving its back open. Taking the opening, a warrior struck the ogre's back, but the ogre's skin was too thick. The ogre, enraged at being hit, turned to attack its attacker, only to have another warrior take advantage and strike it.

While the ogre wasn't taking any real injuries, it was no longer causing the mayhem that it had been previously. Seeing this, Sarus shouted to those inside the manor. A group of warriors surged out of the manor. They had no crests or symbols representing their families, and charged Aris and the warriors with murder in their eyes.

With the addition of these warriors, they were no longer able to give their full attention to the ogre, and the beast was able to break free. With a swing of its hulking arm, it grabbed a warrior and ripped the poor man in two.

The scene became chaos as warriors on both sides fought while trying to stay away from the berserk ogre. Just as Aris and her warriors were getting the situation in check, they heard another roar from behind them.

Turning around, Aris saw the wall of a neighboring building being smashed open. Crawling its way through was another ogre. Six warriors with chains held the beast in check, but as they made it through the hole, they released it.

With the appearance of the second ogre, the scene became a living nightmare. Warriors from both sides fell prey to the ogres' rampage. As Aris cut down one of the warriors, she saw on the man's forearm a tattoo of a red sword. Aris instantly recognized the mark as the crest of the Bloody Blade of Tarsis.

"Sarus! Not only are you a traitor who uses monsters, but you plot with the Tarsises. You have sullied your entire family's grand legacy!" Aris shouted.

Sarus looked at the princess with a smug expression on his face. "After today my family will be the new rulers of the Talov Duchy. Or should we call it the Valens Duchy? As for sullying my family's honor, I'm bringing my family to greater heights than my forefathers could even imagine. You should be more worried about what has happened to that precious brother of yours," he laughed.

Aris paled. As she had thought, the Valenses knew what they had been planning and had set traps for both sides to fall into. Her worrying distracted her, and an enemy warrior nearly took her head off. If it hadn't been for one of her own warriors getting in the way, she would have just died.

"Don't listen to him," Roan said. "The prince has been through more than you can imagine. You have to trust that he will make it through."

Aris knew that Roan was right. Calming herself down, she looked straight ahead and charged into the fray.

+

"Something isn't right," said Kay. His crystal blue eyes narrowed as they peered deeper into the corridor.

The plan had gone off without a hitch. After leaving the Stone Hall manor, they had made their way to the Phoenix Temple, where the naming ceremony was taking place, without being spotted. There, they had been able to get the jump on the warriors guarding the outside of the temple and made their way inside.

"You noticed it too," Lucis said, also looking around as if sensing something the others hadn't. It wasn't only the two sell-swords that seemed to notice this. Brana, too, looked around with an alert gaze.

"Even so, we can't turn back now. We have to push forward and stop Duke Valens before it is too late," Leander said. He trusted Lucis, but he couldn't retreat now, not when they were so close to defeating the duke.

Finally they reached the main part of the temple, the worship hall. Large doors

355

that reached the ceiling were the only things separating them from the duke. Over a dozen warriors stood guard, but before they could alert the duke, they were taken care of. With their target just in reach, they pushed open the grand doors. Leander led them through, but what awaited them wasn't what they had been expecting.

The worship hall was completely empty. There was no naming ceremony being held, nor was there a single soul that could be seen. The altar, where the priest should have been standing as he named Duke Valens regent, stood alone, as if looking at Leander and the rest with contempt.

"What is going on? Where is the duke?" One of the warriors shouted what everyone was thinking.

Now everyone was feeling what Kay and Lucis had been talking about just moments ago. As a slow realization crept over them, it dawned on them that they had made a crucial mistake, that somehow their plans must have been discovered by Duke Valens.

"We have to leave," Lord Altares said, but as he began to order his warriors to retreat, someone ran into the worship hall. The man was one of the Divide warriors they had left to monitor the entrance. He was covered in blood, and he was holding one of his arms, which hung limp at his side.

"My lord, you have to escape now," the warrior weakly said before he collapsed.

Lucis noticed the man wobbling and caught him before he landed on the ground. After catching the wounded warrior, Lucis lifted his hand, revealing a pool of blood that had already gathered in his palm.

"Fletcher, what happened?" Lord Altares asked his dying warrior.

"My lord ... Duke Valens's men are forcing their way in as we speak. They are being led by Drenn of the third chivalric order. You have to escape before ..." The warrior Fletcher tried to speak, but before he could, he coughed up a mouthful of blood. The warrior couldn't hold on anymore and passed away in Lucis's arms.

The sound of many rushing footsteps echoed throughout the worship hall, signaling the incoming enemy forces.

Knowing that they were vastly outnumbered, Lord Altares ordered, "Brace the doors!"

The warriors closed the large doors and began to place whatever they could in front of them as quickly as they could. As two of the warriors were placing one of the pews down, the door suddenly made a booming sound. The duke's warriors had reached them and were trying to break through.

"That door won't hold for long. Is there no other way out of the worship hall? No side door hidden from normal view?" Lucis asked Altares.

"This is a temple, not a castle or fortress. It wasn't made to be ready for a siege. There is only one way in, and that is the main entrance," Altares answered.

Then a certain memory popped into Leander's head. "That isn't so," he mumbled. His voice was quiet but was still heard by all those gathered around the prince.

"What do you mean, that isn't so? Are you saying that there is another way out of here?" Kay asked.

With everyone's hopeful and questioning eyes on him, Prince Leander began to speak. "My grandfather once told me that there is a secret underground passage that leads from the palace to the temple, with the entrance on the temple's side somewhere in the worship hall."

"If there is a secret passage to the palace somewhere in this room, then there must be some lever or switch to reveal it," said Knox.

"Everyone, begin searching," Altares ordered.

He actually didn't have to. As soon as they had learned that there was an escape route, the warriors had begun to look. They weren't afraid of death but feared failing to stop Duke Valens. If they fought now, there would be no one left to face Duke Valens.

With newfound hope, they thoroughly searched the hall, but after a sweep through, they couldn't find the passage. The sound of wood cracking and splintering told them that the door would be breached in a matter of minutes.

As they were about to give up on finding the passage, Lucis shouted, "I found it!"

They found Lucis standing near the altar. As one of the most suspicious spots, they had already searched the altar but to no avail.

Lucis then turned to his brother Kay. "Kay, I need you to help me turn the altar."

Kay and Lucis began to push the large altar. As they struggled with the huge structure the altar began to budge. With this discovery, the rest of the warriors ran over to help. With everyone pushing, the altar rotated all the way around until they heard a click.

An area of the floor that was by one of the walls slid open, revealing a passage. As they were about to cheer, the door behind them gave way with a loud crash. A large battering ram slammed through, opening the way for the warriors to flow in. One of the first was the warrior Drenn, who looked toward them with a murderous gaze.

"Get to the passage!" Leander yelled.

With him and Lord Altares leading the way, they ran to the entrance of the passage. Drenn and his warriors noticed the secret passage and were stunned. There wasn't supposed to be any other way out. As Leander disappeared into the passage with his forces, Drenn roared to chase after them.

The passage was dark and coated in dust. The air was stale from being sealed away for so many years. The scent from the sewers that ran parallel to the passage made several warriors with little tolerance gag. As they ran deeper into the passage, they reached a part where there was a steel gate that hung from the ceiling. A large lever was sticking out of the neighboring wall.

Upon seeing the lever, Leander remembered more of what his grandfather had told him. The steel gate was there to stop those chasing from following those escaping. After pulling the lever, the gate would slam down, separating the groups.

"Pull the lever once we are all past the gate," Leander ordered.

The warrior Knox ran to the lever and pulled it down, but instead of what they had thought would happen, the wooden lever snapped right in half. Knox looked down at the lever in his hands, stunned. From behind they could hear the approaching warriors, and without the gate sealing behind them, those warriors would eventually reach them.

"Your Highness, you go on ahead. Leave the oncoming warriors to Kay and myself," Lucis said.

"Are you mad? Do you honestly expect to fight that many warriors? You two will be overwhelmed," Leander argued back. He may have known how strong Lucis and Kay were, but two facing hundreds of warriors was impossible, even for a Zer'sheen.

"In this narrow passage, their numbers will be a disadvantage. Only around four will be able to advance at one time. Four against Kay and me, we will be able to hold them off until you take down Duke Valens," Lucis answered. Seeing the resolution in Lucis's eyes, Leander knew that he wouldn't change his mind.

Leander didn't wish to send them to their deaths, even Kay, who he didn't get along with.

As he was not sure what to say, the warrior Knox spoke up. "Lord Altares, please allow me to stay as well. I won't let a single enemy pass through here," he declared.

Lord Altares looked at his most trusted warrior. "Very well, but I expect you to return alive," he answered.

In the end, it was the sell-sword brothers Kay and Lucis, the warrior Knox, and three others from different warrior families that chose to stay. Seeing these brave warriors left the remaining warriors feeling respect for them.

Standing in front of Lucis, Leander spoke. "I owe you and your brothers more than I can ever repay in my entire lifetime. You must at least let me try."

"Don't worry, Prince. We will make sure that we return safe and sound," Kay said with his usual jester-like laugh.

Normally, Leander would find insult in this, but he noticed the undertones of his words. So instead of getting upset, Prince Leander gave Kay a nod before wishing the rest of the brave men staying behind a swift victory.

Chapter Twenty-Seven: Karsic, a True Evil

Leander, Lord Altares, and the remaining warriors made their way through the passage. Behind them, they could no longer hear the pursuing warriors chasing after them. The warriors that had stayed behind must have halted Drenn and the duke's forces.

Finally they made it to the end of the tunnel. In front of them was a stone wall with light just peeking through the cracks. It didn't take long for them to figure out how to open the secret door. With a quick push, they found themselves in one of the hallways of the palace.

One by one, the remaining warriors made their way out of the secret passage. Once everyone was safely out, they quietly closed the door behind them. The exit from the passage disappeared into the wall, as if it had never existed.

Leander led them through the palace corridors toward the throne room. If Duke Valens was going to be sworn in inside the palace, then the throne room would be the only place where the naming ceremony could happen.

It didn't take long for them to run into conflict. There was no way that Duke Valens would leave himself unguarded. The closer they got to the throne room, the more warriors they ran into. Luckily for them, Duke Valens must have sent most of his forces to ambush them. The number of warriors guarding the naming ceremony was small—nowhere near enough to halt their advance.

Turning one last corner, they found themselves in front of two large doors—not as awe-inspiring as the twin doors of the Phoenix Temple, but magnificent all the same. From the other side of the door, they could hear the naming ceremony in its final stretch, with the loud voice of the priest finishing his speech.

"We can't let this sham of a ceremony continue any longer," Leander said, vowing in his heart that he would not let Duke Valens succeed.

Looking around, Leander saw the determined faces of all the warriors that were standing by his family instead of buckling under the duke's might or promises. Knowing that the final showdown was about to commence, Leander ordered two warriors to push open the doors.

As they charged into the throne room with swords drawn, many gasps and shouts could be heard. Occupying the large room were the many influential people and warriors of the Talov Duchy. They had all come to witness Duke Valens be sworn in as regent. None of them had expected that just before the ceremony could be completed, the missing prince would suddenly arrive with a force of armed warriors.

Sitting on the throne that was rightfully Leander's grandfather's, and should have been his brother's, was Duke Valens. The duke was looking toward Leander with a gaze of bewilderment and hatred. The duke would never have thought that the prince he had been trying to kill would be able to make it this far, even after his final move.

Next to the duke was a man wearing the robes of a priest of the Phoenix Temple, the one sent by the holy city to enact this ceremony. He, too, looked toward the prince in astonishment. The final words he was about to say became lodged in his throat.

"Valens, you vile and wretched man. All your planning and plotting has been for naught. Today, I will bring my brother, who you killed in cold blood, the justice he deserves," Leander shouted, pointing his sword at the sitting duke.

Prince Leander's sudden declaration caused the gathered nobles to begin discussing the situation among themselves. Many weren't sure what to make of it.

Sitting on the throne, Duke Valens wasn't disturbed by the prince's sudden declaration of his crimes. Leander couldn't help but slightly admire the duke's control of himself. Besides the sudden shock at their arrival, the duke hadn't shown any other trace of emotion.

One of the marquesses, and a supporter of Duke Valens, shouted, "How dare you defame the honor of His Grace like this! Guards, seize this traitorous prince immediately!"

The warriors that had been standing at the corners of the throne room began to surround the prince.

"You dog of the duke! How dare you speak up at this moment!" Lord Altares bellowed. His voice sent the marquess and the incoming guards reeling in panic. After terrifying the marques Lord Altares turned his attention back to the duke. "You have no right to sit on that throne. Get down from there at once."

The duke didn't budge at the hall master's commanding shout. He just sat there, looking toward Altares and the rest of the warriors with his calculating gaze before suddenly sighing.

"To be taken in by Prince Leander's flowery words. You have quite disappointed me, Lord Altares," Duke Valens said, shaking his head as if feeling sorry for Altares. Those who sided with Duke Valens nodded in the background.

The rest who had gathered didn't know what to believe. If it had been only Prince Leander accusing the duke, then they would have sided with the duke, due to the latter's reputation, but Leander hadn't come alone. Not only did the hall master of

Stone Hall support the prince, but many of the nobles and warriors saw that Brana, the trusted warrior of the Red Hall master, was also behind the prince. With both hall masters in support of the prince and accusing the duke of treachery, some began to doubt.

"What is the meaning of this, Your Grace?" the priest asked. He, too, was beginning to think that what Leander had accused Duke Valens of might be true.

Even with him beginning to lose the trust of the warriors, nobles, and family heads, Duke Valens wasn't disturbed. As he picked his head up, his cold gaze scanned the room, freezing everyone in place as they waited for the duke to defend himself.

"I have to applaud you, Your Highness," Duke Valens said with a slight grin. "Never in my wildest dreams did I think that you, the one everyone called worthless, would be able to survive everything that I sent your way, and make it here on time to stop my naming as regent. You truly are a descendant of one of the great founding families."

The duke's sudden admission of guilt shocked everyone. They were all waiting for a confrontation of words. Some even believed that the prince, while not guilty, was accusing the duke unfairly. Never had they thought that the duke would openly admit to his own treachery.

"You traitorous beast! Get off that throne at once!" one of the warriors in the crowd yelled at the duke. After the first, more and more people yelled for the duke to be brought to justice. Some of the duke's own warriors, from his chivalric order, were looking to one another, not sure what to do. Not all of them knew of their lord's treachery, but they had vowed to serve the duke. They were caught between two virtues and could only stand and wait.

Finally some of the warriors couldn't stay still and charged the duke. As they had been attending a ceremony, none of them had brought their weapons, but neither had the duke. Just as they were about to reach the duke, several armed warriors got in their way and, with a swing of their swords, struck the attacking warriors down. These new warriors were the duke's personal warriors, and they knew of the duke's plots in great detail.

This act caused even more of those gathered to want the duke's head on a spike, but without their weapons, they could hardly put up a fight. The only thing they could do was rally behind the warriors the prince had brought with him. After such a showing, only the duke's personal warriors stood by his side. The rest crowded behind Leander.

"Now then, why don't we continue the ceremony?" said Duke Valens. He was still as calm as ever, and that only made Leander and the rest worry at what else the duke still had up his sleeve.

The priest's face turned red with fury. "Do you honestly expect me to name you regent after your confession of treachery?" he bellowed.

The duke sighed. "True, but I guess I don't really need you anymore," he said.

Before the priest could react, one of the duke's personal warriors cut his head right off his shoulders.

As the body of the priest fell to the floor, Duke Valens spoke. "It seems that I will need your assistance after all."

No one knew who he was talking to, but suddenly, a voice answered back. "Looks like, for all your planning, only half of it was successful." The eerie voice echoed through the throne room.

A loud scream came from the huddle of people as one of them was thrown into the air, slamming into the floor with a loud crunch. Walking out of the crowd was a man cloaked in black and wearing a mask of a crying face. The man produced a sinister feeling that sent shivers down everyone's spines, causing those around him to suddenly take several steps back in fear.

Leander instantly knew that this was the man behind Duke Valens, the infamous Karsic, who had sent the Bloody Blade after Kay and his brothers. Leander also felt the disturbance in the air after this man revealed himself, but after everything he had been through, Leander held his ground. Fear no longer had a hold over him.

Karsic turned his attention toward the prince. Leander felt the eyes hidden behind the black eyeholes of the mask staring through him. Karsic calmly walked toward the prince. As he neared, one of the Divide warriors gathered up his courage and attacked.

Karsic watched the man charge him and laughed. Suddenly Karsic let out an agonizing howl, so loud it brought everyone to their knees. As he wailed, Karsic's body began to grow at an exponential rate. His black clothes ripped off, revealing bulging muscles. The bottom half of his mask broke away, showing dozens of sharp fangs protruding out of a bleeding mouth. A large mane grew from his head and flowed down his back, and nine-inch claws took the place of his fingernails. When the transformation ended, Karsic stood there, twice the size of the previous ogre that Leander and the rest had fought, and ten times more frightening.

"Wha... what is that abomination?" one of the warriors cried out, getting the attention of the ogre Karsic.

Not taking being called an abomination lightly, Karsic rushed the warrior with a howl. Before the warrior could let out a scream, Karsic's giant claws reached him, ripping the poor warrior to shreds. The warrior's armor did him little good as Karsic's claws cut through the metal with no problem.

"You dare to call me an abomination? This body was a blessing given to me by my master, the one who will soon trample over you foolish men," Karsic roared.

The warriors, those in the crowd, and those Prince Leander had brought along couldn't help but tremble in fear. Seeing this masked man turn into a monster and kill one of them in a single swipe of his claws made them feel that their ends were near. Not even the warrior's armor had been able to stop Karsic's claws from ripping him to shreds, so what could their identical armor do?

As the morale of his men dissipated, Lord Altares stepped forward. "A mere monstrosity like this has you cowering in your boots? Are you not warriors of the Talov Duchy? We warriors should not fear death but only the dishonor that cowardice brings us," he yelled to his warriors.

Upon hearing their lord's words, the Stone Hall warriors were the first to regain themselves. Mustering up their courage, they faced the monstrous Karsic.

Karsic gave another howl, a howl mixed with pain and anger, as he charged the Stone Hall warriors. As the beast ran on all four limbs, each step broke the stone floor underneath his great weight.

Chaos erupted in the throne room. Those with no weapons began to try to escape, but the warriors still loyal to Duke Valens had already blocked the exit, preventing them from leaving the throne room. In the center of all this madness was Karsic in his monster form, facing off against the forces of Prince Leander.

Letting out an agonizing roar, Karsic grabbed one of the warriors and bit the man's head right off. Using the dead body as a weapon, Karsic began slamming the corpse into the surrounding warriors, only dropping the body when it couldn't take the strain and broke into several pieces.

The dismembered body fell right in front of Prince Leander. Karsic was so crazed by his rampage that he attacked those nearest him and not the prince. Seeing the prince still fine, Duke Valens ordered his warriors to finish him. This caused the fighting to escalate even more.

Leander saw the warriors approaching and turned to several other warriors, who were away from Karsic's slaughter. "Follow me!" the prince yelled, and charged at the new enemies with the warriors following suit.

While the prince and most of the warriors fought against the duke's men, Lord Altares and Brana were left to deal with Karsic. With swords in hand, the two of them threw themselves at the murderous beast.

Brana was the first to arrive. Swinging his great sword, he knocked the ogre's huge claws away, leaving the beast's underbelly open for Altares. Making it under Karsic, Altares thrust his sword into the ogre's belly, but his hide was too thick, and the sword barely pierced it. Luckily, Altares kept his calm and retreated as Karsic felt the hit on his flesh and tried to counter.

"This bastard's skin is too sturdy. Our swords aren't able to do any real damage," Altares cursed.

Angered that his target had gotten away, Karsic continued his pursuit of Altares. Altares fled with the monstrous Karsic biting at his heels. Karsic was so consumed with trying to kill Altares that he didn't notice his other enemy, Brana, come up from behind and strike at his heel. The Top Sword used as much strength as he could muster.

The flesh of the ogre's heel resisted but was cut through. Knocked off-balance, Karsic tumbled to the floor, allowing Altares to escape. Brana tried to take advantage of Karsic's tumble, but as he neared, his intuition screamed at him, allowing him to guard with his great sword just as Karsic's clawed foot shot out, knocking Brana nearly to the other side of the throne room.

The strike was so strong that Brana kept on rolling even after hitting the floor. When he was able to stop, he knelt and coughed up some blood. He may have guarded against the blow, but the force had injured him greatly. If he hadn't been fast enough in his defense, then he would have been dead.

Karsic let out another dreadful roar and was about to go after Brana when something caught his attention. Leander had just dealt with one of Duke Valens's warriors when he felt Karsic's gaze on him. Remembering his real target, Karsic abandoned his pursuit of Brana and Altares, and charged Prince Leander.

"Damn it! Protect the prince!" Lord Altares yelled when he saw that the ogre Karsic was going after the prince. Two warriors heard Altares and tried to stop Karsic, but Karsic simply slashed out with his claws, and the two warriors died, their sacrifice barely slowing the beast down.

With fighting on either side of him, Leander knew that he couldn't get away. As Karsic homed in on him, Leander mustered up all his strength and courage, and faced the oncoming monster head-on. Karsic saw all this and, with fangs open wide, lunged at Leander.

With a shout of his own, Leander used his sword to parry Karsic's claws. The impact nearly knocked the sword out of his hands. Leander could feel his arms trembling and knew that he couldn't do that more than once more.

Karsic stood over Leander, completely overshadowing the prince with his humongous body. When he was about to attack again, Karsic howled in pain. The monstrous Karsic spun about, trying to get something off his back, and that was when Leander saw it.

Sticking out from between Karsic's shoulder blades was Brana's spear. Standing behind the ogre was Brana, having just thrown the spear. He seemed shocked that the spear had been able to pierce Karsic's skin when even his great sword had failed to. Leander didn't miss this chance. Charging forth, he aimed at the one place that he felt his strike would be able to harm Karsic—the beast's eyes.

Prince Leander's strike hit true as his sword cut into Karsic's left eye. Blood squirted out, and Karsic howled once more in pain before turning around to face Leander. Leander tried to retreat, but Karsic's claws reached him before he could, catching the prince in his grip.

As he was lifted off the floor, Leander struggled with all his might but was unable to move a single muscle. As he struggled, he felt warm breath hitting his neck from behind. Turning his head, he found Karsic staring at him. The monster's one good eye glared savagely, and his fangs shifted into a devilish grin.

A low-pitched growl came from Karsic as he slowly began to squeeze the life out of the prince. Brana and Altares tried to save the prince, but several of Duke Valens's warriors blocked their way. As the pressure around him grew, Leander let out a pain-filled moan as he felt his ribs begin to crack.

"Scream. Scream for me," Karsic viciously growled as one of his large claws ripped into Leander's side, causing the prince to scream in pain. Blood poured out between Karsic's giant fingers.

As more and more of Leander's bones broke, his body grew numb, and his mind hazy. He no longer felt any pain as he went limp.

Karsic lifted the prince to his monstrous face, only to find two unfocused eyes staring back. With his goal accomplished, Karsic threw the prince away as if he were a rag doll.

Brana, Altares, and the rest of the warriors looked on in horror as their prince's body fell lifelessly onto the stone floor. Lord Altares was one of the first to take out his anger on the enemy warriors, killing one with a swipe of his sword. The rest soon followed suit, and the fighting grew bloody as the warriors who followed Leander no longer cared for their own safety. Their only goal was the death of Duke Valens and his followers, even if it meant the loss of their own lives.

Lying on the stone floor, Leander held on to his last thread of life, but he knew it was only a matter of time before he was no more. In front of him, everything was in a haze, and he could not make out anything that was going on. The only thing he could see with his fading sight was shapes swirling into one another, but one color was quite noticeable as the darkness engulfed him, and that was the color red.

Chapter Twenty-Eight: Hope for the Hopeless

Aris felt herself stagger as she reached her breaking point. Luckily, Roan was by her side and was able to keep her from falling to the ground. Supported by Roan, Aris looked around the bloody battle that was still going on.

Sarus's ambush was quite the success. Almost all the warriors on their side had already perished. Only a handful of them could still fight, but they were being whittled down. To the side, Jukel Altares was fighting off one of the ogres with some of the Stone Hall warriors and warriors from the Divide. The other ogre was lying on the ground, dead. Roan had been lucky to pierce through the beast's tough flesh and impale the monster's heart, but even with the great beast's death, Aris knew they weren't going to come out of this fight alive.

In the doorway of the Stone Hall manor, Sarus looked on with a pleased expression. Aris wanted nothing more than to cut that vile smirk right off his face, but the young Valens always had several warriors protecting him. Even if they got close, he would ring that soundless black bell, causing the ogre to charge in to protect him. Sarus felt Aris's gaze on him and turned to face his betrothed.

"Ah, Aris," Sarus said. "Now do you see? It is only a matter of time before the duchy belongs to me. Why don't you submit to me willingly? This is your final chance. I promise that I will treat you with all the respect a princess like you should have."

Aris didn't have the words to respond to Sarus, so all she did was scoff.

Sarus's eyes turned deadly. "Very well, then. This day next year will be the anniversary of your death!" he yelled.

In his fury, Sarus lifted the black bell and shook it. The ogre that was fighting against Jukel reacted to Sarus's summons. Plowing through the warriors, not caring for the wounds it got along the way, it lunged at Aris and Roan.

Exhausted as they were, the two of them were still able to move out of the way as the ogre's huge fist slammed into the ground where they had once stood. As the ogre turned to face them, Roan stood in front of Aris in order to protect her, but Aris wouldn't have that. Instead, she moved to stand next to Roan.

"Ma'am—" Roan began, but before he could continue, Aris cut him off.

"If you honestly expect that by throwing yourself in front of me, you will protect me from this beast, then you're a fool, Roan. By yourself, you will be able to stop that beast for what? A few seconds? We have to work together," Aris pointed out.

As she spoke, the ogre let out another roar before it attacked the two. With their death incoming, they faced the ogre with the hearts and souls of true warriors.

Then suddenly the ground began to shake. At first they thought it was an earthquake, but as the sound grew and the trembling intensified, they could hear another sound, the sound of shouting.

Turning around, they found a cavalry unit of warriors charging into the battle. The steeds were adorned with heavy armor, mimicking the warriors' armor. In the horsemen's hands were a mixture of halberds and long swords. Leading them was a large man with the most intimidating presence Aris had ever felt.

Trapped between the ogre and the unknown warriors, Aris and Roan went back-to-back in order to face the two incoming forces. However, as the mounted warriors neared, they divided, going completely around the princess and attacking the ogre, along with Sarus's warriors. As they passed, Aris finally noticed the horns protruding out of the horses' heads, along with a certain crest on the passing warriors' garb.

"That's the crest of the Estelle family. This is the Crowne Cavalry, under the Archduke of the Estelle Duchy," Aris said, surprised by the sudden arrival of their neighboring duchy's famous cavalry forces.

The Estelle crowne mounts lived up to their famous reputation: larger, faster, and stronger than any other horse. The cavalry warriors quickly finished off the enemy, who were either crushed or impaled on the crownes' horns or cut down by the swing of the warriors' swords and halberds. Before long the enemy warriors were in full retreat. The only area where fighting continued was where the ogre was.

As strong as the crownes were, they couldn't rival the ogre's vast might. They did, however, have speed on their side. As one warrior rode past and struck out with his weapon, the ogre would turn to face the warrior, only to find him far away, out of reach. This continued, and though the ogre was wounded, the warriors couldn't get a fatal blow on the beast.

As Aris watched all this, one of the Estelle warriors rode up to her. Unlike the other warriors, this one was slightly smaller and thinner than the rest. The crowne this warrior rode was a pure black color, different from the gray and brown coats of the other horned steeds.

"Looks like we made it just in time," a feminine voice said from behind the helmet. As the warrior pulled off their helmet, Aris was shocked to find that it was the princess of the Estelle Duchy, Elaina Estelle.

"Your Highness? How …?" Roan stuttered. The last time he had seen Princess

Elaina had been at Red Hall, before they had decided to leave her there for her own safety. Roan couldn't understand how she could arrive here along with her family's warriors.

"We can speak after we take care of that," Elaina said as she ordered her mount to charge toward where the ogre was.

Facing off against the ogre was the warrior who had led the charge. Wielding his sword, the warrior faced the ogre on an equal footing. As the princess joined the fight, along with some other Estelle warriors, Aris finally knew the identity of the large warrior. He was the heir of the Estelle Duchy, Crown Prince Aleron Estelle.

With Elaina and the rest of the warriors joining the fight, the ogre was soon overwhelmed. Breaking through the ogre's defenses, Crown Prince Aleron thrust out with his sword, stabbing hilt-deep into its side. The ogre howled in pain and stumbled around, throwing its fists wildly until it fell to its knees. Panting heavily, the ogre didn't respond as Crown Prince Aleron walked up to the dying beast. He raised his sword and finished the beast for good.

Standing stupefied in place was Sarus Valens. He looked on as his men died. He couldn't believe what he was seeing. "This can't be happening," he mumbled to himself. "Today was the day of the Valens family's triumph. This can't be happening!" He yelled the last words.

His shout got the attention of Aris. Noticing the princess staring daggers at him, Sarus tried to sneak away. Aris didn't shout for someone to catch him, because as soon as Sarus turned to flee, he found Roan standing there.

Roan didn't give Sarus a chance to defend himself, hitting the traitor with the blunt end of his sword. Sarus fell to the ground with a loud squeal unbecoming of a warrior. Aris walked to the downed Sarus and poked him with her foot. She scoffed at the young man, as Roan's strike had knocked him unconscious.

"Treacherous filth," Roan spat before sheathing his sword. Not wanting to look at Sarus for even a second more, he walked away, leaving the remaining warriors to tie up the knocked-out Sarus.

After taking care of the ogre, Crown Prince Aleron left the remaining enemy forces to his men. Wiping off the blood on his sword before sheathing it, he made his way toward Aris with his sister by his side.

Aris watched as they came over. Dusting herself off, she spoke. "Crown Prince Aleron, Princess Elaina. I cannot think of the words to express how grateful we are for your assistance. Without your timely arrival, I fear we would all be dead right now." Her words of gratitude were honest and from the heart.

Reaching Aris, Crown Prince Aleron gave a respectful bow. "Princess Aris. It was all my sister's work that brought us here today. She was able to convince me that coming to your aid was the honorable thing to do, and having seen the creatures that the Valenses were using, I am thankful that I listened to her," Aleron said as he looked back toward the dead ogre.

Aris also looked toward the dead beast. It wasn't the warriors under Sarus who had caused them the most losses, but the two ogres. Remembering the scenes of the ogres ripping brave warriors in half made Aris shudder.

"Even if they had won, what honor would they have gained by using such monstrous things?" Aris muttered through clenched teeth. "The Valenses have truly forsaken the path of honor. Only the desire to fulfill their greed remains."

As the anger and hatred for the Valenses coursed through Aris's veins, it was Princess Elaina who broke her out of her wild fantasies. "Princess Aris, I see that you are here, but where is Prince Leander? Or the sell-swords Kay and Lucis?" Elaina asked.

The realization suddenly set in. With their victory against Sarus and the ogres,

Aris had almost forgotten that her brother must have fallen into the duke's traps as well. Both Crown Prince Aleron and Princess Elaina saw Aris turn pale at Elaina's question. Elaina's hand trembled as she waited for Aris to answer them.

"What is it?" Aleron asked when Aris still hadn't answered Elaina.

"My brother led a group of warriors to the Phoenix Temple in order to stop Duke Valens being named regent. If the duke knew of the plan for my rescue, then he must surely have known of the attack on his very person. We have to help them, before it is too late," Aris said, her words quickening as she spoke.

Aleron and Elaina didn't have to be told twice. Mounting up, Aleron called for his warriors to assemble. As Aris watched them prepare to ride, she wished she had her mount with her so she could join them. Just then, Princess Elaina rode up next to Aris and extended her hand toward her.

"Get on," Elaina said.

Aris took Elaina's hand and was pulled up effortlessly. Aris was slightly surprised that Elaina could pull her up so easily despite being a slender girl. As the preparations were finished, Aris looked to Roan, who had no ride. Unlike the two princesses, who were light, the crownes couldn't carry two fully armored men.

"Go. I'll be right behind you with the rest," Roan said, looking at the mixture of warriors who had fought to save their princess. The fight against the ogres had exhausted most of them—the ones who had survived, that is.

Nodding her head, Aris gave Elaina the go-ahead. With a snap of the reins, Elaina's mount galloped away, along with the rest of the Estelle warriors, leaving Roan standing there, watching them fade into the distance.

"May the gods protect you." Roan prayed for Aris's safe return as the princess disappeared from his sight.

+

The magnificence and beauty of the throne room was no more. Corpses littered the chamber as blood threatened to turn the stone floor into a pool of crimson. The wails of those dying echoed throughout the great hall. This was no longer a place of greatness filled with the honor of warriors from long ago, but a place filled with death and despair.

On both sides, the number of remaining fighters was down to single digits. As the few remaining warriors fought to the death, Karsic let out a roar as he swept his giant claws at Lord Altares, who ducked, narrowly keeping his head on his shoulders. Brana rushed in to help Altares, leaving another deep cut on Karsic's forearm.

"We can't continue on like this. If we do, then we will surely perish," Altares cursed as he knelt on the floor, glaring at the monstrous Karsic. During this time, they had left countless cuts and nicks on the beast, but not one was close to being fatal.

Worse was the fact that the hall master was exhausted. He was no longer in his prime, and even though he was one of the most famous warriors, time whittles away even the greatest men. Even now, if it hadn't been for Brana saving him on several occasions, Altares would already be one of the corpses that covered the throne room floor.

"It looks like your resistance will soon come to an end. Pity, the strongest warrior and one of the most powerful men in the duchy are fated to die today," said Duke Valens from atop the Talov throne. His eyes shone with an ambitious glimmer. "But it doesn't have to be. Swear your loyalty to me, and I will spare your lives."

Altares hadn't expected Duke Valens to say such things. "Do you honestly expect me to bow down to you? After all that you have done?" he said.

"Logically speaking, bowing to me is the right choice. With the prince dead and the archduke's health failing him, there is only Princess Aris left in line, and she will be wed to my son by the end of the day. The duchy is already within my grasp. Will you continue to fight against me and bring about not only your own demise but the demise of the Divide as well?" Duke Valens's cold and logical voice was trying to entice Altares and Brana into becoming the duke's followers.

Altares looked to the duke with a dumbfounded expression before bursting into laughter. "You really surprise me, Jarl," Altares began to say, calling Duke Valens by his first name. "I can't believe that someone from such a distinguished warrior family could ask something so foolish."

Duke Valens glared down at the hall master. "Will you really throw everything away just to oppose me?" he growled.

"Wealth, power, and title. To a warrior, these are things that can be tossed away without a second thought. If I bowed down to you, then I would be losing something a warrior must never lose. Duke Valens, I will never submit to your rule. I will drag you down from that throne you unrightfully sit on if it is the last thing I do," Altares declared.

The hall master's shout inspired the remaining warriors to fight with everything they had. Their former exhaustion was all but forgotten as they began to push the duke's warriors into a dangerous situation. Brana, too, fought on, keeping Karsic at bay. The famous Top Sword's heavy swings were able to parry the vicious blows from Karsic's claws.

On the throne, Duke Valens saw that his tempting of Altares and Brana had failed, and he was furious. "If you have chosen death, then so be it. Your deaths today will pave my way to glory," he announced.

Giving out a ferocious roar in response to the duke's declaration, Karsic raised both of his clawed hands as he attacked Altares. Brana tried to halt the beast but was swept out of the way. With the hall master in sight, Karsic ignored everything else. Altares's words angered him, and the only thing he desired now was the hall master's blood flowing down his fangs.

Altares tried to dodge, but his exhaustion made him a step too late. Karsic's large claws slashed into the hall master's thigh, revealing the bone. As he tumbled near the entrance to the throne room, blood flowed from his injured leg. Kneeling on the floor, Altares tried to rise, but the gash on his thigh made it impossible. Unable to move, he could only stare down the advancing Karsic, who looked at him like a wolf would a wounded deer.

Holding his sword as high as he could, Altares shouted, "Come, you abomination!"

With an agonizing howl, Karsic charged. The remaining warriors and Brana were too far away to help. They could only watch as the monstrous Karsic raised his mighty claws to finish Altares. Suddenly the hall master felt someone appear behind him, and before he knew it, he was pulled away just as Karsic's claws slammed down, crushing the floor Altares had just been kneeling on. When he turned to see who his saviors were, the hall master was shocked to find the warrior Knox was the one who had pulled him from death's grasp.

"My lord, I apologize for being late," Knox said. His body was covered in wounds, but his breathing was steady.

"Knox? How are you …?" Altares began, but a howl of pain got his attention. Turning, he found Karsic holding his side. Blood was flowing like a river through a large gash that was now on his side. In front of the beast stood the sell-sword Kay. Blood dripped from Kay's sword as he held it at the ready.

But what Altares really noticed was that Kay's eyes were glowing a bright crimson. Black veins could be seen under his skin, giving Kay a monstrous look.

381

The sell-sword looked almost as monstrous as the ogre Karsic.

As the two faced off against one another, Karsic looked at Kay in shock and horror. Gritting his fangs, he growled at the sell-sword, who he glared at with murder in his eyes. "How ... how could you wound me?" Karsic roared.

Kay didn't answer Karsic but instead turned toward where Prince Leander had fallen. Kneeling next to the downed prince was Lucis, who had made it there without anyone noticing. Lucis quickly held the prince and went over his wounds. As he did, his face turned sour.

"How is he?" Kay asked, not taking his glowing red eyes off the ogre Karsic.

Lucis looked over the prince for a moment before shaking his head. "His wounds are too deep. He has lost too much blood. I'm afraid he isn't going to live more than a few minutes."

Even though both Brana and Altares had seen Prince Leander fatally wounded, they had still had hope that the prince could hold on, especially after Knox, Lucis, and Kay had arrived and heavily wounded Karsic. With their chance at victory returning, hope had returned that they could save Leander, but hearing that Leander couldn't be saved regardless, that hope was quickly dashed.

When Kay heard his brother, the crimson in his eyes grew even deeper. The black veins pulsated as they webbed underneath his skin.

Seeing the savagery of Kay, the monstrous Karsic unconsciously took a step back. When he realized that he was feeling fear for Kay, he howled in fury. "Fear? Is this fear I feel? How can that be? I am one who has transcended humanity and no longer fears anything. How can I fear some lowly human?" Karsic bellowed. Glaring at Kay so viciously that his eyes seemed to bulge, Karsic let out another howl before attacking Kay with all his might.

In his murderous state, Kay was easily able to parry the oncoming swipe of

Karsic's claws. As he did, his sword bit into Karsic's forearm, cutting deep, leaving the arm hanging limp at Karsic's side. Karsic was so enraged at this point that he ignored the grave wound and continued his onslaught.

When one of Karsic's wild strikes found its way through Kay's defenses, Lucis appeared behind Karsic, striking with his own sword against the beast's backside, halting Karsic's attack in its tracks. Howling in pain, Karsic turned to face Lucis, but as soon as he did, Brana appeared at the beast's wounded side. With a swift slash, the deep wound on Karsic's side bled more profoundly, and the monster stumbled to the floor.

Facing the injured beast, Kay, Lucis, and Brana fought on. Two Zer'sheen, along with the demon-like Kay, fought against the ogre Karsic. The fighting was so intense it caused the surrounding people to take cover along the edges of the throne room.

With his back resting on the far wall, Altares could only watch from a distance. At his side, the warrior Knox was in a similar yet different situation to his lord. The warrior had several worrisome wounds and had a slight limp, but compared to Altares, he was in relatively good health. In fact, if it weren't for him worrying about his lord, he would run up and face off against the beast alongside the three of them.

"Go," Altares said. He had noticed Knox's hand trembling with desire to fight. "Go and help them put an end to that evil."

Knox turned and was about to speak but, in the end, didn't. Giving Lord Altares a warrior's salute, the Divide warrior joined the fray. Watching his trusted warrior charge into the carnage, Altares couldn't help but feel proud.

With the addition of Knox, the four of them began to drive the maddening Karsic into a corner. Kay's sword cut into the beast's thigh. Lucis broke off one of his sharp claws, and Brana was able to retrieve his spear, which had been protruding from

Karsic's back, and used it to inflict many small wounds. Even Knox, the weakest among them, was able to distract Karsic by attacking his wounded areas, allowing the other three to cause more damage.

"This can't be. I am one who has transcended. One who has been reborn. How could I lose to a bunch of lesser beings?" Karsic howled as he threw his claws out randomly, but it was obvious that the wounds were taking a toll on him. His large claws were hanging at his sides, and his movements had dulled.

In his rage, he lost track of Knox. Diving under the giant beast, Knox gave a shout and threw his sword, piercing Karsic's one remaining eye.

Blinded, Karsic stumbled about. His howls and roars grew weaker as he tried to find his enemy, but he was unable to. Soon the exhaustion and loss of blood grew too much for the ogre. Falling to his knees, Karsic spat out a bucket's worth of blood. He no longer thrashed around or tried to defend himself. The fight within him had died.

The four stopped their attacks when Knox had blinded Karsic. They watched as the beast thrashed around before finally falling to his knees. It was Kay who finally took several steps forward. He stood above Karsic with his sword raised, then swung his sword down, as if he were an executioner.

"I have failed you ..." was all that Karsic could say as Kay's sword went right through his thick neck, cutting Karsic's head right off his body.

As if satisfied by the kill, the crimson in Kay's eye began to wane, and the black veins no longer pulsed. Pulling out the magical bracelet he had been given by Sage Arvandus, he clasped it back on. The bracelet quickly shrank and gripped his flesh. With the bracelet back on, his crimson eyes faded back into their usual crystal blue, and the black veins receded into him, disappearing from sight.

Sitting on the throne, Duke Valens looked at the dead Karsic in horror. With all his warriors now dead as well, he knew that he had lost. With this realization, Duke Valens gave a hearty laugh filled with a mixture of sorrow and self-ridicule.

"All of my plans. All my carefully laid-out moves. All destroyed by sell-swords," said the duke with another laugh.

Lord Altares ordered Knox and the remaining warriors to apprehend Duke Valens. Knox was all too glad to carry out the command, but before he could, the sound of people rushing toward them came from outside the throne room.

Duke Valens's mood changed upon hearing the incoming people. He had sent out his two most trusted warriors to carry out the ambushes of the prince and princess. With the time that had elapsed since then, they must have been returning right now. Standing from the throne, Duke Valens watched as a torrent of warriors swarmed into the throne room, but seeing who led the warriors, the duke slumped into the throne, defeated.

Leading the warriors was the crown prince of the Estelle Duchy. With him was his sister, Elaina Estelle, and the Princess Aris Talov. Along with the Estelle warriors, they poured in, ready to fight. Aris was the first one to see Leander lying motionless on the stone floor.

"Leander!" she screamed as she rushed to her brother's side. When she knelt at his side, she felt the blood on the floor stain her dress, and her face paled. She knew Leander had already lost too much blood. Holding her brother's body to her chest, the princess began to cry.

The downtrodden duke was easily apprehended and ushered out of the throne room toward the dungeon. Afterward everyone began to circle around the prince and princess of the Talov Duchy. Many had sorrow in their eyes and on their faces seeing the prince's cold body in Aris's embrace.

The silence was deafening as no one dared to speak. Princess Elaina knelt by

Aris's side. Searching her pocket, she pulled out a vial. If Leander had been awake, he would have recognized the vial as the one that Arvandus had given her at Red Hall. He would also have noticed that Elaina had crimson peeking out from her clothes, staining her abdomen.

"I thought that this could be useful, so I dared not take it," Elaina said, handing the vial over to Aris. "Have Prince Leander drink this. It was given to me by Sage Arvandus himself. I was told that it could even bring someone back from the brink of death."

Aris looked at the vial incredulously, but quickly she put the vial to Leander's lips, as she knew that Leander had very little time before his heart stopped. The thick blood slowly made its way from the vial and into the prince's mouth. Those gathered around watched as the prince's pale flesh gained some color, but the prince's heart still only beat faintly.

"Please, Leander. You have come so far. I know you can make it," Princess Aris prayed.

Chapter Twenty-Nine: Honor before All Else

L eander felt as if he were perpetually falling. He didn't know when he had begun or when he would reach the end. The darkness around him tried to consume him, making him drowsy. The more tired he got, the faster he felt himself reaching the bottom. But every time he felt himself slipping away, he could hear a voice calling out from the darkness.

"Wake up," the voice called out.

For some reason, Leander felt that he knew the voice, but he couldn't remember.

"Wake up," a different voice called. This time he was sure that he knew the woman who called, and for some reason, his chest tightened when he heard the woman's voice.

With newfound resolve, Leander struggled to escape this constant fall. As he tossed about, a small light came out of the blackness. He fought his way toward the small flickering glow. The darkness all around tried its hardest to stop the prince, but Leander pushed forward. Finally he reached the small light.

Stretching forward, he grasped it. As his fingers touched the light, it grew with boundless might, pushing the darkness away. As the light illuminated his surroundings, the blackness changed to whiteness. Pain rushed through the prince. Leander felt that his body was being ripped apart, but compared to the feeling he had in the darkness, he felt that the pain was less terrifying than the idea of losing himself. As the brightness found its way into his head, Leander sat up, panting.

Around him, Leander no longer saw the darkness nor the light. Instead, he found himself sitting up on a bed in a familiar room, his room.

Leander couldn't understand how he had awoken in his quarters. The last thing he could remember was facing off against Duke Valens in the throne room. He remembered being picked up by the monstrous Karsic and being crushed to death. Feeling around, Leander found that his body was perfectly fine.

"How …?" Leander muttered when he found not a single wound on his body. Even the wounds and scars he had gained during the difficult journey to Raven's Nest had completely disappeared.

As he wondered what had happened, the door to his room suddenly opened. Entering the room was his sister, Aris, along with her personal warrior Roan.

When she saw Leander sitting up in his bed, Aris gasped in shock before running to the bedside. Not caring that Roan was watching, the princess jumped into Leander's embrace. She wrapped her arms around his neck and buried her face in his chest.

"Thank the zer' you're awake," Leander heard her whisper.

Not used to seeing his strong sister this way, Leander froze for a second before returning the hug. After so much had happened, from the assassination of his brother to the many trials on his journey back home, he was now reunited with his family.

"Sister, what is going on? How did I end up back in my own quarters? And what happened with Duke Valens?" Leander asked. He had so many questions.

Regaining herself, Aris stood up from the bed. She then explained what had happened while he was unconscious, from how they had been saved when Crown Prince Aleron and Princess Elaina had ridden in with their warriors to how Kay,

Lucis, Brana, and Knox had been able to defeat the ogre Karsic. She ended her telling when she arrived to find him near death, and when Elaina had used a wondrous potion from Arvandus to save him.

Leander could hardly believe some of what he heard. His emotions continued to go from high to low. Hearing of the duke's capture, along with his son's, made him ecstatic, but hearing that Elaina had followed them here, even if she had saved Aris, made him slightly mad at her risking her own life like that. In the end, Prince Leander could only sigh and let all his emotions go.

As they sat, more people arrived. Entering the room was Crown Prince Aleron, followed by his sister, Elaina. When she saw Leander alive and awake, Elaina gave him a warm smile that made the prince blush slightly.

"So, the little prince has finally come to." A voice spoke from the doorway.

Leander looked to see Kay and Lucis standing there. Kay, the one who had spoken, had his usual grin on his face, and Lucis was as calm as ever, but Leander thought he saw relief flash in the Zer'sheen's eyes, if only for a moment.

"Lucis ... Kay ..." Leander began, but then a third figure appeared in the doorway. Helped by a crutch under one arm, with the other arm in a splint, the man was someone who Leander thought he would never see again. "Aer!"

"It's good to see you again, Your Highness," Aer said, giving the prince a slight bow.

When Elaina saw the dumbfounded look on Leander's face, she laughed. "My brother rescued him while he was searching for me." She answered the question in Leander's mind.

Seeing so many friends, new and old, gathered, Leander felt warmth grow inside his chest. Those who had never given up on him, and those who had risked their own lives to help him clear his name. Everyone in this room, Leander trusted with his life. Even Kay and his annoying banter, Leander felt he could trust this sell-sword.

"What about Grandfather? How is he?" Leander asked. Seeing his sister's small smile, he knew he had nothing to worry about.

"He is well," Aris answered. "It seems that Duke Valens was giving him small doses of poison to keep him in a comatose state. After we took him off the drugs, he woke up not too long ago. He has already called for a gathering of every warrior family tomorrow."

+

The next day, the palace was packed. Due to the previous gathering, called by the former Duke Valens, many representatives and warrior family heads were still in the capital. It didn't take long for every warrior family, small and large, to have at least one warrior in attendance for the gathering.

In the throne room, Archduke Ambrose once more sat on his throne. The old ruler looked as healthy as he had before the whole incident had taken place. His white hair and wrinkled face showed his age, but his eyes still shone as bright as they had in his youth. Many of the warriors heaved sighs of relief seeing the archduke sitting on his throne, healthy and well.

The warriors of Stone Hall and the Divide stood near the archduke, a place of honor. Everyone knew that they had played a significant role in foiling Jarl Valens's plans against the duchy, so no one thought this was strange. Along with them stood Brana Ulfenn and a handful of Red Hall warriors. All those who saw the Top Sword saluted the warrior and looked upon him with adoration.

Duke Aleo and Duchess Morwood were also in attendance. After Duke Valens had won the vote to be regent, the two of them had left, leaving behind a representative for the naming ceremony. But after learning of the truth and the capture of Duke Valens, they had immediately left for Raven's Nest. They had arrived just in time for the gathering.

One thing that every warrior thought was curious was that Princess Aris wasn't standing by the archduke's side. As she was the head of the council, it wasn't appropriate for her not to be here for a gathering called by their ruler, especially since she was his granddaughter and a princess. Some felt discontent, and several words of ridicule were said about the missing princess, but with one glare from the archduke, the warriors who were speaking against Aris were silenced.

Finally the large twin doors to the throne room opened, and Princess Aris walked in. Following the princess was a group of familiar and unfamiliar faces. To Aris's side was the crown prince and the princess of the Estelle Duchy. Behind her was her personal warrior Roan, along with three sell-swords who many of the warriors didn't recognize. Only the warriors who had taken part in the rescue of the princess and the assault on the former duke knew the three.

What really surprised many of them was that on Aris's other side was the infamous second prince. All those in the room now knew that the prince hadn't murdered his brother and had been framed by the former Duke Valens, but they also knew that he had been fatally wounded during the final confrontation with the former duke. However, seeing him now, looking as healthy as could be, they did not know how it was possible. Even the archduke was surprised seeing his grandson fully recovered and out of bed.

Led by the four princes and princesses, the group made their way to the center of the throne room. The princes and princesses bowed to the archduke and raised their heads while the rest waited for the archduke to allow them to raise theirs.

"Leander, come closer," the archduke commanded.

Leander nervously made his way to the archduke. The archduke may have been his grandfather, but from an early age, he had been taught that he was their grandfather second and the Archduke of the Talov Duchy first and foremost.

Standing no more than two steps away, Leander waited, as did all those gathered. The elderly archduke lifted his body off the throne. Staring into his grandson's eyes, he wrapped his wrinkled arms around Leander and gave him a warm embrace, much like Aris had a few moments ago.

"Thank the zer' that you are all right," whispered the archduke, so that only Prince Leander could hear him.

After his sister's shocking display of emotion, Leander had thought he wouldn't be as surprised as he was. It took him a second for everything to register, and he hugged back. During this fleeting moment, they weren't Prince Leander and Archduke Ambrose. They were simply grandfather and grandson.

After a few seconds had passed, the archduke released Leander. As he did, the warmness in his eyes was replaced by the cold and calculating look that Leander had seen his entire childhood. The Archduke of the Talov Duchy was back. Returning to his sister and comrades, who had found their place at the sides of Lord Altares and Brana, Leander waited for his grandfather to speak.

"Warriors. Warriors are not afraid of death. They are not afraid of pain. Nor do they fear sorrow. They are the ones who uphold the honor and dignity of our people." The archduke began to speak, and everyone waited for his next words.

"Sadly, a corruption has sprouted in the hearts of some of these warriors. They have chosen to forsake honor, forsake duty, and deny the Phoenix God the sacrifice he deserves. These treacherous men nearly succeeded in turning this duchy, our home, into a place of sin, where only the conniving would rule, while those with a warrior's spirit would dwindle and perish."

The archduke spoke vigorously, and his words landed heavily on many of the warriors who had gathered. Some had seen the signs but had chosen to ignore the truth in front of them. Now they felt guilty for not speaking out or acting with the warriors who had fought with the second prince.

"But these vile men did not succeed, for all their plots and tricks could only protect them for so long. Those with a warrior's spirit rose to challenge this corruption. Those who personify the three virtues and hold the teachings of the Code of Valor in their hearts vanquished this darkness and led our land into Ridian's light once more," the archduke said. He then turned to those gathered with his grandchildren. "Brave heroes of this troubling time, step forward."

All eyes were now on the prince and his group. These were the warriors who had risked their lives to stop the former duke's schemes. Many of their fellow warriors had died, but their spirits had never died, and they had fulfilled their duty. Many felt envious of these warriors, but none felt that they didn't deserve such regard from the archduke.

Led by Leander and Aris, everyone who had taken part in the rescue came forward. Some had faces beaming with pride, like the hall master's son, Jukel. Others mourned for their fellow warriors who had died, like the warrior Knox. Others had faces of nonchalance, like the Top Sword, Brana. And a certain person had on a smirk that many of the warriors watching wished to wipe off the smug man's face.

"First, I would like to thank Crown Prince Aleron and Princess Elaina for coming in our time of need. If it hadn't been for your timely arrival, my granddaughter might not be standing here right now," the archduke said.

No one thought it was strange that the archduke had started with the two foreigners. They might not be from the Talov Duchy, but they were royalty and ranked higher than all the others. It was proper procedure.

"Your Undaunted Majesty, our families are so close we are practically relatives. Helping one another is the right action," Aleron responded, ignoring the glare that Elaina was giving him. Only she knew that her brother and father had wished to stay out of the situation for fear of causing a rift between the two duchies. If it hadn't been for her persuasion and Aleron's change of mind at the last moment, they would never have come to the Talovs' aid.

"Nevertheless, I thank you," the archduke said. He then turned to Lord Altares and Brana. "Lord Altares. You risked your own life and your own warriors' safety to stop the Jarl Valens. Your son also helped in the rescue of my granddaughter. The warriors of Stone Hall and the Divide will be justly rewarded. The same goes for those of Red Hall. Brana, send my regards to your hall master."

"Thank you, Your Undaunted Majesty," Altares and Brana said in unison, giving the old archduke another salute and bow. The warriors of the two halls followed suit soon after.

Finally, the archduke turned toward Kay, Lucis, and Roan. "You three. I have heard much of what you have done for my grandson. You are neither from a warrior family nor from the duchy itself. But even so, you three have done more than any other."

Aer was the one who stepped forward to speak for the three of them. "We do not deserve such words of thanks. We are but simple sell-swords. The prince hired us to do a job, and that is all," he said, bowing to the archduke.

Clamoring quickly consumed the throne room. Most of those gathered hadn't ever heard of the three sell-sword brothers, much less seen them. The only thing that most had known was that some people were helping the prince escape the duke's clutches. When the duke's treachery had been uncovered, many had begun to see the ones who had helped the prince in a dignified light.

Now many of them sent gazes of scorn and hatred toward the three brothers. In the three duchies, sell-swords were not uncommon. People who sold their sword to the highest bidder. These people mocked the virtues and traditions of the warrior, and most warriors held these sell-swords in contempt. However, the three brothers didn't seem to care. Kay even smirked a little, causing the warriors around to look down on them even more.

When the whispering grew too loud, some of the vicious words were heard by Leander. Furious, he stepped forward. Kay, Lucis, and Aer might not care, but that didn't mean that he would let others speak of his saviors like that.

"You are all so quick to judge, but what did you do when Duke Valens moved against us? You all just played dumb and let it happen. If you hate them for what they do for a living, then let me judge you for what you have done during all of this," Leander shouted, causing everyone to snap their mouths shut. They couldn't believe the usually docile second prince could act in such a way.

Even the archduke hadn't expected this from his grandson, but after seeing the prince standing with his back straight and no fear in his eyes, he looked at Leander with pride in his old eyes.

"Leander is right. Whether they are sell-swords or not hardly matters. What matters is that they acted in accordance with the Code of Valor. Even if they were hired by Leander, it doesn't change what they have done for the duchy," the archduke said, nodding in agreement with Leander's words.

The archduke then called for his sword. Everyone already knew what the archduke was going to award the three sell-swords with. Some felt it wasn't right, while other minds had changed after hearing the prince and archduke. Leander looked on with a grin plastered on his face. Altares and Brana both nodded at the archduke's decision.

After his sword was handed to him, Archduke Ambrose unsheathed the mighty blade. The ancestral sword of the Talovs, the one bestowed upon them by Calv Ridian himself and bathed in his flames. Standing from his throne, the archduke stepped forward and stood in front of the three sell-swords.

"Kneel and accept your reward," the archduke said.

The three of them each took a knee and waited.

"In my name, Ambrose Talov, I bestow the rank and title of warrior upon these three honorable men. May your souls one day be found worthy by the Phoenix God and find their way to the Ancestral Hall." The archduke tapped the three of them once on each shoulder. With that, the three brothers Kay, Lucis, and Aer were no longer sell-swords but warriors of the Talov Duchy.

The throne room erupted in applause and cheering, first coming from Leander and the ones who had fought with the three, then from the warriors who weren't as biased as the rest. Finally, even the ones who had disliked them upon learning of their identities as sell-swords couldn't help but clap as well.

"Kay, a warrior? I never would have thought I would see that come to pass," Elaina said in a voice that was a mixture of shock and jeering.

Seeming to hear her through the applause, Kay looked in her direction. Elaina quickly turned her head away and blushed, causing the warriors around her to laugh.

"We gratefully accept, Your Undaunted Majesty," the three said, giving a warriors salute before returning to the side where Leander and the rest waited.

Once the cheering had calmed down, the archduke's face grew cold. In a dominating voice, he yelled, "Bring in the criminals!"

With his call, a dozen armed warriors walked in. Each one carried a chain that bound a prisoner. These were the ones who had conspired with Jarl Valens and knew of his plans. The former highborn warriors no longer held their heads high and kept their faces down as they were dragged into the throne room.

The only exception to this was the former duke himself. Bound like all the rest, he kept his head straight as he looked ahead. To his side, his son was quivering in fear for what awaited them. The surrounding warriors mocked and cursed the traitors, and that made Sarus cower even more.

The prisoners were brought to kneel in front of the archduke, who looked upon these traitors with hate-filled eyes. Some of them pleaded for mercy, but all their words landed on deaf ears. When his gaze reached the Jarl Valens, the former duke looked right back at the archduke, showing no hint of remorse or feelings of guilt.

"Jarl Valens," the archduke said. "Never would I have thought that in my final years, I would be sentencing someone of the Valens family for high treason. You have thrown mud on everything that your father has accomplished. Do you have any last words before your sentence is announced?"

Everyone wanted to hear what the former duke would say. Seeing Jarl Valens acting so calm made Leander furious. The prince's fingernails threatened to cut into his palms with how tight he was clenching his fists. As his anger threatened to break free, Leander felt two soft hands grab his. Glancing to his side, he found Aris looking at him worriedly. Seeing her like this made the prince calm down, and he regained control over his emotions. As his breathing stabilized, Jarl Valens spoke.

"You all think you are like the warriors of old? Honorable men who followed the Phoenix God into battle? I scoff at your inflated egos," the former duke said. His words were sharp and tore at the pride of all the warriors gathered.

Before anyone could speak out, Jarl Valens continued to speak. "Honor, duty, sacrifice. These three virtues are relics of a distant past. We are no longer the warrior kingdom of Mezer. We are the fractured duchies, and you who still cling to your traditions and the old teachings will soon find your futures bleak. I have seen what is coming, and no matter how strong your warriors are, Zer'sheen or not, no matter how much faith you put into your Phoenix God or how honorably you act, nothing will stop your imminent demise."

These last words sent everyone who was listening into a frenzy. Even his fellow conspirators looked at the former duke in horror, as they didn't want to be dragged down with him. Shouts for the former duke's death echoed throughout the throne room. The warriors guarding the throne room had to keep the spectators from assaulting Jarl Valens before the archduke had declared his judgment on the traitors.

"Silence!" Archduke Ambrose shouted. His order quieted the disgruntled warriors, but they still glared venomously at Jarl Valens. Just as he was about to announce his judgment, a warrior entered the throne room with heavy breath. The warrior was one of the archduke's personal warriors who was stationed at the entrance to the palace for today's gathering. The warrior made his way to the archduke and whispered in his ear.

Everyone watched as the archduke's frown deepened even more. "Let him in" was all the archduke said. The warrior gave the archduke a salute and left the way he had come.

The warrior that had just left returned not a few moments later. With him was a man in the later years of his life. The man had an unshaven face and a head of brown hair with streaks of gray. Each step the man took had strength to it, even with a missing foot. On his side, he wore a warrior's sword. On the sheath, there was the crest of the Valens family.

Everyone was struck speechless, except for one.

"Grandfather!" Sarus Valens shouted. His eyes moistened, and hope returned to them, as seeing his famous grandfather meant that he would be saved.

"Who's that?" Aer asked Leander, but he had a guess. Only one person would be called grandfather by Sarus Valens. Even Aer, who hadn't been in the three duchies for long, had heard of this old man.

"Devlin Valens, the former Duke Valens and my grandfather's sworn brother. He has saved this duchy countless times, along with my grandfather's life," Prince Leander answered.

"If he is the father of the treacherous duke, then why isn't he bound with the rest?" Lucis asked.

"After years of serving the duchy, Devlin Valens retired and gave his position as duke to his son before leaving for the countryside," Lord Altares answered. "He hasn't returned to the capital since. It seems that during all of this, Jarl has kept his father in the dark and kept news from reaching the old Valens."

The old warrior didn't respond or even look his grandson's way. After making his way to the archduke, he knelt in front of the throne. He didn't move a muscle as he waited for the archduke's words.

Looking at his grandfather, then at the old Valens, Leander couldn't believe that they were close to the same age. The elderly Valens looked decades younger and looked more like the older brother of Jarl Valens than the man's father.

"My brother. Didn't I say before that there is no reason for sworn brothers to kneel or bow to one another? Please rise," Archduke Ambrose said. The archduke and the elderly Valens were closer than brothers. Even after everything that had happened with the latter's son, the archduke hadn't thrown away his feelings for his closest friend.

"I dare not, Your Undaunted Majesty, for I have sinned. I have failed to teach my son the virtues of a warrior and don't deserve to stand before you," the elderly Valens answered, refusing to stand from where he knelt.

The archduke didn't say anything else. Everyone knew that the elderly Valens wouldn't change his mind, even if the archduke demanded he did. With a sigh, the archduke asked, "Why is it that you have come?"

"Your Undaunted Majesty, years ago you told me that you would fulfill one request no matter what, as long as it was within your power. I wish for you to honor that pledge," Devlin Valens answered.

The archduke's eyes narrowed as he looked at his old friend. "One request, no matter what, as long as I could. That is what I promised, and I will honor my word," the archduke said, nodding his head.

When Sarus heard the archduke, he became ecstatic. Just moments ago he had been looking toward his death, but only a few seconds had passed since his grandfather had arrived, and he was already free. As Sarus celebrated, the remaining warriors looked on with trepidation. Many still respected Devlin Valens. He had been given that promise decades ago and could have used it to rise higher than anyone, but the man hadn't. If he did use it to save his family, those who had plotted to overthrow the very duchy he had protected with his life, then their faith and adoration was all for nothing.

The strange thing was that his own son didn't seem fazed by his arrival. Jarl Valens only took a glance at his renowned father before looking away. Many had missed this, with only a few warriors catching this strange action.

"Let me be the one to swing the sword for my son's and grandson's executions," Devlin Valens requested, shocking everyone in the throne room. Even his sworn brother, the archduke, thought he must have misheard.

"Grandfather, what are you saying? Didn't you come here to rescue us?" Sarus shouted. He couldn't believe what he had just heard his grandfather say.

It was then that the old Valens looked at his grandson for the first time. His eyes were filled with pain, seeing his own blood in such a situation, but he was resolved.

"Sarus. Do you remember, many years ago, when you told me how proud you were of being my grandson? Remember what I told you after you said that? I said that I am but a warrior, sworn to carry out my duties and uphold honor, no different from any other warrior in the Talov Duchy. Before anything else, I am a warrior, as are you and your father. You have betrayed all that comes with being a warrior. We were given power and responsibility not for our own gain but to protect others."

"Please, Grandfather. Please give me another chance. I promise to uphold the honor of a warrior without fail," Sarus pleaded. Tears flowed down his face as he looked at his grandfather, hoping for the old man to change his mind.

The elderly Valens answered. "Sarus, if you had only dishonored our family, then I would risk my all to save you, but that wasn't all you did. You betrayed the duchy itself. How many warriors died because of your and your father's greed? How many families were destroyed during all of this? It is too late to repent and change. At least with me being your executioner, you will be left with a sliver of honor in your deaths and be buried in the family tomb rather than an unknown plot of land."

With his final hope gone, Sarus fell to the floor. He had neither the strength nor the heart to raise his head. The warriors gathered looked to Devlin Valens with newfound respect. Even if it meant executing his own flesh and blood, he had chosen a warrior's virtues and valor over familial connections. Not many could do that. He had even used his only request to allow them to be buried with their ancestors.

"Very well. I will allow you to redress your family's sins," the archduke said, allowing the elderly Valens to be the one to end his own descendants' lives.

With his declaration, the other prisoners were sent away, their judgment postponed. Only Jarl and Sarus Valens were left. Everyone watching knew that they wouldn't escape execution for their crimes, but they hadn't known that the execution would happen today and be carried out by Devlin Valens himself.

Pulling out his sword, Devlin Valens stood over his grandson, who knelt motionless. The young man, who had been full of vigor, was now no more than an empty husk of his former self. "Let your death wash away your sins, and may you be born anew," Devlin prayed. He then swung his sword down and cut down his grandson. Devlin was old, but his strike was clean and sharp. Sarus felt no pain as he died.

Wiping the blood from his sword, Devlin then stood in front of his own son. As he raised his sword, he said, "Sage Arvandus warned me that your desire would bring you to the height of power but also threaten to consume you. I failed to see that your greed and desire had turned you into something I could hardly recognize. I will now release you from your obsessions."

Watching from the side, Leander thought he saw Jarl whisper something under his breath, but he was too far away to hear. The prince thought he must have been seeing things, as Devlin's sword didn't falter, and with a single swing, the traitorous former duke met his end.

After killing his son, the old warrior didn't wipe the blood off his sword. He simply stood there motionless. No one dared to speak. The scene was too intense for anyone to handle. The famous hero seemed to age right before their eyes. The streaks of gray in his hair looked to double, and the wrinkles around his eyes folded over one another. The sword he had held so steadily before now trembled in his hands.

Looking at the sword, which was still covered in his son's blood, the elderly Valens let out a painful sigh. Without a single word, the old warrior sheathed his sword, lifted the bodies of Jarl and Sarus, and with heavy footsteps, left the throne room. With the weight of his family on his shoulders, he disappeared from sight.

Chapter Thirty: Farewells and New Beginnings

In the courtyard of the Talov palace, the Estelle warriors were busy strapping bags and saddles onto their mounts. It had been three days since the executions of Jarl and Sarus Valens. Afterward the archduke had sentenced the rest of the conspirators. Some were executed while others lost their ranks and were sent into exile. With everything coming to a close, it was time for Aleron and the rest from the Estelle Duchy to leave.

Sending them off was the archduke himself, along with Prince Leander and Princess Aris. They weren't alone, as many other warriors stood behind them, including Roan and the newly named warriors Lucis and Aer. Lord Altares and Brana had already left. They had much to do at their respective halls.

"Crown Prince Aleron. I wish you well on your journey home," said Archduke Ambrose, shaking the prince's hand. "As for what we discussed, I hope you send my thoughts to your father. I believe he will have more insight into this."

"Thank you, Your Undaunted Majesty. I'll be sure to discuss everything with my father the moment I return," Crown Prince Aleron answered.

As the prince and archduke were saying their farewells, Elaina made her way toward Prince Leander and Princess Aris. At her side was the warrior Kaine Malis and her attending maiden Hali Malis. After their reunion, when the princess had gone to get her brother's help, the two of them had each given the princess a piece of their mind. They had been worried sick after the princess had run off with Roan and Kay to follow Prince Leander's trail into Verilis Forest. Once they had been reunited, they had refused to let the princess out of their sight, fearing that she would disappear again.

Elaina felt particularly bad for Kaine. When they had escaped, she had been the one who had knocked him unconscious. Afterward, because he felt responsible for the princess's escape, he had constantly punished himself. While he hadn't personally told Elaina this, his sister had. So even if their constant surveillance annoyed Elaina, she didn't dare to turn them away.

"I can't thank you enough. If it hadn't been for you, Jarl Valens would most likely have succeeded," said Aris.

"You don't have to thank me. We grew up together, and I think of the two of you as family," Elaina said. She couldn't help but notice how Prince Leander flinched when she said this. She felt bad for not being able to reciprocate his feelings, but her heart didn't move for Leander.

"Princess Elaina, I wish you a safe trip home. Hopefully, it won't be as adventurous as mine," Leander said with a slight laugh.

Elaina smiled back at the prince. Looking around at all the people she had met during this whole fiasco made her feel strange. Before all of this, she would never have thought that she would face off against monsters, find herself at the Grave of the First Zer'sheen, and even work together with a sell-sword. Thinking of that annoying smirk of his, she looked around but only found his brothers, Lucis and Aer.

"Where is Kay?" Elaina asked them.

Lucis and Aer looked at one another, then sighed.

"Truth be told, we don't know," Aer answered. "Our brother doesn't really enjoy gatherings like this. It was a hassle to make him go to the gathering a few days ago."

"I see," Elaina said. She didn't know why, but she felt upset that Kay wasn't seeing her off. That emotion was soon followed by anger. After everything they had been through, the least he could have done was show his face.

As she was lost in thought, Lucis walked to her and whispered in her ear. "Don't blame Kay. He has trouble with farewells, especially saying goodbye to someone he cares deeply for."

Elaina blushed slightly when she heard Lucis. In her embarrassment, she completely forgot her anger toward Kay.

As she was talking with everyone, Crown Prince Aleron suddenly called for her. It was time for them to go.

"Everyone. Till we meet again," Elaina said as she mounted her black-coated crowne. With a pull of the reins, she and the Estelle warriors rode out of the courtyard and out of the city.

At the rear of the riders, Elaina looked around the large city. As they made their way through Raven's Nest, Elaina thought she caught a glimpse of a familiar silhouette in one of the narrow alleyways. She wanted to check to see whether what she had seen was real, but with Kaine and Hali on both sides, she couldn't get away.

"Go," Kaine suddenly said, moving away so that she had a direct route to the alleyway. "Say your goodbyes."

Elaina looked at Kaine, shocked. She looked to Hali for understanding, and when she saw her friend nod, she understood. "Thank you. I'll be back before you reach the city gates," she said before turning her crowne toward the alleyway. She rode away before her brother could notice.

405

The alleyway was quite narrow. Elaina had difficulty riding her steed in such a confined space. Deeper she rode, but she found no hints of the one she searched for. She began to think that she had only imagined him.

When she was about to give up and turn back, she saw the stairway. The stairs led to the top of the large building she was standing next to. After dismounting from her crowne, Elaina began to make her way up the stairs. Her heartbeat quickened with each step. When she reached the top, she found who she was searching for.

Looking in the direction of the city gate was Kay. His crystal blue eyes never strayed as he concentrated fully ahead of him. Elaina's heart raced as she gazed at the former sell-sword, not knowing what to say.

When she took a step forward, her foot made the roofing boards creak. Kay quickly turned around to find who had sneaked up on him, but seeing that it was Princess Elaina, he was shocked silent.

When Elaina saw him like this, she couldn't help but laugh. "So, instead of seeing me off properly, you watch from alleyways and rooftops," Elaina said.

"What are you doing here?" was all Kay could think to say.

Elaina gave a soft snort. "You refused to see me off, so I had to come to you," Elaina said, then glared at him. "After everything we have been through, you decided not to say goodbye. I have never met someone as pompous as you."

"And I have never even heard of a princess as rowdy as you," Kay mocked back.

After Kay's words, the two stood there in silence as they looked at one another. Neither knew what to say to the other. With tension growing between the two, Elaina decided that she had to speak now, since she couldn't stay for much longer.

"For everything that you have done for me, thank you. You have shown me things that I never would have seen otherwise. A world that is so much vaster than my previous small world. For that, I will always be grateful," she said, then turned to leave. "Goodbye, Kay."

As she walked away, she suddenly felt someone grab her hand from behind. As they were the only two on the roof, Elaina knew that the person was Kay. Feeling Kay's hand holding her own made Elaina feel secure.

"Elaina …" Kay began, but he didn't finish.

"What is it?" Elaina asked.

Kay opened his mouth to speak several times, but no words came out. Finally he let go of her hand, smiled, and said, "Stay safe on your way home."

Elaina felt her heart beat wildly in her chest. Returning his smile with a bright one of her own, she answered back, "I will."

+

Kay did not know how long he stood there as he watched the Estelle warriors ride off. It was only after they were long out of sight that he turned around to leave.

As he returned to the palace, Kay found his two brothers waiting for him. Aer had a knowing grin on his face, while Lucis was as calm as always, but Kay could see a light twinkle in the Zer'sheen's eyes.

"Were you able to say farewell?" Aer asked.

Kay only nodded for confirmation.

"Then let us go home. Lucis and I have found the perfect place."

Dustin Farris

Be on the lookout for the next
warriors of Mezer Novel

The Stone Bed and Mountain Gate

It has been two years since Duke Valens attempt at the throne. Tensions between Raven's Nest and the Divide are growing. Thrown into the middle of this conflict are the former sell-swords Lucis and Kay.

With tensions high in the Talov Duchy the Estelle Duchy goes to war. Old enemies emerge, ready to conquer the plains of the Estelles. Plagued by nightmares Elaina fears what vile plot the Tarsis have in store. For the one who leads the march against them is the mysterious Ghost King himself.

About the Author

Dustin Farris grew up with a love for fantasy. There were very little days he was not off in his imagination, going on epic quests and discovering mystical lands. This love led him to the realm of written fantasy and he quickly consumed any books of heroism he could get his hands on. 'The Prince and the Sell-Swords' is Dustin's debut novel and will certainly not be his last.

Dustin Farris

Made in the USA
Las Vegas, NV
07 January 2021